I0788588

THE MISPLACED HERO
What Do You Mean the Demon Lord Has Already Been Defeated?

Tom Black

Look for more books
by Tom Black:

The Longest Quest
The Kingdom of the Pass
Port Royal (A Short Story in Caleuche Chronicles)
Tairn: A Hero Appears (Coming 2024)
Raiders of the Black Sun (Coming 2024)

Tom Black

The Misplaced Hero: What Do You Mean the Demon Lord Has Already Been Defeated?

Printed in the U.S.A. and Great Britain

1st edition

Cover Design by Wong40K

For more information search for TomBlack on Royal Road

ISBN: 978-1-944621-30-8

Library of Congress Control Number: 2024912828

Table of Contents

Foreword

This series began with a simple argument in an online forum. Well, maybe not simple, exactly. The basic question was; which is the proper way to view anime, subbed or dubbed? Simple, right?

The two sides generally come at it in simple terms. The sub fans want to hear the original voice actors perform the lines in Japanese, and are willing to do the extra work of reading the translation. The dub fans want to watch the anime and be able to pay attention to the visuals without having to concentrate on reading.

There is a secondary argument that watching subs will somehow allow you to pick up Japanese through osmosis or something.

Now, the more astute of you might chime in, "But author! How would you learn the language from localized translations?"

That's a good point. But the argument never seems to elevate to that level.

So, I thought to myself. What would happen to a guy who only watched dubs if he got isekaied to a world where they only spoke (the local equivalent of) Japanese? How would he even get there?

Why, he'd have to have been misplaced, of course.

Prologue

His men at arms lay where they'd fallen, scattered in his wake, their bodies intermingled with the legions of demons and lesser dark minions who'd contested their advance through the fortress' first sixty-seven floors. They had fought bravely and beyond any expectation, but for all their skills, for all their abilities, they'd been only mortal men.

The last of them had spent his life's blood midway up the passage to floor sixty-eight. No single one of them had given up the struggle. Not one of them had fled.

The priest had perished on floor sixty-two, wading unafraid into the horde of undead who'd blanketed it. He'd given over every last vestige of his will, his spirit, and finally his life in the grand banishment that followed. Those few stunned dregs to survive had been easily cut down by the last of the men at arms.

An arcane trap had taken the master thief on floor sixty-nine, but not before he'd managed the final lock barring their way to the stairway.

The artificer had followed the last of his toys into oblivion in order to fell the great guardian dragon Noringa on the seventieth floor. The steam cannon's explosive projectiles hadn't managed to finish the task, but its subsequent self-detonation had, tearing both its creator and the dragon to bits and scattering their remains across the hall.

All to place him here on floor seventy-one with his enchantress, in the Great Chamber. But here was as far as he would go. He knew that now.

The two of them were all that was left of the expedition to breach the Obsidian Fortress and slay the Demon Lord Mohrtgauth. Their plan was a shambles, as were the backup plans as far down the list as they'd calculated. It was unlikely they would survive. His only hope was that he would take the demon lord with him when he went to join his ancestors that they not look down on him.

"I am Ishihara Kenjiro!" he shouted up at the towering creature, easily three times his own size. Its bat wings were half unfurled, its four arms askew, one of them culminating in a dripping stump rather than a hand.

"I am Samurai!" he announced hard upon his introduction. "And I will take your life now as you have taken so many before!"

On the floor some distance behind him, just within the chamber entry, lay the enchantress Rosaluna Galbradia, her body half covered by the severed hand of the demon lord, her mouth pouring blood.

Mohrtgauth had surprised them badly.

All evidence had pointed to its never venturing below floor seventy-five. It had been one of the few things about which they'd been confident. They should only be facing lesser spawn on this floor. But the moment they'd entered the Great Chamber of floor seventy-one with Kenjiro well in the lead and Rosaluna hanging back to support, Mohrtgauth had sprung upon her from above.

It had snatched up the girl and sliced out her tongue with its razor talons before either she or Kenjiro could react. As though it had already known who each of them were, and where their powers lay, and who would be more immediately dangerous.

It had been taking flight again, raising her feebly struggling body to its gaping maw when Kenjiro had made his leap, shouting his focusing cry. The gleaming blade of his nodachi had sliced through the wrist of the arm holding Rosaluna in a spray of ichor, severing it cleanly.

For all his training, then, he would have dropped the nodachi and dived to cushion her fall, but the demon, roaring its rage, was already slashing down with its three remaining hands, and it took all of his concentration to fend them off. He was mostly successful.

There followed a series of blow and counterstrike that carried the combatants across the floor and away from the injured girl.

And now, here he stood. Wounded, weary, heartsick, but unbowed. Mohrtgauth was in little better condition, for Kenjiro's nodachi was no ordinary weapon. Its true name was Kami no Seigi no Katana. The most holy of holy swords, won at great cost from its guardian for this specific purpose.

Alone among the blades of Mund, Kami no Seigi no Katana was able to pierce the hide of the demon lord, and Kenjiro had been making extensive use of that property. Along with removing one of its hands, the holy sword had carved out scores of deep wounds in the beast's flesh and had shredded its wings.

For all his strength, however, all his speed…. For all that he was a hero endowed with extraordinary powers by the god of Mund, he was yet a man, and the fight through the fortress had been long. He was at the end of his strength. The plan, if such it could be called, should only the two of them survive this far, had been for Rosaluna to fortify him with her magic for the last push. But without a tongue, even did she yet live, her ability to cast magic was severely limited.

Even as the thought passed through his mind, he felt a touch, gentle as a breeze. "NO!" he shouted without turning from Mohrtgauth, forcing his voice to the guttural of command. "Heal yourself first! You are of no use to me dead!"

LIAR! Even as the words were true, the implication was utterly false. She *must* heal herself first because *sh*e must *live*. Above all else, Rosaluna must *live*. This was the single driving force of Kenjiro's existence at this moment. She must live! All else was secondary. Saving the world, avenging his comrades, killing the demon lord. All was as nothing compared to her life. Even his own.

He felt the touch fade and smiled grimly to himself. That was it, then. He would not survive. But she might. If he could strike down the Demon.

Mohrtgauth, perhaps sensing the spell, weak as it was, turned toward the fallen enchantress. Kenjiro moved to block its way. He had the strength for one last strike. He would make it count. He closed his eyes to slits and adjusted his stance, focusing, concentrating. All of his chi. All of his spirit. All of his mana.

Everything into the blade of his nodachi. All of his will, his history. The honor of his family, his ancestors.

Kami no Seigi no Katana's blade began to glow the fierce yellow-white of a rising sun. He was humming now, deep in the back of his throat, bringing everything that was in him to the fore. This strike would be the sum total of his entire existence. Everything he'd been striving to from the moment of his birth until this single instant. And it would destroy the Demon Lord Mohrtgauth for once and for all. And she would live.

Mohrtgauth saw the glow and crouched more deeply, bringing its fangs into the contest, long as daggers in their own right. It would have taken flight then, but the sword in the hands of the impossibly quick human had rendered its wings incapable of supporting it.

The hum was growing louder. A prayer now, as well as a spell. The glare of the blade altered slightly, shifting more directly to white as its holy powers manifested.

Without warning, and with the last of its strength, Mohrtgauth pounced, attacking before the sword could be fully activated. Kenjiro stepped into it, sweeping the blade up and around in a wide diagonal slash as he called out the blade's binding command with the greatest volume he could muster.

The hundred-twenty centimeter blade of Kami no Seigi no Katana bit deeply into the chest of the demon, sinking half its length into the otherworldly flesh. One of the demon lord's foul hearts was cleaved in two and one of its lungs clipped before the blade encountered a thick rib and snapped off short.

An explosion rocked the Great Chamber, centered at the point where the two halves of the blade had parted, sending dust and chips of stone down from the ceiling and up from the floor. A flash of brilliant light momentarily rendered the entirety of the chamber invisible. When it abated, the combatants had been pushed several meters apart.

Mohrtgauth was on its knees, all three hands pressed against the gaping hole in its chest, struggling ineffectually to pluck the stub of the blade from its flesh. Ichor ran from its mouth and nostrils, pouring onto the flagstone floor to join with that gushing forth from its chest wound. It rocked back onto its heels, breath thundering in harsh, bubbling gasps. It glared down at the human warrior for a moment before collapsing onto its side. It began to drag itself away. Slowly, painfully, centimeter by centimeter, coughing ichor and curses.

During the entire span of the demon lord's snail-like escape, Ishihara Kenjiro stood immobile, hands down, still gripping the stub of the holy sword. At last, with only the fading echoes of the creature's retreat remaining, he dropped to his knees. A moment later, he toppled forward onto his face and was still.

The hall was quiet save for the strangled sobbing of the girl, clinging to a life that had now lost all meaning.

The surviving commanders of the army —those who had remained outside the fortress to guard against such of the demon lord's lieutenants as hadn't been present— broached the walls early the next morning and retrieved the enchantress and the bodies of their brethren, along with the corpse of the dragon Noringa. Even with the ichor trail laying thick as a small river, none dared follow to determine whether the demon lord yet lived.

Tom Black

Truck… er… Bus Kun Pays a Visit

The world returned slowly, bathed in darkness and searing pain. His face felt wet. Hot and sticky wet. His chest felt tight, shot through with stabbing agony. It was nearly impossible to breath, and he thought he might have a collapsed lung.

His legs…. It was as though someone were hammering on his bones with a sledge. His right arm wouldn't move so he tried to reach down with his left hand. The attempt only resulted in more pain. Strangely, he wasn't frightened. Not yet. For now, he was just angry and confused.

What was happening? He tried to remember, but it was difficult through the sawing torment washing through his body. This had already happened, hadn't it? Years ago. Hadn't it? Or had the past several years just been a dream to keep his mind occupied while he lay here in the wreckage of the MRAP bleeding out?

No, he thought as his wits began to return. That had been different. The smell had been different. The pain had been different. That was in the past. He'd been out of the military for years. He wasn't a grunt anymore. He wasn't in the desert anymore. He was home. In the States. He had a normal job. A normal life.

The only thing Uncle paid him for these days was going to school and physical therapy. Or, at least he helped. And the meds, of course. Mustn't forget the meds. They kept the ends from fraying… mostly.

So, concentrate. Remember. He'd been sitting in his living room, hadn't he? Yeah. Kicked back in his easy chair after a hard day's work, followed by a night class and a couple of hours of homework in the school's shop. Unwinding with a video game while he waited for the latest episode of one of his animes to air. He'd been waiting weeks for the dub to finally release, and he'd been looking forward to it.

Steam and Chaos, it was called. The game, not the anime. It had been on sale through one of the online clearinghouses for stupid cheap, considering its breadth of content. A godawful western/JRPG hybrid with greedy graphics and ludicrously complex controls, but a deceptively broad and compelling story.

Just something to kill time at this point, though. After all, he'd beaten it, what, ten times now? Or was it eleven? Each time taking a slightly different path? Always good, though. No surprise. There were evil paths available, but he just couldn't seem to work up any enthusiasm for them. The choices tasted sour in his mouth.

So how did that—? Wait! Something else had happened. It was coming back. He'd looked up from a boss fight at a horrible screeching, squalling, ululating wail coming from outside the house to the sight of bright, strobing lights racing through his front yard. Almost as he'd realized what he was seeing, his front wall had come crashing in, smashing glass, bowling over furniture and hurling the TV across the room dead at him. He'd had time to start his leap sideways from the chair, but he couldn't remember finishing it.

He lay there on his back, the world fading in and out with the waves of pain, wondering if these were real memories or some weird dream. Had he really been run over by a chicken bus, in his own house, in the middle of the United States? Eleven hundred miles north of the Mexican border, let alone anywhere near Guatemala or points south?

The last thing that went through his mind as his consciousness faded back to persistent blackness was the surreal image of the bus as it had struck him. Of the lighted destination bar that had adorned the area above the windshield of the garishly neon clad vehicle. Twin magical girls with fairy wings flanking the screen, waving sparkling wands at the text separating them in some foreign script he couldn't recognize. They'd almost seemed alive, winking at him and waving.

Then, as the hood of the speeding bus had begun to occlude his vision, their skin had begun to darken, their wings become bat-like. Horns sprouted from their foreheads, and tails slid out from beneath the rear hems of their short skirts. The one on the right had blown him a kiss, and then everything had gone dark, echoing with the blaring cacophony of what sounded like bad mariachi overlain with Mongolian throat metal.

The next time he swam to awareness, the pain remained as fresh as the first. Or was it the third time? He was losing track. How long had he been lying here? What the hell was going on? Shouldn't the fire department be showing up pretty soon? Or at least the cops? Hell, the neighbors ought to be wondering why there was a freaking circus bus sticking out the front of his house, shouldn't they? Even at this time of night? Come to that, where the hell was that goofy bus driver? You'd think he'd at least glance out the windshield to survey the damage.

Something else was wrong. He still couldn't open his eyes, but his ears worked. Or at least he thought they did. Except they weren't hearing sirens. No bus sounds, either. Not even settling rubble. No television, no traffic noise, not even that idiot dog of Ferguson's who *never* shut up. Instead, he was hearing birdsong and running water. How was that even possible? At some point during these musings, despite the pain, he faded again to black.

Light. His eyes were still glued shut, but he could see a glow through the lids. The pain wasn't so bad, either. Like the crazy with the sledge had switched to a rubber mallet. It was even a little bit easier to breathe.

He was still flat on his back for sufficient values of, although maybe not so flat as before. As though he were lying on a slight incline. His arms and legs, if anything, felt more paralyzed than ever. He felt as though he were moving, although any 'about time' notions were quickly quelled by the manner of movement.

Far from the racing vibration of an ambulance at speed, he felt instead, the slow thump, thump of wood dragged along stones. He could swear he heard hooves. Even smell the horse, along with dust and hay. The hell was happening to him, and how did he make it stop?

The journey went on for quite some while, during which he stayed awake for a change. He grew convinced that there was someone else nearby. A single someone, whose plodding progress matched the leisurely pace of the horse. Yes, he admitted to himself, there was a horse. Somehow, there was a horse.

The sounds of hoof and foot falls were close. Combined with the sound of the sticks dragging, he came to the conclusion that he was probably strapped into some kind of travois, being conveyed down a stone paved road from somewhere he couldn't possibly have been to somewhere he knew he probably didn't want to go.

Now he was starting to be a little bit afraid.

The sun felt hot on his face. A soft breeze blew steadily over him. He could hear the sounds of late spring or early summer all around him. At least, such sounds as he'd hear if he didn't live in a city. Also, it was supposed to be early February. The longer he bumped along, the more convinced he became that he'd somehow gotten himself a long, long way from home. And the longer the day dragged, the more convinced he was that this was no dream.

It was almost like one of those goofy isekais he was always watching online. Except that he couldn't remember a single one where the hero arrived crippled, blind, and tied to a sled. Not one of the dozens he'd watched, the scores he'd read, nor the hundreds he'd heard about. Still.... isekai translated out to, *another place*, and this was definitely that.

They'd left the road at some point and were now traveling on grass, he thought. It smelled like grass, and radiated up less heat than the road had.

Some long while after, as the light was waning, the horse finally eased to a halt. A moment later, the front end of the travois let go and he hit the ground with a thump and a yelp. He heard the horse moving away, and for awhile he was alone.

The Cottage

He could see! The thought raced through his mind for the fraction of a second his eyes remained open before slamming shut of their own accord. As though they refused to convey what was being presented to them. Slowly, he slitted one open again, experimentally. Yep. Still a low, dimly lit thatched roof less than a foot overhead.

Then he remembered where he was. Or rather, where he wasn't. How many awakenings was this? All in the same setting? Dreams just didn't work like that. Well, he might be dead, he supposed. He wasn't sure how that worked, although he'd gotten pretty close a couple of times. It did make more sense than a dream, given the whole bus incident.

He heard a familiar thumping and turned his head slowly, beholding a short, slender woman leaning on a gnarled white cane. She was moving away from a glowing hearth from which the ruddy light illuminating the place came, and towards a heavy wooden door on the far side of the room. Seen in profile, her hair was snow white where it peaked out around a tied off floral scarf that covered the back half of her head. Her nose was fine-boned, and her figure somewhat hunched.

He wondered if it were she who'd brought him in from the yard, or if there was somebody else around who'd done it for her. She didn't really look strong enough. On the other hand, the way he still hurt, she may well have just rolled him in like a half empty barrel.

As though sensing his regard, she turned her head and he saw two things at once. The thick white of her hair was bisected by a wide band of orchid down the center, and the face below it bore an expression of inconsolate sadness worn decades deep into the lines of her skin.

Ah, the thought came to him. *Awake now, are we?*

Only just, did he stop himself from shaking his head to clear it. That thought may have come from his own head, but it hadn't been his.

The old woman nodded, confirming his suspicions. *Indeed, young man, that was me.*

"How?" he croaked, surprised at how hoarse and intrusive his own voice sounded in the quiet room.

She turned fully and approached him in her slow, plodding way. He could see, despite the sadness wreathing her like a shroud, that she must have been a very beautiful woman at some point in the distant past. *Magic,* she sent into his head. *How did you think?*

Magic. Somehow, it didn't sound as flip as it might have were they conversing in his living room rather than a medieval looking hut God knew where.

I am called Rosaluna, the woman sent, her calm expression unchanging. *Rosaluna Galbradia. How are you feeling?*

Stifling the torrent of questions he was mad to ask, he laid back to take stock. "Like I got hit by a bus," he said to the ceiling.

I see, she replied. *And these bus things. They are large?*

"Very," he answered. "They range from holding a dozen people to more than fifty."

Ah, she nodded. *Conveyances, then. Like large carriages?*

He shot her an eye to see if she was making fun of him. "One of the older terms for them was motor carriage," he wheezed.

Well, she suggested. *That would comport with the amount of damage you'd sustained.*

He returned his regard to the ceiling. "Right. About that. Given what I remember, it's kind of hard to believe I'm still alive. More magic?"

Indeed, she favored him with the ghost of a smile. *There are still a great many spells which may be cast without a tongue, if one devotes sufficient study to their execution. Healing spells particularly.*

"I'm sorry," he struggled with some effort up onto an elbow and stared, eyes going wide. "Did you just say, without a tongue?"

Indeed, she repeated.

He waited, but she did not continue and he was loathe to pry, given the circumstances.

After a moment, she turned back to the hearth, eventually returning with a bowl of something steaming hot and smelling more or less of beef stew, although the aroma bore the scents of unfamiliar spices.

He'd flopped back down in the interim, exhausted by even the small exertion of raising himself partway up. Eying the bowl, though, he felt he might manage another go. Experimentally, he hoisted himself around and to a sitting position, wincing at the effort, his face paling. He swung his legs slowly around and off the side of the straw covered pallet he'd been lying on.

He took a moment then, resting elbows on knees, taking deep, ragged breaths. Nothing fell off. At least not yet. Looking down, he was somewhat surprised to discover he'd been stripped down to his underwear. Not that he could see much skin through the strange bandages covering him all over, all of them slathered over with strange, very precise writing in multiple colors and a very strange script.

After a few moments to steady himself, he took the bowl with a nod of thanks and dipped the wooden spoon into the brew. Before he knew it, he was staring down at the bottom of an empty bowl. Looking up, he saw her nod toward the pot hanging beside the hearth. He frowned, but gave it a shot. He was still struggling, sweat bursting out on his face, when she relented and took the bowl from his trembling hands, shaking her head and frowning.

He was scraping the bottom of his third bowlful when the next thought entered his head.

You don't look much like the others.

"Others?" he asked, looking up. "What others?" He was once more thinking about where he might be and how he might have gotten here.

She measured herself and raised an eyebrow. Was he making sport of her? Sitting there tall as a doorway, broad-shouldered as a dwarf, with his wheat colored hair, bronzed skin, and bright blue eyes. Not mentioning the most glaring difference. *The other heroes, of course,* she frowned. *Who else might appear in that glade?*

Heroes, he thought to himself. *Okay, So I was right. More or less. But what kind of screwed up isekai is this? First, I get hit by a bus instead of a truck.... and in my own house. Then I carry my injuries with me to wherever. And now I meet my first magical girl, and she's, like, a hundred! I just cannot catch a break!* At which point, it came to him that he'd already accepted what should have been a much more difficult concept for a rational person to believe.

"Others, you said," he asked once he'd gotten himself used to the idea that he believed he was no longer on mother earth, and was supposed to be somebody's hero. "How many others, exactly?"

You are the twelfth hero to appear in the Hero's Glade, she sent matter-of-factly.

Oh, boy, he thought. that wasn't good. Just how dangerous *was* this place? What was that grading system they all seemed to use? F, E, D, C, B, A, S? Double S for the worst of them. If the big bad had already done for eleven heroes, this couldn't be below SS, could it?

"What happened to the others?" he asked quietly.

Most of them, her face fell into even greater sadness and tears began to seep. *Most of them were killed, either by the Demon Lord or its greater minions.*

Most? "And the rest?"

It took her some time to compose herself before she answered. *Only... only the last of them survived. Called the greatest of them,* with a hint of mocking snort. *The grateful people crowned him king after he and his armies had finally managed to vanquish the dread Demon Lord Mohrtgauth, and free the land from its shadow.*

"Uhm..." he blinked. "What was that?"

The grateful people— she repeated, tilting her head in confusion.

"The Demon Lord has already been defeated?" he broke in.

Of course, she replied. *After more than a hundred and thirty years of its—*

"Then what the hell am *I* doing here?" he pressed.

Ah, she nodded, understanding coming to her eyes. *Yes. I, too, would like to know the answer to that question.*

They regarded one another for a few moments, neither having a clue. He stared down into the empty wooden bowl, trying to work through the logic of the situation. He was no longer sure what was happening. He wasn't the hero, it seemed. Not if the big bad had already been dealt with. So what was he doing here? Was this somebody's idea of a bad joke?

"Oh," he realized belatedly. "You've told me your name, but I haven't introduced myself yet, have I?" he raised a hand to his chest. "Jackson Thomas Grenell," he pronounced. "Jack to my friends. It's a pleasure to meet you, Rosaluna Galbradia." he reached out the same hand.

It is my pleasure as well, Jack san, she smiled wanly, somewhat stiffly, taking his offered hand.

Tom Black

Recovery and Discovery

Days had passed, and he had no more of a clue than he'd had when he'd asked the question. He was still the guest of the former magical girl, of whom he'd learned precious little beyond her quiet misery.

She hadn't conversed with him since the first day. Well, the first day he'd been awake, as it would seem she'd kept him sleeping during the initial stages of his healing. For how long she'd done so was another mystery.

Much of each day, she spent in quiet study or contemplation. The rest on works he assumed must be magical in nature, as he could understand none of it.

The only time she seemed aware he was even there was during those periods she was actively working her healing magics on him, which, granted, were lengthy. Or when she was disciplining him for some error or other he'd managed to perpetrate through carelessness or lack of local knowledge.

For his own part, Jack was left to work things out on his own. It wasn't going well. He had no idea where he might be, where he might need to go, or how he might get there. His injuries were by no means healed, and his mobility thus hampered. There was also a considerable amount of residual pain, though he'd grown used to that long before leaving Earth.

And, of course, no meds, which were all back home in his medicine cabinet. Somehow, though, even without them, he wasn't unraveling. Not much, at least. Not anything he couldn't endure with a bit of effort. He was even sleeping, although he had to wonder how much of that had to do with the old woman's intervention.

His local surroundings gave him only marginal information. He was on the edge of a deciduous forest, and well off of any road. Gravity seemed pretty earth normal, so he wasn't doing John Carter on Mars. The horse was just a horse. An old piebald mare well beyond her better years. No fangs or claws, and she hadn't talked to him. Air tasted clean.

Only the one sun. Two moons, though. One large, one small, or maybe farther out. With different rotation speeds. He became neither stronger nor weaker with either or both in the sky.

Long story short, his physical attributes probably weren't going to give him any advantages, even should the magical girl... woman... whatever, eventually be able to put him completely back together.

He had no weapons, not even those he could have sworn he'd had on him when the bus had come calling. Nor any real idea if he'd need any, given that the most recent hero had apparently already disposed of the greatest evil of the land.

Of course, setting merrily off on his way unarmed and finding an immediate need for weapons midway to anywhere was probably not a sound plan. The greater evil may well have been dealt with, but what of lesser evils? Better to have and not need, right?

Weapons, however, were a thing he could not find anywhere obvious within Rosaluna's small domain. At least no weapons he could recognize or use. That ornate cane she leaned on looked more than a little overbuilt merely to support her weight. Nor could he get a good, close look at it without seeming rude, which he wasn't about to do, for a multitude of reasons.

Not that he'd be able to use any of the weapons he might be likely to find in such a place anyway. Always assuming that this was the fantasy world it appeared to be. Sure, he'd done some fencing in college. Community college and sport fencing. He'd messed around with rattan weapons and armor in the park a good bit with those anachronist guys during the same time.

Okay, he had some solid HEMA training under a couple of decent masters from when he'd been stationed in Europe in the army after his last combat tour, and during the year he'd taken off after his release from the hospital.

Granted, an abnormal lot of sword slinging for a modern man, but none of it worth a damn here against people who did it for real. If the desert had taught him anything, it was that using a weapon in combat wasn't anything like playing in the park.

Theoretically, he knew how to build a bow. He'd never actually done it, of course, but he'd watched a lot of videos. There was an internet channel he subscribed to that was devoted to making bows out of all manner of goofy materials. Of course, almost all of his actual archery over the past ten years had been with compound bows. Which were, while he still theoretically knew how to build them, even less likely to be within his skill range to construct.

Then, too, even were he to be able to successfully cobble together a meaningful bow, somehow the subject of crafting arrows had never intersected his search track. He knew what the finished products should be, he could swap out heads, he could repair fletching. But making them? No idea. All of the primitive arrow making videos seemed to start out, 'buy some dowels from the home improvement store,' and he was pretty sure the nearest one of those was too far away to walk to.

So here he sat, many days into his impossible adventure —she was remarkably cagey about letting him know just how long that might be— scraping the bark off of a small ash tree he'd chopped down and split lengthways with an axe he'd found leaning against the hut.

The old woman had given him merry hell over it, too, laying into him about the callous destruction of things about which he knew nothing. He still wasn't sure what she'd been on about. Spirits and magic and stuff that she couldn't or wouldn't clarify. In the end, she'd stormed off, but only after securing his solemn vow never again to touch the axe or venture into the wood without her prior permission.

By the time he got it shaved and shaped, he figured he might end up with a decent quarterstaff. He was still only marginally sure he could use it, of course. He'd trained with staves with the HEMA guys, but it had been awhile ago. Most of his recent pole arm work had been with the SCA, and they were way more strict in the way they fought.

Counter-intuitively, sparring with quarterstaves was

more dangerous than using rattan swords. They built momentum too quickly and broke people. In the mock skirmishes he'd engaged in, fighters weren't allowed to use staves at all, and the pole arms had all required heavy padding. Even then, it hadn't been permitted to rotate them more than ninety degrees at speed, lest they injure opponents.

His problem now was that, were he to use the thing here, injuring the opponent would be the whole point. His brain would be telling his arms to swing, but his muscle memory would be geared to less than full speed. Maybe, though.... Maybe he could fix that. Overwrite the old memories with more practical ones.

But not right away. It was too soon, he was told. He was on a strict regimen of therapy, both magical and otherwise, which did not include stressful exercise. Apparently, his internal injuries had been far more severe than even he'd first imagined, and repairing the damage likewise more involved.

It was some time well into the second month, as near as he could figure, before he was permitted to begin anything like real physical therapy. Or what he called physical therapy in his head. It may have been longer, of course, since she kept putting him to sleep for various procedures without regard to his wishes. But he thought two months.

His phone would know, even without being able to check in, but he hadn't seen it since awakening. Not that it would do him much good after all this time, he supposed. He hadn't seen anyplace he'd be able to plug a USB cable since he'd woke up, and didn't think he was going to any time soon.

His watch would still be running, but he hadn't seen *it* either. Nor any other of his possessions beyond his heavy leather belt, his Leatherman, and its pouch. It was like she was deliberately trying to divorce him from the passage of time.

Anyway, two months and change, he thought, and she'd begun to allow him some measure of autonomy in his physical exercise. Stretching, moving, plodding across the yard clinging to the increasingly ornate quarterstaff. A rehash of what they'd had him do at the military hospitals during his recovery after the

IED. It surprised him how vividly he could recall the programs.

As time progressed and his recovery grew more complete, he became more active. His sessions grew longer, his movements broader. The pain diminished.

They'd settled into a sort of rhythm, the two of them, during this period. He'd awaken with the dawn to find Rosaluna already up and about. She'd examine him intently, as though she could see into his very bones. She'd engage in various antics to ensure his continued recovery, taking anywhere from a few minutes to a really long time before turning away and ignoring him for the rest of the morning.

For his part, once he'd been seen to, Jack would be free to take care of his morning necessities, after which he'd be free to either do the chores he'd taken up doing or work on his physical conditioning and training.

Whenever he wasn't doing either of those, he worked on the staff with the blade of his Leatherman, carving various decorations into both it and his fingers. he still wasn't altogether steady, and there were slips. Chiefly, the carving involved knotwork, but there were stretches where he experimented with floral or other designs, to see if he could manage them.

He added a sling hook to one end against the possibility that he might someday try to use it as a sling staff. He'd never tried one before, but he'd seen videos and knew the theory.

Unsurprisingly, she had neither TV nor internet, nor could he make heads or tails of any of her books. This severely narrowed the variety of pastimes available, and carving on the staff gave him time to think without having to work at it.

At some point, he began carving a waster from the other quarter of the same tree. A basic cruciform with a long, narrow blade. Not for any particular reason beyond boredom. Maybe the vague notion that he might someday find a real sword he could wield, even here, and so he may as well get in some practice.

Once the waster was done, he'd started on a long knife. At which point the old woman had confronted him, seizing the remainder of the felled tree and stalking out into the forest with the pieces clutched under an arm. He watched her progress, dumbfounded, the Leatherman held in his hand poised over the rough outline of the dagger blade he'd already carved out of the wood. So much for a bow.

Thereafter, his whittling was restricted to finishing and decorating those pieces he'd already started. She didn't seem willing to take them away, although she made her displeasure known whenever she caught him at it. He tried to ask once or twice, but she wouldn't have it, turning away the moment she understood the topic was being broached.

She didn't seem to mind his whittling on random firewood, but somehow, any attempts to create any sort of timeline, regardless of how he hid the marks, resulted in the fire claiming his work. He didn't try anything tricky with his ash projects, fearing their fate should he be caught. But he was chafing at the treatment, regardless of his confidence in her intentions.

Somewhere into month three, near as he could figure, and he was out behind the hut with his finished quarterstaff in hand, training as he'd taken to doing as his strength returned.

He'd wrapped the bole of an old tree with straw from beside the stable and some burlap scraps he'd found inside. Nearby, he'd hung a knotted rope from one of the branches. Off to the side was a crude pell with several rough arms protruding at varying heights.

He'd visualize the movements and recite them quietly to himself as he executed them, as though he were both instructor and student. He was still more than a little amazed at how clearly the memories of those lessons came to him. Just like those of his physical therapy. Clearer every day, it seemed. As though they'd been mere hours back rather than several years. Like his mind was becoming sharper.

Somehow, though, even beneath the amazement, it didn't occur to him to connect this with his new circumstances. If anything, he put it down to the old woman's healing skill.

Mornings, he did the whole routine slowly, concentrating more on the movements than on force, working on getting every motion exactly correct. Slow was smooth, smooth was fast as the old saying went. First with the staff, then the sword and dagger.

This was his afternoon session, though. He'd already done a full hour with the blades, and was now on the staff, alternating between whacking on the tree using the full speed and force of his muscles along with the full range of motion the staff allowed, and practicing precision strikes and counters with the hanging rope.

He'd been at it awhile and sweat was running down his back and chest when he became aware of his audience. "How long have you been watching?" he asked without either turning or slowing.

Not so long, she sent. *This time at any rate. What are you doing?*

Now he did stop, leaning on the staff and taking a moment to catch his breath. Wipe sweat from his eyes. He turned to her, standing there in the sun, leaning on her white cane. "Nothing here is familiar to me," he said as evenly as he could. "And I don't have any idea why I've been brought to this place... this world. *You* certainly won't tell me anything."

He waited, not expecting an answer and not receiving one.

"I'm kind of expecting to have to defend myself at some point," he continued after he felt he'd waited long enough. "And since you have no actual recognizable weapons laying about, this was the best I could come up with."

So you intended this from the very beginning to be a weapon? she seemed both confused and irritated. *How do you expect to gain expertise with such a thing? You don't have a life crystal.*

You can flail away at that poor oak from now until you're old and grey without earning a single modifier. Without a crystal, you are no more than an ordinary ungifted, despite where I found you, destined to rank zero for life. The first gifted or monster of any significant rank you confront will simply smash you out of hand regardless of any effort you can make.

Your toy sword, she nodded towards the wasters laying near his crude pell, *I could somewhat understand. You seem at least competent with it. Should you find a true blade before you're slaughtered, you may survive a low level encounter or two. But this? No, young man, forget this folly. Perhaps you should better practice running.*

Those were more words than she'd thrown at him at once since he'd first awakened. It was a shame they weren't making much sense. "Life crystal?" he asked. "Modifiers?"

Life crystal, she repeated, motioning to the air above her head. *Such as mine, do you see?*

He looked. He squinted. He peered. "Not really, no."

I beg your pardon? She asked, alarmed. *You cannot see my crystal? At all?*

He took a few steps closer, twisting his head this way and that. Nothing. "What is it I'm supposed to be seeing?" he asked.

She blinked, frowning. *A glowing blue crystal, perhaps a hand's length, palm to fingertip tall, spinning slowly about a hand's width above the crown of my head. You truly don't see it?*

"I'm afraid not," he admitted. "Perhaps it's because I'm from ano—"

Kenji saw it instantly, she insisted. *Nor did any of the others have the slightest difficulty. What's more, each of them had crystals of their own, bright and clear. And yet you have none. And now you say you cannot even see them? How is that? Am I to believe that you truly are no more than an ungifted peasant after all?*

Ah. He remembered the abortive thread of conversation from his initial awakening, when she'd observed that he wasn't like the others. It must have been his lack of one of these crystals.

"Any idea where I might acquire one?" he wondered rather than answering. "Or am I doomed?"

Her initial thought was doomed, but she didn't say it. The answer she did give was awhile in coming. *I do not know,* she admitted. *I will have to give the matter some study. It is not something that I've ever encountered before, you see. People are either gifted, or they are not. I have never so much as* heard *of anyone who was both.*

She turned back for the hut without ceremony or word, leaving him to his apparently pointless practice. She hadn't addressed the subject of modifiers, but he supposed he'd seen enough anime and played enough video games to guess. She'd been talking about a leveling system of some sort. A system that he was locked out of due to his lack of this life crystal thing.

He stood there for a few minutes, giving it thought. Such a system meant that he'd be encountering things stronger than normal humans, be they monsters or people. Probably a whole lot stronger. Pretty much anything with one of those crystals would be tougher, stronger, and faster than he was, if he had it right.

If he was really to be encountering enemies at all, of course. There was nothing to say he would with their demon lord gone. The question now was, did he continue to train, or say screw it and get used to the idea of being weak.

As though that were a question. Shrugging, he turned back to the tree. Absence of modifiers meant that he'd need his baseline to be higher. And there was only one way to do that.

Tom Black

Another Magical Girl

Another month had passed, as near as he could tell. He was currently doing wind sprints, having given over the first couple of hours after breakfast to sword and staff respectively. He was surprised at how easy it was these days. His knees weren't bothering him at all. Fifty yards, stop. Fifty yards back, stop. Ten repetitions and then some calisthenics. His wind still wasn't what it should have been, but he was getting better. The sprints were helping.

Jack san, the voice came to him. *Would you come here, please?*

He looked around, but she was nowhere to be seen. Out front, then? He grabbed the rough towel and wiped some of the sweat from his torso and shoulders before shrugging into the ill-fitting tunic which was his only upper covering. He shuffled over to his arch nemesis and retrieved the staff he'd leaned against it. "Don't think I'm letting you off this easy," he warned the tree. "I'll be back," in his best Austrian accent.

He was leaning on the staff more than he probably should be when he rounded the corner of the hut and brought up short. The old woman was there, of course. But she had company. A girl of perhaps fifteen or sixteen, dressed in white robes piped with purple and cyan, and carrying a tall, elaborate shepherd's crook staff capped with a gaudy blue jewel the size of a robin's egg woven within a maze of colored metallic threads inside the eye of the crook. Over her shoulder hung a leather satchel, dyed pink and embossed with brightly colored flowers and colorful gems. Her eyes were the purest violet, and her hair a true silver bisected by a familiar band of orchid. It was obvious who she was before the thought confirmed it.

This is my granddaughter, the old woman raised a hand to indicate the girl. *Tiarraluna Galbradia.*

He turned to the girl, who placed her hands together on the fronts of her thighs and bowed formally from the waist. "Hajimemashite, Jackson sama," she said softly. "Watashi wa

Galbradia Tiarraluna desu."

He leaned his forehead against the staff and groaned. Of course she was speaking Japanese. What else could he expect at this point. He suddenly regretted all of those dubs he'd been watching. 'I *watch* anime and *read* books' he'd always insisted to the haters. Hah! If only he'd known.

Seeing his reaction, Rosaluna frowned. *Is something wrong, Jack san?*

"Not really," he sighed. "Except that I don't speak Japanese."

But she is not speaking Japanese, Rosaluna corrected him. *She is speaking Tandrian, the language of this land, although I'm told it sounds a great deal like Japanese. Are you saying that you are speaking something else?.*

"English," he said, raising his head. "I'm speaking English. I'm an American."

A-mer-ick-an? Her eyes went wide. As though she knew the word, and didn't much care for it.

Another error, I'm afraid, she said a moment later, shaking her head, her tone harsher. *You must forgive an old woman, Jack san. I have been listening in here,* she tapped her forehead, *rather than here,* indicating an ear.

She looked back and forth between the man and the girl. *This will be a problem, I'm afraid,* she told him.

"Ya think?" he groaned. Then, "I'm sorry, Rosaluna. I owe you more than I can say, and I'm being rude. I'm just... I'm...." he sighed and banged the staff lightly against his forehead. "I'm lost."

In more ways than one, I'd imagine at this point, she came back. *The question is, what are we to do about it? How is it that you alone, of them all, do not speak the local language?*

"Same reason I don't have one of those life crystals?" he ventured without raising his head.

He lifted his head from the staff and looked towards the hut. "Perhaps it might be better if we moved this conversation?" he suggested. "I think I need to sit down."

She smiled stiffly and waved, glancing towards the con-

fused girl and indicating the hut.

"We have legends on my world," he began once they'd settled to the wooden chairs arrayed just outside the door and beneath the shade of the thatch. "Going back many, many years. Each of our countries, of worlds beyond our own, and of heroes from our world who journey there, to those worlds, in their times of need. Many of those legends are told in the land that we in the west know as Japan. But not all of them. My own country has tales going back even further, although they are more rare."

He paused to sip from the mug of water he cradled in his lap, and to allow Rosaluna to translate for her granddaughter.

"One, almost universal trait of all these legends," he resumed, "is that the hero from Earth can somehow understand the locals when they speak. It never really made sense to me, and I'd always put it down to author's convenience. Makes for a dull story if the dashing adventurer has to spend his first month or so in the new world learning the basics of the language from nothing. Not counting how short the story would be if he were mistaken for a barbarian and murdered by the locals before he'd built up the skills to save them."

Again, he paused while the old woman conveyed the story.

So, she turned back to him. *You believe that some sort of spell is used in order that we... ah, that these heroes may communicate with the residents of the worlds to which they travel?*

"Possibly," he allowed. "Or possibly it's some function of the worlds themselves. See, usually gods are involved. Some to better purpose than others."

I see. She tapped a finger against her cane. *And yet, you cannot understand my granddaughter, and would no doubt fail to understand me, were I speaking normally.*

"Clearly stated and correct." he nodded, frowning.

And do you have any idea how that might be possible?

"I'm afraid I'm beginning to," his frown deepened. "I'm beginning to think that the spells aren't cast on the heroes, but on the worlds."

World spells? An eyebrow went up. *That is a grand notion, indeed,* she allowed. *Although I'm not sure I'm ready to believe in such things.*

He shrugged. "If it was supposed to affect me, I'd be speaking Japanese. Or at least something closer to what you're speaking. Don't you think?"

She nodded slowly. *As you say, I'm beginning to.*

He sighed again. "The evidence is building that... well, as a great sage on my world once said, 'I t'ink I may'a took a wrong toin at Albeqoique.'"

That one took her a moment to work through. *You believe you were sent here by mistake?*

"Not even," he shook his head, remembering the peculiar nature of the bus. "I think I was pushed. Redirected. Deliberately."

The silence this time was longer. The sending when it finally came was tinged with more than its usual degree of sadness. *You believe that somewhere there is a world that desperately needs you, and that, instead of saving it, you are stranded here battering at my oak tree with a stick.*

Another shrug. "That's the theory that makes the most sense at this point."

That makes what we do here even more important, she stated firmly.

"And that is what, exactly?"

While I cannot aid you in your search for a life crystal, she said. *There is one who might. Tiarraluna is here to escort you into the town so that you may petition him for his aid. There is no other way for you to reach the capitol in a single piece.*

"The capitol?"

The new king, she told him. *He is from your world and a mage in his own right. If anyone on Mund will know of a way for you to reach your true destination, it will be him.*

But you must needs be able to communicate with him. And, for that matter, with my granddaughter.

"Yeah, that's the—"

Not so much as you might think, she said contemplative-

ly. *Perhaps after all, the problem is not so great. At least, there may be some limited remedy over the short term. There are magical devices, you see. Some used to facilitate long range communication, some for privacy, some to allow the user to communicate with the fell beasts or even demons.*

"And you have some of these things?"

She snorted. *Young man, I craft such things to earn my living. A skill I learned long ago...* tears formed at the corners of her eyes. *in another life.*

She turned once again and spoke to the girl, who nodded and disappeared into the hut. Moments later, the girl returned, bearing a pair of plain gold rings. Bowing, she handed one to Jack. The other, so soon as he'd donned his, she placed on her own finger, blushing prettily.

Rosaluna seemed to chide her for the blush. Probably something to do with the fact that the items were rings, and the connotation of exchanging them was similar here to what it was at home.

Her ring firmly in place, Tiarraluna stood before him and repeated the bow. "I am pleased to meet you, Jack san", she said. "I am Tiarraluna Galbradia, and granddaughter to the great and wise Rosaluna Galbradia."

He stood and bowed in turn. "Jackson Grenell," he told her. "Knucklehead from Earth."

She giggled, though Rosaluna didn't seem to find it so funny.

You know about sticks, Jack san, she sent sternly. *Do you know anything of horses?*

He smiled, feeling better already at having doubled the number of locals he could converse with. "I know which end to stay clear of after a big meal," he laughed, although her stern gaze wiped the laughter from his voice. "Grew up with them, madam," he held to a small grin. "Need one shoed, curried, doctored, or broke, I'm your boy."

I will settle for your putting her between the traces and walking her into town, she said, slightly less sternly, in spite of herself. *When I scraped you off of the grass of the Hero's Glade,*

I was forced to leave my cart behind, loaded with trade goods for the shops. Tiarraluna knows the spell to undo the wards, but she is not versed in the workings of our four legged friends.

"Got it," he said. "I appreciate your efforts, I truly do, and I'm sorry if I messed up your plans."

Delayed them, only, she assured him. *My buyers can afford to wait a few months. The prices will only rise.* With that, she stood and turned for the door.

Accustomed by now to her manner, Jack nevertheless stiffened. "You mean right now?" he called to her back.

What better time? She answered without turning. *I assure you that you will never defeat the tree without a larger stick.*

Who's Escorting Whom?

Turning to the girl, his eyes just a bit concerned, he raised an eyebrow. "Now?"

She laughed, a tinkling sound that hinted at a much gayer sense of humor than her elder.

Regarding her closely for the first time, he could better see both the family resemblance, and that Rosaluna must have been something special when she'd been young. She was a pretty, well put together kid standing about five foot nothin', with the proper amount of curves to be perfect, but no more. Tiarraluna's blush returned and deepened, and he realized that he maybe was putting too much into his inspection.

"Grandmother has prepared provisions and equipment for us," she motioned to the doorway somewhat breathlessly. "The journey should take us two days, although we will have reached the cart by tonight."

Sure enough, there beside the door was a large pack. Large even by eleven-boo standards. His back hurt just looking at it. He would apparently be carrying all their gear. He cast a quick glance within the cottage and another back to the girl waiting expectantly. There really wasn't anything inside for him to gather, so why wait?

He rolled his back, leaned over to grab a strap, and shrugged into the pack. Then he breathed a quick sigh of relief. It was lighter than it looked. So much so that his eyes narrowed, and he was tempted to haul it off and look inside. There was no way he was carrying enough gear and supplies for two people for two days on the trail.

At this point, however, he had developed a certain amount of faith in the old woman. If she thought it was good, it probably was. Anyway, he doubted she'd change anything in the loadout even did he mention it, so he let it go and turned to follow the girl to the stable.

"This is Jelia," Tiarraluna smiled as she stroked the muzzle of the piebald. "She has been grandmother's companion for as long as I can remember. She is very smart, but not so swift as once she was."

Jack looked her up and down and clucked his tongue. Yeah, he could believe that. Twenty years if she was a day. And she still pulled a cart? The velocity of his journey here made more sense now, even with the old woman's pace taken into account.

There was a pack saddle on the half wall of the stable's inner room, so he figured why not? Despite being from another world, he was able to work it out fairly quickly. Utility, form, and function, right? Similar tasks bred similar design. It might have been considered cheating, but he rigged the saddle, and tied the pack onto it. What was it his old commander had always said? No point practicing to bleed? He also took a few minutes to fetch the waster and dagger now that he wouldn't need to haul them on his own back. Never know when they might come in handy.

He cast a last look at the small stead as they left it behind, swishing through the tall grass on their way to the road, still unseen over the horizon. He'd only been here a couple of months, but he was going to miss it. Yes, and the grouchy old woman who called it home. He'd never see either again, he supposed. For some reason, that made him feel melancholy.

"G'bye, you grumpy old magical girl," he whispered under his breath.

And goodbye to you, too, young tree's bane, came the reply, making him jump. How much range did she *have* with that trick?

They reached the road by late morning, taking it easy. Jack wasn't sure if the pace the girl was setting was for his benefit or the mare's, and he didn't ask. He'd already been working himself stupid for a couple of hours before she'd shown up, and wasn't exactly fresh.

Tiarraluna called a halt when they reached it. There was a small stream on the far side along which the road traveled, so it was a handy place to water the mare and have a quick bite.

Jack didn't have to be asked twice. He settled himself down with one knee up and the other crossed beneath it. He accepted the apple and chunk of bread she dug from the pack and got to work, taking the odd sip from the water bottle hanging from a strap across his shoulder.

Watching him, Tiarraluna frowned and took a moment to observe before starting on her own lunch. He'd flopped down loosely, with apparent abandon, but she noted that his pose would allow him to rise rather quickly should he decide to. She noted also that he kept his staff close to hand.

And yet, as grandmother had said, he bore no life crystal. Not any trace of one, no matter how hard she concentrated. No status indicators of any sort, in fact. Very strange. By all visible indicators, he was the most utterly ungifted of all ungifted. But the feel of him.... the feel of him told a different story. If only she could read it.

He *was* a hero of some sort. Grandmother had assured her. And gifted. In some fashion, at least. She'd seen something of it as she'd stood beside Grandmother this morning soon after her arrival, watching him practice at the old oak. His movements had been precise beyond the level of any ungifted she'd ever seen. His speed greater. She suspected he'd be stronger as well, for his given frame. Yet none of it would matter unless they could understand it. Unless *he* could understand it.

Without making a show of it, she called forth a bit of power. Her staff barely changed hue, so faint was the glow. There was a thing she might try. Grandmother would certainly not approve, but Grandmother was back at the cottage. Closing her eyes, Tiarraluna began to hum a seeing spell. One normally not used for this sort of task. Something to find lost things. Something to open ways.

Quietly, slowly, she opened her inner eye and raised her point of focus in the man's direction. Her eyes popped open and she hiccuped in a great gasp of air, reeling back just a bit.

Jack jerked and looked up at her, puzzled. "Something wrong?" he asked.

"No-nothing," she replied too quickly. "Nothing at all,

Jack san."

He shrugged and went back to his meal, although he seemed to give it less attention than he had been. Seemed a bit less open. More wary.

Tiarraluna remained where and as she'd been, one hand upon her now quiescent staff, the other in her lap. Her food lay beside her, forgotten. A cage, she'd seen within him. With hammered bars, thick and grey. And curled far back within the depths of that cage, a mass of darkness, black as the bottom of a well, radiating power that lapped at the bars. And from within that blackness, a pair of red, glowing eyes had gazed back out at her. His gift? Or his curse?

* * *

"Hold up," Jack warned, suiting action to words.

They'd traveled about ten miles since leaving the cottage, and the sun was heeling over into dusk. They were already running behind their self-imposed schedule.

"What is it?" Tiarraluna asked, turning her head this way and that, searching for the cause of his concern.

"There's something up ahead," he said, moving forward and to the side.

Turning back, she studied the road ahead. "What is it?"

"Dunno," he admitted. "Something. I can feel it."

She whispered a command to Jelia and moved forward, bringing her staff up and to the ready. She couldn't sense anything herself, but that wasn't really her field of expertise. A few muttered words brought the jewel to a dull glow and prepared the staff for combat. It was her job, after all, to protect the man until he could reach the town.

"No," he said softly, waving her back. "This feels wrong. You watch from here."

That was stupid. She was— but he was already moving off, quartering away from the roadway. She shook herself free of the nonsensical command and had already moved to follow him when he stopped and flung a fist sized rock he'd picked up somewhere into a scraggly bush on the far side of the road.

The rock landed behind the bush with a meaty thwack,

instantly followed by a chorus of deep-throated howls. Five creatures the likes of which Tiarraluna had never seen burst forth from undergrowth she wouldn't have guessed would conceal a large cat, all of them rushing straight at the man. None of *them* had life crystals either!

Tom Black

Teufeljaegers

Something wasn't right, Jack thought, moving forward and quartering away from the area that was giving him the itch. The girl, for the moment, was staying behind with the horse. That, at least, was good.

There was something about that jumble of bushes over there across the road that didn't look quite right. Nothing obvious. He couldn't even articulate to himself what it was. There was also the hint of an odd smell in the air. Something that tasted of rotting garbage and mildew. Not anything he'd ever smelled before, not even in the 'stan.

If this was an ambush, it was a pretty good one. There wasn't any indication anywhere that this might be a good place to lie in wait. The grass wasn't overly tall, there were no real terrain features beyond those bushes, and *those* didn't look substantial enough to conceal a coyote.

He was carrying his staff in high guard, so he shifted it to his shoulder, fishing around in the possibles pouch the old woman had included with the replacements she'd given him for his ruined clothing. He'd picked up a couple of good sized rocks back along the way for just such occasions. Scanning his surroundings one last time before committing, he chucked the rock into the bush with everything he had.

The projectile hit something obviously alive, and things instantly went south. Half a dozen creatures with the heads of bats and the bodies of stub-tailed, humanoid werewolves leapt up from nowhere, howling doom at him. They were armed with short swords. The one farthest from him —the one who'd been behind the bush— also had a buckler. Worse, the nearest one was almost on top of him already.

He got the staff into low guard barely in time to divert the first sword blow, fumbling the move enough so that the riposte was late and only grazed one bat ear rather than caving in the skull. He knew these things!

Teufeljaegers! They were from that damned game! Level

ten to twenty monsters, they were bio constructs, and the most prolific lower mid tier mobs you encountered until you started running into guns in the second area at around level twenty-one. They came in packs of eight to ten. There were usually crossbows mixed with the melee fighters, but he saw no hint of any here.

Their hide had the same Armor Class as boiled leather, and was resistant to cutting or piercing. That was okay, he didn't have anything that did either of those. They were fast and decently smart, but their base tactics ran along the lines of charge and chop. The one with the buckler would be a champion. Stronger, with a better weapon skill and a deeper health pool.

He took a wide step back, trying to keep his near opponent between him and the others as he maneuvered. They'd be on him in a second, so he had to be quick.

GrandmotherGrandmotherGrandmotherGrandmother-GrandmotherGrandmother! Tiarraluna took two steps back at the appearance of the beasts, shocked to her very core, and very frightened.

Child? Came the worried sending.

Grandmother? She thought, surprised to be answered. *How—?*

You are at the far edge of my range, Child, the reply was worried. *Were we not tied by blood, I'd not have heard you at all. What is happening? You sound—*

Grandmother, Tiarraluna's sending bore the hint of a squeak. *We are set upon! Creatures such as I have never seen! Huge and hairy! They bear no life crystals!*

Ten miles away, in her small cottage, a giant claw squeezed around Rosaluna's heart. *How many, child?* She struggled, eyes squeezed tightly closed to maintain the concentration the spell required in the face of her dread.

Five, Grandmother, Tiarraluna sent. *They have swords, and one a small shield.*

What is Jack san doing? The old woman demanded.

He... he is fighting them, Grandmother!

In the hut, the old woman chuckled without humor, an ugly sound due to her handicap. *Of course he is,* she sent. *That is what they do,* with a tinge of bitterness. *Regardless of how impossible the odds. Even to their certain doom.... That is what they do.*

Quickly, child, the old woman ordered now, straightening and squaring herself, reaching for her bag and the tools therein. *You must cast ironwood on Jack san's staff, and name it!*

But Grandmother, the girl quailed. *I cannot. I do not have the power or time to name—*

I will aid you, child, the old woman insisted. *Do it now!* She withdrew a phial of smokey liquid from her bag and dashed it to the floor, shattering the fine crystal vessel and releasing a cloud of pungent vapor into the room. Dashing also the stab of regret at what she was about to do to her old friend.

The girl began the spell, uncertain of how much good would come of it. Even were she to successfully name the weapon, without a crystal, Jack san could not wield such a thing. Nevertheless, she forced her eyes closed and gave over her entire concentration to forming the spell. An aura of azure light grew around the jewel in her staff as she opened her eyes. Eyes that now showed no visible pupil, only a pale, blue-white glow.

The glow emanating from the jewel expanded beyond its physical confines, darkening into a nimbus of pulsing sapphire energy before lancing across the field to envelop the staff and the hands holding it. "By my power and my will, and my bond with this land," she hissed the incantation's final stanza. "I name thee now and forevermore... er... FoeSmite!"

Far off, the old woman rolled her eyes. *Now, child! RUN!*
Grandmother?
Run, Button! Run away! The man has no chance. None at all! He will die. You have given him an opportunity to perhaps buy you some time to escape. Jelia will carry you home; she has one or two runs left in her old bones. But you must flee! NOW!
Grandmother, I cannot!
Heroes are not immortal, child, the old woman insisted.

You above all should know that!

I will not. Tiarraluna was firm.

Button...! The sending bore the tone of a wail.

Wait, the girl interjected. *Something has changed. Grandmother! He is fighting them!*

Of course he— the old woman started.

No, Grandmother, Tiarraluna insisted. *He is* fighting *them!*

The jaeger was charging hard, and Jack nearly missed his next parry, but he made it, just. The instant his staff had broken the sword's line, he swung high and around, sliding his left hand down the shaft. *Hard, now,* he grunted unconsciously. *Break something, damnit!*

Even as the staff sliced the air, he felt an electric pulse race up both arms, felt the hair stand all along them. Felt an even more intense shock race up his spine and crash straight up through the crown of his head. His eyes went unfocused.

An instant later, he heard a sickening crack. His heart sank. He'd broken the damned staff! He was done for.

But wait. There was no overbalance or any of the follow-through he'd get if he'd broken the thing off short. Instead, there was an agonized yowl as the jaeger buckled at the shoulder, going nearly to one knee.

He didn't have time to be amazed. Even as his vision came back into focus, the next monster arrived. Jack danced sideways, struggling to keep his first opponent in range without opening a line for its friend.

He shook his head struggling to clear the buzzing in his ears. He felt like he'd been tazed.

The creature was still howling. Hell, they all were. It was an area effect attack that was supposed to paralyze its victims with fear. But it wasn't a surprise mortar attack at oh-three-hundred, or a five hundred pound bomb buried in the road beneath a soda can, so it had little power over him. His sense of terror had long ago been anesthetized. He could power through it now.

The others were halfway across the road already. He could see them from the corner of his eye. Had to hurry. He parried the incoming sword, slapping it offline and bringing his staff up into the riposte. The jaeger had seen its friend fall to that move, and ducked quickly aside. That was fine, *it* wasn't his target.

Swinging the staff in a full arc, using his entire upper body, rolling the shaft off his hip and around, Jack let it slide out of his grip until he held the shaft with a single hand, grasping it at its very base. Six-and-a-half feet away, moving faster than the eye could follow, the far end struck his first dancing partner in the side of the knee as it was gaining its feet. The crack was louder this time. The knee buckled sideways and the beast collapsed into a muddy heap.

Another two steps back, drawing them away from the girl and the horse. Four to go. They weren't charging quite so quickly now. As he'd noted; smart. The near jaeger had its sword up en garde trying to work out how to attack him. He remembered there were no staves in the game. Spears, yes. Polearms, for certain. No staves, and his use of it seemed to confuse them. Good. Any advantage was useful.

He moved in at middle guard, waving the staff like a spear, to draw them in. Every second he spent in this encounter tipped the probabilities in their favor. He had to get things over quickly. So, small circles, holding the staff at the base in one hand and about a quarter of the way up with the other. Small circles to keep them guessing. Maybe he was a spearman, maybe not....

At once, he thrust forward and up, straight in for the face of the nearest. The jaeger parried, attempting to break his line as though facing a spear. Jack swept his trailing arm up and back, curling the fore end of the shaft down and around the sword blade, spanking it well clear. In the same motion, he punched down at the rear while pulling up at the fore, smacking the creature under the chin and measuring it. Another thrust, this time to the groin with a good yard of travel to build momentum, and the head was right there, waiting. Up to high, and down atop that misshapen skull, and he cracked it like a melon.

Three steps back, two to the right. Three of them left. But something was wrong with his left arm. It was on fire and he was losing strength in it. A quick glance down showed him blood on the staff. Red blood. Opening his hand, he saw the wound. His first exchange, then. He hadn't gotten his hand clear of the initial, clumsily parried blow, and the bastard had shaved the pad from his fingertip. And, oh, yeah, he remembered now. Poison. A dark stain was spreading down along the finger and wicking out into his hand even as he watched.

He was still backing away as the three remaining teufeljaegers maneuvered to surround him. His position was still pretty dire. Moreso, in fact, than before. Unlike in the game, he had no way to deal with poison, which meant that he was probably already dead. Thankfully, without the crossbow mooks, none of them had any ranged attacks, so he at least stood a chance of taking them down with him and saving the girl.

Do not attack, Button, Rosaluna was ordering sternly. *If you must refuse to flee, at least do not draw attention to yourself. Just try to keep him alive as long as possible. It will not be easy. He has no armor at all, and against swords, well.... I will aid as I can, but I am weak after so many months of putting him back together the first time and now granting him a named weapon from this distance. There is little more that I can do.*

As you wish, Grandmother, Tiarraluna replied taughtly.

Button, please reconsider, the old woman pleaded.

Mere seconds had passed since the eruption of the monsters from seeming invisibility, but much had happened. Tiarraluna had managed to enchant the staff and the man had already weathered two attacks. More, the first creature to attack him seemed sorely injured.

FoeSmite never stopped moving, swinging about and darting in as though it had a mind of its own, and the man merely holding it back. Was it glowing? It looked to be glowing. She must be imagining that. Ironwood should not cause such an effect.

She gasped when he missed his first chance at the second beast, but had to throttle a shout of joy when the blow struck its true target. How was he doing this? She had never seen a true hero fight. She was too young. Was this how it always was with them?

He is not doing so badly, she sent to her grandmother.

How can that be? Came the reply. *Even with what we've given him, he cannot hope to prevail against five—*

There are only four now. Tiarraluna couldn't keep the pride from her voice.

What was that? How?

Now three, Tiarraluna smiled wide as Jack san's latest victim went down. *The others are growing wary. Grandmother! He has a life bar!*

Oh, Button, you didn't! the claw tightened around the old woman's heart.

It is not very bright, the girl sent. *Almost transparent, but I am sure it is a life bar.*

Do you see any sign of a crystal? The old woman's sending sounded resigned.

No, she admitted. *Just the bar. Wait. There is a status effect in play. I do not... Grandmother, his health is dropping. They are not touching him but it is dropping.*

Poison! The old woman warned. *You must cleanse it, Child! Quickly!*

Wasted effort. Tiarraluna was already chanting the spell. She felt her gorge rise as her spell touched the poison. Vile stuff, grown of ichor and hate and evil. She grounded herself more firmly and began to draw mana from her surroundings as well as from herself and her grandmother. The glow of the purification spell began to brighten as she fed more power to it. A very powerful poison. Such that she would not have the power to heal him or close his wounds while dealing with it.

One of the creatures raised its head and sniffed at the air. Its head swiveled around, coming to bear on her. Without pause, it turned and charged.

Far away, Rosaluna felt the fear take hold of her little

Button and quailed.

It was getting harder to use the arm. That was bad. A quarterstaff was one of the most two handed of two handed weapons to wield. It wasn't the pain, either. The muscles were under attack. His tormentors were holding back now, waiting for the inevitable.

All at once, he felt a sensation of warmth wash through him, and the pain began to diminish. He could feel the strength return to his arm, bit by bit. He didn't dare turn away from his enemies, but he knew that this must be the girl's doing.

He shuffled farther to his right, shifting to low guard, his right hand high, drawing evil eyes further away from her. He could see her now. What's more, he could see the glowing trail of what he could only consider a magical spell connecting them. And if he could see it....

One of the jaegers straightened. The one closest to the girl. It sniffed the air, as if sensing the magic. It turned, and charged.

"NO!" he shouted without conscious thought. He reared back, and flung the staff spearlike with every ounce of strength left in him. It sailed like a bullet and impacted the base of the jaeger's skull. The thing crumpled bonelessly to the dirt nearly at her feet, the staff bounding away and over her head.

Okay, *NOW* he was screwed. But it wasn't in him to give up. He dove back in the direction of his first kill as the remaining pair of teufeljaegers charged with renewed rage.

He hit the ground rolling, snatched up the dead jaeger's sword and lunged to his feet just in time to clumsily parry the first onrushing assault.

Tiarraluna did not scream. She wanted to. She needed to. But she would not. Not while he needed her. She held her concentration and pulled the poison from his body even as her vision was filling with a mountain of stinking fur, teeth, and claws. She didn't even step back as the beast collapsed at her feet, or duck as FoeSmite sailed over her head to disappear behind her. Only when the poison was gone did she drop to her knees with reaction.

Then the realization hit. FoeSmite had sailed over her head? Her heart caught, and she turned to look, but it was nowhere to be seen. Back to the battle, and she saw that Jack san had taken up one of the swords.

He has thrown FoeSmite away! she sent raggedly.

He can't have, the old woman sent with utter assurance. *That would be idiocy.*

He is fighting the remaining two with a sword now, the girl told her.

A monster's sword? The old woman wondered, even as she absorbed the notion that he'd somehow struck another of the enemy down. *How can he even hold one?*

Tiarraluna shrugged helplessly. She knew no more than her grandmother. *He is not very good with it,* she admitted. *But he seems at least to know its working.*

The sword was crap. The hilt felt like rebar, the heavy pommel like a lump of untempered ore. The quillons were loose and undersized, and the blade felt like an iron ingot that had been poorly cast and sharpened on a rock. It was too short, there was no real point, and the balance was completely wrong.

He was still nominally on his knees when he parried the first attack by the simple expedient of bashing it out of the way, feeling the shock of the blow travel all the way to his shoulder. He didn't stick around to riposte. Instead, he dug in his toes, took a runner's knee, and launched himself clear. He began circling away from the big one with the buckler. That guy was going to be no end of trouble.

He was waving the sword back and forth as he circled, not so much to fend off any attacks as to try and get the feel of it. It hung from the end of his hand like an iron club. Hold on. Time for a change of perception. Don't think of it as a steel sword. Think of it like it was a rattan stick. Heavier, but just as bulky. Just as poorly balanced. Just a long club with a hilt. Just like with the Anachronists in the park. Except with these things, he didn't have to moderate his strikes.

His first victim was still alive and still clinging to its weapon, though it was reduced to crawling, dragging itself along the ground with one arm and one leg. It was raging at him, a string of invective and curses that he could clearly understand. Well, the words, if not some of the curses. That thing had an imagination.

A quick feint at his pursuers, and he took off running, arcing wide to intercept the crawling jaeger. He didn't even bother to parry the feeble chop that came up at him. Instead, he stomped down on the wrist and swung for the neck with his entire strength. He stooped to catch the sword from the slackening grip as the head bounced along the grass. Another thing the game hadn't had was dual wielding.

Okay, he thought, his breath coming in gasps. *Now, we're talkin'!*

He has changed his stance, Tiarraluna informed her grandmother. *And he has picked up another sword. He is holding two of them now. Grandmother, he is smiling.*

Jack was dancing back, shifting his feet, one blade held upright in each hand. They may as well have been cleavers for all the finesse they allowed, so as cleavers he'd treat them.

They moved in, and he shifted aside, keeping the lesser jaeger between himself and the champion. They were the stronger, but he the more agile. The creature shifted with him undeterred, striking swiftly. Jack parried with his right sword and slashed downward with his left, the crude blade skittering along the tough hide and shaving off a hatful of hair.

Oh, right. Resistant to cutting attacks. Another strike, which he parried with his left, this time striking straight down across the forearm with his right hand blade, grunting with the effort. The thick blade bit deep, cleaving the arm nearly in two.

The jaeger yowled, dropping its sword and clutching at the ruined arm. Without warning, then, the creature lunged directly forward. The big one had kicked it bodily into him. He managed to feed it a hasty shot to the teeth with a sword pommel as the pair of them toppled backward to the ground, with the wounded jaeger on top, knocking the breath from the man as they landed.

The only thing that saved Jack then was that the jaeger was also stunned, and so didn't tear out his throat with its teeth. As it was, it was bleeding all over him, and its stench was hampering his ability to think.

Aaaand, he is poisoned again.

He'd freed a hand and had begun to push the recovering beast aside when he became aware of the pillar-like legs flanking them. He tilted his head around to get a better look and realized the big one was going to run its subordinate clean through and pin them both to the ground. *Yeah, no.*

He cocked a leg and fed the big guy a heel to the ankle, feeling the shock travel clear up past his knee and into his hip. It was enough, though, and the champion staggered back. Jack took the opportunity to roll the dazed jaeger off his chest and run the sword he hadn't dropped in the fall into its throat, leaning into the thrust with both hands and bathing his face and upper body in its ichor

Very, very poisoned.

Jack had only managed hands and knees before he felt the brutal slam of the big foot into his chest. He was hurled backward several feet, landing in a tangle, the sword flying well clear. His whole body was on fire now, as the poison ate away at him. He rolled himself onto his side, struggling to rise, but that kick had really hurt him. Another try, and he'd almost made it before the boot hit him again, hurling him even further. He groaned when he hit. Okay, that one had broken a rib or three.

He was slower getting over this time. The pain in his chest combined with the fire of the poison was overwhelming. He made it halfway to one knee, then flopped over onto his back. The jaeger champion was taking its time, calling taunts as it strolled toward him. It had won, and it knew it.

Call to me, an unknown voice drifted into Jack's brain. Different than Rosaluna's communication. Voiceless. A whisper coming from both within and without. *We are one now,* it urged. *Call to me.*

The jaeger was standing over him now, grinning its toothy grin. "You will never inconvenience my master now," it laughed gutturally. It raised its misshapen sword to split him in half.

"Come!" Jack croaked, holding his arm at full extension, willing the staff to him.

The sword came down with a mighty clack! Intersecting the shaft of the staff midway, bowing it with the force of the swing. With a mighty heave, holding the staff centered, hands wide, Jack thrust the blade to the side, shifting his grip and pushing up with his left arm as he pulled in with his right. The end of the shaft arced up into the side of the jaeger champion's head with a sodden thunk.

He reversed then, swinging wide from the ground, slipping his grip farther back, and took the disoriented jaeger's knee. As the staff rebounded from the breaking joint, he brought the far end around and down against the ear of the falling monster almost exactly where he'd already struck it.

As the creature lay stunned half atop him, Jack kicked himself painfully clear and climbed the staff like a ladder, pulling himself painfully up along its length, leaving bloody streaks along its surface. The foot he'd kicked the jaeger with wouldn't hold his weight, so the staff became a crutch. Moving to the hairy, bat head, he looked around. The fallen sword lay too far away for his comfort. The jaeger might come to by the time he reached it, and he was all out of fight. So he took his balance, raised the staff high, and rammed it down into an eye socket with a sickening squelch. Then, just because his chest *really* hurt, he pulled it clear and slammed it down again, sinking at least eight inches of its length into what passed for the creature's brain.

He raised his head, then, and groggily surveyed the battlefield, his breath coming in shallow, croaking gasps. The horse stood calmly, not a care in the world. The girl knelt nearby, working some sort of spell by the looks of her. Hopefully something to do with the fiery sludge coursing through his entire body like cut rate biryani from a questionable street vendor. All else was still. He'd apparently won. Hooray for him. With that, he collapsed, out before he hit the ground.

Tiarraluna's heart skipped at the man's collapse, but not so much as it had when FoeSmite had shot past her and into his hand a few moments earlier. He was not dead, at least. She could feel his life through the connection of the spell she was still working to clear the poisons he would insist on bathing himself in. His health bar was no more than a sliver of red, but he would probably live if his physical injuries weren't too severe. She was ruinously weary.

It is done, Grandmother, she sighed.

* * *

In her cottage, Rosaluna joined her, though her sigh was more drawn out and deep. *By your tone, I take you to mean that he has succeeded rather than succumbed?* She sent hopefully.

They are all dead, Grandmother, the girl affirmed. *Whether he succumbs or not remains in question. It was a near thing, but he has defeated them.*

Oh, and he has a mana bar now.

Rosaluna leaned forward and lay her face in her hands. How tightly was that idiot child binding herself to this strange man? Did she not see the calamity of such endeavor?

He called FoeSmite to him, Tiarraluna went on. *At the end. He was about to die and he called. And it came.*

Did she now? Rosaluna wondered absently to herself before asking, *how far?* She was struggling against the urge to order the girl to bring both the hero and the staff back to the cottage for examination.

I am not sure, her granddaughter sent back. *I do not know how far it was behind me when he called. It was flying like a crossbow quarrel when it passed me, and he was nearly a hundred yards beyond. It was a strong call.*

Can you go to him yet? The old woman asked. She could feel the weariness in the girl through their connection. Feel the pull of mana indicating that she was yet casting.

Soon, Grandmother, came the reply. *It seems the blood of these things is horribly venomous, and he got quite a lot of it on him. The cleansing is taking some time.*

Do you need me any further? The old woman asked. *Are you strong enough to finish alone?*

Yes, Grandmother, Tiarraluna sighed again. *I am strong enough.*

Good, then, the old woman wheezed. *In that case, I must rest for awhile. Call for me again when the both of you are up and about.*

I will, Grandmother, Tiarraluna assented. *And when I do, will you tell me please how I managed to perform a three hour naming ceremony in as many seconds? I must confess to being somewhat confused.*

In her hut, the elderly enchantress laughed aloud, so much as her deformity allowed her. *Perhaps I will, Button,* she smiled inwardly. *Perhaps.*

She broke the connection and flopped backwards against the thin cushion of the chair, breath coming in tearing gasps now that she'd no need to hide her condition. The claw at her heart had loosened only moderately. Button had joined herself with this man somehow. She had become his companion. That was a bond that did not go away regardless of how fervently one wished. It was a life bond that promised only heartbreak. How had she managed it? And so quickly?

And what of the man himself? What sort of creature was he, who could summon magic and wield higher order weapons, and even monstrous weapons, all without a crystal?

And yet the staff. FoeSmite now, she was. She had returned when called? That was very unexpected.

* * *

Jack san was still unconscious when Tiarraluna reached

him. That wasn't terribly surprising. She'd already shut down the purification spell twice, thinking herself done, only to have the rot spring forth anew after only a moment. It was pernicious stuff. Finally, she'd decided it best to simply allow it to spread for the time it took her to reach him. If she could lay hands on him, the spell would be that much more powerful, and draw that much less mana. She would wring that horrid putrification out of him if it took the last dribblings of mana she could gather.

In the event, it took nearly that, even once she'd drenched him in purifying water. Once he was truly free of the invasion, she settled to the ground beside him, exhausted. Resting on one arm, she looked down at his still face, wondering at the place he'd come from. That place where heroes spawned. Were they all like this? They couldn't be, surely.

She caught herself and cut her introspection short. He was still grievously wounded, and she was now without the mana to aid him. Not for some time would her reserves build sufficiently to do anything of note. The local area even longer. Nor would she call upon Grandmother again so soon. The old woman might think her fooled by bravado, but Tiarraluna could sense full well the degree of strain the battle had put her under.

Gathering herself with a deep breath, she pushed to her feet and moved slowly to Jelia. The pack would contain basic first aid equipment. Perhaps enough, perhaps not. Enough certainly to stop the bleeding, at least. What she'd use to replace the horribly fouled tunic she'd had to cut him clear of she had no idea.

Anger, Gifts, and the Passage of Souls

Jack awakened slowly, painfully, to the powerful stench of dead teufeljaegers. The fire was gone from his body, but there remained sufficient pain to do the job. He tried to catalog the different areas without moving. An old trick that had served him well over his misspent life. Sliced finger, stinging like somebody had soaked it in lemon juice. Another cut, apparently, along his stomach. He didn't remember getting that one. Throbbing ache of a sprained and swelling ankle. That one he did remember. Somebody was strumming the muscles of his back from his right shoulder blade to his spine with a steel guitar pick soaked in brine, using his arm as a fretboard. And, of course, the cracked rib. Or maybe two. Had he really survived that fight? At the moment, he wasn't altogether sure.

"Awake at last," the girl's musical voice intruded on his self pity.

He cocked an eye open and regarded her as calmly as he might. "Healer, right?"

She smiled and laughed lightly, a surprisingly unsettling sound for the way it made his stomach tighten. She was way too young for him and that wasn't counting the wrong world angle.

"I am a mage, Jack san," she told him. "Not a priestess. I *can* cast low-mid rank healing spells, but not just now. It will be quite some time before I am able to generate so much as a fairy light after you put me to so much trouble with the keeping of you alive. Have you no sense of self-preservation at all?"

He started to answer, but she hadn't stopped.

"I mean," she went on. "Grandmother always told me how you heroes were, but I had always thought her to be exaggerating."

He sighed. He wasn't sure which one she was, yet, but he figured here was where he found out. He'd originally thought deredere, but the snark was confusing him. Obviously not tsundare, since she hadn't clobbered him yet even once. But she didn't fall into any of the other categories either. He closed his eye again, reminding himself, *Too young, wrong world*. Therefore, whether the universe was hitting him with best girl tropes or not, it didn't matter. Couldn't matter.

"Define, 'quite some time', please?" eyes still closed, voice strained.

"Some time tomorrow, at the earliest," she said. "I cannot express with sufficient clarity how near you came to dying out here, Jack san." she scolded. "I am not an arch mage. I am only a rank ten. I am not even officially a full mage yet, merely an advanced novice.

"The venom is gone," she let out an exasperated breath. "You have stopped bleeding, and I have bound your physical wounds as best I can using mundane methods. I suggest you settle for that."

"Fine," he relented. "I'm sorry, alright? I promise, I probably won't do it again."

"Probably?" her voice squeaked. "Jack san—"

"Best I can do," he opened the eye again, grinning at her panicked expression. "It wasn't like I *invited* a mob of teufeljaegers to jump us."

"Jack san?"

He winced at the coldness that had come to her voice. "Tiarraluna?"

"You know these things?"

"Kind of?"

"You have fought them before?"

"Sort of?" he winced and tucked in his head. If she was tsundare, he'd find it out now.

"They are from your world?" her voice was ice. "This is why they bear no life crystals?"

He opened both eyes when the rain of blows didn't come. Okay, not tsundare. "No."

"Then where?"

"Can we move clear of the bodies before we discuss things any further?" he asked. "They stink something awful. Am I well enough to move?"

"If you are careful," she allowed.

"Where's my staff?"

"FoeSmite is beside you, on your far side. I cleaned the goo from it as well."

"FoeSmite?" he asked quizzically.

"Your staff," she clarified. "Grandmother and I enchanted and named it. Did you really think you had successfully bested five monsters with a green heartwood stick?"

"But... FoeSmite?"

"I was in a hurry!" her cheeks reddened. "Be grateful it is named at all. That fact probably saved your miserable life!"

"Alright," he held up a placating hand. "Alright, I'm sorry. FoeSmite it is."

He rolled to his side and took up the staff, noting the lack of any fresh gouges or dents. Yeah, that didn't jibe with the thing he'd carved. As he had before, he climbed it like a ladder, accepting the girl's additional aid without comment. Now that he could pay attention, the wood was darker than he remembered. Sort of reddish, like cherry wood. It felt warm to the touch. He looked to the girl and back to the staff. FoeSmite. Whatever she'd done had indeed changed it.

Then he remembered the call. Had that been real? He'd been down and unarmed, and then he wasn't. *You called me?* He wondered. As if in response, he felt the wood warm beneath his hand.

He looked back to the girl. "Rank ten, you say?"

She sniffed. "Grandmother helped, alright?"

"Grandmother?" his eyes went wide. "You can connect with her all the way out here? Just how powerful *is* that woman?"

"I can," she smiled proudly. "And very. My grandmother, Rosaluna Galbradia, is rank two-hundred, and one of the most powerful enchantresses in the land. If not *the* most powerful. You have her as well to thank for your life. Again."

"Well," he nodded. "She may consider herself thanked. Again."

They'd reached the horse by this time, which was a good thing, as both were exhausted by even this token effort. Jack sort of slid himself down FoeSmite's shaft and lay back down for a little rest. He shuddered to imagine what continuing on to the cart would be like. He hadn't been this beat since running mountain patrols in the 'stan humping a mortar tube.

"How far are you expecting to go before we camp?" he asked experimentally.

"I think five or ten yards from the road should be enough," she answered casually. "I do not want to venture beyond the wards."

He raised his head, and stared. "You mean camp right here? What if those bodies draw scavengers?"

"Do you not know how to start a fire?" she asked. "If not, I do. We shall be fine."

"But why here?"

She glared. "Because I will not abide those... things... to foul the land," she said. "I will purify their souls and give their bodies to Mund." she drew in a breath. "But not until tomorrow."

"Mund?" he wondered. "Who is Mund? Your god?"

She looked at him as though he were an idiot for a moment, before remembering that he was not of this world. She looked to the ring on her finger, frowning, and then back to him. "Mund is the world," she explained.

"So you're going to consecrate the bodies and give them over to your world?" he ventured. "Good luck with that."

"And what is that supposed to mean?"

"Means," he yawned, "that I doubt your world will have them."

Tiarraluna would have to gather the firewood and kindle the fire on her own. Jack was asleep.

She sat watching him for quite some time before rising to do so, her mind working through the day's events. She'd been fully prepared to find him strange, based on Grandmother's warnings. She hadn't expected to find him so infuriating. Moreover, she hadn't expected to find herself so readily falling into the role of a follower.

Grandmother had given over to her the task of conveying the man to the town. She should have taken the lead and held to it. But when he'd told her to stay back, she'd unthinkingly done so, like it was the most natural thing in the world. Worse, he'd fully expected her to do so. As though it were her place. And his place to order such.

Atop it all, he'd gone to sleep without clarifying where he'd previously encountered the like of these teufel-things. Sighing in a put-upon fashion, she rose and moved into the treeline to hunt for kindling.

Jack was up with the sun to find that she'd apparently managed to roll him onto a blanket and drape the loose end over him. Good thing, too. The air was brisk. Smiling, still using FoeSmite as a crutch, he staggered to his feet and into the woods while the girl slept.

She was stirring by the time he'd returned, sitting up and primping her colorful hair. Girls etcetera. He debated flopping down beside the embers of the fire and seeing if she'd feed him, but decided he needed to see the results of his prior day's efforts with a clear head more than he was hungry. He settled for grabbing the blanket and draping it over his shoulders. That was the trouble with having only one set of clothes to your name while living a life of adventure. Too easy to iterate the one down to zero.

The jaegers hadn't derezzed. He'd been half convinced they would, despite the girl's comments. Yeah, they were teufeljaegers alright. Far uglier in life than in the game, but there was no mistake. He hobbled completely around the champion, trying to get a better notion of what he would be dealing with moving forward, since he did not doubt for an instant that he'd be dealing with more of these things as time progressed.

Having satisfied himself that they were indeed from the game, he was coming to the decision that they'd been sent specifically to take him out before he could spoil their master's plans. The champion's final comment helped that theory.

Now he was wondering if maybe the bus had been sent for the same purpose. He'd been going under the assumption up until now that it had been a more or less typical isekai delivery system gone deliberately awry. But if its purpose had simply been to kill him without shunting him anywhere, how had he ended up here? And how had they known where to find him?

He was still standing over the champion's body when the girl arrived some while later. He glanced up as she moved to his side. "Good morning, Tiarraluna," he nodded. "Sleep well?"

"Jack san," she replied, looking down at the dead monster rather than up at him.

"They're supposed to be bio-constructs," he ventured experimentally.

"Golems, then?"

"More self aware," he said. "Fairly smart on the scale of the creatures their master employs."

"Yes," her voice was low, contemplative. "Their master. About whom you were going to inform me yesterday, but instead decided to hibernate."

He gave her the eye. This attitude was in danger of becoming tiresome. "Is there something you want to address with me, Tiarraluna?" he asked with an edge to his voice.

She started and looked up, directly into his eyes, blushing slightly.

He twisted around on the staff to address her more directly. "Look," he said more softly. "I'm very grateful for all the help you and your grandmother have given me. For my life, in fact, since I'm sure that my continued presence among the living can be laid entirely at your feet. But you keep treating me like your ex-husband on visitation day and I think I might just as well say goodbye here and go on alone."

She ducked her head and lowered her eyes. She had almost no idea what the man was talking about, but his tone was clear, and she could guess its cause. Upon some short introspection, she thought that she *could* perhaps see where it *might* be that she could *possibly* be seen as somewhat infuriating in her own right. Maybe. In a certain light. Her blush deepened.

"Very well, Jack san," she said without looking up. "While I do not know what visitation day is, nor how one becomes an ex-husband, I will attempt to guard my tongue more aggressively."

He raised an eyebrow, playing back through that statement in his head. So, she'd still think him an inconsiderate idiot, but she'd try harder to keep it to herself? Was that what he'd heard? *Ah, well,* he thought. Tomorrow they'd be in the town. Next day at the latest. And then she could find somebody else to look down on. He'd be out of her hair, and she wouldn't be his problem anymore.

The silence stretched on for minutes before the girl gathered herself once again to speak. "And you will tell me now where you have encountered these monsters?" she asked in what she hoped was an even tone.

Now *he* was on the spot. Did they even have video games here? He kind of doubted it based on the level of technology he'd seen thus far.

"I've never encountered them in person," he admitted after some thought. "Only in simulations."

"Simulations?" she wondered. "I don't understand."

"I'm pretty sure these things are from the world I was supposed to be sent to," he explained.

"We had already worked that out, Grandmother and I."

"Right." he scratched at the back of his head with the hand not holding onto FoeSmite. "In my world, we have... machines... that allow us to simulate being elsewhere. Spells, I suppose you'd call them here, though they aren't technically magic. That allow us to practice," *Or pretend*, his subconscious confessed silently. "engaging and defeating obstacles. So that when or if we encounter them for real, we aren't entirely unfamiliar."

"I see," she ruminated. "War games, yes?"

"Sure," he smiled. "Close enough."

"And so, you already knew how to defeat them before you went forward on your own?"

"I, ah..." he cleared his throat. "I didn't know it was these things until they jumped up out of the grass at me."

"Ah," she frowned.

"Look," he shot back. "I lived, they didn't, okay? Just do your thing and let's be off down the damn' road, alright?" he waved a hand in the direction of the stinking lumps of matted fur. "Just get my ass to town and I'll be out of your hair for good. Won't that be nice?"

She'd taken a step back at the increased volume in his voice, but it wasn't enough. Somehow, his sudden anger hurt. She felt her chest tighten at his proclamation. But that was silly. Why should she care if he was angry with her? Why should she feel pain at the notion that she wouldn't see him again? That had been the entire plan from the beginning, had it not?

"I... I cannot," she stammered back. "Not yet, at the least."

He rested his head against FoeSmite's shaft, eyes squeezed shut, forcing himself to calm. Where had *that* come from? As if he didn't know. He'd done the best he could. From the moment he'd awakened in this crummy place. Just like he'd always done in that other crummy place. His very best.

Sometimes, that hadn't been enough, though, had it? Who was he, Clark freaking Kent? And every time... each and every God—! Every time he'd come home after something had gone sideways —his fault, somebody else's fault, nobody's fault— somebody had always been right there handy to look him dead in the eye and say, 'Ah. Too bad. If only you'd been stronger. If only you'd been quicker. If only you'd been smarter.' And all too often, if there'd been no one else to lay blame, that look, that 'ah,' had come from the mirror.

"—ill take at least the rest of the morning," the girl's voice intruded on his thoughts. "Before I have regained enough mana to attempt a soul release."

"Fine," he said into the wood of FoeSmite's shaft. "I'm gonna take a turn around to scout for sign. See if I can figure out where these things came from. And then I think I need to rest a bit more."

Tiarraluna stood stock still as he turned and hobbled off, the tortured cast of his face burning itself into her memory. Had she been the cause of that? How? What had she done? Was his ego so frail that a bit of sarcasm could damage him?

Shaking herself loose from that train of thought, she turned back for the fire circle. Jelia would need water, and there was a bit of sweet feed in the pack that would help her along. She was an old mare, and deserved more rest than Grandmother gave her.

The sun was heeling over and Jack seemed to have recovered his temper by the time Tiarraluna was ready to assay the task for which they'd held themselves from the trail.

"I've been meaning to ask," Jack ventured as they moved towards the bodies. His voice was much subdued, but not hostile. "You're a mage, right? For sufficient purposes of? Isn't this the sort of thing for a priestess?"

She shrugged, herself still uncertain how to feel. "Ideally," she said. "But there is some overlap in the abilities and duties of our professions, and many things that any gifted can accomplish. For instance," she waved a hand in the direction of his wounds. "A priestess of rank ten could have cleared the poison out of you *and* healed all of your physical maladies with relatively little effort. But she would not have been able to enchant or name FoeSmite, regardless of how much assistance she might have."

"I see."

"Any gifted," she went on, "with any sort of mana manipulating ability, can cast healing spells. It is often the first thing adventurers learn. Even you," she nodded his way. "With the mana you possess, could perform up to, I would say, higher order low level healing."

"Wait," he stopped, causing her to bring up short. "Mana I possess?"

"Or course," she frowned.

"When did this happen?" he asked. "My acquiring mana, I mean?"

"Everyone and everything has mana," she pointed out. "It is merely that only those with life crystals —the gifted, as we are called— may use it in any directed manner.

"As for you, personally?" she admitted. "I have no idea. For all I know, you have had the ability all along."

"But you know it all of a sudden now?" he asked. "How? Rosaluna told me that I had no status bars. No crystal, no nothing. No way to read or even ascertain *if* I had abilities of any sort."

"Well, you have status bars now," she shrugged. "Not that I can read them properly. They are very strange. And you still have no life crystal."

"I repeat my question," he persisted. "When?"

"Oh," she half turned as she resumed her trek to the dead jaegers. "Yesterday, when you dec— ah," she managed to overcome her natural inclinations. "When you... when you were fighting. They were just there. First your life bar, and later, when you called FoeSmite to you, your mana bar."

"Hmmm," he hmmmed, moving to follow as he worked this new information into his internal logbook.

She'd stopped several feet short of the smallest of the bodies. "Stand back, please," she requested as she began the incantation.

The jewel in her staff began to glow. Initially, the same dull azure as yesterday, but as the incantation continued and grew in power, the light took on a different hue. Blue-white, shifting to nearly pure white, hot as an electric arc.

Jack averted his eyes. Tiarraluna's voice rose, took on urgency, took on strain. He squinted one eye open. The body was bathed in a thick coat of brilliant luminescence, easily a foot thick. Nothing else was happening. He opened his mouth to ask a stupid question, but shut it again without voicing it. To paraphrase Lincoln, better to remain silent and be thought a fool, than to speak up and foul the spell, to who knew what horribly unintended consequence.

Tiarraluna ended the incantation with a demanding crescendo, smacked the butt of her staff against the ground, and went quiet, breathing heavily. Jack opened both eyes to see what was what. The girl had sagged to the ground, but seemed unharmed. The coat of luminescence remained. The creature within remained as it had been.

"You were correct, it seems, Jack san," Tiarraluna's tired voice came to him. "Mund will not accept the creature, nor Jehsha its soul."

"If it has one," he muttered low enough that she might not hear.

After a few moments, the glow began to dissipate. They watched quietly for a few minutes more, wondering, each on their own, what they were going to do with the thing. At which point, the substance of it began to bubble. The first bubble burst with a small pop, emitting a puff of thick, black, foul-smelling smoke. Quickly then, tempo increasing, more bubbles burst, adding their own small puffs, gathering together into a thick, noxious cloud, rising straight into the air. Like a burning latrine, Jack thought.

Both humans moved back, well clear of the billowing black pillar. Five minutes later, the only sign the jaeger had ever existed was a scorched patch of ground, a small sprinkling of gold coins, a smooth ochre ovoid of some sort of gemlike sub-stance, and an oversized, stylized bat ear of some crystalline substance.

Jack stumped forward, sliding down the staff's shaft to a knee to examine the gold. He had no idea what sort of value the coins held on this world, or if they'd be useable, but he scooped them up and stashed them in the pouch. Pretty good haul for a jaeger, if he was remembering right. He'd count them later and divvy them up with the girl. "This, he gestured with the dull or-ange gem, "will be the core."

"What we call a life stone," the girl supplied. "And what is that supposed to be?" she asked of the bat ear.

"Magical component, obviously," he laughed. "I'd think you'd know that."

She scowled. "I have never seen anything like that," she said. "I would not dare to touch it, let alone work it into a for-mula."

He shrugged. "That one," he closed his eyes in thought. "I believe, is part of a concoction that grants temporary sonar."

"Sew-nar?" she seemed confused. "And what is sew-nar, Jack san?"

"Oh," he scratched his head. "Uhm, it's a device or skill that uses sound waves to echo locate objects, or your place within a given space."

"Of course," she said quietly. "Naturally it is that. But what is it?"

She was being snarky again, but he'd give her this one. "You have bats here, don't you?"

She nodded.

"This allows you, for a time, to navigate as they do, even in total darkness."

"And you know the formula to create this wonder?" she asked.

He tried to remember. "Pretty sure, anyway," he told her. "Although, I'm not at all certain we'll find any of the other ingredients anywhere on this world."

"Still," she mused. "I am loathe to simply leave it laying there next to the road. Do you suppose it is safe to touch?"

He shrugged. "Am I poisoned?"

She held back her snarky retort this time, and instead looked to his health bar. "No."

"Then you should be fine," he said. "It's no more than an object at this point. like the coins and the core."

So, she thought. *Much like our native monsters. How re-freshing.*

The second monster's disposal went much more quickly. As an experiment, she didn't try to fully release it, merely building a thin blanket of cleansing light to allow it passage on its own. This time the light dissipated much more quickly. The ordeal of the bubbling horror proceeded exactly as the first had. This one yielded coins and core, but no components, as did the third.

The fourth gave up a crystallized venom sac, which Jack explained could be used to create antivenom. Which came in very handy when fighting jaegers and their ilk..

The champion, however, in addition to a much larger

pile of coins and a larger, clearer core, gave up a pair of eyes and a narrow sword of much higher quality than the creature had wielded alive.

"Is this normal for your world?" he asked, picking the weapon up and swishing it through the air, testing its feel. He'd used one of these in the game for a number of levels, but had never held one in his physical hand. It was an Imperial infantry officer's saber, and a pretty high level drop for a jaeger.

He tried to remember the lowest level at which he'd ever seen one of them as a random drop, but couldn't put his finger on it for sure. Forty, he thought. Maybe. Not being one to particularly enjoy wading into close range and soaking up damage in exchange for dealing it, he'd only done a single playthrough as a melee build, just for the purpose of having done it. More as a challenge than for enjoyment.

It had been enough to convince him that a sword was what you used when your ammo ran dry. Consequently, he'd generally been more interested in the firearms than blades by the time he hit the mid levels. So, fortyish. And jaeger champions topped out at about twenty-five.

"The components," she said, eyeing the sword critically, "yes. The gold, also yes. I have never heard of a random monster below rank fifty dropping anything beyond those, however."

So, another difference. "Oh, just to be clear," he asked. "The local monsters... do they just naturally derezz and drop, or is that ritual required?"

"Only the ritual releases the gifts of Jehsha," she told him once he'd explained the term.

"Gifts of who, now?" he asked. "You mentioned that name before."

"Jehsha," she scowled again at the ring. What was wrong with the silly thing? Again? Were there words it simply refused to translate? "Jehsha is our god, of course," she told Jack. "The god of Mund."

"Oh," he kept his face straight. "Sorry. I'll remember that."

She allowed her expression to ease. "Thank you."

"So," he pressed. "If the ritual isn't performed?"

"Nothing," she shrugged. "Nature takes the beast's body as it does any other living thing. The difference is that the beast's soul is chained to the underworld for eternity and forever lost to Jehsha. Being a just and benevolent god, Jehsha morns the loss of even these creatures, and so holds back his gifts."

"Even evil creatures?" Jack was dubious.

"Monsters are not evil in and of themselves, Jack san," she scolded. "They cannot help their nature, and so deserve the chance at salvation."

"Even things like orcs or evil wizards?"

"Orcs?" she asked. "I have never heard of such a thing.

"Evil people, of course," she frowned. "Wizard or otherwise, must also be given back to the earth and their souls freed."

She paused for a moment, thoughtfully. "You see, Jack san," she intoned seriously. "Jehsha, while benevolent, is not all forgiving."

She shook her head slowly. "For those who live lives of unrepentant evil, Jehsha insists on judgement. Some, should they not be completely beyond redemption, are sent back to Mund as lesser creatures with but a single chance to earn their ways back to heaven. It is a difficult path, and many, even most, fail."

"And those beyond redemption?" she had him hooked now.

"Jehsha has more potent torments at his call than the underworld in its chaotic hellscape can manage," she shivered.

Wards

They didn't make the so-called Hero's Glade that night. Sunset found them still trudging along the thus far empty road, exhausted again, or perhaps still. The only silver lining was that Tiarraluna's mana had recovered sufficiently that she was able to heal the deeper sword wounds, along with both his cracked ribs and broken —yes, broken—ankle. The lesser cuts and bruises would have to abide. They were annoyances anyway as far as he was concerned. Pain was an old companion to Jack Grenell, after all.

The following day —day three of their two day adventure— found them leaving the road shortly before midday, and heading south into a deep forest.

"Is this seriously the way to this town of yours?" Jack wondered irritably as he slapped at another of the mosquitos that the animes never seemed to mention.

Tiarraluna smiled a not entirely humorous smile. "We are not heading into town at the moment, Jack san," she told him. "We are going to the Hero's Glade. Did you think the gods had placed it in the middle of the road? Or that the citizens of Ardia would build a road through it, even leaving aside the wishes of the gods?"

Okay, he'd grant her that. "So how did your grandmother happen across my most annoying near-corpse on her way to town," he asked not entirely seriously. "If the place is so out of the way?"

She turned full face to him over her shoulder, frowning. "Do not jest about such things, Jack san," she scolded. "You are very lucky Grandmother is as sensitive to that place as she is, or you would truly *be* a corpse."

"Sensitive?" he ignored the rest.

"Obviously," she said. "How could she be otherwise, given her history?"

"You mean the history I know nothing about?" he asked dryly.

She stopped full in the trail, turning around to block his passage and glare at him. Her expression changed only when it became clear that he wasn't making a jest. "Are you trying to tell me that you did not know?" she was astonished.

"I know exactly jack, and —" he stopped himself. Clearing his throat, he started over. "Your grandmother told me almost nothing, Tiarraluna," he said, not quite growling. "She threw maybe a few hundred words in total to me the whole time I was there, and a quarter of those were not complementary."

"I am truly sorry, Jack san," she frowned. "I... I did not know. I thought that she would at least— that she would...." she paused, putting hands to forehead, frowning deeply, wondering if it were within her right to speak of, given that Grandmother had apparently decided not to reveal the story herself.

"Did she tell you anything of the others?" she inquired without moving her hands.

Jack looked around, then back at the frowning girl. "Some," he said. "But can we continue this as we walk? I'd like to reach this mythical town before we either run out of supplies and starve to death, or I'm completely drained of blood by these damned mosquitoes."

"She told me that there had been eleven of them," he said some time later, after they'd put some distance behind them. "And that the last of them had finally defeated the demon lord and become the king of Tandera not too long ago."

"Only a little more than a year ago, she confirmed. "Nothing about the others?" she wondered then. "Nothing at all?"

"That they were all dead," he shrugged. "Even that was hard to get out of her."

"I see," her frown deepened, along with her reticence to reveal what her grandmother had held back.

Another mile had passed beneath their feet before her decision formed itself within her mind. "The first hero to pass through the gate," she began hesitantly, "was called Ishihara

Kenjiro. He was, perhaps, the strongest of them. He perished battling the demon lord in its very hall."

Another hundred paces passed in silence before, "he was also my great, great grandfather."

That revelation punched Jack right in the guts. In a blur, his every interaction with the old woman zipped past his inner eye. Each and every grimace or frown, each long dried tear that could be seen by its track upon her face. Each of his corny comments, each of his unguarded ponderings. He felt his throat tighten. He felt like a total and complete ass.

"I'm sorry," his voice trembled. "I didn't know."

She nodded, not slowing her pace. "Rosaluna is not so much my grandmother as my great, great grandmother," she clarified. "She is far older than she appears.

"She called me, " she continued slowly. "Because your presence at her cottage was causing her physical pain. The very notion that you were alive and he so long gone tore at her." the old woman's other opinions regarding him she forswore to mention.

"And yet she put everything else aside and helped me," he groaned. "Saved me."

"Do not punish yourself, Jack san," she told him softly. "This is her way no less than battle is yours."

He frowned more deeply, nearly a scowl. "What do you mean by that?" he asked. "Is it because these heroes of yours aren't good for anything else?"

She glanced at him again, seeing that the tortured look was back. What sort of wound, she wondered, could be so deep that the merest breeze would suffice to so inflame it? Then she remembered the red eyes within the iron cage and forced herself to stop.

"I say that because of what Grandmother found while healing you," she clarified. "Wounds and injuries years old, improperly healed. Bones and joints damaged far beyond anything reasonable for such a young man." another few paces. "How long had it been before these past months that you were not in constant pain, Jack san?" she wondered.

Hmph. He had to think about that. Years, easily. Since well before his discharge. It was a common trait of vets in the modern era. Messed up backs, bad knees and hips. Chronic, they called it. Totally not duty related at all. "A long time," he confessed.

"And now?" she asked.

What? He looked over, but she was serious, "Little girl, I hurt like hell."

She blushed at the name, but clarified. "In the same way? Or are you only feeling the pain of your most recent wounds? Remember those, what did you call them, wind sprints, you were running the day I met you? When was the last time you were able to do those before arriving on Mund?"

He thought about it and had to nod. She had him there. He hadn't even realized at the time. "Your great—"

"Just grandmother will suffice, Jack san,"

"—grandmother did that as well?"

She nodded.

"I'll be damned," he muttered. Five years at the VA, and all they'd managed was pain pills and unproductive therapy. "Another thing I have to thank her for."

"Jack san?" she asked after awhile.

"Hmm?"

"Why do you suppose whoever sent you through a hero's gate did so?"

He started to answer, but hard against what they'd just been talking about, he paused. That was, come to think of it, a very good question. One he couldn't answer.

It was growing dark beneath the trees when Tiarraluna alerted Jack that they were nearing the glade. Not a moment too soon, he thought. He was dragging, despite the healing she'd done, despite the time he'd been putting in to rebuild himself since the old woman had started allowing it. Obviously, stamina was something he'd need to work on. Funny how those guys in the stories could instantly go from office monkeys or shut-ins to Olympic grade trekkers with no transition. Another instance where the tropes had failed him.

He tensed suddenly, bringing FoeSmite up reflexively, unsure of what it was. He stopped, calling softly for Tiarraluna to do the same. She hadn't quite begun to reassure him before the creature loomed out of the darkness. It was a wolf. Dark grey, golden eyed, and the size of a horse.

"No!" she hissed when he'd bring the staff to high guard.

His eyes went round at the command. What the hell was she thinking?

"They are Grandmother's outer wards," she hastened. "I had not expected them to be so far out, or I would have told you about them already."

"Constructs?" he asked.

"Do not be ridiculous," she shook her head. "They are dire wolves, obviously. They are merely friendly ones. Or," she gave him a sly smile. "At least, they are friendly to Grandmother and to me.

"Now, she ordered. "Hold FoeSmite out before you parallel to the ground in open hands. Let Alshantar see that you are not a threat."

Alshantar. He'd save that question for later. He held the staff out as indicated, feeling the hair stand up on the back of his neck as the huge beast padded forward and huffed at the weapon. It raised its massive head and looked him in the eye. He looked back, seeing far too much intelligence behind that amber gaze to suit him. It was dangerous, looking it in the eyes. This close, if it decided to take the exchange as a threat, he was a goner, even with a magical stick.

"Alshantar is the pack's alpha," Tiarraluna explained. "He is, for all intents and purposes, the king of the wood."

"I see," he answered, his gaze locked with the wolf's.

"Alshantar," she called lightly. "Come, your majesty. I have treats."

With a last dismissive huff of breath into his face, the wolf turned and padded over to the girl, twisting his head to have his ear scritched before accepting something from her hand. Then he moved around behind and stood framing her, tail out and ears up as other wolves of varying size began to materialize from all directions out of the deepening shadows. Each of them received their scritches and offerings in turn before fading back into the darkness. Including a dozen pups who tumbled out of the undergrowth to receive their due. Each of them, despite the diligent application of puppy eyes, received only half a piece.

Once the ritual had been completed, she called Jack over.

"That some sort of control animals concoction your grandmother mixed up?" he asked as he drew near."

"Absolutely!" she smiled, popping a piece into her own mouth, giggling at his shocked response. "Dire wolves will do almost anything for chocolate."

"Choc—?"

"Want some?" she asked, holding out what, at close range appeared to be a chocolate brownie.

"Seriously," she insisted. "Take it, but do not eat it."

He narrowed his eyes, but took the offered confection.

Turning to the giant alpha, Tiarraluna closed her eyes for a moment, her expression going still.

The dire wolf lowered his head, but did not otherwise initially move. When he did, it was only to raise his head and issue a series of yips and growls in the direction of the trees. A few moments later, another, slightly smaller wolf appeared, head lowered.

"Well," Tiarraluna sighed. "Not ideal, but still better than I should have expected, I suppose. That is Belthasat. He is the beta. The prince, if you will."

Jack was still trying to decide what that meant when the creature arrived before him and stopped expectantly.

"Offer him the brownie, Jack san," Tiarraluna ordered.

He held out the treat and the great maw moved to his outstretched hand. He felt the dagger teeth scrape his palm as the brownie disappeared. Without thinking, he reached up to scratch behind the beast's ear, quickly bracing against the pressure when the dire wolf twisted his head and leaned into the ministrations.

"Very good, Jack san," Tiarraluna laughed. "You have defeated his caution."

"Yeah," he smiled despite himself. "Twenty years of having dogs gives you the touch, I suppose." he had to shift his feet to brace against the not inconsiderable weight that was pressing against his hand threatening to bowl him over.

Another yip from the alpha and Belthasat withdrew his head and turned for the darkness. In another moment, Alshantar also faded into the night.

"Belthasat will be your guardian within the wood, now," Tiarraluna told Jack after she'd given the wolves time to achieve some distance. "If you are in need," she continued. "Anywhere within the confines of this forest, you may call, and he will come if he can. But I caution you, Jack san," and her eyes went stern. "Do not call him to aid you against those teufel things."

He snorted. "There is no way in creation I'd ever call anything that relied on tooth and claw to confront poisonous constructs," he said. "Not even to save my own life. I'm kind of hurt you'd even think it necessary to warn me."

The Glade of Heroes was something of a letdown. It bore no remarkable attributes. No more than an area of about a quarter acre and surrounded by trees, in which there were no trees. There wasn't even a path. No quaint little pond or bubbling brook. Even the grass cover was spotty. In fact, other than the still cart at its near edge, the only vaguely interesting feature of the place was a suspiciously Jack-shaped gouge in the loam, indicating that his entry had been less than graceful.

"Seems...."

"Yes?" Tiarraluna wondered when he didn't finish.

"I dunno," he mumbled half aloud. "I was kind of expecting something more..."

"Grand?" she asked. "Something with marble columns, perhaps? Befitting a true hero?"

He gave her the eye, wondering if she was back to being snarky for its own sake.

Instead, she was hauling things out of her bag and arranging them about the cart. "Many people expect many things to be more grand than they are, Jack san," she said distractedly as she readied herself to release the final wards on the cart. "This glade is no more than a location. Its import lies not in itself, but in where things come from to arrive here, and where they go once they leave."

"Things," he said. "Heroes, you mean."

She looked up at that. "In this place, yes," she agreed. "But understand you, Jack san, there are more gates on Mund than this one. There are gates to the underworld, and from the underworld. There are places where monsters or spirits spawn, seemingly from the very air. Many, if not most of them no more remarkable than this small open place in the wood."

"I see," he said. And he was beginning to. Looked at as no more than a spawn point, what really had he expected?

The undoing of the wards took quite some time, or so it seemed to Jack. He was dead on his feet and wanted desperately to find someplace to curl up and sleep for the next three or four days. Tiarraluna seemed to notice as he was putting Jelia between the traces and she was busy stowing magical gear into her amazingly capacious bag. "We cannot camp here, Jack san," she warned. "Not only because it is a portal area. We will encamp nearer the road, but still within the wood. We will be safe with the wolves guarding us."

Mohrdrand

They began to encounter junctions in the road by midmorning and started seeing traffic soon after. Not much, to be sure. Sparse hardly covered it. As the morning drew on, Jack began to feel uneasy. What people they saw looked frightened. Holding close to their wagons and carts, as if ready to bolt at the merest noise. Most carried knives or axes or long handled scythes, but nothing that might be considered a dedicated weapon. They saw not a single patrol, nor even solitary guardsman. Even Tiarraluna was frowning as they finally drew near the town.

Mokkel Town, it was named, she told him, although it was more commonly called Mokkelton. There was a wall and a gate, although the man guarding it looked no more than a tradesman, and bore no arms. What did he expect to do if he should encounter somebody or something that needed to be kept out? Jack wondered. Maybe the world was just that peaceful these days? No. The demeanor of those citizens he'd been seeing suggested otherwise. He cast a sidelong glance at Tiarraluna, but didn't say anything. Something was going on here that he didn't like, but this was neither the time nor place to discuss it.

Tiarraluna flashed a strange stone and paid two silver reals for their entry into the town with the horse and cart. Jack remained silent. While he could understand her end of the conversation perfectly, he had no idea what the local was saying. The guy seemed curious and uneasy. Whether because of the blanket Jack wore in place of a normal garment, or the sword hanging from his hip was unclear. Jack was willing to wager both.

Here, too, he got his first look at Tandrian cash. A stamped silver, or more likely, silver washed coin, given its large size and low purchasing power. It had a rough castle embossed on the side he could see. He didn't get a look at the other before it vanished into a box standing on the ledge of the gatehouse window.

"Come, Jack san," Tiarraluna ordered once the coin had been paid.

"No stamp or seal or anything?" he wondered.

"Would you like one?" she asked. "There are, it would seem, insufficient soldiers or guards to throw you in jail or eject you from the town, but if it would make you feel better...?"

Then why a wall? Were things so peaceful that they'd disbanded the guard? That made no sense at all. But he kept his yap shut. He could see that she was worried no less than he, despite her flippant tone, so he let it lie for the moment. But he meant to find answers at some point. The whole place offended his sense of order.

Also, if the desert had taught him one single thing, it was that you paid heed to hunches that were telling you something was off.

She led them into the depths of the town for several blocks before turning right at a wide square. Then several more blocks trending mostly southward, though the street twisted and turned more than a bit.

He was coming to realize Mokkelton was larger than he'd at first guessed. More a small city than a town. Which made the guard situation even stranger. What did they do about crime? Surely there were criminals here, even without a demon lord. There should be dozens of city guard, if not hundreds.

Tiarraluna brought the cart to a halt at an unmarked door on the left side of the otherwise featureless walled street, no different than two dozen others they'd passed since turning south. She knocked three times, then three again. Then they waited.

After a short while, the door clicked. Without waiting for it to move, Tiarraluna opened it and stuck her head in. "Uncle!" she called. "We are here with Grandmother's toys!"

Another hundred count and there came another, louder click from a dozen or so feet down the roadway. Jack followed the noise to see a double door swinging slowly inward a few inches.

"That is the stable," Tiarraluna informed him. "Bring the cart inside, please, and unhitch Jelia. There should be hay in the manger already, so she will be fine. Join me here once you are done."

"Yes, Mu'um," Jack couldn't resist, bowing deeply. "As you say, Mu'um. Your will be done, Mu'um," he finished with a flourishing genuflection as he backed toward the cart.

He ignored her scowl as he took Jelia's halter and moved her to the small stable, chuckling to himself. That was a girl used to getting her own way.

There was no way that he could see to lock the stable door once he was done, nor any other way into the rest of the property. He settled for closing the double doors and walking over to the previous one, which, it turned out, remained ajar.

"Hello?" he called as he stuck his head into the dark room beyond.

"We are back here," Tiarraluna's voice drifted from deeper within.

The place turned out to be quite large. The front room consisted of some sort of shop, its shelves populated by all manner of odd shapes and colors. He found them two rooms in, seated in comfortable looking chairs fronting a cold hearth. Fragrant tobacco smoke filled the upper reaches of the room, emanating from the bowl of an ornate pipe clamped between the teeth of a strange old man whose long black beard sported a wide silver stripe down its center.

"Jackson Thomas Grenell," Tiarraluna gestured to the old man. "My uncle, Mohrdrand Hollandria." Then she leaned forward and whispered mock-conspiratorially, "he is not really my uncle, we just like to pretend."

"Right." he turned to the old man and bowed, resigned to go through the whole language rigamarole. "Ah... hajime-mashite, Mohrdrand sama. Wa... uhm... watashi wa Grenell Jackson desu."

The old man stifled a chuckle, and bowed in turn, not getting up. "And a pleasure to meet you as well, Jackson Grenell," he said in what could be pure Oxford English.

Jack turned to Tiarraluna and gave her a scowl.

"Uncle Mohrdrand is a wizard, Jack san," she giggled. "Quite a powerful one, and a good friend of Grandmother's going back many decades."

"He knew we were coming," Jack said grumpily.

"He knew we were coming," she confirmed. "And that you did not speak Tandrian."

Turning back to the old wizard, he raised an eyebrow. The old man held up a hand bearing a familiar looking gold band.

"Have a seat, young Jackson," the old man waved to a couple of unoccupied chairs. "Button tells—"

"Uncle!" she hissed. "I have asked you not to call me—!"

"Button?" Jack grinned, watching as her face turned red.

"Yes, Button," she snarled. "It was a name my grandmother called me when I was a toddler, alright?" She turned to the old wizard. "But I am no longer a toddler, Uncle. I am a—"

"You will always be Button to me, I'm afraid," the old man shook his head. "And look at you now, still cute as a flowered porcelain button."

She growled at him.

"Well, Button," Jack began."

"*You*, I will burn with fire," she warned him, eyes flashing.

He couldn't hold the laughter back. Countless weeks, even months of confusion, pain, terror, and fatigue, and the fuming girl had overpowered it all. And the madder she got, the cuter she became. Like a true anime heroine. He almost expected her to go full chibi and start flying around the room shooting lightning bolts everywhere. And that image made him laugh even harder.

He missed the part where the old man made a couple of surreptitious gestures, locking down her staff to keep him from finding out how serious her threat had been.

Once the mirth had run its course and he could focus again, Jack rubbed the tears from his eyes and apologized. He couldn't make it entirely serious, but he did his best.

"Button—" Mohrdrand flinched and corrected at her glare. "Tiarraluna," he soothed. "Perhaps you might brew us up some tea?"

She glared for a moment longer before hurling herself to her feet and stomping wordlessly off deeper into the environs of the building, leaving her shepherd's crook staff behind.

"And do try not to poison any of them," the old man called after her back.

"I promise nothing!" her voice drifted back.

Returning his gaze to Jack, the old man chuckled. "You are indeed a brave one," he remarked.

"Sorry," Jack said again. "Couldn't help myself. And she *is* cute as a—"

"What is it?" the old man asked, leaning forward as Jack choked to a stop. "Is something wrong?"

"Button," Jack deliberately used her toddler's name. "What is she, fifteen? Sixteen?"

"Ah," the old man nodded. "Fifteen as of this past Summer's Dawn." he said. "In your land, this is significant?"

"In my land, this is prison time," Jack husked. "Among other, less savory terms. In my world, she is a child."

"I see," the old wizard nodded solemnly. "And how old are you, Jackson Grenell? If I may ask?"

"Twenty-eight this past November," Jack told him. "Three months or so ago."

"When you left, then?" the old man asked. "In your world?"

What difference does that make? Jack wondered. Then he asked.

"Have you seen yourself since you arrived, Jackson Grenell?" the old man wondered. "Have you looked upon your own face?"

"Not really," he said. "Not in anything more accurate than a water bucket. Why?"

"There is a mirror against that far wall," the old man pointed forward towards a room immediately behind the shop. "Open the window for some light and have a good look. Let me know what you see."

"Okay, that's not ominous at all," he muttered. But he followed the directions.

He found the window latch and the mirror. Then he just stared for awhile. *Well, of course.* He turned his face this way and that, pulling at his cheeks and chin. He'd been twenty-five before he could generate a decent beard or mustache, so, his body had been thrown back at least farther than that. Not too far into his teens, thankfully. He thought he'd have noticed his voice cracking or an explosion of pimples.

Twenty or twenty-two, he thought. His mustache wasn't second lieutenant wispy, but his beard was embarrassing enough to get rid of. *Maybe there's some sort of magical beard growing spell,* the thought meandered through his mind as he turned away

He was subdued when he regained the chair. "What the hell?" he wondered aloud.

Inwardly, he was going through various storylines, fishing for averages. About thirty percent, he decided, particularly if you got grabbed young, you kept your original age and body. About thirty percent of the time, you got catapulted back to fifteen or sixteen, regardless of your real world age. Another fifteen or twenty percent, you went in as the character of a game you were good at, or had written, or managed. Again, regardless of your original age. Reincarnations of course, where you started over from scratch or woke up suddenly after five or six years of your new life comprised a big chunk. The remaining cases, where they turned you into a monster or an inanimate object, or a little girl or something, were outliers, he supposed.

The old man was regarding him bemusedly during this introspection. Finally, he broke in. "And does this allay your fears at all?" he asked.

Jack looked up. "Still twenty-eight in here," he said, pointing at his head.

"You would be surprised to know how little that really matters," Mohrdrand chuckled. "Particularly in a land where girls often marry at fourteen and boys at fifteen."

Jack started to protest, but remembered that it hadn't been all that long ago on earth for those ages to be apt. Well under two hundred years. Still. "Where I come from," he told the old man. "She's still jail bait." he paused while the old man worked through the term.

"And in your world, Jackson Grenell," the wizard wondered. "How many years must unwind from your skein before you are no longer a child?"

"Eighteen, for some things," Jack mused. "Twenty-one for others. Various idiots in authority are trying to run that either up or down for various things in order to gain more power. Hell, there's a sizeable portion of my country's population that may as well still be children well into their thirties or forties. Even beyond."

"You must indeed live in a sanguine land," Mohrdrand rubbed at his whiskers, "for children to be allowed to be children for so long.

"Why, our new king," he informed his guest. "Was barely twenty-one when he led his army to Storm the demon king's obsidian fortress, hard upon several years of travail. Many of his soldiers did not live to see their sixteenth year.

"Tiarraluna has been an adult for more than a year, and has been plying her trade in a not undangerous world."

"Anyway," Jack groused. "I said she was cute, I didn't say I wanted to... to...."

"Oh, *no*," the wizard shook his head broadly. "*Obviously* not."

"She just escorted me to town," Jack explained. "Just a chore for Granny, right?"

"Of a certainty," the old wizard confirmed, leaning forward and steepling his hands, a wide grin on his face. "How could it be anything else?"

"Here I am in town," Jack hurried on. "Job's done, I'm on my way. Bam! Never see her again. Problem solved."

"Problem?" Mohrdrand asked. "And what problem would that be?"

"Problem?" Jack asked, voice rising. "No problem. Done

problem, see? Away I go. Done."

The old wizard was openly chuckling now. "And what of Tiarraluna?" he asked merrily. "Has she no say in this?"

Jack was struggling to get a grip on himself, wondering what the hell was happening to him. Was there something in the smoke of the old man's pipe? Was that it?

"I've known the girl less than a week," he insisted. "Anyway, she'd rather burn me alive than spend another minute with me," he lowered his voice with some effort. "Didn't you see? Aren't you the one who warned her not to poison me?"

"I could have been asking her not to poison me," the wizard pointed out. "After all, It was me called her Button first."

Jack closed his eyes and took a few deep breaths, gathering his wits. The old man was making sport of him and not even trying to be subtle. Everybody on this world thought themselves a jolly joker, it seemed.

When he opened his eyes, Tiarraluna was returning with a tray upon which rested cups, a pot, and several small jars. These she set on a small cart, which she wheeled to stand between the chairs. She was looking back and forth between the two men, an odd expression on her face. While she seemed to have gotten her temper under control, it was difficult to say how well.

"Now," the old wizard began once she'd seated herself and they'd all acquired and fixed their tea. "Where were we again? Ah, yes. Your adventures along the road."

He turned to Jack, his face going serious. "I am led to believe that, in spite of having no discernible sign of a gift, you fought and vanquished a significant number of higher rank monsters on your way here."

Jack shrugged uncomfortably. "I suppose so."

"Hmm," the old man waited for further elaboration. Then, "Tiarraluna has told me that you had encountered these creatures before? Or at least their proxies?"

Jack nodded.

"And their ranks?"

"Ten to twenty," Jack supplied. "I can't say for sure,

since I wasn't able to see any stat bars or identifiers myself. Going by the way it was armed, the champion was probably a bit higher."

"I see," the old man stroked his beard. "And how do you suppose you managed this?" he asked.

Another shrug. "Partially," Jack gestured to FoeSmite, leaning against the wall beside the door. "I've been advised that my staff isn't quite normal. Partially, it was a case of my enemies not understanding either me or my weapon style. I surprised them. I think that if I hadn't, I'd be seriously dead right now. I nearly was anyway."

"I see," the old man repeated. "If I may?" he indicated the staff.

"Be my guest," Jack told him.

"Oh, no, no, no!" the wizard shook his head violently. "You misunderstand, Jackson Grenell. I would not touch that thing if you held it out to me and my only other option was falling from a tall cliff."

Jack's eyes narrowed, but he rose and retrieved the staff, holding it out when the old man requested.

Mohrdrand leaned in close, tching and clucking as he ran his gaze up and down the shaft, requesting Jack rotate it in his hands to provide a full, three hundred-sixty degrees of examination.

"This text here," the old wizard indicated with an outstretched finger. "FoeSmite?"

"I was in a hurry," Tiarraluna huffed. "It is not *that* bad, is it?"

The old wizard clucked his tongue. "Insufficient, more like," he chided gently. "There is will here, child, in this object. A very powerful will." He looked up from the staff, expression serious. "Bone cruncher seems more apt," he postulated.

"Jackson Grenell," he wondered. "What were you thinking? At the exact moment this weapon was enchanted, I mean? The moment it was named? You were holding it, yes?"

"I'm not sure," Jack admitted. "I don't exactly know when it happened."

"As you were striking your first foe," Tiarraluna provided. "I named it as you struck your first decisive blow."

Ah, he thought. *The tingling in my arms and back.* "I was thinking, 'break something'," he told the old man. "It was more a prayer."

"Indeed," the old wizard muttered. "That would do it, I suppose. And you struck bone immediately after?"

"Clavicle, I think," Jack nodded.

"Yes, yes," the wizard muttered. "But not yet sufficient, I think, to explain all of this."

He rose and hobbled off into the depths of the building, leaving his guests to wonder at his purpose. He returned a few moments later with a polished crystal lens clamped within a gold collar. He played the lens over the staff, clucking and tsking some more.

"There are strange forces at play within the enchantment you've laid upon this device," he said finally, presumably to Tiarraluna. "I see your grandmother's touch, and yours as well. But there is a third. With a strange feel to it. A strong aura of purpose and strength." He looked to Jack. "By process of elimination," he informed the man, "I'm going to say that was you."

That he could sense faint traces of yet a fourth, he kept to himself for the now. It felt old... primal. He'd want more time to think before starting that conversation. And perhaps a few words with the lady Rosaluna.

"And what's that mean?" Jack wondered.

A broad shrug. "Who's to say? The old man answered. "Tell me, you fashioned this staff yourself originally, yes?"

"I did," Jack confirmed. "I felled a small tree close in to Rosaluna's cottage, then trimmed and split it. One half I split again and then carved FoeSmite out of one of the quarters."

"And this carving? The knotwork? The embellishments?"

Jack nodded.

"you didn't happen to feed it any of your blood during the process, I suppose?"

Jack narrowed one eye. "Feed it?" he asked uneasily.

"No. I mean, I may have gotten some blood on it over the course of the process. There were times I wasn't as steady as I'd have liked, and I did occasionally slip and draw blood, but I certainly didn't *feed*—"

"So," the old man smiled. "You cut down a tree from a magical forest, fashioned the living wood with some care and with your own hands into a weapon. You infused it with your own blood. And then, while it still bore life, you helped to enchant and name it. Is that what you're telling me?"

Jack looked to Tiarraluna and back to the old wizard. "I guess? I mean, if you look at it a certain way...."

"And what sort of training did you provide?"

"Training?"

"He spoke to it constantly," Tiarraluna supplied. "I saw him at Grandmother's when I first arrived."

"What?" Jack turned on her.

"You were whacking on her old oak tree," Tiarraluna told him. "And with each whack, you were speaking to the staff. I could not then tell what you were saying, but you were definitely speaking to FoeSmite."

He tried to recall. He'd been speaking to himself, really, he supposed, but he'd been doing it out loud, as he was prone to do. Each strike, each technique. He'd recite them out loud as he ran through the drills. To sort of hone his concentration.

"What's it all mean?" he wondered to the wizard.

Mohrdrand leaned back in his chair, not unhappy to have some distance from the uncomfortable feeling bar of wood. "You three have created something quite unique, it seems," he informed his guests. "And something not entirely unalive."

"Unalive?" Jack questioned.

"Mohrdrand rolled his shoulders. "Your FoeSmite is not quite alive," he stated evenly. "But neither is it quite *not* alive. It is, at this moment hovering somewhere in between, and I cannot tell you why."

He gave the situation more thought. "Moreover, I cannot tell you for the moment whether this situation will remain as it is or whether it will slide in one direction or the other. I suppose that will have much to do with how you treat it going forward."

"And what that means is...?" Jack pressed.

The old man shrugged. "As time passes," he told the younger man. "It may revert to an inanimate object, retaining no more than the enchantments you've placed upon it." He paused. "Or, it may take on a life of its own and become much, much more."

"You mean self aware," Jack posited.

"That," the old wizard nodded. "Other things. Personality, drives... for all I know, it may even begin advancing in rank as though it were an adventurer in its own right. I really cannot fathom what form of change the influence of your alien mana may have infused into it, nor of your will."

"Its ranking?" Tiarraluna asked timidly. "I cannot read it, nor its effects."

"No," the wizard smiled. "I don't suppose you can. Not at rank ten in any case."

"Well?" she asked with more force.

"Keep in mind, Button," he cautioned, ignoring her quick glare. "That I'm only rank one- seventy-nine, myself."

Only? Jack thought. *I thought Rosaluna was the highest rank in the land at two hundred?*

"I cannot read it either, I'm afraid." Mohrdrand admitted, drawing a soft gasp from the girl. "It seems to follow the proper formulae, but there is something off about it. I suspect from the otherworldly mana."

"So what *can* you see?" she asked.

"My appraisal skill tells me eighty-two," he told them both. "But I've no doubt it's higher than that. Possibly much higher. I just don't know."

"Would Grand—?" she began before stopping herself.

He chuckled and shrugged. "Perhaps? She does more enchanting than I do, so her appraisal skill is most certainly better. But I'm not certain that will help. As I told you, there is something off about the staff. I can clearly see a ranking and the effects it bears, even the name. But the rank is overlain with shadow. A shifting hint of another modifier, perhaps. Perhaps an entirely separate rank added to the one I can read. I cannot say for certain. Even the name seems to slide around a bit, as though it might not be complete."

"But at least eighty-two?" Jack asked, looking down at the dark wood. "So how can I use it? If I've got the rules of this place straight, I shouldn't even be able to lift it."

"Simplicity itself," the old wizard smiled. "You made it. You trained it. You infused it with a part of yourself. And, finally, you were holding it when it was named.

"I would wager," he said mock confidentially. "That in all the world, only yourself, Button here, and perhaps Rosaluna are able to so much as touch it without injury, regardless of rank or class.

"Now," he waved. "If you please? Being this close to it is not comfortable."

Jack nodded and returned the staff to its former position against the wall, feeling the shaft warm as he released it. As though it were self-satisfied at the wizard's distaste. He favored it with a frown.

"Adamant," the old wizard told them. "And, of course, ironwood."

He was less certain of the final effect, although he could describe its function. "Foe Shatter," he finally decided, naming the enchantment on the spot. "It is the ability to sunder anything it strikes with sufficient force and will, regardless of composition. Of course, the harder the target, the harder the contact must be, and the stronger the will behind it. The concentration. Other enchantments notwithstanding."

The old wizard examined the sword next. It was just a sword. A very fine sword, befitting a legendary drop from a higher ranking monster, and very different from the swords most local warriors wielded. But no more. The strangeness of it lay in how it came to be rather than its innate properties. He judged it to be around rank thirty-five, but would not guarantee that assessment. It could, he warned, be lesser or greater by some margin.

The rest of the afternoon was spent discussing the pair's journey there, and Jack's problem regarding his lack of a life crystal.

Elsewhere

The great chamber was vast. Larger by some significant measure than the chamber on floor seventy-one of the Great Obsidian Fortress of Mohrtgauth the Soul Eater. Thick columns of heavily ornamented marble, hundreds of them. Thicker, each of them, than the span of a tall man's wide-stretched arms, they soared up into the darkness above. Their ranks marched into the dimly lit distance in all directions, disappearing into stygian blackness from which could be heard a thousand unnatural calls, chittering, growling, rumbling. The susurrus of... things, not of the mortal realm.

Affixed to the center row of these massive columns, electric lights in lavish sconces struggled vainly to impart some small glow into the oppressive shadow that wreathed the entire space as though it were a physical construct deliberately injected into the air. Pools of light, they shed, widely separated, like the blood spatter of a fleeing and wounded animal.

Far off in the distance, from an area bathed in a greater pool of brighter light, a pair of mumbling voice could be heard, seemingly arguing, but too muffled to be clearly understood.

The man who stood in the outer doorway between slowly opening double doors tall enough to allow a delivery truck passage and thick enough to stop cannon shot, did not immediately enter as the four sweating guards pushed, straining, to open the way. Only once they'd gotten them fully opened and regained their posts outside the chamber did he step forward and into the oppressive space.

Ernst Jungmann, his name was. A cabinet minister highly placed in the government. Chief Secretary of Scientific Discovery and Cognition was the title he bore. An important one, to be sure, as these things went. He was as near indispensable a figure as the Dread Lord numbered among his minions. Near, however, was the operative word. No one was completely safe when in the presence of the Dread Lord.

It took him some time to traverse the hall. Moreso because his pace was beyond measured. He might have been marching behind a casket in a funeral procession for the pace of his ponderous gate. He did not want to be here, and even less did he want to have to impart to the Dread Lord the news he carried.

The larger pool of light grew closer. Details within made themselves known. A great and ornate dais lay at its center, atop of which an elaborate throne rested behind a low and lavishly decorated table. A single figure could be seen slouched forward in the throne, both voices issuing from its single mouth. This was the Dread Lord of Tarr.

His appearance wasn't particularly imposing, even in this setting. He was shorter than the average Tarrian. Slight of build, with a boyish, clean shaven face and black, mid length hair, a tuft of which fell down and between his eyes, forming a fork over his nose. He was wearing the dark blue uniform of a Nuverian High Marshall, devoid of rank, insignia, or medals.

He wore no weapons. What use would he have for such things? On his right hand, he wore a white glove with gold piping, its upper surface decorated with crossed lightning bolts in silver and red. His left was bare, gnarled and scarred, covered with coarse hair. Long uncut nails resembling talons jutted from its fingers.

He was playing a game of Castles and Kings on a board of precious metals built into the table before his throne. Against himself. Or, rather, his right hand was playing his left.

Jungmann shifted his gait slightly, trying to bring it into measure with the game. He must be excruciatingly careful to arrive within notice of the Dread Lord at the proper moment or his very life was in peril.

The dread lord was observing the board critically, his chin resting on the back of his gloved hand. Jungmann quickened his pace. All at once, the head raised, and the white gloved hand shot out, shifting the Paladin of Light and withdrawing in a single, slashing movement.

Oh, no! Jungmann's face went ghastly pale and a wild shiver ran through his body, hard enough to make his bones creak.

"What is it?" the voice issuing from the Dread Lord's mouth was graveled, and seemed too low to have come from a human throat. The chin was now resting on the gnarled left hand, one taloned finger tapping at the pale cheek. The left eye regarding the secretary was the glowing orange of flowing lava, its sclera the hue of fresh blood, set within skin blackened and scarred from brow to upper cheekbone. Pale smoke drifted up from beneath his eyelid. More from between his down-turned lips.

"We've recently recovered a flit from one of the watcher teams, Dread Lord," Jungmann informed his master, ducking his head momentarily in a precise bow, struggling to keep his voice firm. "From the starting zone of U-14365, W-21019. Uhm, Mund, I believe the locals call it."

"And?" the response was more growl than spoken word.

"We believe that we may have found him, Dread Lord." he croaked, "but we're not completely sure."

The head came up, a Dark Mage held poised above the board between the fingers of the clawed left hand. Both eyes were open now, as the dread lord peered at the uncomfortable Secretary. The right was black as midnight, and sharp as a teufelsoldaten's bayonet. "Elucidate." the dread lord ordered coldly in the basso growl that told Jungmann the beast was in charge.

He swallowed broadly and tugged at his collar with a nervous finger. With the beast in control, not even *he* was safe. "The individual encountered seems to fit the description of the Grenell, Dread Lord," he husked. "But some facets of the encounter have led us to believe that it may be another who merely resembles him. Thus, we are not one hundred percent confident in our identification."

The dread lord remained as he had been, holding his glare.

"Er... yes," Jungmann gave his collar another tug. "You see, Dread Lord, while the time constant on this Mund runs a small increment more quickly than it does here on Tarr it is no more than a few months per year at most."

Another pause answered by more silence. Jungmann gulped. Dealing with the darker side of the dread lord was always a trial.

"Given the time frame, Dread Lord, and the injuries we feel confident the Grenell had sustained in our initial fai—" he froze, his face going even greyer. The dread lord's eyes narrowed to slits, the left moreso than the right.

"Th-that is to say," Jungmann stuttered, "given the life-threatening injuries he'd sustained in our first, ah, valiant strike....

"Ah," another gulp. " the highest ranking we had reasonably expected him to have achieved, regardless of grinding, would have been level five. Perhaps six if the prognosticationators miscompiled the time flow differentials.

"And what has that to do with anything?" the voice was a volcanic hiss, and the smoke trailing from the demon lord's lips grew thicker.

Jungmann was panting heavily at this point, the fear overcoming his ability to suppress. "We had stationed teufeljaegers in that zone, Dread Lord," he explained. "Only five, unfortunately, although one of them was a champion. Still, we thought the force to be more than adequate."

"I begin to see where this is going," the demon lord grated. "Why only five? Have we so few that we are forced to deploy less than a minimum mob? Have the machines stopped making them for some reason unknown to me?"

Jungmann bowed deeply, partially to hide the tears of terror that were forming at the corners of his eyes at the prospect of what might occur at any moment. He hadn't yet gotten to the bad part of the report.

"I beg the Dread Lord to understand," he quavered, still gazing wide-eyed at the floor without daring to look up. "This was in a starting zone, and the portals in these zones, we have come to realize, will only permit five life forms to pass at a given time. And there is a hard limit on the levels such life forms may possess. We did initially send a full mob through, Dread Lord," he insisted. "Only five survived passage. We are working on expanding that number, Dread Lord," he explained. "But have thus far met with no success. It is as though we are being actively hindered."

"Given that more than six months have passed," the demon lord's voice remained harsh. "Why had you not bolstered their force? Surely ten or twenty jaegers would have guaranteed more success than five."

"I beg the Dread Lord to understand," Jungmann's voice quavered. "There are literally tens of thousands of worlds in the many universes. At least a thousand of them lie along the potential paths the Grenell might have been propelled by the force of the initial spell's misfi— ah," he gulped spasmodically. "Th-the spell's v-vast p-power.

"The machines are running at one hundred percent capacity, and we are building as many jaegers we can, but the required number is vast.

"And even should we have been able to create sufficient of them," he pressed. "Our scientists have not yet been able to break the respawn coding that requires those sent through the portals be eliminated before the timers begin to count down.

"Eighty-two levels of teufeljaegers should have been more than enough for a single level five or six *anything,* Dread Lord, even a hero." this last more a plea.

"And yet they obviously weren't," the dread lord was fully upright in his throne now, the Dark Mage still clutched in his left hand, its surface smoldering with the heat of contact. Despite his otherwise completely human appearance, he seemed to have grown to half again his normal size. "And how did he defeat this unstoppable force you arrayed against him, then? As a level five?"

Jungmann gulped again, tears flowing freely from his eyes, snot from his nose. He felt that his next pronouncement would result in his grisly and immediate demise, and he was loathe to voice it. "He... He beat them to death with a stick, D-Dread L-Lord."

Jungmann felt the ground tremble as the dread lord

leapt from the dias. He heard the initial phase of an enraged roar before a sudden silence descended upon the throne room.

After a long moment, he raised his head just enough to take in the form of his master. The Dread Lord had frozen in place, his body twice and more its normal size, a rictus of inarticulate rage etched upon his face, the clawed hand halted mid-slash as it had made to strike him down. Long minutes passed, counted by the panicked beating of his throbbing heart.

He watched as the rage washed slowly from the Dread Lord's face. The clawed hand lowered, and the Dread Lord began to shrink until he'd once more resumed his normal size. He calmly straightened his uniform tunic and swept his hair smooth with his gloved hand. He turned and paced calmly back to his throne, resuming his seat. The claw now lay in his lap, with his white-gloved right hand resting atop it. He was once more fully Kanzaki Haruo, former hero, and one time savior of a world far removed from his current domain.

"A stick, you say?" he asked somewhat genially.

A violent shiver of relief surged through Jungmann's body at this miraculous reprieve. "Technically, Dread Lord," he straightened all but his head, which remained bowed, but not so much that he couldn't see his now more benign master. "He only beat four of them to death, including the champion. One, he killed with a jaeger short sword."

"I see," the Dread Lord frowned. "And the stick?"

"About seven feet long and perhaps an inch and a half thick. The flit wasn't close enough to gather fine detail. Like a thrusting spear from which someone had removed the head. The stick did appear to change at some point during the encounter, so it may have had special properties."

Kanzaki nodded to himself. *A bo or western quarterstaff, then. A highly unusual weapon for a hero to wield.* "I believe that I would like to see the recording," he said. "Bring it to me as soon as possible.

"Also, while we're discussing possibilities," he stopped Jungmann as the man was turning to leave. "Is it possible that we might send soldaten through that portal while Grenell may still be in the general area?"

"Alas, Dread Lord," Jungmann shook his head. "Given it's a starting zone portal, we cannot send anything ranked higher than level twenty, save a single champion accompanying lesser creatures. That much we have gleaned from the code. And even then, nothing higher than level twenty-five will survive passage."

"I see," the white-gloved hand came up to stroke Kanzaki's chin. "Jaegers, then, I suppose. "And find a portal somewhere on that rock that *will* allow soldaten through. In fact, let's just see how many we can suborn. Surely not even the great and wondrous Jackson Thomas Grenell can hope to defeat an entire army at level six."

Jungmann neither moved nor answered for a good long while. And when he did speak, it was with a tremor. "Is the Dread Lord certain we are ready for this?"

"Ah," Kanzaki smiled an off kilter smile. "Invasion, yes?" then he shook his head. "No, Ernst, I don't believe I am. Not yet, at any rate.

"Have your brain trust determined at what point the Grand Council of the Gods decides that an incursion has become an invasion?" he wondered.

"Ah... I'm sure the Dread Lord understands that such... studies... are a delicate matter," Jungmann answered carefully.

"Given the vanishingly few times such events have occurred, there are no patterns to find. And given that the first hint one has that the gods have decided to take direct action is when they arrive in force, I'm sure the Dread Lord understands that we must tread... carefully."

"Yes, yes," Kanzaki nodded, waving his concerns off with the white gloved hand. "How do they feel about flits?"

"Dread Lord?" Jungmann was taken aback.

"Flits, Ernst," his master reiterated. "Do they count against the totals allowed through the portals?"

"I, ah, do not believe so, Dread Lord," Jungmann smiled, beginning to understand what his master was getting at. "It was allowed through with the five we sent, and the portal countdown began without its having been eliminated."

"Good. Then send another force of jaegers through, with as many flits as they can carry. Program them for the widest feasible spread. And see that at least a couple of crossbowmen are sent through, if nothing else.

"Meanwhile, get me that recording."

Jungmann bowed himself out, relief heavy on his face.

Kanzaki Haruo, former hero, and the current Dread Lord of Tarr, relaxed back into his throne, rested his elbows on its arms, and steepled his fingers together.

"I knew that stupid bus gag was a mistake," he said amiably. "All flash and no action. Typical demon lord nonsense.

"Should have gone with *my* plan and just hired somebody to shoot him in the back of the head when he wasn't paying attention. Less effort, better results."

His face went hard and he scowled. "He is not here, is he?" he answered himself in the rumbling growl that had so terrified Jungmann. "Your information regarding his strength must have been faulty."

His face relaxed back into a casual grin. "You were right there when I got it," he chided. "If you had doubts, you could have voiced them then. It's not like I can ignore your prattling."

The scowl returned. "You should have dug harder. You were always one to take shortcuts. Always ready to race forward without sufficient preparations."

"I defeated *you* before I hit level fifty," he laughed lightly. "And with only two companions."

"And yet I remain," his scowling face replied. "While your lover and your closest friend are long cold beneath the ground. And soon I will become dominant, and you will be subsumed."

Kanzaki went silent, his face stone, his eye fixed ahead as his gloved right hand curled into a tight fist. He held that pose for over a minute before his features relaxed, and the casual smile returned. "But you *don't* remain," he chortled as though he'd not a care in the world. "You're an after image. A shadow.

"We're already well on our way to conquering the whole

of this world and subjugating the populous. Without their hero, they've nothing and no one to stand against us. You've lost your chance to weaken me. From here on out, you're a battery whose sole purpose is to keep me hale and hearty, no more."

The red eye went half-lidded, and an evil grin spread across half the face of the Dread Lord of Tarr. "We shall see," as the smoke trickled from between the tight stretched lips. "We shall see."

Tom Black

A Plan Forms. For Sufficient Values Of

"I'm afraid there is no help for it," Mohrdrand admitted late in the afternoon, having poured over several volumes from his library. "You either have one, or you don't. It's a thing for the gods, not for humble workers in magic such as I."

"I see," Jack frowned.

"Do you, I wonder?" the old man raised an eyebrow. "Jackson Grenell," he leaned forward, his voice growing serious. "You wield a mythic grade weapon and have vanquished monsters of some substantial rank. I think it safe to say at this juncture that you are most assuredly gifted, and will do perfectly fine without a crystal."

"But—"

"She is wrong every twenty or so years," the old man laughed. "Although you'll have a devil of a time getting her to admit it.

"Sitting here with you," he went on. "I can just see your status bars, as we are on friendly terms and wearing these rings. They are faint, granted, and health and mana only. I see no status effects, no alignment, no guild affiliation, nor your name, class, nor species. But I suppose that should be enough. Button?"

She still wasn't happy at being so addressed, but she'd apparently decided to put up with it, at least for the time being. "I see the same," she announced. "Although his health and mana bars are clear and bright for me. And during the fight, I was able to see status and affect modifiers."

"As they should be for you," the old man nodded. "Given your connection."

"And you, Jack?" he asked, ignoring the look she shot him.

"Nothing," Jack told him after a short span of staring at him through narrowed eyes. "Nothing over either of you."

"Hmm. Is this normal on your world?"

"Mine or the one I'm supposed to be going to?" Jack

wondered.

"Yours first, I believe," the old man said.

"Same as I'm seeing now," Jack admitted. "Nothing."

"Wait," the wizard straightened in his seat. "Are you telling me that, on your world, no one has status bars or identifiers?"

"Pretty much. We also don't have 'gifted' people as you understand them. At least as far as I've ever heard."

"Then how do you determine friend from foe? Monster from farm animal?"

"I'm told," Jack grinned. "That more people are killed by cows every year than by sharks." when that response garnered only confused stares, he clarified. "We pretty much have to guess."

"Guess?" Mohrdrand gaped.

"Well," he clarified. "Guess based on observation and experience. It does lead to trouble. We're forced to judge people by their actions. Or by cues in body language. Sometimes by affiliation. It gets kind of muddy, and frequently there are issues caused by misidentification, or by basing decisions on the wrong cues or just bad information."

"I should imagine," the old man shook his head. "How do you manage? I mean, how do you know who to be cautious of and who cannot fight?"

That drew a burst of laughter. "Friend Mohrdrand," he said. "On Earth, you have to be cautious of *everything*, and *everything* fights. Even a mouse will take a chunk out of you if it's cornered."

"Well, of course," the old man agreed. "But a mouse does not rank up and become more dangerous. The ungifted will fight if cornered, but they're awful at it and cannot use weapons or armor stronger than rank zero. This renders them mostly harmless to the gifted. Even low ranking gifted.

"And the world you are journeying to?" he ventured then.

"A bit more like here," Jack said. "But not exactly. First off, any sort of identification requires a learned skill. Often, several skills. And you have to be actively using them to get any sort of information. Otherwise, there's no difference at all between active characters and NPC— er, ungifted.

"Even then, from a distance," he went on uncomfortably. "It's like home. Nothing, even with skills. As you get closer, though, and depending on the situation and which skills you've learned, some designators begin to appear. General at first, but more specific the nearer you get. A monster, for instance. At range, the first thing you'll see is the species. A troll, say. Of course, by then, if you know what a troll looks like, you'll already know, so it's kind of useless.

"Closer in, you'll get the level. That's like your ranks. That is, if your own level and skill modifier is high enough. If it's too low, all you'll see is a black or red skull. That generally means it's one of two flavors of get the hell away, it's too powerful for you.

"Once you're really close, and with the proper skillset, you might see weaknesses, strengths, and specials. But that takes a lot more training —like your appraisal skill— and isn't available until you've leveled up a ways."

"Indeed," the wizard was stroking his beard now, leaning in.

"You won't see enemy life bars or health indicators until you enter combat," Jack finished. "There's a point, though, when you just stop messing with it. After you've gotten familiar enough with who and what you're going to be up against, you just know. So you use the concentration you'd ordinarily spend on the identification skills and apply it to fighting."

"I see," the wizard said after a bit. "And friends?"

Jack gave it some thought. "Party members, you'll see names, life and mana bars. But that's it. Any other information you have access to will be in men— er... visible by other means."

Mohrdrand narrowed his eyes, a hint of suspicion edging his face. "But nothing like the life crystals?"

Jack gave it some thought. "Monsters drop cores," he said tentatively. "I think that's the closest it gets."

"Monsters, but not people?"
"Right."
"Indeed."

At some point during their discussions, an old woman let herself in the front door, quietly passing them and vanishing into the depths of the building where Tiarraluna had previously ventured. Shortly thereafter, the aromas of cooking began to fill the structure, setting mouths to watering. It grew more difficult for the old wizard's guests to concentrate on the topics at hand.

Eventually, Mohrdrand called a halt to the discussion and they adjourned to the dining room, a more cheerily lighted venue with brightly glowing lamps set in ornate sconces arranged along the walls. Dinner was served by the still silent old woman, who vanished into what was undoubtedly the kitchen while they ate, and emerged only to clean the table.

They were back in the previous room, a fire now lit in the hearth, when she passed them on her way out. She'd uttered not a single sound the entire time she'd been there. The wizard offered no explanation, and Jack didn't inquire.

The topic for the remainder of the evening fluctuated between Jack's descriptions of his true destination insofar as he could extrapolate from the game, and questions regarding how he might cope in the world in which he currently found himself. The old wizard tried various trinkets in an effort to allow Jack to see the status indicators and life crystals of others. None worked. He tried various spells. None of them worked either.

Eventually, the effort was curtailed in favor of a night's sleep. Jack was shown to a small, sparsely decorated cubby. Tiarraluna apparently had her own room, arguing that she was a more regular guest, or had been so at some point in the past.

Jack lay awake for a long time, gazing at the ceiling, his head resting on one forearm as he stared up into the darkness. He was beginning to chafe at the delay of his journey. In his opinion, the past several hours had been a complete waste of time. Mohrdrand didn't really need to know about Tarr, and he didn't, he thought, need to be able to see crystals or stats. His plans involved avoiding fights on this side if possible. Failing that, knowing how high the levels of any opponents were was pointless, as he'd have to fight them anyway. That was the way unavoidable fights were — Unavoidable.

The big question, though, hadn't been addressed at all. What was going on around here that had everybody afraid, and the guard missing? True, it wasn't really any of his business. These weren't the people he was supposed to protect. Of course, that hadn't ever stopped him in the past, had it? And he knew in the back of his mind that it wouldn't stop him now if he decided that something had to be done.

Somewhere during these contemplations, sleep took him.

Breakfast was already on the table when he rejoined the others early the next morning. There was no sign of the old woman. Perhaps Tiarraluna had prepared it. The meal certainly lacked some of the complexity and flair of the previous evening's endeavor. Simple cereal cakes and oatmeal. Substantial looking, but rather bland. However, and this made up for all the rest, the old man had coffee! and sugar.

"Where do I go from here?" Jack asked the old wizard as he was savoring his second cup. He wouldn't ask about the local situation. The subject had been conspicuously avoided by his hosts up until now, and he figured his asking would only cause friction. He'd find out somehow once he left the wizard's home.

"The capitol," the wizard said around a thick chunk of cereal cake liberally smeared with butter. "I have it on good authority that the king has access to an exit portal. The one that he, himself, was supposed to use to return to his home before he decided to remain and rule Tandera.

"I'm no expert on portal dynamics, so I'm not sure whether it will help or not. It may be possible to select a destination, or it may simply return you to your world. It's a chance, at least, and the best I can think of."

That made sense. "Fine. How far is it?"

A shrug. "As the calta flies, around three thousand lenn."

Jack narrowed an eye as a stab of pain shot through his forehead. He looked down to the ring. It seemed to be having trouble converting the term to a concept he could understand. "Lenn?"

"Ah," the old wizard nodded. "Ah, a lenn is a measure of distance. Let's see... Ah, this house is slightly more than two-thirds of one lenn from the city gate by the way you traveled."

Jack nodded. If he had his distances right, they were about a mile in. Which put a lenn at around a mile and a half. So, forty-five hundred miles. Whoof! "And what sort of terrain am I looking at between here and there?"

"At least two mountain ranges," the old wizard ticked off on his fingers. "The Sessik plain, which is more a desert, assuming you don't go around and add another four hundred miles to your—"

"Hold it," Jack interrupted. "Did you just say miles?"

"Did I say what?" the old man asked. "No, I said miles."

Jack frowned and gave the ring another scowl. So, once he learned a word, it would add it to his dictionary. Good to know.

"In any case," the wizard went on, "there are marshlands to the south that you'll want to avoid if you can."

"So," Jack mused. "It's gonna take me awhile."

"In all probability," the old man agreed.

"Hey," Jack snapped his fingers. "You're a high ranking wizard, right? Can't you guys teleport or something? Wizards can always teleport to wherever they want, or so I've always heard."

Mohrdrand frowned, quirking a lip. "Wherever do you learn these supposed facts?" he wondered.

"So you can't?"

A shrug. "Not exactly," the old man admitted. "No such spell or magic exists here. There is a spell which allows us to... travel *around* time... but the mana requirements are massive, and while the distance traveled is certainly less, the journey only *seems* instantaneous from the outside."

"So, you can't just take my hand and sling us to the capital," it wasn't really a question.

Mohrdrand let go a bark of laughter. "I would do well to sling myself to the capital in less than a couple of weeks," he said. "It would require many castings, much travail, and even using the most powerful potions I possess more rapidly than is remotely safe, enough mana that I would be a year fully recovering." he paused for the magnitude of the task to take hold. "And that would be proceeding on my own. I wouldn't dare to contemplate dragging another along with me."

"So," Jack frowned. "I'm walking or riding. Any estimates?"

"Depending on mode of travel and route," the old wizard contemplated. "Close enough to a year as doesn't matter. If you proceed directly there, which you will not be able to do."

"Oh?" Jack straightened in his seat. "And why not?"

The old man rocked back and raised his eyebrows. He looked to Tiarraluna, and back to Jack. "How would you go about it?" he asked, his voice serious. "Is it common for your people to just take off walking on long journeys without even a proper shirt to wear, let alone provisions of any sort?"

Oh, yeah. Jack thought, his face reddening.

"I may have an old tunic that will go over your shoulders," the old man postulated. "Although it would be quite snug. Nor is it armored in any way."

"There is also the inconvenience of your not speaking Tandrian," Tiarraluna pointed out. "You will be unable to communicate with the citizenry. Not to ask directions, nor to purchase food or lodging."

"Which you would not be able to pay for in any case," Mohrdrand took up the warning.

Right. Money. "I don't suppose this will help," he fished around in his satchel and withdrew the gold coins the teufeljaegers had dropped.

The old man leaned forward and took a few of the coins, examining them closely before handing them back. "I'm afraid not," he shook his head. "They appear to be of a much higher gold content than the local currency, but I doubt you'll find anyone willing to take them as payment."

"So what you're not quite telling me," Jack frowned, shoving the coins back into the satchel. "Is that I'm gonna need to find a job."

"Not precisely," the wizard stroked at his beard. "Mokkelton isn't exactly the sort of place someone of your... attributes is likely to find gainful employment. At least of the normal sort."

Jack's eyes narrowed. "You're leading up to something. We arriving there any time soon?"

Mohrdrand didn't answer him right away. Instead, an uncomfortable silence grew between them. Finally, "Bounties, Jackson," the old wizard heaved a great breath. "Somehow, you're going to have to convince the local adventurer's guild to accept you so that you may go out searching for bounties."

Jack blinked.

Mohrdrand held up a hand before he could say anything. "Face the facts, Jackson," he urged. "You will not earn sufficient gold at any sort of mundane job you're likely to find to finance even a journey to the next city, let alone the capitol. You'll be ten years reaching the king. Your only hope is to garner some bounty money, and perhaps a bit of plunder."

"In a city where, as it's recently been pointed out, I don't speak the language," Jack grumbled. "In a land where my lack of a life crystal marks me as a peasant, not a fighter."

"I will act as your interpreter," Tiarraluna offered.

"You most certainly will not," Jack turned on her. "Your task was done when you brought me here."

"And so I shall begin a new task," she seemed undeterred.

"I won't expose you to—"

"If you say danger, Jack san," she warned, "I shall have to smack you with my staff. I am a rank ten advanced novice mage, and have been, I would wager, on more adventures than you."

He doubted that, but he was saved from the folly of saying so.

"I may have a solution to your other problem,"

Mohrdrand interrupted, a small smile quirking his lip.

Jack turned back to him, his mind still working on what to do with the girl.

"I will write you a letter of recommendation," the old wizard informed him. "Explaining your situation. I'm sure Guild Master Jonkins will accept."

"And then what?" Jack wondered.

"Why, you look at the bounty board and pick a mission," the old man said. "Something you're strong enough to accomplish, but not so ruinously dangerous your journey ends here."

"That's it?"

"What else would you need?"

Jack scratched at the back of his head, wincing. The list would be voluminous. He looked over at FoeSmite, leaning against the wall. Melee. The sword, too. Melee. If he was expected to go monster hunting, he needed something with range. He'd had quite enough of wading into contact distance to start trouble.

"Unless I'm gonna finance the trip by killing gophers," he said, irritation tinging his voice, I'll need more equipment than I currently have."

The old wizard nodded. "I suppose you will," he commiserated, though he didn't offer solution.

Tiarraluna drew breath to speak, but Jack turned to her again, "No," he said, voice flat.

Her face drew into a volcanic frown.

Back to Mohrdrand. "This recommendation," he asked. "Can you make it clear enough that I don't need a translator?"

The old man shook his head. "I'm a mage, Jackson," he chuckled. "Not a seer. I cannot predict all that you would need. Nor could I possibly predict the totality of the bounties that may be present on the board. And before you ask," he gestured with the hand again. "No, I cannot accompany you. I've business of my own to attend to that I've already put off for longer than I ought."

Jack scrubbed at his face, irritation growing. This was why the world spells on language existed. "Another ring, maybe?" he asked forlornly. "Something I can hand over to whoever I need to speak to?"

Mohrdrand frowned. "Just exactly how much is it you anticipate I owe you, Jackson Grenell?" he asked quietly.

"Huh?"

"What I have done," the old man announced. "And what I am doing, I do as a favor to Rosaluna, who is an old friend. I owe no allegiances to these people you travel to save. My loyalties lie with Mokkelton and Tandera.

Jack gave it some thought. "And the rings are expensive?" he asked after a short while.

"*Very* expensive," the old man nodded. "I don't mind feeding you for a day or two, or giving you an old tunic. But I must draw the line at equipping you with high order magical items, or performing magical tasks beyond the minor. The recommendation, I will provide because it costs me nothing more than these discussions we've been having. Beyond that, I'm afraid I will have to begin charging you for services."

So. Back to square one. Or was it two? He cast a sidelong glance at Tiarraluna. Button. Her face remained angry, but still focused on him.

"I don't imagine you'd consider a small loan?" he wondered of the old wizard. "Just enough to buy a decent bow and maybe some sort of cheap armor."

The old man rested his elbows on the arms of his chair and steepled his fingers, his face stern. He drew breath to speak, but hesitated, his eyes shifting slightly to his right.

Jack followed the shift and caught Tiarraluna glaring silently at the old man.

"I'm afraid not," Mohrdrand sighed still regarding the girl. "I have no idea when or if I might ever see you again, Jackson. It would be a poor investment."

Now it was Jack's turn to glare. "Tiarraluna...."

Her glare was gone, her face benign. Smiling, even. "Jack san?" she beamed. "You will listen to me now?"

He scrubbed at his face once more. He wasn't in control here. Not even close, and it bothered him. Reminded him too much of other places where he'd been forced into situations against his better judgement.

But the push to move had him. Ever since his realization that he wasn't where he was meant to be, and particularly once he'd encountered the jaegers. There was a place —people— who needed him, and sitting here wasn't getting him there.

"Alright, Tiarraluna," he sighed without removing his hand from his face. "Let's have it."

Her grin widened. "I will accompany and translate for you," she started. "And I will loan you the money to ready your-self for your first adventure. I do not have much, but it should be enough."

"And in exchange?"

"You will pay me back," she said simply.

He peeked through two fingers at her, smiling smugly over there. His eye shifted to the old wizard, who seemed strangely relaxed. "And what would that look like?" he won-dered.

The question seemed to confuse her. "Jack san?" she wondered, eyes narrowing, "Just how is it you imagine I make my living?"

His eyes widened and his hand moved from his face.

"Yes, Jack san," she grinned. "I am an adventurer. How is it, I wonder, that you have not already come to this conclusion? How did you suppose one became an advanced novice mage?"

He really hadn't given it any thought. His mind had been otherwise engaged the whole of the time they'd known each other. "You want to come along, then."

"Do I?" she giggled. "Jack san," she informed him then, a patently false sonorous note to her voice. "I am afraid you do not understand your situation here. I am rank ten. You are... something other. It is you who will be coming along with me."

The old wizard seemed to be getting a kick out of this. Jack less so. So he was the sidekick, huh? He didn't like the sound of that. Oh, it made sense now that she'd laid it out in the open, but that only made it worse.

"So, the letter?" he asked the old wizard, his voice re-signed.

Tom Black

The Adventurers' Guild Part One: Jackson Grenell, Demon

The tunic was, indeed, snug. What's more, it was a faded purple and covered in quarter moons and stars. Jack felt utterly conspicuous, not to say ridiculous, trudging along beside Tiarraluna toward the city center.

They ran into trouble almost immediately. Adventurer's Row, which Tiarraluna insisted had been thriving during her last visit, was empty. Abandoned. From one end to the other, nothing could be seen but boarded up shops or vacant stalls. What's more, they looked to have been in this state for quite some time.

Their luck was no better among the normal merchants. What few of them had bits or pieces of the sort of gear he needed refused to sell him a single piece. Nor would they sell anything he might use to Tiarraluna.

They managed a couple of larger tunics, two pairs of pants, and a decent pair of tall boots to replace his worn through steel toes, but that was it before Jack called a halt to the exercise. Tiarraluna, despite being the nominal head of the party agreed. It was time to see what was going to happen at the Adventurers' Guild hall.

The building itself wasn't particularly grand. Three stories, rough stone, small windows. The entryway was overlarge, but that was the most remarkable thing about it. And the sign, which was somewhat garish, although Jack couldn't read it to know whether the text was as overblown as the imagery.

Tiarraluna entered first. Jack followed. Without warning, and too quickly for him to react, bars slammed down from the ceiling and sprang up from the floor, caging him tightly in the doorway, neither inside nor out.

Without thinking, he spun on his heel, drew FoeSmite high, and smashed its butt down onto the base of one of the bars, shattering it. He was angling for a strike at a second bar when Tiarraluna's frightened voice came from within the building.

"Jack san," she cried. "HOLD!"

He froze in place, hearing a clatter from behind and above. Turning his head and craning his neck, he spotted a grizzled looking old guy holding a strangely glowing crossbow. Yeah, he wasn't gonna dodge that. Nor was he likely to get around quickly enough to have FoeSmite block it. He held himself absolutely still.

The old guy was yelling down angrily while Tiarraluna was calling up beseechingly. Jack could only understand her side.

"He is no demon!" she insisted. "We are here on official guild business!"

Jack turned slowly, his movements very deliberate, arms held as wide as the cage would allow. If things went south, he wanted the staff between himself and that incoming bolt.

"Cursed?" Tiarraluna showed her first hint of anger. "It most assuredly is not! My grandmother and I enchanted that staff ourselves!"

Closer inspection of the old guy revealed a scarred and mustachioed visage, on a balding, grey haired head. He might have been sixty or seventy, but his arms still showed muscle. Importantly, he was alone. If this was the guild hall of a sizeable town, what did that mean?"

"I have a recommendation letter from the wizard Mohrdrand," Tiarraluna was calling. "Requesting you admit Jack san into the guild."

She listened to the still angry reply before turning back towards the cage. "Jack san," she sighed. "Would you please, very carefully, slide FoeSmite out of the cage and into the room?"

He narrowed his eyes, hesitating for several heartbeats before he complied, crouching and sliding the staff well into the room and off to the side.

She turned back to the balcony from which the old guy was covering Jack. He called something down.

"The sword as well, Jack san," she translated. "If you

please?"

Jack slid the scabbard out from behind the leather belt he'd cinched around the tunic, sliding it clear as well. Not towards the staff. He didn't trust FoeSmite to make contact with it and they not both in his hands. FoeSmite was maybe a little cursed, Jack admitted to himself. Certainly willful.

Once Jack had been nominally disarmed, the old guy, who, no surprise, turned out to be the local guildmaster, stumped slowly down the stairs, crossbow still trained on the damaged cage's occupant. He sidled across the room to a long bar and behind it, the prospective path of the crossbow bolt never veering from Jack's chest. As he reached the midpoint of the bar, the guildmaster reached down and activated something.

With an audible clack, marred somewhat by the scraping of the stump of the broken bar, the cage retracted into the floor and ceiling respectively. Jack didn't move.

"What the hell was that all about?" he asked Tiarraluna.

"The trap," she informed him without moving from her own position. "Activated when FoeSmite was detected entering the guild hall. Apparently, the ward mistakenly identified it as a cursed weapon."

"And the bit about me being a demon?"

She smiled without humor. "That was the guild master's interpretation of an individual with no visible life crystal bearing a high ranking cursed weapon. In his eyes, what else could you be *but* a demon? Or demon possessed."

Huh. "This something I'm gonna have to get used to?" he wondered.

"Let us hope not," she frowned. "That would be most inconvenient."

The guildmaster called something to Tiarraluna. She nodded and approached the bar, staying well clear of the prospective trajectory of the crossbow bolt as Jack remained rooted.

"You!" Borea Jonkins, the guildmaster, commanded the

novice mage. "Girl! What is the meaning of this? What has Lord Mohrdrand to do with this... this thing, and who is your grandmother?"

"To answer your last question first," she replied as she approached slowly, careful not to foul his aim. "My grandmother is Rosaluna Galbradia. You may have heard of her. And Uncle Mohrdrand has sponsored Jack san into the guild. Is this somehow unacceptable to you, Lord Jonkins?"

He was scowling as he took the letter from her hand. Rosaluna Galbradia? Of course he'd heard of her. Everybody'd heard of her. Even the question was insulting. And Mohrdrand? Sponsoring an ungifted? Even with the troubles, that was nonsense.

He took the letter and read it. Then he read it again, more slowly. Then he examined the seal. All were genuine.

"Is this true?" he demanded, looking up from the parchment at the girl. "Your grandmother found him in the Hero's Glade? What's that supposed to mean?"

"Well, obviously," she replied, her expression less cloudy. "It means that he is a hero."

"But the demon lord is gone," he told her unnecessarily. "What need have we of another hero?"

Now she frowned and pursed her lips, lowering her head in a contemplative manner. "And when, Lord Jonkins," she asked smoothly. "Did I claim that he was *our* hero?"

Now he was even more confused. Who else's hero would he be? Even then, why would he appear here rather than wherever there was? "That makes no sense."

"And yet," she stated confidently. "Grandmother has determined it to be the truth, and Uncle Mohrdrand has concurred."

Belatedly, it occurred to the guildmaster that he was taking her identity on faith. While the letter screamed authenticity to him, and she did, upon closer examination, resemble the powerful enchantress more than a little bit, he was naught but a rank seventy Battler, and neither mage nor wizard. "Your guild token, if you please?" he asked gruffly.

She smiled a self-satisfied smile and handed him a smooth, rectangular stone about three fingers width by five, and no thicker than a peach seed at its center. The same token she'd shown the man at the town gate. He fed the stone into a device behind the bar. While he had no personal magic beyond the basic spells most all adventurers gleaned, the enchanted reader would not be fooled, no matter how clever the forgery.

A translucent image of the girl, appearing slightly younger, bloomed into view above the machine. Tiarraluna Galbradia, it verified. Rank ten, advanced novice mage. Her various stats and skills pertinent to her membership followed. So she *was* Rosaluna's great, great granddaughter. "Heatherton guild, eh?" he noted. "That's a ways off."

"You have already seen that Jack san is capable of bearing ranked weapons," she said to his back. "And now you have verified that I am a guild member in good standing. So, will you aid us or not?"

The guildmaster removed the stone, tossing it in his hand a couple of times before turning and passing it back into her hand. "And what would you have me do?" he asked.

"Obviously," she said. "He will need a guild token."

"And what would I have that token convey?" he wondered. "I can see nothing about him to indicate his rank or skills. I cannot even clearly understand how he bears those weapons."

She gave that some thought, finally turning to Jack and explaining their current dilemma.

"How do you guys assign levels?" he wondered. "Does it just happen whenever your experience warrants, or is there some sort of testing procedure?"

Her eyes lit up and her face brightened. She spun on the guildmaster. "You shall test him," she announced. "As though for a new rank assignment."

To Jack, she said, "it is some of both. Our statuses rise whenever we reach the appropriate level of proficiency and experience, but we must test for the new rank to be recognized by the guild, and to manage skills should such become available."

The guildmaster was thinking it over, rubbing a hand

along his bearded chin. "It will cost you the standard fee," he cautioned. "Do you have the gold?"

She frowned. She didn't. At least not if she expected to retain enough to purchase equipment. "Could you deduct it from our first bounties?" she asked hopefully.

He frowned harder and gave his beard another go.

"As a favor to Uncle Mohrdrand?" she wheedled.

His hand dropped and he made a sound that might be a growl. "Fine," he conceded. "But there will be interest accrued. This isn't a charity, little miss."

She nodded happily. "That is acceptable. Now, what do we do?"

He looked to Jack, standing still and mute. "And you say he doesn't speak Tandrian?"

"Not yet," she admitted. "He is learning, I hope," she held up her hand displaying the gold ring, to which Mohrdrand had added a supplemental spell.

"Alright," he nodded. "You repeat everything I say to him, and everything he says back, got it? Exact translations. As though you yourself were a ring."

"Understood," she nodded uncertainly.

"You," the guildmaster ordered, pointing to Jack. "Strip."

Tiarraluna's eyes went saucer wide and her blush threatened to leak blood.

"Go on," the guildmaster insisted.

She repeated the demand. And Jack's refusal.

The guildmaster's hands went to his hips and he quirked an eyebrow. "I thought you wanted him registered?"

She tried again. This time, his answer was, "not with the girl in the room."

That wouldn't do, of course. Tiarraluna was the sole venue of communication between them. "How about if I have her turn away?" the guildmaster asked.

Tiarraluna needed no urging. She turned her back on the pair of them even before translating the message.

Jack moved slowly into the room, caution in every step. He still didn't trust the old guy with the scarred face. Tiarraluna rotated so as to keep him out of her line of vision. Finally, he brought up before the old guildmaster.

"What's this about?" he asked.

"I need to see if you've ever been in a fight in your life," came the reply. "Or if you're just some farmer putting on airs."

That didn't sound quite right to Jack. If he had it right, the vast majority of heroes had zero experience before embarking on their journeys. "Why?"

The guildmaster chuckled dryly. "Because it costs money to test you," he said as though it were the most obvious thing in the world. "Money which you'll have to repay at some point. Would you rather I started you at rank one and charged you for each rank increase?"

Okay, that made sense. "Fine," he relented, suiting action to words.

The guildmaster whistled once Jack had gotten down to his undergarment. "Alright," he admitted. "So you aren't a farmer," taking in the partially healed wounds from his most recent encounter and moving on to the fainter traces of those injuries Rosaluna had been treating. Then he looked over the older ones. Those that Jack had been carrying for years. "What's this one?" he pointed to one such scar on Jack's leg.

"Piece of a truck I was riding in," Jack explained. "We ran over an IED. There are a few more. Here, here, here, and here," indicating the places where blast fragments had been removed from various parts of his legs. Then he had to explain what a truck was, and then an IED. Those explanations took longer.

"And this?" pointing to a three inch scar along his left forearm.

"Knife," Jack said dryly.

"Here?" pointing to a pair of puckered circles low on his midriff. "Arrows?"

"9X18 Makarov," Jack explained. "Got surprised by a twelve year old jihadi when I should've known better." then he had to explain bullets.

"That must be one strange world you come from," the guild master ventured.

"Stranger by the day," Jack agreed.

"Tiarraluna," the guildmaster addressed the girl directly. "He's clearly seen battle. What do you say to starting him at rank five?"

She gave it some thought. She'd seen rank fives fight, and she'd seen Jack san fight. "I would suggest seven would be more likely."

The guildmaster's face tightened. "You know," he cautioned, "you pay per rank whether it's up or down, right?"

"Seven," she confirmed. "I think that he will be fine."

"If you say so, he shrugged. To Jack, "what are your primary and secondary weapons preferences?"

Jack coughed back a burst of laughter, stopping himself from saying 'M4 and Glock.' "Given my druthers," he told the man, "of the weapons I might find here, bow first, followed by the staff or sword."

That raised an eyebrow. "Why don't you have a bow, then?" he wondered.

"No one would sell us one worth owning," Tiarraluna skipped the translation. "Nothing more than a rank zero hunting bow, in any case. Not without a guild token."

"And yet, he's got that ridiculous staff and an heirloom grade sword."

"He fashioned the staff with his own hands," she pointed out, "and the sword was a monster drop."

"A what, now?" his voice rose.

She nodded without turning to face either of the men. "A creature he fought on our way to town dropped it after I had released its soul."

"That can't be right," the guildmaster insisted. "Those sorts of drops just don't occur until the creatures top rank fifty. There's no way he defeated a rank fifty monster."

She smiled a self satisfied smile, though neither of the others could see it. "It was four monsters of ranks ten to twenty," she told him. "And one —the one who dropped the sword— of, we think, up to twenty-five. Perhaps that explains it?"

The guildmaster was looking a good deal more critically

at Jack now.

"I will confess," Tiarraluna added somewhat self-consciously. "He *was* wielding FoeSmite when he killed them."

Yes, the guildmaster thought. *The cursed staff.*

"Put your clothes back on," he sighed. "And we'll go about seeing what sorts of missions you might be capable of.

Tom Black

The Adventurers' Guild Part Two – Test One: Jack Versus the Bow, and Rosaluna's Ulterior Motive

"**F**ollow me," the guild master turned and set off towards the rear of the building as Jack was struggling into his spanking new boots.

He led them through the entire building and into an enclosed area behind it. Archery targets of various sort were scattered about at varying ranges from what appeared to be a firing line. He moved directly to a small shed, opening it to reveal a fairly large array of bows.

"Choose one," he ordered, standing aside.

Jack looked them over. He dismissed the crossbows out of hand. Yes, they were powerful, but they were also slow. There were no compound bows at all, more's the pity. He'd gotten pretty good with the couple he'd owned at home. They were also capable of being wielded with higher draw weights than regular bows for the same effort. Where he'd probably top out at a fifty-five or sixty-five pound simple bow, he could easily handle an eighty or ninety pound compound bow.

The long bows would most likely be what he'd end up choosing from, but he moved past them to the row of recurves. In the various games he'd played, recurves were higher level weapons as a rule, but why limit himself because of preconceived notions? After all, how many other things on this world had subverted his expectations already?

The bows were all labeled, not that he could read the labels. "Tiarraluna?" he asked.

She moved down the line, pointing to each in turn. "These are listed draw weights, Jack San. Thirty. Forty. forty-five. Fifty. Fifty-five. Sixty. Sixty-fi—"

"That'll do," he smiled, withdrawing the bow from the rack. He quickly strung it and tested the draw length a couple of times. He suspected, his draw was a little longer than would be average here, based on the people he'd seen so far. If the bow didn't break, he'd be drawing an extra couple of inches, and the weight would be a little more than the advertised sixty-five pounds.

His next problem was arrows. They all looked kind of short. He typically used thirty-one inch shafts. What he was seeing looked more in the twenty-four to twenty-eight inch range. While that wouldn't normally be a problem, if he got into a hurry it wouldn't be entirely out of the question for him to overdraw one and shoot himself in the freaking hand.

"This it for arrows?" he asked, looking over to the guild master.

"What's wrong with them?" the man wondered.

"They're kind of short for my draw," Jack explained, wondering why he'd need to.

To his surprise, the guildmaster smiled. He was nodding to himself as he came over and opened another of the shed doors. More bows and more arrows. Some of them very long. Jack had to revise his opinion of the stature of the people of Mund. There were eight foot bows on these racks, and forty-eight inch arrows.

"How many will I need?" he asked.

"Twenty ought to do it," the guildmaster explained.

Nodding, Jack moved to the first door and grabbed a quiver. Back to the second door, and he counted out twenty-two of the proper arrows. Done, and the quiver hung from his belt, he pulled out a twenty-third and faced downrange, nocking and drawing fully, holding the draw for twenty or thirty seconds. Yeah, these would work.

He released the draw slowly, glancing contemplatively at the rack of bows. This one felt kind of light and he wondered if he might try a heavier bow before proceeding. Then he shook his head and turned back to the guildmaster. This wasn't the time to get too full of himself. He had no idea what sort of testing he was in for, after all. And it wasn't like he couldn't grab a heavier bow when it came time to purchase one for himself.

"That was the first test, huh?"

The man nodded. "First, second, and third," he said.

"You'd be surprised how many fail them."

The first course consisted of no more than standing at the line and plunking away at targets, starting with the nearer and working his way out. Four in each, with the farthest target around eighty yards out. Pretty serious range for a sixty-five pound bow to hit with any authority.

The second course had him mixing ranges. The third had him doing that and doing it for speed. Still, he wasn't doing too badly.

The fourth course had him moving and shooting, which was a thing he'd never done before. The movement added a whole new level of complexity. And then, as he was drawing near the final firing stage, an unexpected target leapt up from the grass to his right and nearly at his feet. He twisted and went to a knee, but managed to loose his arrow into the soft wood at around groin level. Almost, he stopped to rest, but then he remembered. He still had one last target. Rolling quickly on his rump, he slid one of the three remaining arrows clear of the quiver, nocked it, and let fly. Forty yards or so. He didn't exactly hit it clean, but he hit it.

He was running sweat at this point, and none too steady. He hoped there wouldn't be a fifth stage.

"How'm I doing?" he asked as he trudged back to the main firing line after collecting his arrows.

"Fine so far," the man said as he threw Jack a rough towel. "You need to rest before the next stage?"

* * *

A circular patch of air some forty or fifty feet from the cottage doorway began to shimmer, waves of translucent energy lapping about the plane of its surface. A second or so later, an arm poked through, followed by the rest of the wizard Mohrdrand. The circle collapsed in on itself the instant the trailing edge of his heel cleared it.

Rosaluna Galbradia seemed almost not to notice, remaining where she'd been, in the same chair she'd occupied on the day her granddaughter and Jackson Grenell had left. On the table beside her were a tea pot and two saucers, one of which held an empty porcelain teacup. Precognition wasn't supposed to be one of her talents, but some days that was easier to believe than others.

"Rosaluna," he bowed slightly as he approached. "And how are you this fine summer's day?"

She looked up at him at last, as though only just noticing him, and he noted that the perennial sadness of her features seemed etched more deeply today than when last he'd seen her.

Mohrdrand, she nodded. *And what brings you to my humble cottage so far from the bustle of civilization?* Belatedly, she waved him to the other chair flanking the small table.

"Simply returning your wandering bird," he replied, producing a small cage from within which a brightly colored bird slightly smaller than a pigeon looked out upon the world through large, star-flecked eyes.

Indeed? She wasn't convinced. *I'd wondered where she'd gotten off to after having delivered my message. And why did you not simply allow her to return on her own once you'd retrieved it? I'm quite sure she would have had sufficient mana remaining for her return journey. Wandering around time is her species' gift, is it not?*

He didn't bother answering as he walked past her and into the cottage. He returned a few moments later, sans cage, and took the seat she'd previously offered, taking up the cup after filling it from the pot. "I've had some interesting visitors," he ventured after a sip.

Have you now? Despite having both sent them and warned him of their impending arrival.

"Indeed," he nodded. "And in our talks, I began to wonder a thing."

And what might that be? She was looking out into the trees again.

He looked over to her across his freshly filled teacup. "Rosaluna..." he cleared his throat. "Rosaluna, why do you hate that boy so?"

Hate? Her eyes widened as she turned to give him her

full regard. *Hate, Mohrdrand,* she frowned. *Is not, perhaps, the correct term.* A short, uncomfortable silence followed. *Resent, perhaps, better describes my feelings. Yes,* she nodded. *Resentment sums it nicely.*

"And what has he done to deserve that?" he wondered, taking a sip of tea.

She didn't answer immediately. Instead, turning to stare once more out into the forest, her eyes losing focus.

You have met him, yes? She asked after awhile.

He snorted. "Of course I have. And I'll agree he can be a bit of a trial. Yet, I ask you."

You know that I am... less than happy with my life, she sent after another long silence. *And still, I confess to a certain... contentment.* Another silence, followed by a glance in the old wizard's direction. *A peace, of a sort. Out here with the beasts and the trees and the forest spirits. With few reminders beyond my work of... of losses... suffered.*

"Mm hmm," he nodded slowly, watching the tears form.

And yet, her sending took on an underlying bitterness. *The gods.... In their infinite wisdom.... in their cruel disdain....* she paused to dab at her eyes with a handkerchief she'd taken from a sleeve.

Why, Mohrdrand? She pleaded. *Why would they do this to me? Why, after all of these years...? to inflict another of those maniacs upon me? What more can I give, Mohrdrand? What more can they ask? Have I not given enough?*

"Ah," he understood now.

And now he's taken my Button, her mental voice was uneven. *I never should have—*

She bit off whatever she'd been about to say and raised her eyes to regard him again, tears streaming freely. *Perhaps, Mohrdrand,* she admitted finally. *Perhaps I hate him a little.*

* * *

The fifth stage consisted of running a variant of the fourth, but with projectiles coming back at him. Blunts, fortunately. He had no idea how the guildmaster was managing it. His first run, Jack managed to come away unscathed, but he was growing weary. The second run through, he caught a projectile in the arm. The guildmaster called a halt, and Jack slowly gathered his spent arrows. The third run through, he took a grazing hit to the thigh, but no halt was called.

"Well and good," the man told him. Then, to Tiarraluna, "that's a dead draw at rank eight," he said. "I'm impressed. You want to try for higher? I'd advise against it."

"Does that grant the rank or no?" she queried.

"Grants," he allowed, "but at threshold and with no bonuses."

"Jack san?" she called. "Are you content with your performance thus far? The guildmaster has granted you rank eight with the bow. Would you like to continue with more difficult stages?"

He thought about it as he ran the towel over his neck and down beneath his tunic. "Nah," he shook his head. I'm good. "I think that last one about showed me my practical limit."

"Good," the guildmaster nodded, smile growing. "So, he has sense, too. Ask him if he'd like to begin at this rank for the staff stages."

* * *

"You could have sent him off fully equipped," Mohrdrand pointed out, gesturing with the stem of his pipe. "It's not like you haven't got the gold to spare. Or the treasure."

I could say the same of you, she returned. *I take it, then, that you have not?*

He shrugged. "I almost offered," he admitted. "But Button glared me down."

She glanced over from her perusal of the trees. *I suppose she did,* she sighed. *By the gods, Mohrdrand,* she insisted. *Had I known this might be a possibility, I would have kept him here until I was able myself to escort him, regardless of how long that might be. I never should have summoned her. It was just so painful to have him about, do you see?*

"As to that," he drew on the pipe. "Couldn't you have simply drawn him a map and sent him on his way?"

She sighed again. *I could have,* she admitted. *I probably should have. It would have solved a great many problems, looking back. I simply didn't anticipate the attack on the road. How could I have? I've lain so many wards so thickly over that way down through the years that a great dragon would struggle to pierce them. And yet these creatures managed somehow. Better for him to have faced them alone, I think, than to have drawn Button into it.*

He took some time to digest that. "You think he'd be dead, then, and the problem thereby solved?" his face closed down into a deep frown. "And what of the folk of the world he's supposed to be saving?"

She waved a hand. *People die, Mohrdrand,* she sent. *I am far too familiar with that fact. Time would pass, and eventually the gods would send another. They always do.*

Something about the way she was— "You *want* him here!" he accused, straightening in his seat. "You wanted to give him a head start, but not enough to carry him to the capital.

"The troubles!" he snapped his fingers. "You would use him—"

Thus is the path of the hero, she sent quietly. *Is it not?* She allowed a small, secret smile to peek from behind her veil of sadness. *Still,* she allowed. *Had things gone to plan, Button would have conveyed him to your door and been done with him. If not for that damnable attack on the road.*

"Such a thing has that much power?" he wondered. His path to wisdom had lain along different lines. He'd been a military mage, and while he'd fought many, many battles through many, many campaigns, he'd never once directly followed a hero.

Now she looked to him, her eyes steady, her face grim. *He fought for her, Mohrdrand,* she sent. *And she for him. He bled for her, and together they vanquished powerful foes. She delved into his being to heal him. With such as he, these things are a powerful, compelling force.*

She looked back to the forest and rested back into her chair. *The fact that he is strong and handsome will have played a small part as well, I suppose,* she sighed. *Button is still a young girl for all her mastery of magic.*

"You needn't worry about that," Mohrdrand assured her. "Jackson considers her a child, and will allow himself to harbor no such feelings."

She snorted, nearly going into a coughing fit. *Believe that as you will, old friend,* she laughed croakingly. *But it means nothing. Kenji felt the same about me at the beginning.*

Mohrdrand didn't answer. He hadn't had much faith in his assurance himself. He'd seen the children together.

"And so," he refilled his pipe. "What are we to do about them now?"

How can I know, she sent back, *when you have not yet told me what is happening with them?*

"She's taken him shopping for proper attire and equipment," he told her. "And then to the adventurer's guild."

She raised an eyebrow, though she didn't turn back to him. *And this will aid them how? And he with no crystal?*

He cleared his throat. "I, ah... I wrote him a recommendation, based on his experience along the road, and suggested Jonkins allow him entry, despite his handicaps."

I see, she narrowed her eyes. *I suppose it is for the best. He cannot address the crisis without credentials, regardless of how powerful he might be.*

"As to that," Mohrdrand began.

The Adventurers' Guild Part Three – Test Two: Staves and Dolls and Rosaluna's Resignation

"You're sure?" Jonkins the guildmaster asked. "I remind you that each stage will cost, regardless of whether he succeeds or fails."

"Rank twelve," Tiarraluna insisted. "With a staff in his hands, he will be fine."

He shrugged and excused himself to make the preparations.

"Remember, Jack san," she called to Jack, standing in the center of a large training floor. "You are not allowed to call Foe-Smite to you."

"What was that?" the guildmaster asked over his shoulder.

"Hmm?" she put hand to mouth. "Nothing, Master Jonkins. Nothing."

Jack ignored them. He was busy trying to get the feel of the staff he was holding after growing accustomed to the weight and heft of FoeSmite. Outwardly, the only differences between his own staff and the one the guildmaster had provided were color and ornamentation. The weapon he was holding looked to be ordinary ash, a light blond in color. Practically, it felt far lighter than he liked, but without a corresponding increase in speed. Was added speed a function of FoeSmite's enchantment?

Across from him, lining the far wall of the arena, were arrayed a couple of dozen or so large mannequins. He wasn't sure how this was going to work, but the hair was standing on the back of his neck. They didn't really look like practice dummies.

He was wearing a heavily padded gambeson now, with wide gaps at the joints for freedom of movement, and a barred helmet. Some protection, but by no means proof against injury. A fact magnified by the waiver Tiarraluna had been made to sign. If something in this process killed him, the guild was off the hook.

"Ready on the floor?" the guildmaster called through Tiarraluna's voice.

"Ready!" he called back.

Three of the mannequins lurched into motion, causing Jack to jump a bit. They strode with increasing steadiness to the rack from which he'd drawn his staff. Two of them took up staves, the third continued until it had reached the rack of swords, taking up a cruciform waster of about thirty-four inches in the blade. They turned to him forming a shallow triangle, and began to approach.

He cast a nervous glance to the ready area where Tiarraluna was observing with seeming calm. The guildmaster didn't seem so sure.

Jack began to back and shift. Did he take out the sword first or the staves? The mannequins seemed pretty fluid. Not so much as the jaegers had been, but moreso than what he thought a puppet ought to be.

As they approached, the sword wielder moved to the center and slightly forward. Ah, so the staves could cover it as it closed.

Making his choice, Jack moved quickly to his right and in, somewhat surprised at how quickly the mannequins adapted. He beat aside the near staff and got a spear strike into its face as the sword wielder flowed around its falling comrade. But Jack was already backing away, and now there were no staves to protect the sword. Jack waited for the first thrust and swept it clear, before riding the arm inward and striking the chest. The automaton didn't go down, just like a real person wouldn't. But it did hesitate enough for Jack to swing the staff around for a killing blow.

Except that the remaining staff was there to intercept the strike. He backpedaled and slid to the side. His next attack was a feint and thrust, but that was blocked as well. Okay, so that was the way it was going to be.

He was breathing heavily, and he wondered if these

things were programmed to get tired. Another ignored feint, but now he was in measure, so he rode the feint in, risking a cut. He torqued the staff sideways and struck at the knee of the sword wielder as it came in. It didn't go down, but it staggered and slowed. That was two good strikes. A real human would be starting to grow cautious. Would that hold for dolls?

He'd been using the staff largely as a blunted spear to this point. Time to change up. He struck at the sword again, thrusting, but sliding the grip of one hand forward at the last instant to shove to the side. The staff swung a full three-sixty, and he twirled with it, crowding the sword wielder so it couldn't get a decent strike at him. The staff wielding mannequin parried, but an instant too late, and his shaft smacked into its neck, hard. It collapsed into the dirt.

Late though it had been, the automaton's staff had caught him even as he'd struck. His whole right arm was tingling. His forearm felt broken. He danced to the side, dodging the sword strike coming in at him while trying to keep the body of the staff mannequin between him and the advancing sword wielder.

They circled the body a couple of times, Jack holding his staff couched beneath his left arm as he tried to shake some feeling back into his right. He still had the reach, but with a foreshortened arc, he wasn't going to do the damage per hit. He was betting that the guildmaster would call it after a single clean strike from that waster.

This was actually more difficult than sparring with a living person. With a real opponent, you could read the body language, watch for tensing muscles. More importantly, you could often read your opponent's face. The mannequin had no face.

* * *

"How powerful do you suppose he is?" Mohrdrand asked. "I was unable to perceive more than his life and mana bars. Those, however, were much longer than I'd have expected an unranked to possess."

Give thought, old friend, she sent. *To the notion that, where he was to be sent, rare weapon drops occur at less than half the rank they do here.*

"So," he gave it more thought. "Mund was given the S rank, was it not?"

Eventually, she replied. *After it had... chewed through several heroes. When... when Kenji came through, it was ranked Double-A.*

"So," he mused. "Jackson was meant to be addressing a world considerably more dangerous than an S rank."

So it would seem, she sent. *Nor would it strain credibility to imagine his power to be equal to that task. Look to that basket beside your foot.*

Mohrdrand leaned over and lifted the wicker lid of the woven basket. His eyes went round. "What is that?" he asked, voice catching.

Some sort of weapon, I believe, Rosaluna replied without looking. *He was wearing it. As though it were a sword or dagger. Presumably in his own home, if I have the story correct. Attached to his belt inside his trousers. Here,* she indicated a place on her waist to her right rear. *The other piece looks to combine with the first. Quivers, if you will. They hold small, brass cylinders closed off with copper plugs which I think are arrow or quarrel equivalents, and filled with some sort of alchemical mixture that causes my stomach to turn do I peer too closely. I haven't got the whole of the function of it worked out just yet, but I believe it to be quite dangerous in the manner of old Arvand's steam cannon, and do not wish to suffer any accidents.*

This, Mohrdrand, she pressed, *is the sort of thing he kept with him always. Though he was supposedly living in a peaceful land. He also had a folding knife in his pocket that looked quite dangerous in its own right. And some sort of complicated folding tool, also with a sharp blade incorporated. Again, worn on his belt. Jehsha knows what other sorts of atrocities he might have brought with him had he been given advanced warning of his departure.*

"And you didn't include this with his belongings why, exactly?" he asked.

Now she did look at him. *Truthfully, Mohrdrand?* she

sighed. *I'm not entirely comfortable having such things as this loose in the world. Even do they benefit young Jackson Grenell. That thing smells of fire and brimstone and cold steel death, and I do not care for it.*

Did you get a good look at the sword? She asked, changing the subject.

He nodded. "The sword I held in my hands. It's no more than a sword."

And?

He shrugged. "I'm no swordsman Rosaluna," he admitted. "Oh, I've carried them, and used them over the years, particularly when I was young and the wars were raging. But I've no notion of what sort of fighting weapon this particular one might be. Had an odd, half basketed hilt and a long, straight, narrow blade of a type I'm not familiar with. Single edged, primarily, with the last quarter of the foible also edged.

"The fit and finish appear to be excellent, and it has three upgrade slots, empty at the moment. It's easily the equal of several I've been asked by various of the capital nobility to enchant over the years. Beyond that, I cannot say."

It is a great shame that you did not bring it along with you.

"That would have been quite rude," he frowned. "Also, he took it with him when he left."

"Rosaluna?" he seemed hesitant. "Perhaps you might consider—?"

I am not leaving my cottage to look at a sword, Mohrdrand, she sent in a no-nonsense tone. *If I were willing to venture forth in my current condition, I would not have summoned Button to escort the man to town.*

Which brings me to the subject of Button. You say that she will insist on following him? Regardless of the folly of such action?

* * *

Even one handed, Jack had survived several tentative attacks. The mannequin had, indeed, adopted at least the simulation of caution. The program or spell or whatever looked to be quite sophisticated. It was even favoring the leg he'd hit earlier.

He was starting to get some feeling in his arm again, although most of it was pain. Experimentally, he lunged and thrust with the couched staff, backing quickly and seeing could he get a meaningful grip with his bad arm. Meaningful might be stretching it, but he could more or less hold it with both hands again.

He was struggling to come up with a good avenue of attack. Despite his superior reach, he was under no illusions that he had the advantage here. And he was getting tired.

"Well," the guildmaster observed to Tiarraluna over by the equipment area. "He started out pretty strong, but I'm not really seeing rank twelve performance out there."

"I do not understand," Tiarraluna answered apprehensively. "What is wrong with him? I have seen him wield a staff with my own eyes, and he was better than this."

"That's the way it is with some fellows, I guess," he told her. "They need real foes to bring out their true potential. They just can't seem to take these tests seriously enough to expend their full effort." he watched Jack struggle for a few more minutes. "Doesn't effect the outcome, though. He still needs to defeat the training dolls to earn the rank."

Jack choked up on the shaft about halfway down its length. He still had some reach on the sword this way, and some added speed. It had occurred to him, finally, that he wasn't facing a real fighting weapon. That was a blunt. A blow from that wouldn't damage his staff the way a cut from a service sharpened blade would. Which gave him an idea and possibly an edge.

He moved in, and feinted inside. The sword slid around the supposed strike and back on line as the mannequin began a riposte. Jack took a half step back and a bit offline, nudging the sword from the opposite side and thrusting in, ramming his bad arm forward and sliding the shaft through his lead grip.

The tip struck the mannequin's biceps just above the el-

bow, coming in hard. Swinging further around as the mannequin's sword arm went limp, Jack drew partially back with his trailing hand and forced the forward end of his staff horizontally into the junction of collarbone and neck. As the mannequin started to topple, he drew back and slid his lead hand back to the quarter position, bringing the much longer free end around in a full arc.

"That's enough!" the guildmaster called from the sideline in a voice loud enough it nearly drowned out Tiarraluna's translation. "The match is yours!"

Jack hauled the shaft back, forcing the staff to slow and slide past rather than through the dome of the mannequin's head. He stood there for a moment, hands on knees, the staff suspended between them.

The guildmaster was walking out to meet him, Tiarraluna trailing close behind. "I have to fix these things, you know," he groused in a somewhat aggrieved tone, staring down at the depressions that Jack's attacks had left in the construct's surface.

Tiarraluna handed Jack a towel, taking the staff from him so that he might peel open the gambeson and wipe the sweat from himself. "What is wrong with you, Jack san?" she asked somewhat irritably. "Why are you moving so slowly?"

Slowly? "What do you mean?" he asked, puzzled.

She pointed to the constructs laying in the sand. "Fighting these," she said. "You seemed to be only playing. You moved much more quickly when you faced those teufel things on the road."

Had he? "Could it have been FoeSmite?" he asked.

She gave it some thought. "I do not think so," she shook her head. "Remember, Jack san," she pointed out. "You were already moving and fighting before it was enchanted."

Hmm. He looked over to where FoeSmite was leaning against the arena railing, and then to the staff Tiarraluna was holding. He played the trial back through his head. Had he been holding back? If so, why?

"Hold this," Tiarraluna ordered as he was thinking, gesturing with the guild staff. Once he'd taken hold, she placed

both hands against his injured arm, muttering to herself. The familiar blue glow manifested, this time from the palms of her hands, only traces of the light leaking out from around the edges. He felt warmth, and then heat wash through the arm as her muttering increased in tempo. In a matter of minutes, the glow was gone, as was the pain.

He smiled as he worked the arm through its full range of motion. "I could get used to this," he laughed.

"Do not," she frowned. "Healing magic does not fully repair damage, it only speeds your body's natural processes along. Yes, yes," she grumbled at his raised eyebrow. "I know what you are thinking. But Grandmother's brand of healing is not normal. You should not expect it of anyone but her. Particularly not from a rank ten such as me."

Right. He bounced the staff in his hand once or twice, considering. He looked again to his enchanted staff, trying to call, trying to get some response. *Is the speed from you?* He didn't hear anything coming back. Aside from that first request, it hadn't spoken to him. If it had then. But he seemed to sense a negative response. Nothing overt, just an impression.

So. "Hey," he called to the guildmaster, who was supervising a small gang of functioning mannequins in the removal of their fallen brethren from the field.

The man paused and looked back.

"What happens if I break this?" Jack asked.

The guildmaster laughed out loud at Tiarraluna's translation. "I stand you for drinks for the night, laddie!" He called. "You ain't nearly high ranked enough to break *my* weapons. Even my staves."

Jack nodded and smiled. *Full on, then.*

The second stage had him facing two swords and two staves. Jack stood quietly, eyes closed, staff grounded and held vertically before him, both hands gripping the middle of the shaft, waiting for the call. When it came, he opened his eyes but didn't otherwise move. He watched the mannequins lurch into motion, noting the additional opponent. He watched them gather their weapons. His breathing was deep and even throughout all of this. He was concentrating, calculating. Psyching himself up. Making himself ready. No holding back. Like they were trying to kill him.

The four automatons moved forward, going into two loose ranks, swords to the fore, as though they'd seen the earlier fight and knew what to expect. When he didn't move they hesitated, just out of measure, seemingly unsure. That's when he exploded into motion.

Rather than shift to the side and draw them out, he drove straight in, throwing the upper end of the staff forward with his left hand, allowing his right to slide along the shaft as it flew. The tip met the throat of the nearest sword wielder as it came forward in a lunge to meet him.

Pulling back just enough to clear the jaw of the falling mannequin, he brought the staff up to deflect the incoming strike of an opposing staff, slamming hard to bring it well offline.

Now he was moving out of line himself, sliding left and in, crowding the staff wielder nearest him. He brought the butt of his staff down on its foot, going halfway to his knees to impart force to the blow. He heard things snap inside the foot, so there were at least bone analogs in there.

As the thing fell, he hooked the upper end of his staff around behind its neck, lunging to his feet and forcing the staff down and around, powering his opponent into the sand. Two quick steps back and he brought the full length of the staff up and then down against the bowed neck. The mannequin collapsed and went still.

Now, rather than move back to assess things, he raised the tip of the staff and lunged across the body, parrying the incoming strike of the remaining staff as he dodged the sword blade accompanying it. A quick leap to the side and he was inside effective range. He bum rushed the staff wielder, knocking it into its companion. As they grappled, he forced the staff up and horizontal, pressing in with his whole body, trapping his opponent's weapon. He got one foot around behind the mannequin's and planted it.

He let go of his own staff with one hand, hauled back and smashed it right in the face with a closed fist. He had no idea if this was allowable during a skill test, or even if it would work against one of these things, but he wasn't quite in the moment anymore. A second, shorter punch to the throat, and he pushed the thing clear of him, towards the maneuvering sword wielder.

Unconsciously, he reached behind himself for the knife that should be there but wasn't. The realization that he was gripping air was what brought him back. He stepped back and grabbed the staff with his free hand, going into the spearman's stance as the sword wielder cleared its falling companion. He hit the shoulder first, then the throat, and was drawing back for the finishing blow when the guildmaster called it.

The man was looking at him oddly as he moved clear of the tangle. In real combat, the staffman would almost certainly still be alive. The swordsman? Fifty-fifty without the finisher. In either case, he supposed, the fight would be over.

"So, you're a grappler, now?" the guildmaster's voice was gruff, his face clouded. "And you've used a knife in anger before, it's clear. Just how many weapons *are* you qualified to use, I wonder?"

Jack was impressed. That was a good catch just from his reaching back to an empty spot on his belt. "Whatever it takes, Sir," he smiled. "I'll throw rocks if there's nothing else."

"It is true," Tiarraluna added to the translation. "He began his last battle by throwing a stone."

The guildmaster was just shaking his head. "Toss me that staff," he demanded irritably.

Shrugging, Jack complied. The man looked the thing up and down carefully, running a thumb along one particular spot along its length, about a quarter of the way from one end. His face was stern as he looked up from it. "One drink," he pronounced. "That's all you get."

"Uhm...?" Jack started.

"Cracked isn't truly broken," the guildmaster insisted. Turning, he threw the staff towards the weapons storage area with some force, bouncing it off the wall. "It's not even that big a crack," he was mumbling. "Pick another!" louder, and without turning his head.

Jonkins the guildmaster was still frowning volcanically when he brought up beside Tiarraluna. Jack was still retrieving a new weapon. "That last bit how he moved before?" he grumbled.

She hesitated. "No, Master Jonkins," she decided. "Somewhere between the two bouts. His strategy was more like the former, his speed and force more like the latter."

"Mmm hmm," he crossed his arms and watched as the supposed hero moved out into the center of the arena. The man's final two victims hadn't gone down for good, thanks to his intervention. They were up and clearing the others away.

"Well," he decided, watching them and calculating in his head the amount of work he had cut out for him already. "While his first performance was definitely not up to rank twelve standards, that last slaughter, I'd rank well above."

"I see," she said noncommittally, watching Jack herself.

"I'm prepared to grant him thirteen without further proof," Jonkins offered. "With a ten percent experience bonus. Call him back."

"But you said—"

"I know what I said," he grumbled, "but I also know that I don't want to spend the next ten days putting broken training dolls back together."

The Adventurers' Guild Part Four – Test Three: Swords and Rosaluna's Gifts

Rosaluna stood and vanished into her cottage. Mohrdrand remained as he was, not particularly concerned nor insulted. This was the way she was, and he was used to it. She returned after several minutes, bearing a large satchel of burgundy dyed leather. The strap was frilled and flowered, but also of subdued hue. Various jeweled crests and gems, some of them of considerable size, adorned both case and strap.

"Isn't that—?"

It is Button's now, she replied without emotion. *It is completely stocked, with additional items she will no doubt find useful in her travels. I've also included notes regarding its contents, and some tomes of spells she will be able to learn from as she gains experience. Along with a blank journal, which I expect her to keep current.*

I have also included a not insignificant sum of gold, she stated somewhat grimly. *Enough to outfit him properly and start them on their way.*

She set the satchel on the ground beside his chair.

He nodded, face inscrutable. "And what has brought about this change in attitude regarding his safety?" he wondered.

Her lip drew back at his airy tone. *It should be obvious even to you, my dear friend,* she near growled. *That he is now her protector as well as her companion. Shall I place her in yet greater danger simply because I dislike the boy? You think so little of me?*

"Never," he consoled. "I suppose I just wanted to hear you admit it."

From within her robes, she withdrew what looked like a brooch, gleaming dully. It oozed magic. *She will wear this against her heart,* she ordered. *Against the skin. It will attach itself to her flesh. It will be... uncomfortable, at first.*

"And it accomplishes what in exchange for this discom-

fort?" he wondered.

The enchantment should be proof against the venom the two of them encountered along the road, she sent. *Not one hundred percent, but a notable reduction in potency.*

"They took no samples," he noted. "And haven't returned here. How have you managed such an aid?"

I was with her when she cleansed the rot from his body, she replied. *At least the first time. I understand that he was foolish enough to become tainted multiple times.*

"You were that deeply embedded into her mind?" he was surprised.

There is a price which must be paid to lend such strength as I gave her, she said. *It involves sending life along with power. Which,* she admonished, *is something she need not ever know, although I'm sure she is already suspicious. Mark me, Mohrdrand,* she waved a finger for emphasis. *What I did, I did to save her life. I would do it again were circumstances similar, and I will not be shamed for it.*

He watched her stow the brooch in the satchel which had been her own traveling bag for almost fifty years, wondering a thing. "And you don't anticipate *he'll* fall afoul the stuff ever again?" he ventured. "Even with the wonderful armor she'll no doubt provide him now she'll have the cost?"

She scowled at him, eyes going narrow. He returned her regard calmly, his face mild and innocent.

With an angry grunt, she spun from him and stomped back into the cottage. When she reappeared, she bore a second brooch, which she must accidentally have made at some point in the past, for she certainly hadn't had the time to do so between her recent departure and subsequent return. She tossed the brooch into the satchel with a disdainful flip, as though disposing of a mouse carcass.

What? She demanded as she resumed her seat with more force than was necessary.

"Nothing," he smiled. "Not anything at all. May I refresh your tea, my dear Rosaluna?"

* * *

"You want to test with the spear?" the guildmaster wondered. "Looked like some of those moves would translate well."

Jack shook his head. "Not for the moment," he said. "I won't be carrying both a spear *and* FoeSmite, and I'm not about to leave it behind, so it would be a waste of time. Later, maybe."

"Fine, then. Let me see that sword,"

Jack retrieved the weapon and passed it to the guildmaster. Jonkins drew it and stepped clear, taking a few passes with it. He ran a finger across the blade and nodded. Then he looked up at Jack and frowned. He resheathed the sword and bade Jack pick a waster from the rack. The boy had already surprised him a few times this afternoon, and he didn't want an embarrassing visit to the healer out of being overconfident.

Jack was frowning of his own accord. The Mundians didn't, it appeared, go in for bell guards. He found a couple of swords with blades similar to his, but none with a similar basket. Eventually, he settled on a five bar swept hilt number with a blade a couple of inches longer and a bit wider than his own. It felt alright in the hand, so he figured he'd give it a shot.

Returning to the center of the arena, he was surprised to see the guildmaster standing there, a sword in his own hand. A much more substantial weapon than Jack himself was wielding. He looked to the sidelines where Tiarraluna was standing, an apprehensive look on her face.

"He will be testing you himself," she called.

He looked back to arena center and his eyes narrowed. The man simply waved him in.

"Alright," the guildmaster ordered through Tiarraluna when Jack had come nearly within measure. "Offend. I'll be blocking for now."

Jack hesitated for a second or two. This had an eerily familiar feel to it. He went into en garde and looked for an opening. Hah! Like he was going to find one against *this* guy. Still, it was a test for a change, not a fight, so he figured he'd go through the standard progression, striking through the nine standard lines, their cuts and thrusts. Not a single one went through, but the guildmaster was true to his word, and didn't counter any of them.

"Alright," the man ordered. "Faster." and again, "faster."

After four or five minutes of this, the man called a halt. "Not bad," he nodded. "I'm going to start offending. You defend. Feel free to parry if you think you can."

He started slowly, almost like Jack's original instructor. Then, gradually, without losing his air of casualness, he increased his speed in stages, until finally, it was all Jack could do to hold him off. He hadn't managed more than a token cut the whole time.

Again, the man called a halt. "That it?" he asked. "Is that your best?"

Gasping for air, sweat running down his face and back, Jack nodded.

"Fine. Okay, go find yourself a shield and we'll start over."

Half an hour later, he called that segment.

"I'm told," he ventured as Jack turned to dispose of the shield, "that you are able to use two swords."

"I can," Jack answered hesitantly, giving Tiarraluna the side eye. "I'm better with a sword and dagger, but I've done some dual wielding.

"Let's see that," the guildmaster told him. "That ability is pretty rare, and I'd like to see if you're telling the truth or if you just think you can."

"I can bring the dolls out," the guildmaster offered some time later. "You might do better, but I'm willing to call you a rank four without."

"I'll take it," Jack gasped, glad just to be standing.

"Out of curiosity," the guildmaster asked. "How'd you like a go with your own blade? I'd like to see if it makes a difference. I promise not to cut you."

Jack frowned at the barb, but couldn't argue with it. "Give... give me a minute," he panted. "And we can have a go."

The jaeger drop sword did feel better in his hand. And the bell guard somehow gave him more confidence. When Jack moved back out into the arena after a short break and some water, he thought he might do noticeably better.

The guildmaster moved in first this time, assaying a leisurely thrust with his larger blade. Jack parried and drove in smartly, causing the guildmaster to take a step back for the block. His face grew more serious, and his second attack bore a bit more speed. Jack blocked, parried, and sideslipped.

Now Jonkins' eyes took on a glint, and a small smile crept out from the corners of his mouth. He beat aside Jack's thrust and followed his blade, boring in. Jack managed the block, but it was awkward, and left him badly placed. The followup would have been the match, but at the last instant, there came a clang as Jack brought his basket up, his wrist at a painful angle, to intercept very close to his face.

Now it was the guildmaster who was overextended, and Jack flipped his lighter blade up and in, going for the guts. Jonkins sucked in his gut and slapped the blade away with his off hand.

They went on like this for a few more minutes before the guildmaster called a halt.

"Still only a four," he laughed. "But a high four. Say, a four plus ten. When you can come at me like that with any sword in your hand *but* that one, *then* I'll call you a five.

Also," he added. "You should find yourself at least a good parrying dagger to go with that blade. You really aren't that bad, all things considered."

They were at the sidelines with Tiarraluna, cleaning their weapons, when the guildmaster voiced a thought. "You've never fought a man in a real face to face fight before, have you?" he asked, voice casual.

"You mean a with sword?" Jack asked with half a chuckle. "To kill? No. Until I got here, all my sword work was strictly sport. On my world, we're a good century beyond killing one another with swords. I'm actually considered something of an oddball for even owning one. Even the guy who got the knife into me got shot for his troubles."

Jonkins eyes were wide. "Those bullet things, then?"

Jack nodded. "Among other things," he told the man. "The war I was fighting, the only bladed weapons we used —*my* people, at least— were knives, which I *have* used in combat, and hawks. Uh, tomahawks. They're a kind of specialized fighting axe. Even at that, we only used them when things got very, *very* squirrelly and we were already in serious trouble.

"Some of the enemy still used swords, but it was mostly to murder prisoners. They loved to lop the heads off of just about anything or anyone they didn't like."

He told them some stories, most of which they probably didn't believe, while they finished cleaning and stowing the weapons.

"Do you want to test with the knife?" Jonkins asked when they'd done.

"Will it give me any benefits?" Jack wondered.

The guildmaster shrugged. "I confess, I'm still not sure how you can wield the weapons you do. Nor am I certain you'll gain any benefit from being tested with them, or whether or not you'll accrue any sorts of skills or bonuses. To be honest, without the life crystal to show us, I'm only guessing at where you'll rank."

"Damn," Jack frowned. "In the stories, there's always this magical machine where the hero just goes up and puts his hand on a mirror or crystal ball or something and it tells everybody everything about him from age, to rank, to magical abilities. Bam! No muss, no fuss. I don't think I've ever even heard of anything like the tests you've been putting me through."

Jonkins and Tiarraluna were looking one to the other, faces very still. Jack queued to this along about the time he'd finished complaining. "What?" he asked.

Mirror Mirror

"**Y**ou are speaking of Jehsha's Window," Tiarraluna confessed. "It does accomplish all that you say." At his surprised expression, she continued. "The window is used to gauge the abilities of new apprentices as they begin their journeys along their chosen paths of adventure. And later, to grant them additional skills or traits when earned."

"And why am I only just now hearing about this?" he wondered.

"You are not twelve years old, Jack san," she replied with some chagrin and a glance to the guildmaster, who was now speaking. "And," she added, "the device imprints upon a life crystal, which you do not have. It simply did not occur to either of us."

"Still," he said. "Worth a shot, no?"

She spoke to the guildmaster. Back to Jack. "We are already indebted to the guild for over one hundred-seventy gold rondels, Jack san," she told him, voice low. "For the tests you have already undergone, the issuance of a guild token, and the damage you did to the demon trap. Are you prepared to add an additional ten gold rondels to that debt on something that stands almost no chance of working?"

"One hundred and seventy rondels?" he asked, his voice raising.

The guildmaster chucked a thumb over his shoulder and groused for a bit. Tiarraluna translated this as, "he says that you are getting a bargain, and asks if you have the slightest notion how expensive the dolls are to repair."

"Fine," he supposed.

He gave it some further thought. "I'd know better whether I was willing to incur additional debt if I had any idea of what sorts of bounties we're looking at per job," he said.

More back and forth with the guildmaster, before she informed him, "it is impossible to say before we know what sorts of bounties we might qualify for," she told him. "He says that, in this area, they range from fifteen or twenty silver reals for lower level quests to upwards of a thousand gold rondels for grand quests."

Okay. "And, say, I'm at least close in level —rank— to you. Where would that put us?"

She arched an eyebrow, but turned to the guildmaster to convey the question.

Back to Jack, and, "a small party of two rank tens might be able to garner in the range of eighty silver rondels at the low end to forty gold rondels at the high end," she sighed. "Not as much as I am used to earning, but Mokkelton is in a very low ranked area with, one presumes, lesser threats."

So they were probably already underwater for their first four or five quests, and possibly their next three as well. He paused to consider how easily he'd fallen into that 'we' territory in his thinking. Then he shook his head to clear it. It wasn't like he had a real choice. "Let's hook me up," he said. "Worst case, we come home broke an extra couple of times. Best case, we rate for higher level quests and break even on our first."

"So cavalier," she sighed. "Grandmother was right about you, was she not?" But she translated to the guildmaster, who nodded reluctantly and promised to give the device a shot. After they'd put everything away, of course.

* * *

He has night terrors, you know. She was looking off into the wood again.

"I did not," he replied. "They must be quiet ones. Or perhaps my walls are thicker than I'd given them credit for."

Oh, she shook her head slowly. *Not so quiet as all that. And not every night. There are nights, however, when he is quite vocal. Early on, I was forced to render him limp more than a few times when his thrashing about threatened to undo my hard work.*

He nodded without immediately answering, waiting for her to continue on her own.

He isn't like the others, she mentioned after awhile. *Beyond his size, his skin and hair and eyes. Beyond even his lack of*

a crystal. Despite coming from the same world.

"And how is that?" he prompted as though reading lines in a play.

The others, she sighed. *Save perhaps my Kenji and that poor haunted boy. They were innocents. Prior to their arrival here, they lived lives of peace and relative safety. Their land was very civilized, and no longer engaged in war.*

"I see."

Do you? She wondered. *Jack san's land is different. He is from a place called America. Kenji told me about them. Savages, he called them, with no honor. Barbarians. They had only just finished conquering their own lands, and were setting out to intimidate the whole of their world with their so-called Great White Fleet of battleships.*

Their world was marching to war, and these Americans seemed eager to be a part of it. Japan was still an empire then, and so she studied them. In the case that they were drawn into that war. Kenji was summoned to Mund scarcely a month after 'the first shots of that war were fired', as he described the initiation of conflict, and so he never learned of its outcome or whether Japan had been drawn in.

And yet by the time the fourth hero, the haunted boy, came through, that war had been over for some decades, and yet another had been fought. And Japan had found herself a conquered and occupied nation. I'll leave it for you to gather by whom.

"I suppose I might work it out," he told her. "Given your clues."

I wonder, Mohrdrand, she posed. *Did you ever have opportunity to speak to the haunted boy?*

He shook his head, wondering where she was going with this line of discourse. "I was barely Tiarraluna's rank back then," he confessed. "Little time would a hero have for the likes of me."

America played a large part in that war, Mohrdrand, she told him. *Towards the end, when Japan refused to surrender, they used flying machines against her, blackening the skies like vast murders of crows over a carcass. Night after night, they dropped fire upon her cities, in great sheets, burning whole populations alive.*

And in the end, when still she opposed them, they created weapons such as should not exist. Two of them, at the least, Mohrdrand. Each of them for a city. Do you understand me, Mohrdrand? A city! And they used them. Two infernal devices, two cities filled with people utterly destroyed. She snapped her fingers. *Like that.*

That is what the haunted boy told me, she sighed raggedly. *Among other tales. He himself bore the scars of horrible burns suffered in those last days before the American soldiers set foot on the home islands.*

You see, perhaps, why I might not want a weapon created by such a people loose in the world?

Even now, her jaw tightened and her eyes hardened. *America is fresh from her latest war, although her foes were different. According to Jack san, as I have it through what he's told Button, she has been at war for most of his lifetime. Oh, they are far off wars, against those who rule and conquer through terror. Nor do these wars discomfit overmuch the majority of those who live within her borders.*

But him? She grunted in lieu of a chuckle. *He volunteered to fight in them. You see, Mohrdrand, he was a warrior before ever he set foot on Mund.*

"And that fact is what causes his terrors?" he asked.

No, she replied. *Not exactly. And yet, wholly.*

"I'm not sure whether you expect me to understand," he chuckled, "or are merely building drama."

She shot him an eye, but clarified. *He is not only different from the others, Mohrdrand but would seem to be as different from his own people, if what Kenji and the haunted boy told me was the truth.*

"How so?" he asked.

Far from being a soulless barbarian, Mohrdrand, she sent, *he is... He is mortally terrified of not being where he is needed. That he will be late, or not strong enough. That others will suffer or die due to his shortcomings or his absence. That innocents will suffer.*

He clucked his tongue. "That sort of guilt can burn a man dry," he observed. "It's not rational."

Rational? She shrugged. *My old friend, I suppose the measure of rationality is a matter of how many children you've had die in your arms. How many friends. How many atrocities you've seen. For some, the acceptable number is surprisingly small.*

"So?" he asked, frowning.

I did not count, she hastened. *Grief enough of my own, have I, without borrowing from others. But enough. For good or ill, he is driven. And the gods, in their wisdom, have given him to us. Given him a new war to fight. Many more people to save.*

"Many more opportunities to be late," Mohrdrand grumbled. "He is only one man, Rosaluna, and Mund is vast. He will not be able to save everyone."

He will save many, she sent. *Perhaps that will be enough for him. Certainly, each of those saved will be happy enough for it, don't you imagine?*

He is very strong, I think, in many ways, she nodded slowly to herself. *Perhaps strong enough. Particularly if they take him to the window and Jehsha chooses to see him. Oh, but would that I could be there to see the look on Master Jonkins' face should that happen.*

"You say that as though you already know his class," Mohrdrand chuckled.

But of course I do, my old friend, she smiled grimly back, eyes still hard. *Now that I know him truly to be gifted in a way that Mund recognizes? How long was he in my care, after all?*

* * *

Finally. Something that looked like it was supposed to. This Jehsha's Window appeared to be an extravagantly elaborate full length mirror consisting of the standard isekai fantasy world reflectionless black glass. Its thick frame was all gilt and filigree, inset with jewels, slathered with glowing symbols and arcane script. He couldn't *wait* to try it!

"So," he held up a hand. "I just press my hand against the glass and the mirror does its thing?"

"Both hands, Jack san," Tiarraluna corrected. "And your forehead, although I am still more than a little unsure whether the window will be able to produce any viable result without a life crystal to interact with."

The guildmaster moved around her and removed what had appeared to be a jeweled ornament from the mirror's frame. Turning to Jack, he motioned for him to hold out his hands, palms up. Two quick jabs from the thick pin protruding from its reverse side and blood began to flow from the punctures on the balls of Jack's palms. Another jab to his forehead, almost too quick to follow, and the guildmaster stepped back.

"Now, Jack san," Tiarraluna prompted. "Quickly. Palms out at chest height and to either side. Face the mirror close enough that your nose nearly touches the glass without stretching. Close your eyes, and concentrate on opening yourself up to Jehsha. Then place your palms flat against the glass and touch your forehead to it as well."

"And then what?" he asked as he closed on the mirror.

"And then we wait to see if anything happens."

The glass felt icy cold at first, but warmed quickly, becoming uncomfortably hot within a few heartbeats. He tried to ignore it as he strove to 'open himself up' without really knowing what that felt like.

"Is it working?" he asked tightly after a few moments had passed.

"Shhh!" she scolded. "I do not know. I do not think—"

"Oh," the guildmaster interrupted. "It's working alright. I'm not sure how, but it's working. It just isn't doing so in any way I've ever seen it work before."

The glass had grown smokey, its surface roiling slowly, flecks of grey-green light flashing as if from some deep cavern beyond the smoke. A soft keening grew up from beneath the audible range, faint, yet clear. Lightning seemed to be arcing from beneath Jack's fingertips, tracing deep into the dark field; an odd sort of blue-white, fractious display. His forehead felt as though somebody was going at it with a diesel powered tattoo pen.

Above, and deep within the field, wavering text seemed to be trying to form, shifting and sliding away even as it manifested. The whole process was taking longer than the guildmaster thought it should, and he said so.

"Should we stop?" Tiarraluna asked nervously.

"Not yet," he cautioned. "As I said, it's working, just not normally. We'll give it a chance. You pay either way, right?"

"Jack?" she asked after translating.

His teeth were clenched at this point, his palms on fire. The tattoo pen had been replaced with a fiery jackhammer. Faintly, through the pounding, he could swear he heard a gruff voice. As though someone were standing before and above him, within the mirror. *Endure, lost child*, it ordered. *You must endure.*

"Give it a bit more," he winced without opening his eyes. "I'm good."

She didn't believe him, but she nodded to the guildmaster.

They could hear his teeth grinding before the mirror gave up its secrets and formed a mostly coherent message within its depths. His head came away from the surface with an audible pop the instant Tiarraluna gave him the news and the guildmaster's permission. His hands took a bit longer and came away with less skin than when he'd laid them against the glass. His forehead was bright red and blistered. The burns on his hands were worse.

"You put *kids* through this?" he growled, irritated and dizzy.

Tiarraluna gasped at the sight of his injuries and moved quickly to his side. "This is not normal behavior, Jack san," she explained taughtly as she began a healing incantation. "I have never seen a window *harm* anyone before." He merely stood with his hands held out, swaying on his feet, panting and glaring at the tale of the trial as it slowly vanished from the glass.

"Well?" he grated after Tiarraluna had done what she

could.

The guildmaster was scratching at his beard and squinting hard at the displayed text, widening first one eye and then the other, as though changing focus might alter what he was seeing. "Well, it kind of worked," he said, hesitantly. "Sort of. I suppose."

"What does that even mean?" Tiarraluna demanded without bothering to translate.

"It means," Battler Borea Jonkins, guildmaster of the Mokkelton Adventurers Guild replied stiffly, "that it seems to have worked, but that the results make no damned *sense*."

"How so?" she asked, at least translating his response for Jack this time.

"Three classes?" Jonkins demanded. "Three? *Nobody* is three class. And this first one?" he pointed broadly.

* * *

"Surely not!" Mohrdrand's eyes went wide. "There hasn't been a sentinel walk the face of Mund in nearly a thousand years. I know you don't like to hear this, Rosaluna," he shook his head. "But you must be mistaken."

Look with your inner eye, Mohrdrand, she urged. *What were the forces that drove the old sentinels? What was it sent them out from their castles and cities into the wilderness? Sent them forth from lives of wealth and potential ease and onto paths that more often than not led to early and painful death? I submit to you, my good wizard, that they were the same forces which drive our young Jackson today.*

No, friend Mohrdrand, she waved a finger at him. *Jehsha will not so much grant him the class as see within him that he has already been a sentinel for most of his life.*

* * *

"Sentinel?" Jonkins lowered his gaze to Jack, narrowing his eyes. "Sentinel. Him."

"And what is wrong with that?" Tiarraluna demanded. "Is there something wrong with being a sentinel?"

He cut short his bark of laughter to answer. "Nothing at all, little miss," he grated. "If it was a thousand years ago and he a first rank nobleman.

"Sentinels," he explained more slowly, as if giving a lecture. "Were the wardens —the guardians— of the frontiers when the world was wild. More sparsely populated with humans or demihumans than it is today. More heavily populated with manifestations of the dark. And before the gifted were as common as they are these days, and able to hold the darkness in check. They traveled the world, mostly alone, righting wrongs, battling monsters, freeing princesses, defending villages. Bringing hope to the downtrodden....

"They were the heroes ordinary heroes revered. Storybook legends. Almost exclusively," he went on, "they were royals. Kings and princes who gave up everything to protect the land."

She looked to Jack, slowly rubbing his forehead with the back of a hand while he glared accusingly at the once more pristine glass of Jehsha's Window. She giggled. "Alright, Lord Jonkins," she allowed. "I will grant you that he does not look the part just yet. But his heart is true. He will grow into the title, I think."

She forcefully pushed away the image that popped into her mind of the dark thing in the iron cage. That was not him. It could not be him.

"Yes, well..." he grumbled. "Not the greatest of the those who came before him pretended to be a sentinel. Even our esteemed new king whatsisname was no more than a battle mage."

"Pretend, Lord guildmaster?" she asked. "Is this what you call the pronouncement of the window? The recognition by our Lord Jehsha?"

His scowl freshened, but he scrubbed it away with a hand. "I suppose not," he conceded. "It's just... I'd always thought of sentinels as the province of *our* people is all. Mundians. Not these imported heroes."

"And the next?" she turned the subject away from this sore spot. "Do my eyes deceive? That truly says artificer? As a *secondary* class? I do not believe I have ever heard of such a thing."

"I suppose once you've been granted... sentinel..." he grated with ill humor, "*every*thing else must be. Though where *it* came from I no more know than his being.... Certainly not from carving a staff, despite what you lot have done with it after the fact."

"The books!" Tiarraluna clapped her hands together.

"Books?" both men asked at once.

"When grandmother found him... you," she spoke to them both. "Your —his— feet were tangled in the straps of some sort of knapsack. Filled with books and papers it was, and strange devices. That must be it."

My textbooks! Jack realized. *My notes! My homework!*

Hard upon that realization, came another. He had his explanation now for why his leap away from the path of the on-rushing bus had been so spectacularly unsuccessful. After eight hours of work, three hours of class, and a couple of hours using the trade school's machine shop, he'd stumped into the living room dead beat, tossed his backpack full of school gear onto the floor beside his easy chair, tossed his jacket onto the couch, and flopped down to try and relax with some gaming. When he'd jumped, he must've gotten his legs caught in the rigging of the heavy pack. *Wait a minute!*

"My pack?" he demanded of Tiarraluna, catching her arms in his still stinging grip. "My pack is here? My books? My tools?"

"Jack san!" she squeaked. "Jack san, release me this in-stant!

"Yes," she said somewhat agitatedly once he'd released her and stepped back. "Your books, in any case. I am not sure about tools, though. Grandmother said that there were some strange contraptions in there, but nothing about any tools."

He was grinning so hard it was painful. Then his face fell. "Where are they?" he demanded. "Why didn't any of you tell me about this?"

She was frowning now as well. "*I* saw no need," she sniffed. "I had assumed you already knew. Why grandmother did not tell you I cannot say.

"As to their location, I should imagine they are still in the pack we brought from grandmother's cottage."

"Are we finished with our little drama yet?" the guildmaster broke in.

They left off staring at one another and returned their regard to him, faces stern.

"An artificer," he began, but stopped. "There's no need for me to explain," he told the girl. "You know what they are as well as I do."

She nodded and gave it to Jack in her own words. "Artificers are... builders, I suppose," she told him. "Engineers, perhaps. They design and build engines, tools, weapons. Devices with magical properties, mostly." She pointed to the mirror. "This device was crafted by an artificer, in fact."

"I see," he mused. "So I do have magical abilities, then."

She tilted her head. "As I have indicated, Jack san," she clarified. "You have mana. As Uncle Mohrdrand has said, you have the ability to infuse a thing with that mana, and perhaps affect its properties. Whether you have magical *abilities*, however, remains to be seen. Considering how you interact with FoeSmite, it is probable but by no means certain."

"Oh, it's certain, alright," Jonkins informed her.

She turned questioningly.

"Part of being a sentinel," he told her. "Sort of baked into the class."

"Ah," she nodded. Then back to Jack. "You see, Jack san," she went on. "Magical ability is not a hard and fast trait of artificers. Most of them have it, but not all."

"But you've already told me—" he began.

"Do not fret, Jack san," she soothed. "Apparently it *is* a hard and fast trait of sentinels. You will simply require training in its use."

"Ehem," the guildmaster reminded them that they weren't alone. Again, they turned to him.

"This final class," he said a bit worriedly. "I can't begin to say. I can't read it, nor is it solid enough to say that it's an active class or merely a potential. That alone is strange beyond anything I've seen before. Even given the rest of today's events and revelations."

"But...?" Tiarraluna started.

"As I said," he cautioned. "Not normal. It shouldn't be there, and yet it is. It should be comprehensible, and yet it isn't. I don't even recognize the script or language."

Tiarraluna translated. Jack gave the mirror his full attention. Yeah, he could see where they'd have trouble. The script was indeed strange, and the translucent quality of it made it more difficult yet. But the language? Yeah, he could read it.

"It says rifleman," he chuckled dryly. "Rank twenty-four. In English."

It took the Mundians awhile to absorb that information.

"Ryfl-man?" Tiarraluna wondered.

"The way my people wage war," he reminded her. "Our primary personal weapons, remember?"

"The bullet things, yes." the guildmaster acknowledged. "But we don't have those here."

Jack smiled dryly. "That's why it's funny."

Accepting Their First Bounty

Jack squeezed hard, feeling the sticky spread of his blood as it oozed out against the slick surface of the stone. *They sure love their blood magic, these Mundians*, he thought. In any case, he kept up the pressure, supposedly infusing the token with his 'essence'. Presumably Tiarraluna had done the same, along with every other member of the guild. Seemed overly complicated, but whatever.

"Alright," Tiarraluna translated for the guildmaster, who tossed him a towel. "That is enough. Wipe the stone clean with this cloth and give them both to me."

He did as instructed, looking down at his new ID before handing it over. It had gone from a sort of clear quartz to a smokey dark, almost black onyx. Far darker than Tiarraluna's had been from the short glimpses of it he'd gotten earlier.

The guildmaster fed the stone into the reader, and the translucent image of Jackson Grenell, gentleman adventurer sprang to life above it. Every detail, from his current tunic right down to the fiery red, suspiciously hand print shaped splash the size of a pancake smeared across his forehead.

His hand went instinctively to the place the burn had been, though there was almost no trace left after Tiarraluna's ministrations. Obviously, the reader and mirror were connected somehow.

"Well, now," Jonkins muttered. "Eighteen years old?" he looked over at Jack. "The way you handle yourself?"

"The transfer affects the physical body, Grandmother says," Tiarraluna answered for Jack, who had no idea what had been said. "So far as Mund is concerned, Jack san is apparently eighteen."

"Right." Jonkins looked back to the projection. Agility and strength were both stupidly high for his rank, perception even moreso. Oh, right. That was the effect of the sentinel class adding two points to each of those stats. As was his ability to use just about anything he picked up as a weapon.

Intelligence was a cut or two above the norm, but nothing spectacular for an artificer. Wisdom was moderately high for his given age, but not, he supposed, for the age he'd been before coming here. Whatever that might be. He'd really like to discuss tactics or philosophy over a pint. He'd wager the journey had shaved five or ten years from him. The only low stat of the lot was endurance, and that one wasn't exactly bad, but for its comparison with the others.

"Well," he waved a hand. "Jehsha definitely saw him, and accepted. He's got the bonuses and traits of his classes noted. Even the weapon ranks and percentage bonuses I granted out on the floor, and *that's* a neat trick, since I haven't entered them in yet. And an overall level of nine?" he looked to the boy again, shaking his head. "Nine. Well," he shrugged, throwing up his hands. "Who'm I to gainsay Jehsha? Let's go look at the board." he slid the token from the slot and tossed it to Jack as he made for the far side of the guild's main hall. Jack would have preferred to have examined the field awhile longer. Maybe have the girl explain some of those class traits to him.

The bounty board was huge, covering the whole of the long wall, from knee height to a good stretch above for a tall man. It was, Tiarraluna explained, divided into sections, separating quests of differing levels for differing party ranks.

"I have a few questions," Jack announced as the guildmaster came to a halt before what would be the section for rank nineteen parties. In truth, the banner read ranks fifteen to twenty, but he still couldn't read Tandrian.

Tiarraluna translated, fearing what the questions would be. Jack san was no fool, and she thought that she already knew their general thread.

"We've been here all morning," Jack began. "And yet I haven't seen another soul enter the hall. Nor have I heard any noise beyond what we've been making ourselves. The section of the market that would normally cater to adventures is a ghost town, and looks to have been so for awhile.

"I haven't seen anybody who might be mistaken for a guardsman since... well, at all. Not a one. Not inside the town, nor outside on our way here. And every living soul I saw outside the walls looked terrified."

Tiarraluna sighed resignedly, but duly translated.

"Astute observations," the guildmaster allowed. "But I've heard no questions."

"One question, then," Jack frowned. "Why? Where is everybody? The guards, the adventurers who should be around? The army? Oh, and another. This area, if I'm not horribly wrong, shouldn't be dangerous enough to have so many unfulfilled bounties. Why aren't they being served?"

Again, Tiarraluna translated, her voice low. The guildmaster sighed this time as well, rolling his shoulders. He looked up at the bounty wall and out the doorway into the street before answering.

"There are five guardsmen in Mokkelton," he said slowly, voice somber. "The highest ranked among them, their captain, is rank four. And that's counting his bonus for being within the walls. He crosses out through the gate and he's back down to three. He's thirteen and a half years old.

"As for adventurers," he said with no more vigor. "With Tiarraluna here, and now that you're officially one of us, the total number within the walls has gone up to four, counting your friend Mohrdrand. There's two more out on a quest, and they'll complete the rolls of the Mokkelton guild as of this moment. One of *them* is also a freshly minted rank four, although he's four at baseline."

Six. In a town of this size? Jack thought, stunned. *No, make that four. I've only just gotten here, and Tiarraluna's from out of town.* "How is that even possible?"

Tiarraluna didn't bother to translate. "You must understand, Jack san," she told him earnestly. "The demon lord may be gone, but he was defeated only slightly more than a year ago."

"And?" he prompted.

She raised her eyebrows in surprise. "Did you think the hero simply marched himself alone up the dark road to the demon lord's obsidian fortress to slay him? No, Jack san," she shook her head firmly. "Every soldier. Every adventurer. Every guard, even, marched with him save a very, very few. Mohrdrand and grandmother," she clarified. "Despite their power, are very old, and no longer fit for the battlefield or its trials. And so," she finished. "Only they were left to guard the town." She half turned to the guildmaster. "And lord Jonkins, who's duty is to Mokkelton and the guild, which must always be manned.

"Surely," he started, but she stopped him. "I remained behind because I was not old enough to go when the last of the reinforcements marched out nearly three years ago.

"It's the same for Tiglund and the guards," Jonkins supplied then. "Cable was brought home by a group of the ungifted before the final campaign began. Wounded beyond the ability of any save Rosaluna to heal, but stubbornly clinging to life. By the time he'd recovered enough to walk on his own, the demon lord was gone, and so he stayed. He's been working to keep the worst of the problems at bay, but he's only one man trying to cover an area that used to be served by a hundred or more."

"But aren't there always gifted being born?" Jack asked, confused. "Always some ready to begin training?"

Tiarraluna rocked back as though she couldn't believe what she was hearing. "Jack san," she narrowed her eyes. "How many of us do you think there are? Do we grow on trees, perhaps? Or are we planted like vegetables for harvest?

"One child, or perhaps two of a hundred is granted any gifts at all," she told him. "And most of those are born to the nobility. Even then, of all those born with gifts, no more than a third have any useful talent with them. Even of those, most gifts are not particularly useful in adventuring. We are rare, Jack san," she repeated. "And, even were there dozens of us milling about, Who do you suppose would train us? Lord Jonkins, perhaps? His skills are not unlimited, nor universal. I was fortunate enough to have my grandmother to train me. Most are not so lucky."

He stood for the scolding. He deserved it, he supposed. What were there around Mokkelton, five or six thousand people, maybe? Lucky they had as many as they did.

"But," he had a thought. "You told me the demon lord was killed over a year ago, didn't you?"

"Approximately."

"So where is everybody, then?" he wondered. "Why haven't any of those who went off to fight come home?"

Neither the girl nor the guildmaster had an answer, and there was the problem.

"Fine," he ran a hand across his face, glaring up at the board, temper flaring. "You know what? Fine. Which of these is the most urgent then?"

"That you can handle, you mean?" the guildmaster prompted.

Jack looked over his shoulder at the man, his eyes steady. "What's urgent?" he repeated. "What's getting people killed?"

Jonkins returned the stare thoughtfully. Drifting through his mind were the memories of watching the boy in the arena and the improbable class he'd been given. Sentinel. An old class. A special class. There were powers at play here. Powers he wasn't privy to. But he'd been at this game a long time, had Guildmaster Jonkins, and he knew a thing or two.

"I think I probably know the answer already," he asked sort of casually. "But you ever kill a man? I mean close up, at arm's reach, while you looked him in the eye." The way Jack's eyes went to flint told him everything he needed.

To Tiarraluna. "You, little one?"

She shook her head. "Beasts only," she admitted. "Beasts and low level monsters."

"Could you?" he asked. "If it came down to it? If you had to? Could you end a human being?"

"I..." she stumbled. "If I must... if...."

Both men were giving her the eye.

"What's the bounty?" Jack asked into the silence.

"On its face?" the guildmaster replied after Tiarraluna's stuttering translation. "No more than a scout, with the potential to turn into a cleanup.

"We've been getting reports of troubles to the north. Travelers waylaid, mostly. Bodies found on the roads, stripped of valuables. Now some of the locals have gone missing. Some steadings have been raided and pillaged.

"Bandits, obviously," he nodded when Jack would speak. "But we haven't gotten any clear notion of how many or who. That's the job. Find out who's doing it. If it's only normal brigands, see if you can bring them in, but don't be silly about it. Dead or alive, ungifted bandits are worth two silver rondels each.

"If they're gifted, and there are only a few of them and they're low enough rank, feel free to take them out. The pay is two gold rondels per rank for each of them you bring back proof of death for. Plus, of course, whatever plunder you retrieve from them.

"If you decide that there are too many of them, or if they're too strong," he went on. "Hie yourselves on back here and we'll try to figure something out. In that case, you get ten gold rondels for the location of the camp."

Jack gave Tiarraluna a long look. He was ready, but he doubted she was. "How about it, little sister?" he asked finally.

The name got him a hint of her old glare, but she didn't follow it up. "I... I will try, Jack san," she said slowly. "I... I cannot promise..."

"No need," he shook his head. "Just try, that's all I ask. I'll take care of the rest."

"You are very sure, Jack san," her eyes narrowed.

"Not my first rodeo," he smiled, though it was a cold sort of smile, and the rodeo part had her frowning at her ring again.

"We will take the bounty, Lord Jonkins," she nodded to the guildmaster.

"Are you sure?" he asked dubiously.

Another look to Jack, before, "yes, Lord Jonkins," she nodded again. "We are sure."

Back to the counter and he took their tokens, sliding them together into the reader, sliding the bounty into another slot. "As the higher ranking member and leader," he wondered over his shoulder to Tiarraluna, "do you want to assign a name to your party?"

"No thank you," she answered quickly, without consulting Jack. "Perhaps later," she added, casting a sideways glance to her companion.

There was no keyboard to the device. Notations were made longhand with a quill pen within a shimmering field. Notations done, a bounty token slid out the bottom of the reader and into the guildmaster's hand. Similar to the guild tokens, it was larger, and engraved with a glyph. He withdrew it and their guild tokens and passed them back to their owners. "You're now officially assigned the bounty," he smiled. "Good luck to you both. Now get lost, I've got work to do." He turned without further ceremony and vanished into the building's interior.

"Is this normal here?" Jack asked softly as he regarded the empty doorway, thinking of his erstwhile hostess and her habits.

"Not really," Tiarraluna replied equally softly, herself giving attention to the empty portal. "At least, I do not think so. I remind you, Jack san, this is not my home guild, and their ways may be different. In any case, shall we be on about our business?"

Jack stared down at his guild token, really wanting to get a more in depth idea of what was going on with it. But they'd pretty clearly been dismissed, so he turned towards the outer door, nodding. "May as well," he shrugged as he slid the token into his pouch.

Tom Black

An Evening of Counsel

They ran into troubles almost immediately. Now that Jack had a token and the few tradesmen with anything to offer were willing to sell to him, it turned out that equipping him would be a significantly more costly undertaking than they'd earlier imagined.

Bows, for instance. He could settle for a rank three longbow of forty pound draw or so and Tiarraluna would possibly have enough gold left for some cheap armor, if they could find any. Or he could purchase a rank five sixty pounder and go hunting bandits in his shirtsleeves. The one recurve they found was well beyond their current wherewithal, and the trader wouldn't even allow Jack to test its draw without a show of gold beforehand.

As to armor, they determined that he could purchase either a worn set of rank four boiled leather that had seen better days but sort of fit and have enough left for the cheapest bow they'd found, or a better fitted coat of rank six brigandine and settle for a hunting bow that might or might not launch an arrow farther than he could sling a rock. And he'd be going out without a helmet, which he'd never liked.

"Perhaps we might speak again with uncle Mohrdrand after all," Tiarraluna posited nervously as Jack was scowling down at a dented spangenhelm with visible rust along its edges and a price that seemed farcical even to an outsider.

He looked down at her, his face still hard.

"I would like to speak to him in any case," she pressed. "Now that we know your class, he may have more advice."

He tossed the helm back onto the plank table, causing the vendor to jump a bit and scowl back. "You think it makes that much difference?"

"I do," she nodded. "You are a sentinel, Jack san," she pointed out, causing the vendor's eyes to widen. "That is an exceedingly rare class, and may well require special equipment. Equipment we might not find at all in a place such as Mokkelton."

Jack heaved a great breath and, with a last scowl for the merchant, acquiesced. It wasn't like they were going anywhere today in any case. The afternoon was waning, he was bone weary, and his stomach was grumbling.

They surprised Mohrdrand coming in through the back door as they entered through the front, as though he were himself only just returning. Then Tiarraluna did a double take and stopped in her tracks. "Is that grandmother's bag?" she demanded.

The old wizard smiled and shook his head. "Yours, now, according to Rosaluna," he chuckled. "With a tome's worth of instructions and advice to go with it, to complement a heaping ration of stern warnings."

"Whatever could have caused her to decide that?" she squeaked. "I... I have... I do not deserve such a prize. What shall she do without it?"

He shrugged. "Build a new one, I'd imagine," he laughed. "In all probability, a much more powerful one. In any case, she was quite insistent that you have this one." he moved forward and held the burgundy satchel out to the flummoxed girl where she stood rooted in his hallway.

She reached out and took it after a good while, holding it before her as though she couldn't imagine what to do with it. Mohrdrand took her by the shoulders and led her to one of the chairs before the hearth, all but bending her knees for her to sit before he retreated to the kitchen.

Jack hung back, waiting to see what would come of this new development. It seemed pretty momentous, and looked to indicate a significant shift in the old woman's stance on him. He'd already worked out that the old wizard must have visited the cottage while they'd been gone, but that was about all he'd worked out. He sidled around the distressed girl and took the seat she'd occupied the day prior. He was itching to get himself out to the stable and look for his pack, but that would now have to wait.

Mohrdrand returned to the room awhile later. He'd brewed coffee for Jack and tea for himself and Tiarraluna. He used the same tray and cart she'd used and took the same seat he'd occupied before. And then they sat in silence while Tiarraluna struggled to work out what was happening.

"What does this mean, Uncle?" she asked finally. "I do not understand."

He smiled for her, warmly this time, and without mirth. "It means, child," he said kindly, "that you have her blessing. You have her support insofar as she is able to support you."

"In what?"

He chucked his head in Jack's direction. "In your entanglement with the misplaced hero there," he said not unkindly. "She is not happy about it," he cautioned. "Very not happy. But she understands, and she loves you, and so she is doing what she is able."

Then, while she stared down into the bag, he related his conversation with Rosaluna, and the old woman's wishes. The high points, at least. There were yet secrets Rosaluna wished kept, and he would keep them. No mention of the strange weapon with the tiny copper quarrels, for instance.

He explained the wards and the journal and the gold. That Jack was now her protector. And now he included Jack in on the conversation, conveying the warning and cautions.

While this was going on, the old cook let herself in and began preparing the evening meal.

As they ate, Tiarraluna seemed to regain herself somewhat. "Uncle?" she ventured at one point. "Jehsha saw Jack san."

"I suspected as much," the old wizard answered over the rim of his cup.

"Uncle," she continued. "He is a—"

"Sentinel?" he asked, covering his grin with the cup.

She stopped dead, her mouth open. "You *knew*?"

"Your grandmother knew," he corrected.

"I see," she lowered her head. "Is there, I wonder, anything at all she does *not* know?"

"If so," he laughed as he reached for the tea pot. "I ha-

ven't discovered it in all the years I've known her."

Jack, meanwhile, ate in silence. He was working things through in his own mind, completely irrespective of either of the Galbradia females. His urge to be on his way was battling his need to address the dangers facing the area surrounding Mokkelton. He was having to do casualty math, and that was a subject he'd never been able to tolerate. Who did he protect? Who did he save? And for each of them saved, how many others would perish? He was one man. He couldn't be everywhere.

Mohrdrand's eyes were going narrow, even as he bantered with the flustered girl. Jackson was cutting his food as though he were slaying an enemy, his face grim. He could almost read what was going through the boy's mind. Rosaluna had been correct again, it would seem. The question was, how much could the boy stand before he started coming apart at the joints?

The table was cleared and the three of them back before the hearth, which had been lit and was a good long way into warming the room. Jackson had retreated more deeply into his funk, which even Tiarraluna had now noticed. It was time to address the dragon in the room.

"Jackson Grenell," the old wizard shot the address like an arrow to pierce the boy's concentration.

Jack looked up, his face closed off.

"What have you been told of sentinels?" the old man asked.

"Heroes' heroes," Jack said with no real feeling. "Fairy tale stuff. Rescuing princesses, that sort of nonsense."

"Ah hah," Mohrdrand nodded. "Balderdash, the lot of it."

Both Jack's and Tiarraluna's eyes went round.

"And would it surprise you overmuch to hear that Rosaluna has claimed you to have been one most of your life?" Mohrdrand gestured with his freshly lighted pipe. "Not merely since this afternoon? Did you rescue many princesses in your old life, Jackson Grenell?"

Jack shook his head. "Yes it would, and no I didn't"

"Sentinels were lunatics," Mohrdrand went on forcefully. "Idiots who took the woes of the world onto their own shoulders of their own volition. Fools who believed that each and every life on Mund was their own personal responsibility. Sound familiar yet?"

Jack was flushing, his face closing down into hard planes.

"Jehsha blessed them because Jehsha loves fools, and they were useful and occasionally amusing."

"Uncle!" Tiarraluna scolded. "That is blasphemy!"

"The truth is never blasphemy, child," he chortled.

"Maybe not," Jack's voice matched his expression. "And maybe they *were* fools. Does that make their pain less valid? You think I *want* to torture myself like this? But if not me, who?"

Tiarraluna was looking at him strangely now, wondering what was going on. Looking back to the old wizard for answers.

"Where you are isn't your fault, Jackson," Mohrdrand insisted. "If anyone is to blame, it would be the gods. Those who allowed you to be hurled here without warning. Those who should have protected you at least until you'd gained the field."

"You'd be surprised at how little that knowledge helps," Jack replied with no great force.

"Then how about this?" the wizard ventured. "Our god, Jehsha, the god of Mund, has seen you. Acknowledged you. Blessed you."

"I'm painfully aware," Jack managed a bit of snark. "So what?"

"So," Mohrdrand held out his hands, palms up, as though offering Jack a tray piled with reality. "You are now, for all your original goals, *our* hero as well, misplaced though you be."

Jack's expression didn't change, nor did he offer comment.

"See here," Mohrdrand tried. "Examine the facts of the situation you're in.

"One. Here is where you are. On Mund. No amount of wishing will land you on this other world. You're stuck, at least for the time being.

"Two. You have been made a hero of the land by the

very god of our world. Perhaps not by *your* choice, but when do *any* of us get to choose when the gods decide to use us? Or where? Were you allowed a choice before the decision was made to send you to this other world? I think not.

"Three. The way ahead is long, and not one you will traverse in a short sprint. You've neither the money nor the skill. Nor will either be particularly easy or quick to gather. It will take you a long while. You may as well help some people along the way.

"Four. Inasmuch as the demon you were on your way to fight was strong enough to gain a march on the very *gods*, I would think that the stronger you were when finally you made landfall in his realm, the better, yes?"

Jack closed his eyes and lowered his head. Those were all good points. Back home, he'd been able to hold his personal demons at bay with the knowledge that he was utterly unable to do anything to help. That and keeping himself too occupied with things like video games, HEMA, and trade school to think. And the meds, of course. Couldn't forget the meds. Meds which he no longer had access to.

Earth's demon lords were too powerful, too far removed, and too well concealed behind their rank upon rank of minions, with their mountains of byzantine laws stymying even the most ardent challenger. Hell, even defending yourself against armed criminals was cause for arrest in the dystopian garbage dump the west was becoming, while the criminals often went free. The east was even worse. Hundreds of millions murdered by their own governments in the twentieth century alone, exclusive even of war.

Here, at least, he had the ability to do *something*, small though that something might be. What had that Burke guy said? *'All that is required for evil to flourish is that good men do nothing'*. And what had he been doing *but* nothing? Well, here was a place and time he could change that. Even if it wasn't where he was *supposed* to be.

He opened his eyes tand regarded the old wizard from beneath his brows. "Points taken," he sighed. "I'll try to take things as they come. Can't promise anything, though."

Mohrdrand shrugged. "Nor can I blame you," he grinned.

"Now, what say we get the two of you ready for your first trial?"

The Adventure Begins

Midmorning found them well away from Mokkelton, trudging up the northern road on their first official adventure.

Tiarraluna had donned a hooded cloak, as the day was cooler than had the previous few been. Brightly colored and bedecked with flowers and baubles, much as her robes were, and of similar hue.

For his own part, Jack was freshly garbed and armored from the skin out. With the added funds supplied by the old woman, they'd acquired for him better boots, undergarments, leather trousers, a more substantial tunic, and a legitimate arming doublet and cap.

In addition to the fresh clothing, and after scouring the market, they'd purchased a rank five mail hauberk and coif with only a little rust, which he wore beneath the blue rank six brigandine he'd been looking at the previous day.

He'd also found some steel rank four shoulder cops painted mostly black and not too dented. Steel bracers and greaves painted a dull red were now strapped to forearms and shins. The sallet he'd found would need a good bit of TLC when he got the chance, but was as solid as it was a particularly ugly shade of yellow. He looked like a walking yard sale, and none of the new gear bore any enchantments or upgrades, but they'd done the best they could and he was decently protected from anything they should encounter in the area.

Atop it all, he'd found a cloak of his own, much more subdued than Tiarraluna's and of roughspun wool. Long, hanging well below his knees to conceal the armor beneath, and dyed a dark forest green. It was just a cloak, though, and offered protection only from the weather.

Trudging along beside her, hood up, he gave the appearance of a servant. An appearance buoyed by the pack he bore. The larger one they'd brought from Rosaluna's cottage.

The recurve bow lay unstrung against the pack's side, not readily apparent as a weapon. At least, not at first glance.

Nor the thick quiver of arrows lashed to the opposite side. It was a risk, carrying them this way, as they'd not be readily accessible should an immediate need for them arise. But they were still close to the town, and strolling along the road with a strung bow at the ready seemed sort of impolite, leaving aside the inadvisability of trying to juggle both the bow and staff together.

Worst case scenario, he could hurl FoeSmite at any ambushers they might encounter with some hope of calling it back in time to do any good. He'd done it once, right? He could do it again, he figured.

He might also be able to use the sling he'd rigged for it, but he hadn't practiced with it at all. Not here nor back home. It was only something he'd seen once in a video on the internet and decided to try.

They'd spent the morning scouring the market for goods and items the old wizard had advised they lay hand to and which they could now afford. Along with those things they'd known from the beginning they should have, but had lacked the wherewithal to acquire. Basic traveling gear for him for the most part, as Tiarraluna already had her own. A bedroll and such.

Some of the other items Jack understood, some were a complete mystery. He clung to the hope with some small part of his mind that, at some point, Tiarraluna would let him in on their secrets.

The greater part of his mind, however, was involved in other pursuits, and he was in a bad mood for it. Beyond even the pain of the so-called protective broach he could still feel burrowing into his flesh like a giant blood sucking tick.

He'd finally gotten a look at the pack the previous night, after their discussions with the old wizard. Tricky bit of business it was, too. Bigger on the inside than the outside sort of tricky. Much bigger.

He'd found his personal day pack inside, somewhat the worse for wear. Stuffed into an inner pocket that may as well have been a small shed. All his books were there. His micrometers and other instruments as well. Homework, laptop —which had somehow, miraculously, survived the bus's impact, along with his subsequent and precipitous arrival on Mund— the works. Everything he'd had on him or in the pack, right down to the empty gum wrapper he'd had stuffed into a pants pocket. With five glaring omissions.

All by itself, his pack weighed as much as the entirety of the larger pack did, so the inner pocket not only made size vanish, it did the same for weight. What did they call them again in the RPGs? Portable hole? Wait... was this an RPG or an isekai? If the latter, it'd be, what, a dimensional box? He'd heard it called dimension home, Item box, bag of holding, inventory box— wait... that one had been an isekai *about* an RPG. That seemed most common, but didn't really seem to fit a physical object. In any case, and for so far as it went, all good news.

But then there were those five glaring omissions. The main reasons for his foul mood of this morning. The nagging question eating at his mind. Where in hell was his G20? Or its holster, the mag holder, and spare magazines for that matter. He'd been trying for the better part of the day thus far to remember what he'd done with them, but to no avail. Between the attack, the shift in worlds, and the time elapsed, it just wasn't as clear as it could have been.

He'd been using the machine shop that night, hadn't he? On such occasions, he traditionally stuffed the holstered pistol and mag holder into the lockbox behind the seat in his pickup. But he also usually put them back onto his belt after he was done. Had he this time? He could swear he had. But even if he'd just grabbed them out of the box, stuffed them into the pack, and headed straight home, the pistol should still have been in there, right? If not... if he'd put the holster and mags on his belt upon leaving the shop, he should still have been wearing them when the bus came calling. But he hadn't seen them since awakening here. The old woman had returned his Leatherman early on. His folder and flashlights he'd found in the pack. No pistol, no ammo.

So where was it? Had he taken the holster off and set it

on the end table beside his chair? If so, why this time of all times? So used was he to having it on him after so many years, he didn't really even feel it anymore, so why take it off? And if he hadn't, he circled around, where the hell *was* the damned thing?

Tiarraluna was watching him as they strolled up the road, noting his grim face. Was he still worried about those people who would perish without his aid? Or was this something else? Traveling with him should this prove his default mood would be difficult. Eventually, it would become impossible. Perhaps this was why so many of the old sentinels had traveled alone. None other could stomach them over long periods.

They stopped for their midday meal late into the afternoon, having gotten such a late start. Light fare only, for they had a ways to go and didn't want to have their bellies too full.

"Why do you stop so often?" Jack wondered around a mouthful of travel cake. "It's like every half mile."

She gave him an eye, at once relieved that he seemed over whatever ill wind had been blowing between his ears the day long, and nettled that he'd need such a simple thing explained to him. "I am freshening the wards, Jack san," she said simply. "As part of the duty of my class."

"Wards?" he wondered.

"The protection wards which make the roads safe to travel," she said. "Have you truly not seen them? Or wondered how the ungifted may travel the roads at all without being accosted by roving beasts or monsters?"

He hadn't, truth be told. The fear he'd seen in the faces of the few citizens they'd encountered on the way to Mokkelton had led him to believe that the roads *weren't* all that safe. "You didn't do it on our way to Mokkelton," he pointed out.

"Along *Grandmother's* road?" she laughed. "A *dragon* could not burrow its way through *her* wards!"

"The jaegers didn't seem to have much trouble

"No," she frowned. "they did not, did they?" She gave it a few moments thought as she munched on her own travel cake. "Perhaps," she ventured then, "it has something to do with their not being from Mund."

"Possibly," he shrugged. "So this is something you do wherever you go? This business with the, what, ward stones?"

"Very good, Jack san," the frown vanished. "Yes, they are called ward stones. And yes, wherever I go, should the wards need strengthening, I do so. Really, it is the duty of every adventurer, but particularly mages and priests.

"This road," she waved a hand, "is not so well traveled as the East or South roads, nor has it had Grandmother to lay powerful spells upon it for three quarters of a century. So I will do what I may as we travel."

"How's it work for bandits?"

"Not well, I am afraid," she admitted. "Men are not fooled by uneasy feelings. Or most men are not. And being human, the wards are not directed specifically at them.

"Perhaps elsewhere," she suggested. "But this part of the country has not traditionally been beset by evil humans, and so there was never a need. I will try and remember to ask Guildmaster Jonkins upon our return if there are other wards that may be used."

They made camp well after dark, having pressed on into twilight against Jack's protestations. Despite his newfound powers, which he didn't understand and wasn't able to apply terribly well, he was firmly opposed to wandering down dark roads in strange territory without backup or, at least a good set of NVGs. *Anything* might be out there in the deep shadows, waiting to pounce. Tiarraluna, meanwhile, insisted that there would be a waystation up ahead, roughly a day's walk from the town. One which they'd already have reached had they left first thing rather than spent the morning shopping.

In the end, it was there. A wide spot in the road, cobbled and circumscribed by a low wall. There were rails to tie horses, had they managed to purchase horses, and a small spring from which to draw clean water. Once, according to Tiarraluna, long ago, there had been a small inn here, though only vague outlines of its foundation remained.

At present, there was a fire ring, although there was no

wood anywhere about. It would be a cold camp.

Tiarraluna freshened the wards around the circle, showing Jack the way of it. He was supposed to have some magical ability through his class, and it was time to start exploring the bounds of that ability.

Of course there were problems. Weren't there always? Tiarraluna used her crook staff as a focus, as her grandmother used her very deceptive cane. Jack had no such focus. There was FoeSmite, but Tiarraluna quailed at the thought of focusing mana through it. A focus must be neutral, which FoeSmite was most definitely not.

This was, in retrospect, something they should have addressed prior to their departure from town, but had not. It was something a master or teacher would most certainly have understood. Tiarraluna, however, was herself yet more student than instructor, and so she hadn't thought to secure one.

They tried without. Having Jack focus through a hand, holding it out and attempting to funnel mana through it. While he was able to produce a small flow, and might be more successful with experience, he was unable to provide enough mana to power even the low level ward. No surprise, really.

Very few could provide sufficient mana flow without a physical focal point. And the larger that point, the better. Which was why Tiarraluna's shepherd's crook staff was so large, and why grandmother's was... well... what it was. Jewels were best, at least alone. Living wood next, and the combination of them, particularly with the bridging capabilities of certain metals, was best overall. Jack would need a jewel or properly prepared wand at the least to realize even his basic potential. Which they were not going to find out here in the woods at night.

They would have to settle for Tiarraluna's explanations of how the wards were accomplished until such time as they could procure for him a proper focus.

Dawn found them once more northbound, with Jack only mildly grim. He'd given up, finally, on wondering about the pistol. He didn't have it, wasn't likely to get hold of it, and that was that. Fretting over where it might be was pointless, and he had worries aplenty already without adding more.

They were well into the area where the troubles were supposed to be, based on the bounty details. Jack was once more wearing the hooded green cloak, but he'd strung the bow and the quiver of arrows lay low along his right hip, opposite the jaeger sword.

The bow lay still alongside the pack, but was now secured with a slipknot in the leather thong that held it in place. With a yank from his right hand, he could release the bow and slide it down and around with his left. He hoped. He'd tested the rigging to make sure it worked, but hadn't exactly had hours to practice the move. He gave one last, fleeting thought to the G20, which bore the potential of far more power, and double or triple the range. Then he put it away. Wish in one hand, right?

The sun was nearing zenith when he paused, holding a hand out low and to his side, halting Tiarraluna.

"What is it, Jack san?" she wondered.

"Crows," he chucked his chin in their direction of travel. "Good sized murder of them up ahead circling something dead."

"How do you know it is something dead?" she asked.

He looked back and then forward again. "Seen a lot of crows," his voice was low but harsh. "I know what they're like."

Tom Black

Bandits

Jack unslung the bow and tucked it inside the cloak. He didn't draw an arrow from the quiver just yet. Nor would he unless and until he needed one. He was still carrying FoeSmite in his right hand. Whether he used staff or bow would depend on the circumstances of the moment, but he wanted both ready.

As they drew nearer, the raucous calls of the crows became a general din. Nearer still, and the smell became noticeable. Something was indeed dead, and the sun's heat wasn't being particularly kind to it. Jack became, if anything, even more dour, as though he already knew what they'd find.

Death had taken the pair at least two days ago, Jack decided, giving the information to Tiarraluna. "Along about the time I was playing with dolls," he snarled.

The woman lay naked and sprawled out, bruised and bloody even where the crows hadn't been at her. She'd been raped, it was obvious. Over and over from the bruising. The man lay nearby, his face a rictus, whether due to the attention of the crows, or from what he'd been forced to watch was uncertain. His legs had been chopped off below the knees and his arms below the elbows. A scythe lay nearby, tangled in the mess of lopped off limbs.

"He made a fight of it," Jack's voice was flint. "See, there's blood on the blade. Probably when they started in on her. I'm guessing it surprised them. They probably got pretty mad."

Tiarraluna didn't answer. She stood frozen, immobile, shocked to her core at the horrific sight, and with Jack's cold acceptance of it. She was behind him, so couldn't see the whiteness of his knuckles where they gripped FoeSmite. Nor the shaking of the hand holding the bow beneath the cloak. Nor the sheen of his eyes as the tears hovered just shy of rolling.

He'd seen this sort of thing before, had Jackson Grenell. It wasn't new. Nor was the rage it brought. But somehow, he'd never quite gotten used to it.

"Well, well, Dimo," a hearty voice boomed from behind and to the side as a pair of armored men approached from the treeline. "You see? I told you, did we leave the carrion out to weather, it would draw fresh prey. And here they are, a nice, pretty young mage and her ungifted hired man."

Tiarraluna spun about, eyes wide, breath catching. Jack didn't move. He'd been hearing them skulking through the grass since they'd left the treeline some forty yards distant. He had an idea, furthermore, that there was at least one more out there in the trees somewhere. Some special sentinel trick, perhaps. He was trying to figure out how to focus it and find the guy.

"Jack san?" Tiarraluna gasped as she backed away from the oncoming men. The jewel on her staff had come to life, glowing brightly, but her voice bore more fear than confidence.

"I hear them," he told her without turning.

"They are rank twelves, Jack san," she warned.

"Doesn't matter," he said quietly. Ah. He thought he might have the hidden bandit pegged. He turned finally, looking past the two who were approaching. There. Couple of yards into the treeline, he thought. He couldn't really see so much as sense. Like a faint halo of glimmering light in amongst the shadows.

Dropping his gaze, he examined the two bandits who had now stopped moving, faces quizzical. A big, burly specimen better than six feet tall and probably two-forty or so. He was clad in rusty brown plate, with pauldrons, vambraces, and greaves. He had a dented barbute helmet that looked about two sizes too small mashed down on his head, with dark, greasy hair from both head and beard sticking out from beneath it in every direction. With his oversized pauldrons and beefy arms, he reminded Jack of a gorilla.

Beside the big one, a smaller, rat-faced specimen sauntered along, this one wearing scuffed black plate, but without pauldrons or greaves. He was wearing a sallet much like Jack's, tilted back on his head. He was also waving a long, cruciform sword with a rudimentary knuckle bow lazily around, as though he just liked to watch the sun reflect from its blade.

"Hey Lar," the smaller one, who must be called Dimo, paused and pointed his sword at him. "Hired man wearing a sallet. And a sword! And ain't that armor 'neath 'is cloak?"

"No!" Lar laughed. Then he looked closer and an eyebrow went up. "Can't be," he said in an unworried voice. "Pretty girl probably bought him an ornament or three to scare off the rabble. Forgot that such as us knows he ain't got no crystal."

But he was looking at the bow that he could now see peeking out from beneath the cloak, and it was obviously neither an ornament nor a hunting bow. And the hilt of that sword... that weren't no rank zero grubber's blade.

"Girly only rank ten," he laughed, "and we gots armor resists, hey?" but his voice was less certain.

Jack squared on them and they saw his eyes for the first time in his grim face, staring out from beneath his helm's visor. Dimo paled a little, but Lar was made of sterner stuff. Jack started walking. Not fast, but steadily, with a heavy stride. "Who's your leader?" he demanded, voice charged.

"He wants to know who your leader is," Tiarraluna translated.

Now it was Lar who was confused. What language had that been? He didn't recognize it at all. And why would he be...? but the ungifted was closing on them. He raised his axe menacingly, and gave the grubber his best snarl.

Jack saw the axe as if for the first time and something clicked. He stopped and looked over at the dead farmer in the roadway.

"That's right," Lar called tauntingly. "I chopped him up! And I'll do the same for you, grubber!"

Jack turned back to the bandits, and now Lar paled.

"He said—" Tiarraluna started, but Jack cut her off.

"I can guess," he snarled. "Ask him again who their leader is, and where," he pressed. "There's gotta be more of them around, and some sort of chief. This one's too stupid to lead a starving pig to slop."

Tiarraluna repeated the demand and the taunt.

Lar was confused and growing moreso. The grubber... the ungifted. Something was wrong with him. That wasn't the face of a hired man wearing props. That was the face of a killer. Lar ought to know. And there was no fear in it. None! He ran a hand along the healing slash down his arm where that last grubber had caught him with the scythe blade the other day. That one, and now this? What was the world coming to?

Then, too, there was the way the grubber moved. He seemed to be coming straight on, but Lar suddenly realized that he, himself, was now squarely between the oncoming grubber and Stetz's bow back in the woods. He shifted to his right to clear the arrow's path, but the grubber moved with him, like he'd known it was coming. Like he knew Stetz was out there and where.

The man spoke, and the girly repeated. Where was the boss? Well, damn him! Lar wasn't about to tell them anything. He roared his best battle cry and charged, axe up, hearing Dimo break into movement beside him, his own cry ringing.

Jack tossed the bow aside and went to meet them, Foe-Smite coming up and slapping into his off palm. The gorilla with the axe was closer, which was okay. *That* bastard was getting on his nerves.

The axe came down hard, but FoeSmite was there to meet it. Not dead on, but just enough to nudge it off line. As the axe blade whistled past him, Jack brought the butt of the staff up hard, slamming the far end down, shattering both the gorilla's radius and ulna just below the elbow. The axe chunked into the loam beside his foot with a sound that couldn't be heard over the yowl the gorilla let go at FoeSmite's first kiss.

FoeSmite came up and over, smacking into the gorilla's other arm as it came around to cradle the shattered one. The yowl altered in tone, and any dog within miles must surely be hearing it now and wondering who was calling so urgently. The bandit dropped to his knees, eyes closed in pain, snot running from his nose, tears from his eyes.

Jack ducked the swing of the sword the gorilla's buddy

had launched at his head, bringing FoeSmite up at the rear to create a bind, twisting and driving in. The bandit backpedaled, his sword sweeping around in a tight circle as he tried to break the bind.

Instead of contesting, Jack took a couple of paces back to where his superior reach would come into play.

The instant he'd cleared the swordsman, he hit the ground rolling. The arrow the one in the trees had fired so soon as he'd had a clear shot sailed over his head. Good. Now he had a vector.

Surging to his feet, Jack ducked behind the crying gorilla and clubbed down against the kneeling man's lower legs. Tibia and fibula this time, just below the knees, left first, then right, and FoeSmite was shimmering with a faint reddish glow as he brought it straight back and straight in, shattering the gorilla's spine and nearest shoulder blade.

There was a glimmer of movement in the shadows of the wood, and Jack dove for the ground as the hidden archer loosed another arrow at him. Big mistake! Now Jack knew *exactly* where he was. He rolled to a knee, hauled back and hurled Foe-Smite with all his strength. The sound of a far off clang echoed back a moment later. He drew his sword.

Dimo was sweating now. *Ungifted my knobbeldy arse!* He thought grimly, still backing stumblingly away. *He's hiding his crystal somehow.* The man in the green cloak was up on one knee now, a strange looking sword that was obviously not a prop held in his hand as though he knew its use. Lar was done for — he'd heard the shattering of his bones clear. And he somehow doubted Stetz was in any better shape. He'd heard the clang, hadn't he? And there was the man in the cloak just kneeling there with no more arrows coming.

On the other hand, there was the obviously magical stick gone from the fight now, right? Just a sword. And Dimo might not have been the sharpest stick in the bundle, but he did know his way around a sword, didn't he?

He grinned evilly and took a step forward, going into a

guard. But what was this? The man was smiling and pointing over Dimo's shoulder, saying something in that strange language.

"He said," Tiarraluna's voice came from behind, raising the hair on the back of his neck. "That you forgot the girl."

He hadn't time to register the warning, though, before his body was wracked by lightning coming up from the ground through his boots and out the top of his head, searing everything in between. Despite the warded armor, he was unconscious in less than a second, a faint trail of smoke rising from beneath his collar.

Monsters, Kindness, and an Interesting Datapoint

Jack regained his feet, giving some effort to sense for anyone else nearby. So far as his new abilities claimed, they were alone with the dead. There was a clump of light out beyond where he figured the archer had been, but it wasn't human. Might be their horses, but he couldn't be sure until he knew more about how the ability worked. He wished, not for the first time since waking up here, that he could see an actual menu. But thus far, everything he'd tried had failed.

He sheathed the sword and looked around.

Tiarraluna was starting to shake as the rush of battle left her and she began to realize what had happened. "Is... is that man—?"

"He should be," Jack called back.

He took the few steps to the form of the first ape laying stretched out, face down in the loam. He tucked a foot beneath the body and rolled it over. The eyes were fixed and the face grey. "Yeah," he pronounced. "He's dead. Yours?"

"Of course not!" she seemed indignant. As though killing the bandit would never enter her head.

Jack held his tongue on that subject for the moment. Instead, "I'll check on the one out in the woods and see if they had horses. Do what you can to see that yours stays harmless until I get back."

The archer was as dead as his first kill, with a good chunk of his skull caved in above the eye socket. Glancing around, Jack spotted the deeply dented helm off to the side and back a ways. FoeSmite was harder to find. It had sailed off into the trees as it'd rebounded off the helm, and was hidden in the ground cover.

Experimentally, Jack held out a hand, concentrating. *Come,* he thought. Brush rustled further into the trees and the staff came sailing out of the undergrowth like a spear, straight for him. He got his hand out and around the shaft as he ducked aside, hauling the staff around and upright, slowing its momentum with what turned into a flourish. Okay, clearly some practice needed.

He frowned down at the still faintly glowing shaft of wood, holding back a curse. Damned thing *felt* bloodthirsty. He'd need to get a handle on that before somebody got hurt who shouldn't.

The horses he found less than a hundred yards deeper into the wood, tied to some heavy brush. They were decent stock, he supposed. Not particularly well cared for, though. The saddles and tack were in poor shape, but serviceable. More importantly, there were only three of them, so he probably didn't need to worry about any more unwanted company. At least not right away.

Tying the horses together and leading the bay while the others followed, he returned to the body of the archer. He knelt and carefully lay the staff in the grass beside the body, holding his hand close for a second or two in case it decided to shoot off somewhere on its own and break something for the sake of it. When it remained still, he began the process of looting the body as thoroughly as he was able.

Much to his disappointment, the bow the guy had been using wasn't as good as the one laying back out in the grass. The guy was shorter into the bargain, with shorter arms, which meant that Jack wouldn't be able to use the arrows either. There was a sword, but while it was better than what the jaegers had been carrying, it wasn't all that much better. Certainly not as good as the Jaeger Drop sword.

Decent knife, though. Single edged, clip point blade around seven or eight inches in the blade with short brass quillons and scales of some dark wood. Jack bounced it in his hand a couple of times and tested the blade with a thumb before divesting the corpse of its sheath and stuffing it down behind his own belt.

The rest of the gear wasn't worth more than trade goods, even should he be able to sell any of it in a town filled with nobody who could use it. The armor, while also good enough, wouldn't fit him, wasn't up to what he was already wearing, and stank of old onions and rancid grease. He dutifully bundled it all up, though, and lashed the bundle to the saddle of one of the horses. Even the boots might bring a copper or two, always assuming he could find anybody willing to stuff their feet into the things. Waste not want not, right? Ever the rallying cry of the compulsive loot whore.

Tiarraluna was standing beside the bodies of the bandits' victims when he returned to the road. Good. He wasn't quite ready to confront her with what was coming next. Instead, he set about repeating with the axeman what he'd done with the archer. This guy had more cash on him, but his gear was even more unsuitable for anything Jack might desire. The axe was too heavy, the shield the clown had never bothered to deploy too large, and the armor... well, the armor stank worse than the archer's.

Jack wondered whether there were cleaners here. There'd been a cute isekai back home where the protagonist had started up a laundry service using custom slimes. That kid would come in real handy about now. He wondered did they even have slimes here. He hadn't seen any, but he hadn't exactly been roaming the countryside up 'til now, either. Shaking his head and smiling a little despite himself, he finished his unpleasant task, bundling the gear beside the rest.

A glance at the remaining bandit showed him the guy was tied with a good length of rope, hands behind him and lashed to his ankles. The rest of the roll lay coiled beside him. He smiled a bit wider when he saw that she hadn't just used a couple of feet and cut it short. Girl was frugal and knew the value of a good long piece of rope. Nevertheless, he made his way over and tested the knots.

They were good and tight, and the bandit still unconscious. Also, he smelled faintly of burnt hair. Jack whistled and gave her a glance over there by the road. He hadn't expected this level of power from her. He'd kind of expected more of a distraction so he could move in for the kill himself.

She hadn't looted the bandit properly, but she'd taken

his visible weapons and tossed them well clear. Jack, not being a trusting sort and having played this game more than a couple of times, gave him a further patdown. He found another, smaller knife down in his pants. He tossed it over with the others.

She was weeping softly when he finally arrived by her side. She'd covered the savaged woman's nakedness with her own cloak, but hadn't done much else.

"How could...?" she sniffled when she caught sight of him from the corner of an eye. "How could people...?"

"*People* generally can't," he explained. "The creatures who do this sort of thing aren't people, though."

She turned her head to him, her face confused. "But was it not it those men over there who did this? The big man even admitted it."

He didn't even bother to look away from the bodies before him. "When I was little," he said quietly. "Back on Earth. I had quite the imagination. I thought that the world was filled with monsters. All kinds of monsters. That they were everywhere. I used to have nightmares. My parents told me it was just in the stories. That monsters weren't real. They convinced me finally, and the nightmares stopped.

"Turns out though, I was right and it was them who were wrong." Now he did look to her. "But it was only when I'd grown up that I realized it. And that all the monsters on my world were human. For sufficient values of."

She didn't understand. "Jack san? What...?"

"Eventually, I kind of got around to the idea that they weren't human in the same way most everybody else was," he explained. "Some offshoot of the genus. A variant of sorts. Mutants. Nearly human, but not quite.

"Those things over there, little sister," he told her, his voice going harsh. "They're human after a fashion, but they aren't *people*."

She still didn't understand.

"They're not the first human monsters I've killed," he admitted after a bit, looking back down. "Not even close. After awhile... after I'd realized... they're just the enemy now, see? Or any of a number of names we gave them, depending on where us were and who them was."

"Surely that cannot be," she shook her head violently, sincerely puzzled. "We are all—"

"NO!" he spat. Then more softly. "No. We're not. We're us, who preserve life and dignity so much as we can, and them, who destroy both and care for neither. Get used to that, little sister. It'll make things easier going forward.

"Now," and he straightened his shoulders. "First things first. Can you free their souls?" he indicated the man and woman before them.

She was still working on the previous topic, but she forced herself to answer. The other she filed for later discussion, for it was a world altering concept. "Should we not bring them to their relatives?" she wondered. "Won't their family—?"

"Look at them," he interrupted. "You think their family wants to remember them like this? Even if we could figure out who that family was, or if it exists?

"No. Best to deal with their remains here, with as much dignity as we can manage. We'll see what we can find to identify them and bring that back. Perhaps that'll be enough."

The bandits hadn't left much, but they hadn't bothered with the clothing. Maybe there would be something distinctive about some piece or two of it. Jack took care of the man's remains, Tiarraluna the woman's. He took their belongings to secure on the horse while she performed the ritual of release.

"Jack san?"

Jack paused in his task at the tone of her voice. Looking over, shifting his eyes to where she was pointing, his eyebrows went up. *Damn!*

He hustled back and looked down. Where the man had lain, there were a scattering of silver coins and a small gemstone.

"Gifts of Jehsha?" he inquired.

She nodded uncertainly. "But... Jack san.... An ungifted should not drop gifts. Nor a life stone. We perform the ritual merely to send them upon their way, not for rewards."

He knelt and caught the coins up, counting them carefully. "Seven, uh, reals, right?" he announced. "Not much, if I've got the theme right."

"Seven too many, Jack san," she countered. "And the gemstone. Amber only, it may be, but there is power in amber, make no mistake."

The woman's body yielded nothing beyond the glittering light of her released soul. That was curious, particularly to Jack. Then he remembered the blood on the scythe blade. Trotting over to the nearby bandits, he checked them over for wounds he hadn't made. There, on the arm of the big one. A long slash.

"Farmer made a fight of it," he called out. "Got him a chunk of this one before they butchered him."

"That should not matter, Jack san," she insisted. "It remains that he was neither gifted nor a monster, nor yet a wild beast."

"It remains," he persisted. "That he fought them, wounded one, and then dropped gifts. That is an interesting set of data points if nothing else."

He stowed the silver and the amber shard in his pouch. Were they to find any relatives of either, he'd pass the gifts on to them. Along with any other of their possessions he and Tiarraluna might happen across in their travels.

Going up the road a ways while Tiarraluna saw to the remaining dead, he found their tracks, along with traces of wagon or cart tracks, and the prints of a single, plodding horse. They'd probably been leading it when set upon. He circled wide around the scene and found what might be the trail of the wagon's departure heading westward, cross country.

Tiarraluna, meanwhile, saw to the tarnished souls of the dead bandits.

They met back at the remaining survivor, where Jack informed her of his discovery and deductions. Then he regarded the unconscious man. "You hit him pretty hard with that spell, didn't you?" he commented idly. "I'm impressed. Sure you weren't trying to fry him to ash?"

"His armor is warded," she pointed out. "See?" and she

pointed out the telltales. "If you use your inner eye, you should be able to see a faint glow. Had I put any less power into the spell, he would not have been affected at all."

Magical armor, eh? He thought. *So it should be valuable after all. Good to know.*

Then, "Inner eye, huh? While I've heard of the concept, I've got no idea how or if I can use it."

"I will teach you."

"When there's more time," he held up a hand. "At the moment, we need to find out where the rest of them are."

"The rest of them?" she wondered.

"None of these knuckleheads is exactly leadership material," he pointed out. "And I didn't find any horses or carts in their pockets. No, they killed and robbed those people, took their stuff somewhere off to the west, and then came back to see could they catch anybody loitering around trying to figure out what had happened."

"I see," she said softly.

Grim Resolve

Jack oriented on the bandit, hesitated, and then turned back to her. "You understand what this bastard is, don't you, Tiarraluna?" he asked in a serious voice. "You understand what he and his friends did? Probably a good many more times than this, given their ranks."

"They may have been soldiers, Jack san," she tried. "They may have gained their ranks before becoming bandits."

"Coulda, woulda, shoulda," he rolled his shoulders. "They're butchers who prey on the innocent. On those who can't defend themselves. Whatever they may have been before, that's what they are now."

"What are you getting at, Jack san?" her eyes were narrowing.

He heaved a deep, shuddering breath before answering. "We don't owe them anything," he said flatly. "No mercy, no compassion, no empathy. You need to keep that in mind for what's about to happen. You need to focus on that and translate for me."

"What are you planning to do, Jack san?" her voice deepened.

"I'm gonna ask him some questions," he replied.

"And should he not answer?"

"He'll answer," Jack laughed, no humor in it. "Might take a few tries to get the right ones, but he'll answer."

She was still working through that statement when he turned back to the bandit and fetched him a solid kick in the ribs. She thought she might have heard one of them crack.

Dimo howled as he came awake, the pain washing through his entire torso. He looked left and right, owl-eyed with terror, mouth gaping wide. He tried to surge to his feet, but his hands and legs were tied tightly together, and he only managed an ungainly flop onto his face.

Jack grabbed the bandit by a hank of his greasy hair and lifted his head, flopping him over onto his side. "Ask him where the rest of them are," he ordered in a barking tone Tiarraluna had never heard him use before.

"She hesitated, unsure of what he was up to. He was glaring into the bandit's face from only a foot or so away.

"Ask him!" he roared, spraying spittle on the clearly terrified bandit's face.

"Dimo," she called the name she'd heard his dead compatriot use.

"Where are the others?" she went on when his eyes switched to her.

"O-others?" he squeaked.

"The others," she repeated. "Where are they?"

"N-no others!" he cried.

She repeated the claim for Jack.

Jack thrust the man away, rolling him onto his face. He reached down and grabbed hold of the man's right pinkie finger. "Where are they?" he leaned in.

Tiarraluna repeated the demand.

"N-no—! AIIIIE!"

Tiarraluna flinched at the loud snap of the finger bone. "Jack san!" she accused. "You did not even wait—"

"He's not gonna tell the truth on the first try," he told her without looking away from his victim. He leaned in close to the man's ear as he took hold of the next finger. "Where?" he shouted.

"J-Jack san..."

"Translate!"

"W-where are they?" she sputtered.

"I don—" snap! "AIIIIE!"

"Where?"

"Please! The man cried. I can't—" snap! "AIIIIE! Jesha, help me! I don—" snap!

The scream this time wasn't so loud, and trailed off into whimpers. Tiarraluna had her hands to her face, aghast.

"You'd better answer me before I run out of fingers," Jack hissed into the blubbering man's ear. "It gets worse after that."

"He… he'll kill me!" Dimo cried when the next finger went.

"You're already dead," Jack told him. "We're just discussing how much it's going to hurt."

Tiarraluna was weeping now at the brutality of the man she'd been thinking of as a hero. What was more, she was no longer translating. Somehow, Jack san was speaking — shouting— in Tandrian. Was this the black beast? Freed at last from the iron bars?

Jack was well into the second hand when the bandit broke. "A- a d-day's ride to th-the west," he cried. "N-near th-the r-river… Th-three tall trees n-near a promontory! West of the road! An-an old f-ferry st-station!"

"Now," Jack hissed. "Who and how many?"

It took awhile longer, and he did indeed run out of fingers, but eventually Jack had gotten all he figured he was going to. The bandit was a gibbering wreck, and had soiled himself. Tiarraluna was little better.

"Look away," he warned then, his voice returned nearly to normal.

"What?" she demanded. "Jack san, you promised—!"

"I promised I'd make the pain stop," he said.

"I thought we would heal—"

"Look away!"

Instead, she covered her eyes as he reached beneath the neck of the sobbing man with the blade of the archer's knife and let loose his life's blood onto the grass.

"Alright," he sighed. "It's done."

She didn't uncover her eyes, though. She was crying almost as hard as Dimo had been. Jack watched her for a few moments, sighing inwardly. Ah, well. He'd been trying to get rid of her since the second day anyway, hadn't he?

He left her to it as he took care of the dead man's gear and wandered over to the horses. She was still crying when he'd finished pulling all of it apart and re-tying the lot into a single bundle on the scrawniest of the horses; a sorry looking buckskin. He tied the reins to the saddle of the bay and brought

them over.

Then he waited. It took awhile.

"H-how could you?" she wept some time later. "You are supposed t-to be a *hero*!"

He'd long since seated himself in the grass, well away from the corpse. "Look at the bounty, little sister," his voice was calm, without any trace of the rage he'd shown his victim.

When she didn't move, he helped her out. "Scout," he said. "Locate. If possible, eliminate."

He waited some more. "Did you think we were going to invite him back to town for tea?" he wondered. "Or that he'd get a fair trial and be held in some sort of jail by the vast forces of the Mokkelton town guard? After what he and his friends had done? To these people and no doubt others? No, little sister," he gave his head a shake. "He reaped what he'd sown. As the rest of them will."

"I... I cannot...." she struggled to form the words.

"I know," he let his voice go soft. "You're too good for this sort of thing."

Her head shot up, her eyes flaring. "Do not mock me, Jackson Thomas Grenell!" she warned.

He shook his head again. "I'm not," he insisted. "No sarcasm here, little sister. You're genuinely too good a person for this sort of thing. I understand, that's all I'm saying. It takes a certain sort, and you're not it. I'm sorry I got you involved.

"D'you ride?" He asked, now that the flash of anger had burned through a bit of her grief.

"Barely," she admitted. "Why?"

He chucked a thumb over his shoulder in the direction of the pair of horses. "I want you to take those two and the plunder I've packed them with and head back to town," he said. "Maybe you can sell some of it and recoup some of our debt. Leave them with the guildmaster if nothing else. Here, take this," he tried to pass her the pouch holding the gold and silver they'd taken.

She was rubbing at her eyes with the palms of her hands, sniffling. She made no move to accept the offered pouch. "How are you so calm, Jackson Grenell?" she demanded with no great force. "You have just killed three men. You have tortured a man and then *murdered* him. You have made me *help* you to murder a man. Is that nothing to you?"

He tried not to frown at the lack of honorific. He knew what it meant, and was surprised at how much it hurt. Well, he'd been after this very thing, hadn't he? "I'm sorry you had a part in it," he told her. "I'm sorry I caused you to do something so contrary to your moral code. I promise it won't happen again. Now, do you think you can make it back to town alone?"

A hint of the anger shone in her eyes, but only for an instant before she deflated. "I can."

He watched her for a few moments longer, trying to understand what was going through his own head. But he had a job to do.

"How do I handle proof of death without your ritual?" he asked hesitantly.

She fished around in her satchel and withdrew the bounty token, throwing it unceremoniously in his direction. "Touch this to the forehead," she told him. So long as the... the deceased falls within its parameters, The bound spell within it will free the soul and grant Jehsha's blessings, although you will gain no experience from the casting of the spell. You must also gather the life stone for the bounty. It will drop with the rest of Jehsha's gifts."

He caught the token and stared down at it while she spoke. When she was done, and with a sort of forlorn sigh, he surged to his feet, startling her with the suddenness of it, and hied himself off to the last and best of the horses they'd captured. A big chestnut gelding he'd held for himself because he'd known in his heart what would happen. He reined the beast over to where Tiarraluna Galbradia still sat, eyes wet with tears, glaring up at him. He tossed the pouch down to her, a little surprised when she caught it.

"I'm sorry," he said sad-voiced. Then he reined the horse around and kicked it into a canter. Westward, his back straight, his shoulders square. Nor did he look back.

Tiarraluna remained where she was for nearly half an hour before she could bring herself to move. Until the very last, she'd been convinced he'd come back to town with her. Any sane person would. Eleven, poor broken Dimo had wailed at the last. Eleven more of them, all rank twelve or greater, and among them a rank fourteen dark mage. And their chieftain a rank eighteen Plunderer, and alone a match for them all. Jackson Grenell had only laughed at him. And now he went to the west, seeking them out. Alone.

Eventually, she rose up and performed the soul release for the bandit, striving to keep in her mind the evil in his eyes when first she'd beheld him. The evil he'd so obviously been a part of. But as the power built and the glow enveloped him, all she could see was the weeping wreck the man had become, and all she could feel was pity, and guilt at the part she'd played in it.

When he'd gone, she gathered up Jehsha's gifts and the dead man's life stone and moved to the horses. Taking up the reins of the bay with the empty saddle on its back, she set off for Mokkelton, struggling with whirling emotions and trying not to think of the man riding west alone and to his almost certain doom.

On His Own

Jack followed the fading track of the cart through the tall grass for the rest of the day without incident. He was kind of surprised. All day long, he'd been burdened with vague feelings of unease. As though he were being shadowed by something. He could see the occasional glimmer from the edges of his vision, first on this side and then on that. Like the faint aura the archer in the trees had shown but even less distinct.

If he concentrated hard, he developed the impression that he could see his position relative to them. Almost like he was looking at a barely visible map, but without any real detail. He had to stop himself from smacking the side of his head as though it were a malfunctioning monitor in need of percussive maintenance.

It took him an embarrassingly long time to remember the wards they'd spent so much time on during their journey from the city. Wards he was now well outside of. Still, if the bandits could do it, he could, right?

He sharpened his attention, but could not pick anything out beyond the nebulous sense that something was out there. Blotches of amber mist in his mind. Whatever it was, it was small enough to be invisible to his physical sight in the knee high grass. That lack of size would have been a lot more comforting if there hadn't been so many of them.

Sundown presented him with a bit of a quandary. There was no way station out here in the middle of nowhere. No warded circle. Just the grass and the now invisible tracks. Did he push on into the darkness or did he try for a camp. If the latter, he wasn't going to find enough fuel to keep a fire burning all night long, and he had no way of making ward stones. It occurred to him that there was probably a way to do it, given that adventurers would seem to have been roaming the world for at least the last thousand years. Which knowledge helped him not at all.

That was when he remembered the odd things they'd

picked up in town that he'd not been able to identify. What were the odds that at least some of that had been geared towards warding campsites in wild areas? Pretty high, he'd wager. Shame he'd left the whole lot with Tiarraluna when he'd split the gear. Not that he'd have been able to use it, of course. She hadn't got 'round to teaching him much magic during last night's halt, what with his focus issues and all. He could freshen already existing wards, he thought, if he could find something to use as a focus. But as to making them whole cloth? No idea.

The horse was getting nervous as the light dimmed. That wasn't good either. It had been fine under the sun. Argued that the beast was familiar with what came out at night and didn't care for it. And now a new decision. Did he keep to the saddle or take to his feet? He was a decent enough rider, but he didn't kid himself that he couldn't be thrown if his mount really worked at it. On the other hand, he was equally uncertain as to whether he'd be able to hold onto the creature should it take it into its head to be elsewhere and apply its full strength in the effort. And it had his gear on it.

In the end, it came down to FoeSmite. It was a terrible weapon to wield from the back of a horse. Jack dismounted, taking the reins in his left hand, FoeSmite in his right. If it came to a fight, he was going to lose the horse, but there was no help for it. And it wasn't like they were old friends or anything. Then he had a second thought and lay FoeSmite in the grass beside him where it'd be clear of the horse. That done, he untied his pack from behind the saddle and shrugged into it. Losing the horse was one thing, but he wasn't about to risk losing this.

Under way again, he started looking around for someplace with a bit of shelter, or at least substantial fuel. In a pinch, he could grab hanks of grass and twist them into passable bundles, like rolling up newspaper. But wet as the area was, they'd smolder and smoke like crazy. Given the effort required, he'd get about as much rest walking. He'd save the bundled grass idea for plan Z.

And so the night passed, with Jack plodding through the

dark, struggling to keep his path true, straining with his new senses to keep track of whatever the hell it was out there that was so dangerous. He stopped only to drink and water the horse from what he'd brought with him.

He began to encounter the occasional tree. More of them as he traveled along what was increasingly coming to look like a proper trail. He kept moving. The amber blotches had closed in, and there were a lot of them. Staggering tired was one thing, but he did not want to think about what would happen if those things closed on him while he was on the ground in an exhausted sleep

Only when the band of forest was behind him and the sun once more in the sky did he dare to stop. At which point, he simply wrapped the reins around one wrist, shrugged out of the pack, flopped down into the grass where he stood, and closed his eyes, trusting the horse to alert him if anything came close.

* * *

"Thumper! Bonce!" the call rang out through the camp beside the river.

The two thus summoned made haste to the boss's cabin, measuring themselves just outside the door.

"Them three knobheads showed up yet?" the boss demanded from inside.

"Not so's I've noticed," Thumper answered. He was a tall, rough looking rank fourteen highwayman in clean, unpainted, rare grade half plate with two upgrade slots, both occupied. The basketed sword on his hip glowed faintly to the discerning eye, bragging of its own upgrades. It's rank was twelve, but it cut like something higher. "Mayhap they found themselves some juicy prey."

"Not likely," the boss sneered. "'er they'd already be back braggin' about it and wavin' plunder about. More likely, what's 'is head, that rank thirty from th' town has run't acrosst 'em and chopped 'em inter hog slop. They don't show up in th' next hour, you hie your lazy asses on out there and see are they dead or alive.

"But be careful," he cautioned. "You see a trace o' that

one, you skin back here quick as a blink, fer that's something I'll want to know. Don't go anywhere near him, ner let him so much as catch wind of ya. Just get on back here.

"Otherwise," he grumped, "fetch 'em back. Or news they're done, either way. We've a place t' be in two days time, but I'll need t' know if the guild has decided we're trouble enough t' rouse from their nap afore we sets out."

"What if they has?" Bonce, the rank thirteen brigand wondered. His nickname hadn't been applied because he was good at thinking. In fact, he tended to think about as well as one of the mid-ranked hobgoblins he resembled right down to the mishmash of dirty armor he covered himself in.

"Why," the boss laughed. "Then we change our plans an' kill him now rather than when we're closer to taking th' town. Rank thirty 'r no, he'll not live through facing us all to oncet."

* * *

It was an exhausted and bedraggled Tiarraluna Galbradia who staggered up to Mokkelton's north gate an hour or so after noon to present her guild token for entry into the town and hand over a silver real for the horses. She'd traveled the whole of the way straight through, even taking to the saddle and dozing for a time when her own legs would no longer hold her.

She hadn't trusted the roads to be safe, even with her wards so fresh. Not after yesterday. Not until the archway of the town gatehouse had passed overhead did she feel some semblance of safety again.

Nor did she stop there, nor go to her uncle's home. Instead, she headed straight for the adventurer's guild hall, still dragging the shambling horses behind.

The doors to the guild hall were almost too much for her waning strength, but she managed to haul one of them clear sufficiently to squeeze through. There was no trace of the guildmaster in the main hall, so she staggered to one of the empty tables scattered about the room and collapsed into a chair.

Guildmaster Jonkins wandered out into the room a few minutes later, alerted by the draft from the open door. He beheld the girl with her head on the table, her crook staff leant beside her, and rushed over. Asleep. Somewhat the worse for wear, but alive and apparently uninjured. He breathed a sigh of relief. Looking around, though, he could see no trace of the young man. That bade ill.

He spied the horses when he made to close the front door. They stood splay-legged in the street, one tied to the other, too weary to wander off. He clucked his tongue at the carelessness, but moved out to take them up and bring them 'round to the guild's stable, at least for the time being.

The bundle on the saddle of the trailing horse looked interesting, he thought, but he let it be for the moment. They'd need watering, feeding, and a bit of currying before he would give over time for further investigation of their burdens.

Still no trace of the man, and he was beginning to worry. The superficial glance he'd taken at the bundle had shown that the items it contained were of higher order than low rank bandits would be using, and certainly not anything the ungifted could use. Had the lad been killed? Had the girl fled—? But no, she'd hardly have taken time to pack up spoils were she fleeing.

She was still asleep when he'd gotten the livestock taken care of, so he let her be, heading instead for the kitchen. Soup, he decided. Lots of energy in a good, thick soup. Particularly if he spiced it with a healthy dose of restoratives.

Tiarraluna swam slowly up out of the darkness, something pulling at her. An aroma. Enticing, full, rich. She opened her eyes to behold Guildmaster Jonkins seated across from her, a steaming bowl placed between them alongside a wooden mug.

"Feeling better?" he asked kindly. "Get yourself around some of that soup. You look done in."

"My thanks, Master Jonkins," she croaked, coughing and reaching for the mug to moisten her throat.

"What's happened to your young hero?" he asked without preamble.

She coughed, spluttering on her drink. "He is not mine!"

she spat, her voice hot. "And he is *no* hero!" She slammed the mug down on the table with enough force to rattle the bowl. "In any case," she muttered with much less volume, "he is gone."

Uh huh, he thought. "Dead gone, or just gone gone?"

"Just... gone."

"I see," he rubbed at his whiskers with a hand. "And is your bounty done?" he asked. "I see that you've acquired a couple of horses and some loot. Just the two of them, then? I'd have thought more, given the stories."

She was spooning soup into her mouth, suddenly ravenous now that she'd had a taste of it. She hadn't eaten since the previous morning, but had been keeping the hunger at bay with mind games. "We... encountered three," she provided between mouthfuls. "There are supposed to be eleven more at their camp, of ranks twelve to eighteen."

He raised an eyebrow, but held back any further sign of his surprise. That was a much more troublesome bit of news than he'd been prepared for, and one he wasn't sure how to address.

"Jackson Grenell took possession of the third horse and set out for their camp early yesterday afternoon."

"Alone?" his voice betrayed his disbelief despite his efforts. Both at the fact of his departure and her lack of honorific. "And you let him?"

Her face went hard and she paused, spoon halfway to her mouth. "He does as he will," she grated without looking up. "It is not for such as *I* to hold him back. From anything."

Jonkins held his tongue while she went back to dealing with the thick soup, his mind working.

"Perhaps you'd better tell me what happened, young mage," he suggested once the bowl was empty. "All of it, in detail."

In Which Jack's Long Anesthetized Sense of Terror Wakes Up and Has a Look Around

The horse tugging at the reins awakened him, but he didn't move immediately. Glancing around, he decided he'd slept longer than he'd intended, and that it must be well after noon. That wasn't good. He was better than that. Or had been, once.

Stretching his new senses out, he also decided he was about to have company. These felt more like the archer than the nameless shadows of yesterday's journey. Rather than amber, they showed red on his mini map, which was just the tiniest bit clearer than it had been yesterday. They were still a ways off yet, and coming from upwind, which was probably how the horse had picked them up.

He stood and moved back to the saddle bags. There was a picket pin in one of them, and he wanted the horse to stay put during what was about to happen. After a bit of thought, he left his bow and pack twenty or so yards back beside the trunk of a nearby tree. He wanted to look harmless until they got good and close.

He'd moved up a good twenty-five yards by the time the two riders were close enough to make out features, and for them to see that he had no crystal.

They brought up short by about ten yards. Way too close, but they wouldn't know that yet. He simply stood there, FoeSmite grounded and upright in his right hand. His hood was up and low about his eyes, his cloak wrapped tightly around him, mostly covering his armor.

The two bandits were eyeing him critically, their attention shifting between him and the chestnut. They looked to one another and then back to the figure standing before them.

"You! Grubber!" the taller one in the surprisingly clean armor called out demandingly. "Where'd you get that horse?"

Jack had no way of knowing what had been said. Something about the horse, he thought, going by the hand gestures.

He was starting to pick up the odd word here and there, but the man had spoken too rapidly. He remained as he'd been, making no move to answer.

"Maybe he's deef?" Bonce ventured.

Thumper looked at him like he was... well, Bonce. Then back to the grubber standing in the way, between them and Lar's horse, looking way too calm for an ungifted alone out in the middle of nowhere and facing a pair of obvious gifted.

"You know who we are?" he demanded experimentally, yelling louder in spite of himself. "You know what you get, stealing one of our animals? You get gutted, that's what!" still no reaction. "Where's th' man owns that horse?" he demanded, almost as an afterthought.

"Well, then," he decided aloud after receiving no answer. Turning once more to his companion, he nodded in the grubber's direction. "Shall we?"

They clucked their horses a few feet closer before dismounting. Thumper climbed down and moved in, edging to the right and drawing his sword, feeding it a little power to activate the upgrades. Then he stopped dead, about fifteen feet from the still figure, his eyes going grim.

Bonce made it another couple of steps, easing left and waving his mace menacingly before realizing he'd left his companion behind. He looked back, confused.

"Grubber wearing brigandine," Thumper informed him. "See it peekin' out from under the cloak? Blue brigandine. I ain't never see'd brig ranked lower than four, Bonce. You? How he wearing that?"

Bonce swung his head around to give the grubber a closer look. He wasn't much given to thinky bits, was Bonce. He was more a smashy bits sort. But he tried. "Must be rank zero brig, I guess, Thumper," he tried. "He wearing it ain't he?"

"Yeah," Thumper grunted. "And when was the last time you see'd a grubber wearing brig at all, Bonce?"

Bonce shrugged broadly. "Dunno, Thumper," he admitted. " When was th' last time we saw a grubber wearing any armor at all? That village we sacked, what, last summer, maybe?"

"They was guards, Bonce," Thumper growled. "A whole mob of 'em, and inside the village wall, not out here with th' fangeddy weasels, stalker cats, 'n' dire hares all by their lonesomes. An' they was wearing zero rank half plate 'n' kettles. Brig ain't th' sort o' thing grubbers wears, does they?"

"Dunno, Thumper," Bonce repeated. "I ain't exactly a expert on grubber armor, hey? So what we gonna do, then?"

Thumper ignored him. He was busy scanning the grass around out to the horizon, trying to figure out what was going on. Grubber wasn't no normal grubber, that was sure. But if he wasn't really a grubber, how was he hiding his crystal? And who was with him? There wasn't supposed to be anybody like this around. Not for hundreds of lenn. And he was wondering if they shouldn't be hieing themselves back to camp with this puzzle rather than sitting here waiting for an arrow between the shoulder blades. With Lar's horse standing there all Larless, he figured he had the answer he'd been sent to get.

As slowly as he'd drawn it, he slid his blade back into its scabbard, the skin of his back itching where he expected the arrow to sink in. As slowly, he started to backstep, wanting to reach his bow, lashed to the saddle.

Jack, although he hadn't moved while all this was going on, was watching the show pretty closely. He was catching more of what they were saying, although it made his head throb. It was when he saw the less bulky one with the sword start to resheath and back up that he decided it was time to move.

At this point, the big one with the mace was only about a dozen feet off and facing partially away. Jack lunged, sliding FoeSmite out for a spear strike. Big guy was quick, and not as oblivious as he looked. He got his mace up and around in time to swat the incoming staff out of the way, roaring like a bear and crouching down for his own charge. A massive arm flexed and the mace reversed direction so fast it seemed to lack any mass at all, swinging straight back at Jack's head.

He was jerking FoeSmite back towards himself as he ducked the mace, close enough that it sang a song against his helmet, swiping the cloak's hood clear. As the bandit's bulbous face reddened, his eyes wild, that arm seemed to expand again, muscles bulging even thicker.

Jack's left hand was closing on FoeSmite's shaft at the midpoint as he skidded past the man to the right. The instant his grip closed, he jerked full force inward while pushing out just as hard with his right still far back along the shaft, torquing the staff into a blur. FoeSmite sang its own song as it arced into its target.

He was still off balance from the swipe to the head and the yank on the cloak, so the blow didn't strike as true as it could have. Instead of shattering the bandit's spine, the last foot of the staff slammed into the big man's shoulder, cracking the backplate of his cuirass and smashing his scapula like a potato chip. He howled and staggered, but did not go down. That fact alone surprised Jack more than anything had since the first of the jaegers had popped up out of the brush. A flash of terror raced through him on razor shards.

Bonce felt his whole left side go white hot with pain and he howled. He was broken bad, he knew. But he wasn't done, was he? He was Bonce the Crusher, by the eternal. He started the spin that would have the impossible grubber back to his front and in range of his mace, wondering where the hells Thumper had got off to. His left arm was dead, and the pain in his shoulder was making his vision dim, but his mace arm was still just fine, wasn't it?

Jack's brain stuttered for just a fraction of a second before he could regroup and get a grip. This was what it must mean to fight the gifted, the thought came. That blow should have put the guy down for the count just from the pain, let alone the damage to major bones, nerve bundles or blood pathways. Yet it had barely slowed him down.

He had a fleeting instant to wonder what rank the guy was before the mace was coming in again. And there was still another one somewhere nearby.

Jack spun quickly, flipped his lead hand around under FoeSmite's shaft, and put his shoulders into what should have been an effortless redirection. FoeSmite bowed as he deflected the mace clear.

A quick step in and Jack began the lunge that would take the big goon in the throat, but brought up short, just in time to block that mace again as it's impossibly quick return threatened to crush his chest, brigandine or no. Even blocked, the heavy blow hurled him back a couple of paces, to land in a semi-controlled roll.

The bandit was coming in again, still howling, but in rage rather than pain. Jack feinted up from the ground, torquing the staff around with his whole upper body. At the last instant, as the mace whistled in to bash it aside, he raised his trailing hand to slip the shaft under the incoming swing, then back up and over, smacking against the mace's trailing face to speed it on its way. The mace swung wide, moving too quickly even for one of its seemingly massless reversals, chunking into the ground and allowing Jack to bring his own weapon across and into the side of the bandit's anchoring leg.

The big bandit went down, and as he fell, he unmasked his friend, drawing down on Jack with a bow. Jack tucked Foe-Smite in close and rolled, not away from the falling bandit but towards him, and the arrow bit into the ground where he should have been had he a brain in his head.

With no functioning limbs on his left side the bandit on the ground was struggling to maneuver his mace up and out of the dirt. Jack took advantage. Still on the ground, he brought FoeSmite up to full extension above him and slammed it down across the bandit's heaving chest. The cuirass split across the center and the bandit's mouth gaped, his eyes going wide. Another roll tucked Jack in close. Using the heaving form as cover, Jack drove the knife he'd taken from the archer on the road up into the bandit's throat beneath the chin and up into his brain. The man went still.

A second arrow caught at his cloak as it skinned in overhead, letting him know the corpse wasn't the cover he'd have liked it to be.

Taking a deep breath, he lunged up and over the dead

man, going straight in, staff up and in both hands like a rifle at high port. Hopefully before the remaining bandit could nock a fresh arrow. He didn't make it. He watched in horrid fascination as the bandit calmly nocked the arrow, drew, and released in a single, fluid motion, from less than five yards away.

Without slowing, and with no real hope, he shifted Foe-Smite to deflect the incoming missile. To his utter astonishment, it worked. Even the bandit froze for an instant, mouth agape. And that was all the time Jack needed.

The few seconds between the grubber's lunge forward, Bonce's howl of pain, and the resultant exchange of counter-strikes were difficult for Thumper to fathom in the moment. His brain just couldn't process the speed at which it was happening.

Oh, no mistake, Bonce and his Mace of Blinding Speed, he could understand. Bonce was rank thirteen specialized in strength and toughness, and the mace a rank fifteen enchanted weapon with both upgrade slots filled with speed enhance-ments. But the grubber had beat it off with a *stick*. A bloody *stick!* And had sundered warded, rank twelve armor with that same stick.

That wasn't anybody he was going anywhere near with a sword could he help it. He turned and lunged for his mount.

Bonce was going down by the time he'd gotten his bow and quiver off the saddle, and he pegged a quick shot at the roll-ing grubber, but missed. His second shot missed as well, alt-hough he got closer. Then the idiot jumped up and tried to charge. Who did he think he was? Thumper drew a third arrow, nocked, and let fly, dead at the grubber's face at near hand clasping range. And watched dumbstruck as his arrow was bat-ted casually aside.

Right, then! With the impossible grubber right on top of him, he hurled his bow dead in the man's face and drew his sword. This was obviously no grubber, he realized too late. This was a gifted of some rank, somehow hiding his crystal. He'd never even *heard* of such a thing before.

Thumper gave ground, looking for an edge against a

weapon with twice his reach and capable of splitting rank twelve warded plate. He breathed a quiet curse to the gods who'd abandoned him. He should have run when he'd had the chance.

Jack fended off the flying bow and lurched to a stop as the bandit drew steel. He went into low guard and took a couple of deep breaths to clear his ringing head. The sword the guy was holding seemed to glow faintly, as did his breastplate and pauldrons, though in a slightly different hue. Magic, he supposed. Maybe he was growing into the system here now that he'd been recognized. Tiarraluna had suggested he might.

He wanted out of the cloak. It had been good while it was hiding his armor and sword, but trying to fight in it had nearly gotten him killed a couple of times just in the past minute or so. He doubted the bandit would call a truce while he doffed it, though.

The guy was edging back, clearly not comfortable facing the reach of the staff, or its now obvious destructive power. Jack allowed him to gain some distance. The bow had been his greatest fear, but it was out of play. On the other hand, he wasn't about to let the clown remount his horse, which looked to be his intent. He was in no mood for a horse race in the direction of the bandit camp. He took a couple of steps, shifting right to crowd the animal and block his opponent's way

They danced like this for a few more minutes, Jack essaying a strike here and there while the bandit contented himself with evading or blocking, like he was feeling Jack out. And he *was* blocking. None of the moves that had worked on the testing dolls nor with his sparring partners back on earth were working for damn all on this character. His swordplay was on another level. That wasn't good.

He could break the sword, Jack supposed, if he could get a good hard swing at it. But given the obvious skill of the swordsman, he was completely unwilling to give him such an opening. He had a feeling that if he brought FoeSmite too far off line, the bandit would be inside his guard and have that blade in his guts before he noticed movement. Then, too, that damned mace had survived several solid strikes, hadn't it? Mightn't the sword?

Tom Black

Jonkins Explains, Rosaluna Informs, Jack Struggles On

Tiarraluna had broken down again during the tale and it had taken her awhile to get through it. Between the wanton brutality of the murders of the travelers and the torture of Dimo the bandit, she had ventured much deeper into the waters of cruelty than she'd been prepared for. Eventually, Jonkins had come around the table and taken the sobbing girl uncomfortably in his arms, stroking her hair and trying to soothe her grief, as though she were a small child awakened from a nightmare.

For all of her power and rank, Tiarraluna had led a somewhat sheltered life up to this point, particularly for an adventurer. The most of her experience had come from more peaceful pursuits than fighting monsters. And even on those occasions where she'd been forced to fight, the battles had been clean cut and clear against obvious beasts. Even Jack's battle with the jaegers had been honest self defense with no more savagery than had been necessary. Fighting or killing humans was a different kettle of fish. Many couldn't bring themselves to do it to save their own lives. Whether she was one of these remained in question.

"What do you know of sentinels?" Jonkins asked once the sobbing had run its course and he was able to retreat to his own chair. After a slight detour to the bar for a mug of something to soothe his own nerves, it should be noted.

"What you have told me," she sniffed. "Uncle Mohrdrand... he called them idiots. Lunatics. Fools who took the burdens of the world upon their own shoulders for no good reason."

"He was closer than you might believe," he nodded. "I've been reading up on them since the two of you left. We've no great, all encompassing library of lore concerning them, of course. They roamed the world a very long time ago, and there were never that many to begin. A few journals have survived, one or two guild guides. None of them easy to read. Surprising how the language has changed in a thousand or so years.

"The thing you notice," he went on, "when you're reading their journals and comparing them to the histories...." he paused, long enough to take a few swallows of his drink. "The histories go on and on about how many people this one or that one saved. The towns or villages freed. The monsters vanquished. The demons banished. The journals mention none of it."

He had her interest now, even beyond her misery.

"The journals dwell more on those they didn't... couldn't save. Sometimes going so far as to list the names of the dead, each and every one. As though each and every lost life were a terrible burden blackening their souls.

"What's usually the first thing an adventurer asks when he hits town and has a look at the boards?" he asked suddenly, straightening in his seat and looking up.

She reared back a little at the suddenness of it. "Er... I do not—"

"What's the bounty pays the most with the least risk, am I right?"

She nodded uncertainly.

"And what was his first question?" he asked flatly.

Ah, she thought. "What is getting people killed," she answered.

"Right," he confirmed, smacking his hand on the table for emphasis. "No question of pay, no concern for danger. What was getting people killed. That was all he cared about."

"But what has that to do with what he did, Master Jonkins?"

"Everything," he said half to himself as he looked down into his empty mug, as though wondering where its contents had gotten off to.

"You want something stronger than that?" he asked as he stood.

"I do not drink alcohol, Master Jonkins," she demurred. "Grandmother says I am too young, and that alcohol would interfere with my ability to grow into my power."

"Right," he mumbled as he hied himself to the bar and drew another mug of ale.

"Did you get a look at the traits listed for his classes?" he asked when he'd seated himself again.

"I did," she told him. "Briefly. But I am afraid that I do not remember them all, nor their effects."

"I rushed you out," he admitted. "I apologize. I shouldn't have. I was angry, you see?"

"About Jehsha's recognition?" she posited.

He arched an eyebrow. "Yes," he sighed. "I admit it. I was angry at Jehsha. Stupid, eh?

"That aside," he shook himself free and gave her an eye. "Among the traits of the sentinels is one that's maybe not so heroic." He had another swallow of ale before he went on, as though trying to postpone the revelation. "Grim resolve, it's called. Ever heard of it?"

"No," she frowned. "I have not."

"Can't say as I'm surprised," he shrugged. "It's almost exclusively reserved for sentinels. Well, and certain types of paladin that you also don't see anymore, I suppose.

"Once a sentinel has his goal set and there are lives in danger," he explained. "He fixes on that goal. Like a released quarrel. He thinks of nothing but those lives, and will do anything in his power... do you understand me, Tiarraluna Galbradia? *Anything* in his power, to preserve them."

He gave her time to absorb that information.

"In the grip of that power," he pressed. "That drive... they're wont to do some pretty horrible things to those they consider...."

"The enemy," she finished for him, voice strained.

He watched the hard, angry lines of her face for a moment before nodding slowly. "The enemy."

"So," her voice was clipped. "You are saying it was not his fault? That it was a facet of his class forcing him to torture and murder a man?"

"Not at all," he waved the thought hastily away with the hand not holding the mug. "I'm telling you it's a facet of who he

is. Because of what drives him. And what drives him is saving lives. Innocent lives. Likely, it's what makes him a sentinel as well. That same drive.

"As for murder?" he shook his head dismissively. "You did *read* the bounty, didn't you?" At her look, he nodded. "Yes, girl," he told her. "He was correct. Eliminate, not retrieve. Can you not see why?

"There's a reason banditry by the gifted is a capital offense," he told her bluntly. "The ungifted have literally no defense against them. Once they get started and realize how easy it is, there's only one single curb on their depredations. Death. Or the fear of it, I suppose. That's it. And with our esteemed new king having sucked the entirety of the valid fighting forces of the land westward to battle the demon lord, they know there's almost nothing left to stop them. Only us. We few remaining adventurers.

"They have to know in their bones," he stressed, "that, if they start preying on the ungifted, one of us will eventually be coming for them. And that we won't stop until they're dead. We don't have room for it to be any other way. What's more, those men that you... that your... that he, killed? They knew it too. You would have received no quarter, no mercy, from any of them. They'd have left your bodies in the road with the others, and in the same condition, if they'd lived to do it. Make no mistake."

* * *

"Here you go," Mohrdrand placed the cup into Rosaluna's quaking hands. "Are you feeling any better?"

Not particularly, the old woman sent irritably as she swallowed down the decoction the wizard had brought her. *A consequence of being too closely attuned to Button's mind, I'm afraid. When she is like this... I'm afraid there is little I may do to keep her out.*

At least she seems to be calming a bit now.

He took the empty cup from her and set it on the cart, hovering nervously as he waited for the decoction to begin taking effect.

Oh, do *sit down Mohrdrand,* she sent. *Neither am I a chick, nor are you a mother hen. I will endure.*

He took his seat reluctantly, muscles tense. It was seldom he caught the old woman in weakness, and it worried him more than he cared to admit.

I wonder, Mohrdrand, she ventured a few moments later, looking down, a hand to her forehead. *Do you, perchance, remember the class Kenjiro held?*

His brow furrowed. This was even more worrying. She almost never spoke aloud of Ishihara Kenjiro, the first hero. "Something unusual, wasn't it?" he stumbled. "Unique to him alone, if I remember the stories? Samurai, wasn't it?"

Yes, she sighed mournfully. *Samurai. Or so he considered himself. The class originated on his home world, though,* she explained. *In Jehsha's eyes, he was considered an Oathsworn Paladin. Are you familiar with them?*

"I'm sorry Rosaluna," he shook his head. " I'm afraid not."

Don't be embarrassed, she soothed. *I don't suspect many are. He was the first in something in the order of six hundred years.*

"Indeed," he replied, unsure of how to answer.

She allowed him to stew for a few moments before going on. *And you wonder what this demented old witch is on about now?* She teased. *What Kenjiro's class has to do with Button and our misplaced hero? And why I should suddenly darken your door after so recently having refused to budge from my home?*

"Now you mention it," he nodded.

I have been remembering, she confessed. *Some facets of his class that I'd put aside over the years. Things I'd preferred not to remember. The oathsworn and sentinels are not so dissimilar as one might at first believe, now that I think about it. They share a number of traits in common. Some of them... not so noble. Some of them that may cause... but they already have, haven't they? My poor Button is already being made to pay their toll.*

"Oh?" he prompted.

She nodded slowly, sadly. *Allow me to explain to you the concept of grim resolve, Mohrdrand, and the duties and dangers of those whose lot it is to ally with such heroes.*

* * *

Jack was running out of steam. The bandit had gone on the offensive at last, and he was better than anybody Jack had ever faced, bar the guild master. The sword seemed to have a mind of its own, dancing in and out effortlessly, as though weightless. It was all he could do to keep the man at bay, even given FoeSmite's properties.

But, and there was the single ray of hope in this mess. If Jack couldn't land a strike, neither could the bandit. It was a small ray, and dimming. Jack's night had been long and arduous, and he'd already faced one foe before this one, while his opponent was still relatively fresh. It wouldn't be long before one of them made a mistake, and it wasn't difficult to foresee which of them it would be. It was time to get creative.

Jack started giving ground for the first time in the engagement, feigning more weariness than he felt. He deliberately slowed FoeSmite down, just a fraction. Drew it in a couple of inches. It was stupidly dangerous given who he was facing, but if he wasn't getting an opening, he'd have to force one. He drew FoeSmite's shaft back a bit more, slipping his trailing hand up the shaft another inch or so.

He saw the grin slide across the bandit's face as the sword darted in. He slipped it, barely. Again, and he took a greater step back as the tip of the blade flashed far and away too close to his eyes.

There followed a flurry of action as the bandit bore in and Jack pulled him closer, sweat breaking out on his face as the blade nipped at his green cloak time and again. Now he was anteing blood, for a few of those rents were wicking red.

There! The sword was right there, beating against his armor, tearing through the leather outer layer and scraping at the plates beneath. Jack released FoeSmite with his left hand, twisting and thrusting forward hard, allowing the sword blade to slide past and allowing FoeSmite's shaft to slip freely through his right, catching it in a one-handed, Meyer style thrust, lunging far out over his lead foot as he turned side on.

The sudden strike, aimed at a point well past him, caught the bandit in the upper chest, between the breastplate and pauldron, gouging through the edges of the plates, striking the mail beneath and punching through and into the bones of his shoulder. His eyes went wide as the thrust forced him back on his heel, stumbling unsteadily.

Jack pulled FoeSmite clear just as abruptly, pulling the bandit back toward him as the shaft scraped clear of the pushed in plates. In the instant before the man could regain himself, Jack thrust again. He couldn't manage the same force without the extra throw, and so this one only dented the armor. But the placement was better. The man's face went grey-white as his heart took the brunt of the force of the strike. He staggered, and Jack stepped back, finally free to finish this.

Another step back, and he was at full measure again. He whirled FoeSmite back and around, striking this time at the juncture of neck and shoulder. The bandit toppled over onto his side, rolled onto his back, and was still.

For his own part, Jack thumped himself down where he stood. Flat onto his rump, breath coming in tearing gasps, Foe-Smite across his lap. After a moment to catch his breath, he took stock. He'd let that guy in very close to find his opening. There were tears in his cloak and gashes in the leather of the brigandine. There was blood on his left upper arm, and his right thigh. He gave those wounds some attention. His face felt wet and an inspecting hand came away bloody.

His head had stopped ringing, finally, although his headache was threatening to yank his eyeballs out through his ears. He pulled the sallet from his head to regard the deep gouges the mace had dug through the steel. That had been a *very* close call.

Altogether, though, and all things considered, he seemed to have come out of the encounter pretty healthy. Always assuming the bandit's blade hadn't been poisoned.

There was first aid equipment in the pack, and after awhile, he hauled himself to his feet to fetch it. The bodies he let be for the moment. They wouldn't be in any hurry.

Tom Black

Rain, Cable, and Tiarraluna's Dilemma

Tiarraluna was still struggling for calm, still not finding it. Despite the guildmaster's assurances, she could not find it in her heart to forgive Jackson Grenell. He was a murderer, regardless of what the bounty said. She wanted nothing more to do with him. Nor, contradictively, could she stop thinking about him. How could that be?

Button.

"Grandmother?" She sat bolt upright, startling the guildmaster who'd remained at the table rather than leave her alone.

Button, you must come to Mohrdrand's residence at once. I must speak with you.

"You are here?" She squeaked aloud with her sending. "In Mokkelton?"

Indeed, child, the voice came back. *And there are things which we must discuss. Urgent things.*

Nodding, Tiarraluna excused herself to the guildmaster. "I must go," she explained nervously. "Grandmother is here and asks that I meet her."

Guildmaster Jonkins nodded. "Go, then. I'll keep the horses for the time being. What do you want done with the rest?"

"Ja—" she stopped herself abruptly. "Do with it as you will, Master Jonkins," she replied stiffly. "Try to find any of the victims' people. And please apply any value derived from the rest to ou— against my debt to you. Here," and she tossed the pouch Jack had given her onto the table.

The pouch hit the wooden tabletop, bounced, and came open, spilling its contents across the surface. Tiarraluna's eyes went round at the sight of the golden ring laying amidst the coins. Her mouth opened once, and then twice to speak, but no sound came. Instead, she rose and left the guild hall, crook staff in hand, struggling to hide renewed tears.

Jonkins watched her go, not rising from the table for

quite some time after she'd disappeared through the door and out into the street. Giving thought to what must be done about this new development.

Eleven rank twelve and aboves was considerably more than the current guild strength could handle readily. What's more, he had an inkling he knew who they were. A band of such size was all but unheard of in this province, but not completely without precedent.

He feared he might need to involve himself in the hunt, but worried at what such an unprecedented move might mean to the town. The guild hall was one of three bastions within the town's walls to which people might retreat in dire emergency, and the only viable one remaining. A useless one should it be completely undefended and the town suffer a breaching attack.

After awhile, his musings swung back around to the girl and her missing not-hero. He stared sourly at the small scattering of coins life stones, and the single familiar gold ring before rising and moving back to the counter behind which the guild's enchanted auto-chronicler —the reader which had created their tokens and set the bounty as theirs— resided.

He brought up the bounty and wondered how long it would be before she remembered that neither she nor the young man had either forfeited the bounty or disbanded the party. The bounty marker remained active. And, since bounties qualified as quests, the chronicler was still ticking off experience earned. He raised an eyebrow. Quite a lot of experience earned. More than killing three low mid ranks would accrue.

He glanced over his shoulder towards the closed door then back to the chronicler. The boy was alone now. Given his sentinel class, he was earning experience about ten percent faster because of it. The girl, of course, was advancing more slowly. The important bit, though, was that she *was* still advancing, even while having quit the field. An interesting tidbit, that. Quite an extraordinary distance to be separated and still be sharing experience if he was headed to the old ferry station.

He dispelled the field and retrieved his empty mug, refilling it with a heaving sigh. His duty at this point was clear. He was stuck in Mokkelton at least for the time being. Much as he'd like to, he would not —could not— interfere with an active quest. Not without a formal request for aid. For now, the boy was on his own, and Jehsha bless him with thrice extra luck if he came up against a foe double his own rank and he on his own. Particularly if his foe was not.

* * *

One guard, it looked like. Jack couldn't believe his luck. He'd sort of gotten it into his head that levels here were more grudgingly granted than in the games he played back home, and that level twelve was something meaningful. Some of these clowns weren't even up to bush war standard. The first three had been pitiful. And this guy?

Of course, he frowned, remembering the two in the grass, some of them weren't that bad at all. And since he couldn't tell a rank one from a forty with the girl absent, it might be better to not let himself get too cocky again.

Back to the sentry. The idiot wasn't even standing in the tree looking around. He was sitting on a thick branch about twenty feet up with his legs dangling over either side and his back leaning against the trunk. Jack couldn't even tell for sure if he was awake.

He'd gotten the general lay of the camp down over the course of the afternoon, holding well clear and circling slowly. Looked like an old ferry station, right down to the dock. No ferry, though. Couple of shacks, an open stable, and a single more substantial structure with an actual door that was probably left over from when the station had been active.

There was a sort of rough corral where a dozen or so horses and a couple of cows stood listlessly. Several wagons and carts were parked haphazardly behind it. No sign of a dug well anywhere he could see, so unless there was one inside one of the structures, they were probably carrying their water up from the river.

He'd also been watching the camp's occupants. Didn't look like eight guys to him. He hoped that this didn't mean that a couple of them were out doing some light murder to pass the time. With luck, they'd all be passed out drunk in one or more of the shacks. Still, every single one of them was supposed to be higher ranked than him by a considerable margin, so he wasn't about to just wander in and ask.

Clouds had been sliding in from the northwest for most of the afternoon, hiding the sun more often than not as it heeled over towards evening. Nevertheless, he'd gotten himself worked around to have it at his back, using whatever small help it offered. He was crouched low in the tall grass, peering up into the shade of the branches, wishing for a pair of binoculars.

The guard was wearing a plate cuirass, greaves, and pauldrons. He may have been wearing a gorget, but it was impossible to tell, even as close as Jack was to him, which was closer than he'd have liked given the choice. Ideally, he'd be back about a hundred yards with a scoped and silenced carbine. Instead, he was about forty yards out with a bow and hoping he was close enough.

He was using the bow he'd taken from the swordsman who'd tried to skewer him out in the grass, and he hadn't played with the thing as much as he'd have liked. It was heavier than the one he'd used the other day by a good fifteen pounds, though, and at least ten heavier than the one Tiarraluna had purchased for him. It may or may not have had any bonuses baked into it. It glowed softly, but he couldn't tell what that meant beyond some sort of buff. He hoped.

I mean, he thought to himself. *Why would the guy be carrying a cursed weapon around, right?* He cast a quick, involuntary glance at FoeSmite lying in the grass, hopefully quiescent, beside him. *Right?*

Worst case scenario, he'd chunk the staff at the guy if he missed with the bow and alerted him. But that was worst case, because it would make a *whole* lotta freaking noise, and he wasn't in any screaming hurry to take on a whole camp full of high ranking bad guys at once. His bout with those two out on the grass had cured him of any such goofy notions.

Okay, Sergeant Grenell, he told himself silently. *Remember what your dear old sainted Drill Sergeant taught you. Aim small, miss small. Aim small, miss small....*

He couldn't really tell if the armor was warded or not. Probably wouldn't be able to tell if he was holding it in his hands. He was willing to bet it was, though. He certainly couldn't tell what sort of wards it carried, but it didn't take a genius to guess that anti-piercing was probably high on the list.

Aim small, miss small.... taking a deep breath and letting it out slowly, he drew the arrow back, took his sight, and loosed. He was lying on his back in the grass by the time the arrow took the lookout in the neck, passing through and chunking into the tree behind with a loud *CHOK!*

No gorget, then. He lay there awhile, waiting to see if anyone in the camp had decided to wonder at the noise. From here, the arrow wasn't overly obvious. The guy hadn't even sagged all that much. A casual glance might not catch anything amiss at all. Which meant Jack was probably good until they changed lookouts. And with what he knew of this bunch so far, he was willing to — hell, he *was* betting nobody was about to take over unless the existing lookout went down and rousted them out.

Grinning coldly, he rolled to hands and knees and took up FoeSmite, crawling slowly further out into the grass, circling around to where he'd left the horses and wondering how to get the next one alone. He was on the clock now, and needed to pare the numbers as much as possible before they realized they were being hunted.

He hadn't gone twenty yards before he felt the first drop land on the back of his hand. Then another, and another. He cursed under his breath. Well wasn't *that* just wonderful. He stopped and rolled onto his side, just managing to unstring the bow and stow the string inside his tunic before the rain started coming down in earnest. It might have been waterproof, but he wasn't going to bet his life on a wet bowstring.

So much for his plans. He wasn't about to go floundering around in this mess looking for trouble, and it wasn't likely any of the bandits would be wandering around loose for him to find, either.

He needed to get to the horses and find some cover to wait out the storm. He needed to rethink things.

* * *

The main door of the guild hall came crashing in, treating the main hall to a shower of wind driven rain. A pair of cloaked figures hurried inside in its wake, laughing and slapping water from their outer garments.

The larger of the two looked up from closing the door to espy the guildmaster seated behind the bar, tankard halfway to his mouth. He was a big man, curly-haired, square faced, and hearty, his normally clean shaven features stubbled by a week's growth of blue-black beard. "Ho, Master Jonkins," he called jovially. "One pride of stalker cats successfully eliminated! And two days early! You owe us free drinks."

"Cable," the guildmaster called back, his mood picking up. "Tiglund. How was your hunt?"

Cable hesitated at his tone, pausing in the act of hanging his cloak from a peg near the door. He turned full on to the guildmaster, one eyebrow going up. "Something's amiss, isn't it?" the rank thirty demanded.

"You know that bandit problem we've been hearing about?"

"Of course," Cable nodded, finishing his task and moving to the bar. "Stalkers were a priority, but we'll go looking for the bandits first thing in the morning."

Jonkins slid a freshly poured mug his way, shaking his head. "Already found them," he said gruffly.

Cable blinked. "What?" he demanded "How? Who else is there even to look? Some ungifted run across them and somehow live to tell the tale?"

Jonkins was giving Tiglund the eye as the youngster regarded him hopefully. Finally, the guildmaster sighed and poured a mug half full of ale. Then, looking up at the grinning youth, topped it off with water. Tiglund's face fell, but he accepted the mug with thanks.

"Bit of a novice mage from out Heatherton way showed up the other day," he told the big rank thirty. "Rank ten. The

Lady Rosaluna's great, great granddaughter if you can believe it. Had her a strange character in tow it turns out is a rank nine sentinel."

"Whew!" Cable laughed then. "You had me going for a moment there, Bor, old friend," he smiled. "You had me thinking you were serious."

"Deadly," Jonkins brow lowered. "The two of them took the bounty and lit out two days ago."

"A sentinel," Cable chewed over the word. "What's that even mean, Bor? How does a sentinel appear now, so many years since the last, and after the fact?"

Jonkins shrugged and took a swallow of his drink. "Been giving it some thought," he ventured. "Look around, Antel. That goofy new king's taken the soldiers and nearly all the adventurers off west and not returned. The whole of the land's been left to its own devices, with little or no protection for more'n two-and-a-half years. Whole continent is going back to the wild."

"The way it was back when the sentinels first left their castles," Cable nodded thoughtfully.

"Even so," Jonkins nodded.

"So who is it?" Cable asked. "Do I know him? I thought every noble with the slightest viable gift had gone a-demon hunting with the king."

"Not one of the locals," Jonkins told him. "Not even a royal. Another hero, looks like. And even for one of them, he's a strange one."

They went back and forth then, with the guildmaster filling his primary guild members in on this new development. Cable, in particular, took a bit of convincing.

"So, where and how many?" the big man asked finally, smacking his empty ale mug onto the bar. "This whole sentinel business is interesting and all, but these bandits need seeing off. And here, I was hoping to get a night's sleep in a real bed, too."

"Sit back down, Antel," Jonkins waved him down. "There's more to it than just haring off after them. I told you, the bounty's been taken."

Cable sat back down, his brow knitting. "Still?" he asked,

perplexed. "Wait. How d'you know where the camp is, then?" his voice was tight. "Those kids come back somehow without getting killed so they could let you know the location, and *then* went back out after them? Why? What's the point?

"I'm familiar with the bounty, Bor," he said. "If the bandits are too much to handle, you can pay them for bringing the information back, even if they didn't deal with the bandits themselves. If the bandits are too tough for them, there's no need to go back out. If they're not, there was no reason to come in without getting rid of them first. I'm confused."

Jonkins frowned. "What if I told you that this mob was fourteen strong, all ranks twelve and up, with a rank fourteen mage, and that their leader was a rank eighteen plunderer?"

Cable's face went deathly still. "The bunch took down Weilei's Crossing, then?"

"I'm thinkin'."

"And you let a couple of low ranks go out chasing them? Even after you knew?"

So Jonkins explained the day's happenings, including the reduction in bandit ranks, and the sentinel's solo pursuit of those who remained. And of Grim Resolve.

"Well, then," Cable wondered once the tale'd been told, chin resting on a braced hand. "What are we to do? Wait for the bounty to go dark when they kill him? Doesn't seem right. Wait!" he sat bolt upright, snapping his fingers. "Why don't I just go out and get myself invited into his party? *That's* allowed, right?"

Jonkins shook his head. "Won't need to," he said. "They haven't dissolved the party nor relinquished the bounty. Girl's the party leader, and she's still here in town."

"What?" Cable demanded. "Where?"

"Over at Mohrdrand's villa. No doubt getting an earful from her grandmother, who's also in town."

"The lady Rosaluna?" Cable's eyes widened. "That doesn't happen often."

Jonkins shrugged.

"I'd better get going, then," Cable suited action to

words, rising from his seat. Before leaving, he dug through his pouch for the bounty token and life stones he was carrying, sliding them across the bar. "See to the split if you don't mind, guildmaster," he winked as he turned for the door.

"Tiglund," he called over his shoulder without turning. "See to the horses, would you? And wait for me here once you're done. I'll let you know what's going on when I return."

* * *

Mohrdrand's door swung open even as Tiarraluna approached, revealing the wizard framed in the soft halo of light from within. She greeted him perfunctorily and hurried inside. Rosaluna was seated in one of the chairs before the glowing hearth, looking very pale. Tiarraluna rushed to her side, dropping to her knees to embrace the old woman about the waist.

"Oh, Grandmother," she implored, voice ragged. "What have I done?"

What indeed, the old woman replied, stroking her hair gently. *I think that you do not yet realize. Nor its import.*

Tiarraluna drew back and looked up to the old woman's face, catching the hard glint of her eyes. "Grandmother?"

Rosaluna took her granddaughter's head in both hands and drew it in, kissing her forehead gently and patting her hair in the way she'd done when the girl was a toddler. *Fear not, child,* she sent softly. *I will help you to guide yourself through this maze.*

Tiarraluna was growing more confused by the moment. "Grandmother," she tried. "The man... the... hero...."

The sentinel, you mean? The old woman's tone lightened in mirth. *Your Jackson chan?*

Tiarraluna's face flushed and she drew back once more. "He is not my Jackson chan. He is not my anything chan. He is a murderer, and I want nothing more to do with him."

The old woman shook her head slowly, placing a palm against the girl's cheek. *I'm afraid, dear granddaughter,* she sent quietly. *That it is far too late for you to claim such a thing.*

Tiarraluna frowned and drew breath to retort, but the old woman hadn't finished.

You are bound to him, Button, she sent. *And he to you. For good or ill. There is no going back.*

Tiarraluna's denial was vehement. "Bound? Grandmother, by what measure do you say this?"

He is your hero now, Rosaluna might not have heard the protest. *And you are his companion. What's more, you will have to become his conscience.*

"Conscience?" Tiarraluna was confused. "Even were I to desire such a thing, he would not listen. He *did* not listen. He... he murdered a man right in front of me!"

Yes, the old woman nodded. *I'm aware. Grim Resolve is a terrible thing, Button. Unchecked, it may well turn him into a monster.*

Unbidden, the image of the black thing within the iron cage flared into being at the forefront of Tiarraluna's mind, its piercing red eyes fixed on her.

"You knew?" Tiarraluna shook the tableau from her thoughts. "But...?"

But?

"He will not heed, Grandmother. He will not listen to me. He does as he will, in spite of my wishes or my pleas."

Rosaluna cupped the girl's cheek and leaned closer. *Then you must grow stronger, Button,* she smiled. *For it is in your power, and yours alone to temper that base drive within him, and so your duty. As it was mine to do so for your grandfather.*

Of Mice and Man

The rain was still coming down hard, as it had been for the past hour. Jack sat huddled within his tattered cloak at the base of a decent sized fir of some sort, trying to ignore the icy drip of the rain as it dribbled in through the tears in the hood, down the lip of the sallet, and down his back to soak the arming doublet and tunic beneath.

The horses looked to be faring little better, though he supposed they were probably more used to it. His own days of rainwashed, shivering misery had long since been placed behind him and, he'd thought, over for good.

He was wracking his brain trying to determine a path forward that wouldn't see him spitted on somebody's spear or pincushioned with arrows. He wasn't having much luck.

To top it off, he was worrying about the animals. If he didn't make it, what would happen to them? Sure, the bandits might find them, but they might not. So what did he do? He couldn't just leave them out here at the mercy of wandering predators.

"Are you an adventurer?" the voice was faint, high-pitched, and half imagined.

His eyes popped open and his head came up. He looked around, but could see no one.

"Down here," the voice came again. "Beside your right knee."

He shook his head, thinking to clear it, wondering if he were hearing things now. Then he looked down, and was sure of it. A grey mouse, just bigger than his fist. It was wearing a green felt bycocket hat with a bedraggled feather in it, and a green coat of some rough, homespun cloth.

"Okay," he mumbled to himself. "Clearly that guy with the mace hit me harder than I'd thought."

"Are you an adventurer?" the mouse repeated, it's squeaky voice rising.

"Yes?" he answered uncertainly. "Ah..."

"I am Meynardo," the mouse informed him, standing straight, doffing his hat and sweeping it back as he bowed. Meynardo Chee-Ch-Cheep. Called Long Racer. Son of Reynardo Chee-Ch-Cheep, Called The Mouse Who Roars. Grandson of—"

"I get it," Jack interrupted. "What do you want?"

"I need your help," the mouse announced. "*We* need your help."

"We?" he asked in spite of himself.

"My people," the mouse clarified. "My village is besieged!"

The more the tiny creature spoke, the more bizarre the situation seemed. Then, all at once, Jack remembered where he was. Sure. Okay. Why *wouldn't* an oversized mouse in a hat be asking him for help? In a language he could clearly understand? Out in the middle of nowhere in the rain?

"Ah..." he repeated.

"There is no time!" the mouse pressed. "The barrier has fallen! It may already be too late!"

Jack shook his head again, trying to clear it. Trying to shake loose the sense of unreality. He was already in the middle of one dangerous battle. The surviving bandits might find the dead guard at any moment, if they hadn't already. And once they started hunting him en masse, he was pretty much done for. What business did he have chasing off into the night to save a mess of rodents?"

"Please!" the mouse was clasping its hands together in an all too human entreaty.

Damn! "Where," he sighed. "And what's attacking them?"

The mouse's face split into a wide smile and one arm shot out to the north. "Just over a lenn in that direction!" he squeaked. "The village is beset by dire hares. I can no longer say how many. In excess of thirty remain at minimum. Possibly more by now. No matter how many we slay, more seem to appear."

"Dire ha— you mean *rabbits?*" he goggled.

The mouse frowned mightily. "Rabbit-like, but no mere

rabbits, rest assured."

Erudite little bugger, Jack thought. "C'mon, then," he ordered, holding his hand out. "You'd better ride. No way I'll be able to keep track of you in this tall grass. Just point the way."

The mouse scurried up his arm and perched on his shoulder beneath his hood. And yes, he smelled like a wet mouse.

Jack staggered to his feet, groaning at the pain in knees that had been crossed the last forty minutes. Leaning on Foe-Smite for support, he limped to the horses. He swept the saddle of the chestnut clear of standing water and hoisted himself aboard, catching at the reins of the two riderless mounts.

"Where, then?" he asked again.

The mouse pointed, and Jack kicked the horse into motion. He still couldn't believe he was leaving more than half a dozen ridiculously dangerous foes wandering loose behind him to go rabbit hunting with a talking mouse.

With the soggy ground and the rain, he refused to push the horses past a trot, despite the entreaties of his distraught passenger. They'd be no use to anyone if the horse went down and threw them. Still, less than five minutes later, they were approaching their goal. Jack could already see the field in his head, deciding finally that these dire hares must be the vague auras he'd been seeing out in the grass the past day or so. There were way more than thirty.

He brought the horse to a splashing halt well clear of what he assumed to be the battleground, although he couldn't see much between the darkness and rain. "Hang on," he warned the mouse before leaping from the saddle. He hit the ground with his own splash and went to a knee, sliding nearly a foot along the rain-slicked grass, grounding FoeSmite before him to stop his progress.

The vague shapes out in the darkness had stopped moving at the approach of the horses, but apparently a lone man afoot and down presented a much more favorable target. As a single entity, they charged forward, leaping and bounding in his direction with a speed he found alarming. Damn, they were big.

Like German hare big. Like highland terrier big.

The first of them was upon him almost before he could bring FoeSmite up and to bear. It was no contest, and the hare vanished in a cloud of fur and blood. That didn't seem to slow the others, and before he could more than bring the staff back on line, they were on him. They had teeth like dogs, too.

The mouse was tucked deep into his cloak, literally crouched inside his collar for purchase, and from the edge of his peripheral vision, Jack caught a sliver of movement flash past him. One of the hares snapping at his throat froze for an instant and then began convulsing, falling clear a moment later.

He didn't have time to wonder much. He was desperately struggling to stay alive. Another was at his throat. Still another was gnawing on his leg, making short work of his pants. One hit was enough for any of them to go down, but they were all over him, and the fleeting thought came that, if he let them take him down, he'd have one hell of a time explaining to Saint Peter with his head held high how he'd survived three tours in the desert only to be killed by evil bunnies. He smacked the hungry hare away from his upper leg, feeling its teeth gouge out a chunk of flesh as it was ripped clear by the blow.

The mail was doing its job, fortunately, keeping his vitals safe. As long as he kept them off his arms and legs, he wasn't taking too much damage. As long as. He punched and slammed and swung FoeSmite in short, sharp arcs right up against his own body, curled in tight to keep his extremities safe. There was no footwork, no masterful display of agility. Just bashing. Once he'd dismounted and gone to a knee, he'd had no chance to regain his feet. He fought them from the ground, struggling to remain upright as they battered him from all sides.

Meynardo and his bow took care of a couple more who might have torn out his throat; in one case sticking his bow hand nearly between a pair of gaping jaws before loosing his shaft.

And then they were gone. The last two of them had broken finally, and were loping away. The mouse raced out onto his shoulder, and now he saw the bow. A small, toylike recurve with a tiny, four inch arrow nocked. The mouse let fly, and a second later, one of the retreating hares was kicking its life out in the mud.

"None must escape," the mouse warned breathlessly as he reached into his nearly empty quiver. "They breed like—"

"Rabbits?" Jack finished for him. But he took aim and hurled FoeSmite into the remaining hare's body even as the mouse was nocking a fresh arrow.

"Let me down, now," the mouse ordered. Without thinking, Jack knelt and held out his arm. The mouse scurried down it and vanished into the muddy grass.

Jack recalled FoeSmite before limping after, sticking the catch now that he was getting the hang of it. It was still coming straight in at him — at his middle rather than his hand. As though he was more target than master, and that was worrying.

Now that he had a minute, Jack took in his surroundings for the first time. Weathered upthrusts of sandstone pierced the prairie before him. Dozens of them, rising in some cases to more than waist height and stretching out into the darkness for who knew how far. It was difficult to make out much more than their general shapes in the gloom. He couldn't imagine what sort of event had led to their formation.

The rain had let up some, but it was still coming down, and the moon remained obscured. Or moons, he supposed, looking up into the fast moving cloud cover. He still hadn't got the hang of the phases, so he had no idea whether one or both were out. Some faint glow pierced the clouds, casting a wan light and it was slightly easier to see than it had been. Probably moons, then.

Leaving off his examination of the sky, he looked once more to the ground. The whole place was littered with dead rabbits. There must have been hundreds of them, even beyond those he'd slain himself. He crouched down to examine a few as he moved forward. While some of the carcasses looked fresh, many were stiff and cold, like they'd been dead for a couple of days. He whistled low under his breath. Siege was right.

There was no way for him to determine the bounds of

the village, or even locate it under these conditions. There wasn't anything he could see anywhere that looked as though it might have been deliberately constructed. Dead rabbits, scattered stones, and trampled grass was all there was. Wasn't there?

Something laying in the debris had caught his eye. Brightly colored and oddly out of place.   Taking a knee, he picked up what he'd mistaken initially for a tangle of crushed flowers. Bringing it close, he could see that, rather than flower petals, he was holding twigs. They had been fashioned in some way into a solid piece and planed smooth. Roughly oval, around the size of a credit card. It was painted a cheerful blue and decorated with barely visible yellow and white flowers. Halfway along one edge a tiny handle protruded from its surface.

It struck him then that this was a door, ripped from its moorings somewhere by sharp claws. In its upper center was a small opening, like a window, with filmy wisps of tattered and sodden cloth dangling from it. Curtains, or what was left of them. He closed his hand around the small panel, looking up, straining to scan his surroundings more thoroughly. This had been torn from someone's home.

Suddenly, then, they weren't just mice. Suddenly, he wasn't kneeling in a muddy field in the middle of nowhere. Suddenly, where he was kneeling was another shattered village in a line of them that was far too long.

There were no bodies other than the rabbits. At least none he could see. Those incisors the rabbits —No! Dire hares— were sporting would explain that. No herbivores, these. Any bodies to be found would be found inside the corpses of the hares. It took him a moment to wrap his head around that. His gut couldn't decide whether it was better or worse that the village's inhabitants had been eaten alive rather than tortured or raped to death, or had their heads lopped off for a video camera and internet propaganda.

He looked around for his tiny companion after a bit, his mind swimming up out of the old misery. He found him finally by virtue of the clods of mud and spray sailing clear of a deepish hole dimly seen at one end of one of the taller stones. Meynardo was down in the hole, digging frantically with his bare hands, hurling the doughy soil up between his hind legs.

Jack eased up to the edge of the hole, crouching low. He couldn't see anything. Between the rain, the clouds, and the shadow of the upthrust, the inside of the hole was inky darkness. Reluctantly, he fished one of his little cree emitter flashlights out of his belt pouch. He'd been husbanding the batteries ruthlessly as there'd be no replacements probably ever. But this situation desperately needed a little illumination. He tapped the tail switch for low and shined the beam into the hole.

The mouse spared him a fleeting glance before going back to his digging. "The... the inner refuge!" he sent. "Some of them... at least, have... managed to reach it. I... I can hear the young ones wailing."

Some good news, at least. "How many?"

Meynardo seemed to flinch. "I... I do not know," he admitted a second later. "The young ones are terrified. All they send is darkness and death fear. I have been trying to tell them we're coming...." he paused in his digging to swipe at his brow. "I cannot tell if they've relayed any of what I've been telling them to the adults. Perhaps yes, perhaps no.

"In any case, the main entryway at the top of the rock has been collapsed. There is no way through. This was an alternate of sorts. You see the mark?" he indicated a painted slash in the rock face. "If we... I... dig here at an angle of forty five degrees, I should be able to open a way."

"You're sure?" Jack wasn't.

Meynardo shrugged and went back to digging. "Luciandro made the calculations, and I trust his math. If any of the adults survive and know we're coming, they should be digging up to meet us."

Right, Jack thought. "Anything I can do to help?"

"Keep watch," Meynardo cautioned. "The blood may yet draw larger predators, and the wards are a shambles."

"We're alone," Jack assured him. "For a good half, uh, lenn, at least."

Meynardo stopped digging again and stood straight, turning to frown up at him. "And how would you know that?"

Jack shrugged. "Some facet of one of my classes, I suppose," he said. "No idea what it is or which it's from."

Meynardo opened his mouth to ask one of the thousand questions that had just popped to life in his head, but instead turned back to his digging. There was far too much in that short statement for him to try to unpack with so much urgently to be done.

Jack, meanwhile, couldn't help but notice that the hole was filling with rainwater at a worrying rate. He doffed his sallet and held it over the hole with the hand holding the light, juggling the flash to keep it shining into the work area, while blocking what rain he could.

He didn't fail to note that the water dripping from that hand was tinged red. He wondered if rabies was a thing here.

With his other hand, he began scooping mud out of the space behind the mouse, gouging out a sump to channel water away from the rescue operation.

The Party Grows

The door is not barred.

Cable paused, his hand already raised to knock, and reached for the door latch, letting himself in. He gave his drenched cloak a shake in the direction of the street before closing the portal and hanging the dripping cloak from a peg beside it. Then he kicked off his boots, setting them on the mat on the other side of the doorway. He proceeded then, in his sock feet, to where he expected the old woman would be waiting.

"Sensei," he bowed deeply the moment he spotted her.

She was sitting before the hearth with a girl, presumably her granddaughter, kneeling beside her, head in her lap and weeping softly. *Antel kun,* she replied, smiling faintly and nodding. *How fare thee? And your studies?*

He grimaced. He'd been too busy lately to stretch, let alone meditate. "Progressing," he answered noncommittally. "I've been working on fire," he added at her arch look.

And your healing?

His shoulders slumped. "Not so much, Sensei," he admitted. "Even though I'm getting more practice with it. It seems as though I've hit a wall."

We will work on it as time allows, she nodded. *But for now, shall we address the true reason for this visit?*

He didn't waste time. "I'm here to request that your granddaughter invite me into her party."

The girl's head came up, wide eyed.

And why might that be, Antel? The old woman queried.

"Bor Jonkins and I have been giving it some thought," he told them, an edge to his voice. "And we think we know the bunch your young man," he ignored the girl's glare, "is marching himself off to meet."

And? The old woman had picked up his edge.

Cable hesitated for a moment before proceeding. He was remembering Bor's description of how the girl had taken her earlier encounter, and matching it with her current state.

What was coming was orders of magnitude worse.

Out with it, Antel, the old woman ordered.

"We're pretty sure they're the ones raided Weilei's Crossing last summer," he said roughly.

Rosaluna's eyes widened in alarm. Mohrdrand straightened, grunting his dismay. Only Tiarraluna failed to realize the implications of what he'd said. She'd been far away for most of the past two years and hadn't heard about it.

"Killed everything," Cable went on for the girl's sake. "Men, women, children, livestock, right down to the barn cats. Anything they couldn't carry off or couldn't be bothered to carry off, they slaughtered. Didn't even burn the place. Just left the dead to rot.

"Ungifted hunter came across the place a few days later and worked out most of what had happened. Found one starving survivor who'd only lived because he'd been checking traps well outside the village when the attackers had ridden up. Had the sense to go to ground rather than throw his life away raising an alarm wouldn't have done any good anyhow.

"Came up to just about what you two ran into up north, right down to the dark mage.

"Hunter brought him to Bailess, where the nearest guild hall was and a couple of them as were left came out and did an investigation. Nothing left but empty, ruined buildings and rotting corpses."

"Why... why have I never...?" Tiarraluna sputtered.

"Weilei's Crossing's away out west," Cable waved in that general direction. "Out in the higher ranked zones, more'n three hundred lenn from here. It never occurred to us we might run into that same lot in this *province*, let alone this county. Otherwise I'd have been out there myself hunting them down a month ago or more.

"As it is," he pressed, "I need to get up there fast as my horse can carry me. Even three down, those lot are more than a rank nine will be able to handle on his own. Even a rank nine sentinel."

Tiarraluna was staring in openmouthed horror at the

tale. She looked to her grandmother, who nodded.

And you must go with him, Button, the old woman insisted.

Tiarraluna blanched white, drawing back, her emotions a whirling storm of chaos. "G-Grandmother!" she entreated.

No, Button, the sending was grim. *You must go. He is your hero, and you must support him, even against this. Invite Cable. He is a good man and a strong fighter. He will protect you.*

But protection wasn't what concerned the girl just then. The mortal fear that gripped her heart at that moment wasn't of the bandits. Not entirely. The worry that brought her terror was what else she would find at the end of the journey. What sort of monster would she find there at the bandit camp? That was the terror that held her now. What would she find Jackson had become?

"I... I cannot ride well enough..." she stammered. "We will never be able to...."

Mohrdrand? Rosaluna raised her head. *You still have the wagon?*

The old wizard rocked his head, taken aback at the force of the sending. "The Runstable's?" he asked. "Of course I do. It's in the back lot where it always is. You'll need horses, though."

"Horses, I've got," Cable volunteered, eyebrows bunched in confusion. "Even a couple broken to harness. Will two be enough?"

"Four or six would be better," Mohrdrand nodded. "Eight better still. But two will do. Fetch them and I'll get the wagon prepared. You know the back way in?"

He didn't, but Mohrdrand explained it to him.

"Before I go, though," and Cable turned back to the distraught girl. "The invitation, if you please? Have to make it official."

Tiarraluna raised a shaky hand, still struggling with the notion that she was actually allowing herself to be pressed into this folly. "A-Antel Cable," her voice broke. "I... I invite you to join my party."

"I accept," he took her hand, clasping it tight. "The bounty token?"

"H-he has it," she didn't meet his eyes.

Of course he would, he thought, frowning. He nodded, turned, and was off and out the door into the still pouring rain even as his cloak was settling about his shoulders

* * *

Jonkins regarded the chronicler, perplexed, scratching his head with the hand not holding his mug.

"What is it, guildmaster," Tiglund asked curiously. He'd taken the horses to Cable's holding, fed and curried them, and had returned to await further instructions. He was now watching the guildmaster watch the chronicler.

"You know how these things work, right, Tig?" Jonkins asked.

"Yessir," the boy answered promptly. "Cable taught me that right off."

"So," Jonkins mused. "What would you say if I told you that the sentinel has a good chunk more experience than last time I checked? And is still ticking up?"

"Why, that's easy sir," Tiglund beamed. "He's earning experience."

"And yet, the girl... the party leader... isn't."

Now Tiglund was perplexed. "Too far apart, maybe?" he ventured. "You said she's here in town, right? Maybe he's moving away."

"Could be," Jonkins nodded. "Doesn't feel like it, though. Anyhow, we know where he's going, or where he's *supposed* to be going, and it's not all that much farther away than he was earlier when I know for sure they were sharing.

"'S'almost... almost like he's off doing something not tied to the quest at all. Can't imagine why, or how that'd earn him this sort of experience, though. Little jots of it at first, too close together, like he was being swarmed by something small."

"Ran afoul of some wandering monsters, maybe?" Tiglund asked. "Fangeddy weasels and dire hares up that way, not mentioning the prairie wolves, plains lions, foxes, or snakes. I hear there's even some slimes been seen on the far side of the river, up by the sulphur swamps."

"Probably it," Jonkins nodded again, uncertainly. "But why wouldn't the girl share? They're partied up, and should be sharing whether it's directly tied to the bounty or incidental.

"And now, it's just ticking up slow-like and steady. It's almost as though he's taken on a solo side quest. Something not guild related at all. But that would be downright stupid to do up against the kind of adversaries he's already fighting. And he didn't seem all that stupid to me."

Tiglund had nothing to offer to that.

* * *

The outlaw leader stared out the half open door of his cabin, a dismal expression on his scarred face. Bear the Mauler, they called him these days. He'd had another name once, but it had been long ago, and he barely remembered what it had been anymore. He'd shed it when he'd joined the demon lord's armies in his youth and hadn't missed it. Bear the Mauler was all he needed, and was more intimidating to the scum who followed him into the bargain. Particularly now that the lord was gone and what remained of his armies were on their own.

At the moment, he lay, half reclining in his bed, his back against the wall behind him, ignoring the quiet weeping of the naked girl who lay beside him.

She had no name. May have once, but she'd lost it when she'd lost her freedom back in Weilei's Crossing last summer. Now she was just girl. Or whore. Or whatever whichever of them was addressing her decided to call her at a given time. No more than livestock at this point, and who bothered to name the livestock?

No, the girl didn't concern Bear any more than the rain he was staring out into. He was thinking of those three idiots out in the dark, wondering were they dead or alive. The more time passed, the more he figured dead. Had Thumper and Bonce found them anywhere short of the road, they'd already have been back, even with the rain.

While he was staring gloomily out into the darkness, a

splashing commotion interrupted his musing. Narkins, one of his boys, came charging across the yard, splashing mud everywhere. The soggy fool brought up against the doorframe, clutching it with both hands for purchase.

"Boss," he wheezed without preamble. "Willie's dead!"

Bear surged upright, dislodging the naked girl and sending her tumbling to the floor, where she crawled quietly to huddle in a corner.

"The hell you say!" he roared. "Where? How?"

"He were standin' guard," Narkins explained. "Up in that big tree, you know the one. Been out there all day. When he didn't come in after the rain started and it got dark, we got to wonderin' why, so we went to look."

"And?"

"He were a'sittin' up there on that big branch like nothing were 'appenin'," the bandit said, wonder in his voice. "Drenched to th' skin, he were, face all pale... just a'sittin' there, like nothin' to it."

"And?" Bear repeated, voice deepening with rage.

"And when Boz climbed up to see what were wrong, there were a arrow through his gizzard, a'pinnin' him to th' tree," Narkins' eyes were wide. "And he were dead."

Bear was already up, shrugging into his rough clothing and his armor, forcefully ignoring the chill racing up his spine. Something bad was going on out there in the dark, and he meant to find what.

"You see anybody about?" he demanded. "Any sign or anything?"

"In this rain, Boss?" Narkins quailed. "Lucky we were we found th' *tree*."

Right. "Let's go then, dummy. I want to see for myself."

They hadn't bothered to bring Willie down. He hadn't expected them to. He was up there in the tree, alright. Looking like he was still pretending to be on watch. Bear had to get right close even with the lantern light to see the arrow sticking out his neck, and when he did, his face paled, his eyes going to slits.

"That arrow belong to who I think it does?" he demanded.

"Sure do look like one o' Thumper's arrows," Narkins replied.

"Well get him down!" Bear shouted to the mob in general, since they were all just standing around stupidly staring up into the tree at the corpse.

Bear didn't bother waiting for them to finish. He was heading back to his cabin, his jaw clenched as his mind raced. Thumper and Bonce would be dead, then. With Willie and them first three idiots, that was six. Worse, he had no idea who was out there in the dark hunting them.

Boseco was a rank fifteen Dark Skulker, and had been in and out of that town five dozen times in the past four months if he'd been in it once. Wasn't hard given the state of both the guild and guard contingents. So Bear knew just about all there was to know about the place and what sorts of forces they might send against him. He'd been certain the rank thirty would be his only worry.

Rank Thirty was a Spearman, though, with some mage ranks as secondary. If he'd also been ranked with the bow, Bear would have found out about it. So it hadn't been him killed Willie.

Rank thirty's apprentice *could* use a bow, but was a fourteen year old rank four. Thumper's bow was rank ten with a heavy draw. A good four ranks higher than that kid could draw, even ignoring its draw length or weight. So it wasn't him.

Bear didn't even give the guards a thought. Outside the town walls, they were barely stronger than ungifted.

All that left was the mage, and while Bear wanted nothing to do with that one, he didn't fool himself a rank one-seventy would be out in the rain shooting arrows around.

So who the bloody hell was killing his boys?

Survivors

The mouse dug for a good while before anything happened. And when something did, they nearly missed it. Jack was peering down into the ragged tear in the prairie, straining his eyes in the dimming light of his flashlight beam when a trickle of mud nearly at Meynardo's feet fell away and down.

"Hold it!" he warned.

Meynardo stopped his digging, looking up over his shoulder. Jack pointed to the shifting mud. A hand showed at the edge of the trickle, poking up from below and pulling another small plug free.

Either Meynardo hadn't got the angle just right, or those digging upward hadn't, and he'd nearly passed by them overhead. He shifted quickly and began to assist whoever was working from below. In a matter of minutes, a filthy creature with a pot belly and burly arms pulled itself up out of the freshly opened hole.

Jack eyed it skeptically. It was still a mouse, generally speaking, but its form was considerably more anthropoid. More like a cartoon mouse from one of those afternoon kids' shows. The ones from back in the day, when the animators really worked at it. Reaching down, this new specimen helped another of them up. Younger, apparently, although it was difficult to judge. Female, this time. Bosomy and wearing a dress and bonnet, both sodden and grimy. In her arms, she clutched a tiny, button-eyed creature that looked one hundred percent a baby mouse of the everyday variety.

And so they came, straggling up out of the ground. Forty-six of them, ranging from garden variety mice, to a few who, save for their stature, ears, and short snouts, looked nearly human. All were looking apprehensively up at him as they gathered in the rain.

Meynardo was speaking to them in hushed tones, with the occasional gesture or glance over his shoulder in Jack's direction. After a few minutes, they began to disburse, egged along by an older looking, nearly humanoid mouse in mud spattered maroon robes and matching, wide brimmed conical hat.

Jack watched them for a moment as they scattered slowly, some climbing up what he could now see were trails carved into the sides of the sandstone upthrust, presumably to the shattered ruins of what had been their homes. Others moved to the corpses of the invaders.

He wondered at first what the latter were up to until he saw the first of them start working at the remains of one with a tiny knife. He had to turn away then. They were retrieving their dead. Shaking his head, he turned for the horses, moving slowly and with a pronounced limp.

He shucked out of his rapidly deteriorating armor, hanging the brigandine from the chestnut's saddle. He observed the rents in the blue leather and the plates beneath. He wondered as he ran a finger along one of the rents; had he really only purchased it a couple of days ago?

The mail wasn't in much better shape, nor the vambraces. That swordsman had been no joke. He shrugged out of the bloody arming doublet next, and the linen tunic beneath.

He shivered wildly as the rain doused his naked skin, but it would help to cleanse the wounds he seemed to be accumulating like freckles in the sun. He'd gotten the greaves off and was sitting on his hind end in the wet grass gingerly skinning a torn pant leg up over one bloody shin, trying to decide whether he should just peel the trousers off as well, when his companion found him again.

Taking his hat in his hands and bowing deeply, Meynardo addressed him seriously. "Friend Adventurer," he began, voice catching.

"Jack," Jack provided. "Jackson Grenell."

The mouse nodded. "Jackson Grenell," he went on. "I — we— owe you more than you can know. Everything...." he paused, struggling for words.

"But we're not done yet, are we?" Jack sighed into the silence, pausing at his task and staring dismally at the blood washing down his leg.

Meynardo heaved a great sigh of his own and shook his head. "We... we cannot remain here," he managed finally. "Even had we the desire to rebuild in a place of such memories. The scent of death will carry, even in this weather. Other predators... larger, more fearsome, will follow it back, even do we rebuild the wards."

So now he was expected to adopt a tribe of mice? Was he hearing correctly? "And what would you have me do?" he wondered aloud as he stood to dig through the saddlebags for something with which to treat this newest batch of wounds.

"We must find a safe place," the mouse didn't hesitate. "Perhaps a protector of some sort. We are tiny, but we are fierce! There are many tasks we could perform for the right master in exchange for a safe place to live."

Jack paused as he was withdrawing the aid kit, thinking of Rosaluna. Wondering what the old woman would do to him if he brought her a basketful of talking rodents.

"I'm kind of in the middle of something," he ventured without real hope.

"We will aid you," Meynardo assured him.

Right. "You have any idea what I'm up against?" he wondered dubiously as he flopped back down to address the damage the dire hares had done.

"The bandit camp, obviously," Meynardo's voice was firm. "I was headed there when I found you. How many other reasons could there have been for you to be out there under arms?"

"You were heading for the bandit camp?" Jack couldn't believe his ears. "To do what?"

Meynardo raised an eyebrow, an act almost invisible in the darkness and wet. "I was going for help," he said matter-of-factly.

Jack stopped, his leg half wrapped, and stared. "You who the *what* now?"

Meynardo smiled a grim smile. "Oh, granted," he assured the man. "I was not about to request their aid straight out as I did yours. More like I was going to attack them and lead them back here. Introduce them to the dire hares and allow nature to take its course as it were."

Jack shook his head disbelievingly as he finished dressing the wounds on his leg. He started in on his hand, then. One of the hares had gotten a good bite of the back of it, but hadn't taken any chunks out.

"What makes you think you could've gotten them to chase you?" he wondered.

"My arrows," Meynardo stated grimly. "And my bow."

Jack remembered the hare convulsing after being hit. "Poison?" he wondered.

"Indeed," Meynardo nodded. "Derived from the venom of specially bred spiders, cultivated molds, and various plants. Oh, nothing that would kill a fully grown human, I'm afraid. But rest assured, it would be extremely painful, and not something to ignore."

Jack nodded, running his hands along his arms and his other leg, looking for more holes. "So, you just keep pricking them until they've had enough and decide you're trouble worthy of a chase?"

"Indeed," Meynardo repeated. "Although, I much prefer the outcome we arrived at.

"Uhm, your cheek is bleeding as well."

"Thanks," Jack grinned. "You're kind of a hard-ass, aren't you?"

The mouse measured himself. "I am Meynardo Chee-Ch-Cheep," he proclaimed somewhat forlornly. "Called Long Racer. I am a rank eight ranger. And, for my size, a renowned hard-ass.

"Now, will you aid us?"

Jack sighed softly to himself. He'd answered that question already, hadn't he? When he'd diverted to rescue the mouse's village. It was pretty obvious they weren't rescued yet, so what options did he have? "You do understand that I can't promise I'll even be alive by morning, don't you?"

"I have faith in you," Meynardo gave him a quick bow.

"How long will it take them to get ready?" Jack asked resignedly.

Meynardo turned to look up into the darkness of the ruined village. His people were moving about slowly, uncertainly. Many of them were still trying to come to grips with this latest tragedy which had befallen them. He doubted there would be much portable salvage, but there were personal belongings some would want to at least try to save. Some mementos of the lost.

"Not so long," he told the man. "There is not much left. But the dead must be put to rest. Such as we are able at least in this weather."

Having put himself together insofar as he might, Jack stowed the dwindling remains of the first aid supplies. He didn't bother yet to re-don his sodden clothing or armor. He couldn't sense anything out in the grass, and the soaked linen wouldn't warm him. He did throw his tattered cloak over his shoulders, though. Wool was itchy, but it did retain warmth even when wet.

"Anything I can do to help?" he asked.

Meynardo hesitated. "My... friend," he started. "My... brother in arms. We two were among those drawing the hares away to give the rest a chance to reach the refuge." He paused for a long breath. "He fell," his voice broke. "There," and he pointed northward. "It was then that I realized I alone would not be able to... when I decided I would need aid not to be found among my people."

Jack gave him a minute, but he didn't go on. He thought he might understand. Meynardo had shown no fear against the hares, but there were some things that required a different sort of bravery. Some things that you didn't want to be real, so you didn't want them confirmed. Couldn't see them confirmed.

"Let's go, then," he said softly. "He'll want to rest."

"Yes," Meynardo said, eyes downcast. "Thank you. That is the least of the debts I owe him."

"This was just the two of you?" Jack asked a few minutes later.

"Yes," Meynardo nodded. "In this direction. And more him than me, honestly."

They'd passed more than half a dozen dead hares already, and they were barely fifty yards from the former village. Meynardo drew up at an eighth body, dimly seen in the falling rain.

"Here," he announced. "Here is where he fell. My friend. My brother. Osmando Ch-Ch-Cheep, called half-tail. Son of—"

"I'm still alive, idiot!" came a muffled, barely understood voice from beneath the carcass. "Get this thing off of me!"

Meynardo froze for a moment, a look of shocked astonishment washing across his face. Jack, meanwhile, reached hurriedly down and pulled the hare clear by its ears, revealing a crumpled figure mashed into the mud beneath, one arm bent at an odd angle.

This one was more anthropoid than Meynardo, and wore pants, a blood-spattered off white linen shirt, and a black felt vest. A droop hat lay beside it, mashed flat, a bedraggled pinfeather protruding from the tiny silver band.

Meynardo reached hurriedly down and helped his injured friend to his feet, struggling to brush the mud from him as Osmando angrily slapped his hands away with his one good one. "Leave off, you," he grated. "I'm fine. Find me my bow if you want to be useful. It's somewhere over there," and he pointed over his shoulder.

Jack winced in pain as assurance and command infiltrated his brain. Osmando's speech was at once unintelligible and understood. Like a badly out of synch translation — an echo overlaying and overriding what was being said.

Shaking his head clear, Jack examined the hare, finding the cause of death. A needle thin shaft, broken at its midpoint and fletched with what looked to be frilled grass protruded from its throat. As though Osmando had rammed it in by hand rather than firing it from his bow. Well, that would explain his arm.

Osmando was eyeing Jack skeptically while this was going on, tilting his head this way and that. He clearly wasn't understanding what it was he was seeing. Just as clearly, he wasn't liking it.

"Here!" Meynardo called out from a short distance

away, holding aloft a bow very similar to and slightly larger than his own. "Found it!"

"Is it—?" Osmando started.

"It's fine!" Meynardo called back, already returning. "Didn't even break the string."

Osmando took the bow from his smaller friend's hands and turned to Jack. "You..." he ordered, looking up and hesitating. "...whatever you are. Unhand my kill, if you please?"

Frowning at both the tone and discordant delivery, Jack tossed the dead hare to the ground. What came next surprised him more than a little. Osmando approached the corpse, clutching his bow at its grip, and extending one limb out toward the beast.

Jack saw the jewel, then. A shard of aquamarine the size of a grain of wheat. Osmando mumbled something in a low voice and the jewel began to glow faintly. A familiar aura sheathed the hare. It began to fade only a moment later, along with the carcass, coalescing at last into a fountain of glittering sparkles of light floating gently skyward.

It was Jack's turn to stare open-mouthed at the small scattering of gifts that had taken its place.

Osmando, his task finished, gifts gathered, turned back and noticed, one eyebrow going up.

"How did you do that?" Jack wondered. "I thought you needed to be a priest or wizard to free souls like that without a bounty token."

Osmando reared back before turning to Meynardo. Meynardo shrugged. Both looked back to the man. "And why would you think such a thing?" Osmando asked bluntly. "Every child who takes the path of adventure is taught the freeing spell before reaching rank two. Only minor healing is taught before."

"It's true, then?" Meynardo asked. "You *are* ungifted? I thought surely— How, then, do you wield such powerful weapons? Wear such powerful armor? The way you fight.... you spoke of classes."

Jack was getting used to the echoing harmonics of the older mouse's voice now, and it no longer hurt his head. Much.

Scrubbing at his face with one hand, trying hard to cover embarrassment he shouldn't be feeling, he wondered how he could be expected to know? It wasn't as though either of the grand total of two mages he'd encountered since learning of his status had told him or anything, was it?

"I'm... not from around here," he told them after a moment. "Where I come from, things work... differently."

"Ah," Meynardo smiled, coming to his rescue. "Of course."

Osmando gave his friend the side eye, but remained, for the moment, silent.

"So, you *are* gifted?" Meynardo went on. "What rank are you then? What class, if I may ask?"

Jack wasn't sure he wanted to tell them. The older one would be even less likely to believe him. On the other hand, why should he care what a mouse thought of him?

But no. Glancing back at the trail of hares the pair had left in their wake, he realized he did care. He respected warriors. He respected bravery. And, truthfully, he wondered how he, himself, would fare pitted against a couple of dozen or so creatures twenty times his size and capable of swallowing him whole.

"Overall, I'm rank nine," he admitted finally. "Primarily, I'm a sentinel."

Four glowing eyes grew large as saucers in the darkness. Then Osmando snorted disbelievingly. "Of course you are," he sneered. "Because you're not from around here. Where you're from is a thousand years ago, and they don't learn to release Jehsha's gifts until rank ten there, eh? Ridiculous!"

"Osmando!" Meynardo scolded his friend.

"No," Jack held up a hand. "He's right to scoff, Meynardo," he said. "Or he would be if I'd come up the normal way."

He copped a squat so as not to loom so far above them. "Osmando," he began. "I know Meynardo's class and rank. What about yours? If you don't mind?"

Osmando seemed to be having as much difficulty understanding him as he'd been having understanding Osmando. The mouse thought about it for a moment before answering. "I am a March Warden," he told the man. "And my rank is seventeen."

Jack nodded, trying the math in his head, but lacking the background. "How long did it take you to reach nine?" he asked.

The mouse's eyes narrowed. "Two years," he said evenly. "Nearly three."

"And would it surprise you to know," Jack smiled, "that three days ago, I didn't know what a sentinel was? Or a rank?"

"That's absurd!" Osmando spat. "How, then, did you—?"

"Jehsha's Window," Jack told him. "Jehsha's Window granted me both my rank and my classes."

Neither mouse had an answer for that.

"You know about the mirrors, then?"

"We do," Meynardo answered in a subdued voice. "The master had a special one built for us in his castle in the early days. We have not seen one since the castle fell, however."

That wasn't hard to imagine. "So you guys really are adventurers, then?" he smiled.

"Monsters," Osmando growled. "We are classified as monsters."

Jack reared back at that, taken off guard. And by the time he'd gathered himself, the mice had moved away.

He caught up as Osmando was performing the ritual on the next of his victims. "Could you teach me that?" he asked hopefully.

"No," the mouse replied without turning.

"It is a thing for mages," Meynardo explained.

"Why would that—?"

"Because we cannot see clearly enough to know if you're doing it correctly," Osmando interrupted, still not turning from the glistening cloud of disbursing light. "If you were to do it *in-correctly*, there would be no way for us to know how you'd gone wrong, nor how to correct you, and any magic misapplied is dangerous."

Jack looked down at the younger mouse, who nodded agreement. He sighed heavily. "So I'm out of luck until I get

back, then, I guess," he lamented.

"Or perhaps Old Luciandro could teach you," Meynardo shrugged.

"Luciandro?" Jack wondered.

"Our mage," Osmando turned to him finally. "Same as taught us."

The older mouse in the robes, Jack decided. Strange it hadn't occurred to him before. The little guy might as well have been wearing a sign, dressed as he was.

The Bandits Prepare

"**N**othing," Hurgus announced to the bandit leader looming over him. "Oh, hundred or so rabbits, few foxes, a prairie cat and her cubs. But nothing human er humanoid s'far as I c'n scry."

Bear frowned down at the lesser journeyman dark mage where he crouched over a magic circle and a scattering of bones in the middle of the cabin's floor. "So, that'll be, what? Two lenn in any direction?"

"Bit less," Hurgus hunched his shoulders. "More like one. And a bit."

Great, Bear thought to himself. *That's just wondrous great.* Not like anybody hunting them might wander farther out than a single lenn, was it?

He growled like his namesake and turned away, stumping over to the table at the room's end and the bottle sitting atop it. Hurgus was near worthless, but he was what Bear had. Rank fourteen, he was, and had been since Bear had known him. Years, at this point. Which meant that he'd peaked. Regardless of any experience he'd gained or ever would, he'd never be more. Good for basic needs, decent with simple attacks, and a fair hand at wards, he was a mediocre mage without the gift to grow.

Which left Bear with the problem of how to find whoever appeared to be hunting them before whoever it was finished them off. Near half his band was already gone and he hadn't an inkling of what was happening. Damnation!

One thing sure, he'd no intention of sending anybody *else* out looking. Anything could take on Thumper and Bonce together wasn't nothing he wanted to meet with fewer than four or five men at his back. And considering as how that now accounted for just shy his full remaining force, he wasn't about to split them up.

"Keep at it," he growled before upending the bottle and taking a long pull of its rank contents. He stared down at the bottle in his hand as the burn washed through his upper body.

That old feeling was back. The one he hated. From back when that damned hero was wandering around loose and none of them able to stop the whoreson no matter *what* they tried. He shivered involuntarily.

He slammed the now much lighter bottle down and wiped a forearm across his mouth. "Well, keep at it! I wanna know if anything bigger'n a fox comes within a lenn of this camp!"

"Aye, Boss," Hurgus replied without looking up

Bear stood in the doorway, one hand on the frame, staring out into the muddy yard, scowling. Empty. He could see the whole of the station as though it were a cloudy afternoon despite the rain and the clouds, thanks to his dark sight; a rank five skill so common to his class it may as well have been a default.

He stood there for a few more moments, listening for anomalous sounds before grunting and setting out into the rain. They'd all be in the stable, no doubt. Hunkered down and crying for their mothers or some such.

He paused again just out of sight of the doorless opening. Nope. Not crying. They were doing something far worse. Searching around, he spied a tin bucket laying on its side in the shadow of the building. Taking it up and sidling up to the doorway, he swung it by its bail and flung it with some force into the stable, where it bounced from the far wall with all manner of racket.

He stormed in behind it, while all heads beneath the leaking roof were still turned to the clattering bucket. "What's this now?" he demanded in his best crack of doom voice.

Six heads snapped back towards the doorway, fear written upon their features.

"You!" Bear pointed a shaking finger at an older, rank fifteen highwayman. "Ephram! What manner of nonsense are you filling their damned empty heads with now! The Madwoman is a myth! She never existed! She was only something idiots made up as an excuse for losing battles they should've won!"

"W'Weren't neither!" Old Ephram stood his ground not quite steadily. "She were real, and her constructs was, too."

He smacked a hand against his chest. "*I* knowed a hobbie back when th' demon lord was alive, see'd 'er one time and lived t'tell the tale, be it only by a notch."

Bear glowered at him, but the old man didn't back down. True, he had to admit, hobgoblins lived long lives, and it was remotely possible Old Ephram had met one who'd been alive as long ago as The Madwoman was said to have been roaming and slaughtering. Equally true that creatures such as hobgoblins nor bandits were known for their strict adherence to truth telling.

But, and here was the important thing, did he let these chowderheads get it into their minds that The Madwoman might be back, they'd be off into the woods fleeing to the west by morning. That was something he wasn't about to let happen.

"Shut it!" he commanded. "Don't matter if she was or wasn't real." he gave an expansive wave of his arm, encompassing the whole of the world outside the doorway. "Not she nor her creatures ain't been seen in eighty-odd years."

Now he stabbed the finger at Old Ephram again. "So, even *If* she was, and I ain't sayin' she was... *If* she was, she ain't no more. So just you shut it about her and give more thought to what you might do t' keep your*self* alive past mornin'.

"Now...." and he set about putting them into some order. Not spread out higgledy piggledy, or too far out from the station, but far enough out to give some warning before they were, the lot of them, within bowshot of Thumper's bow.

They were none too happy about it, but the lot of them knew better than to cross the Bear when he was in this sort of mood.

Old Ephram, particularly, gave some considerable effort to grumbling when he was sure he was out of earshot. Oh, while he was where the Bear could see and hear him, he was square shouldered and straight backed. He even volunteered to take the least favorable watch, down by the old dock, where the mosquitoes were thick.

The Mauler narrowed his eyes, but nodded for him to go.

Ephram grinned and saluted, heading off for the water.

The Bear would have no way to know that Old Ephram had him a charm against the river monsters, and therefore a way out of this mess the others didn't. First sign of the Madwoman or any of her constructs, he'd be out of his armor and into the water, quick as a shot.

Sure, he'd lose all his gear and most of his plunder, but he'd be alive. His gold pouch was on his belt, and he was high-ranked enough to make it by alone in these low ranked zones. Long as he was careful and steered clear of the Mad Woman or her creatures, he'd make it back to the main force just fine.

Bear and these other idiots could fend for themselves, for all he cared. He'd no loyalty to any of them. He'd warned them, hadn't he? That was *more* than enough.

* * *

The guild hall door burst open, causing a dash of rain to enter and Tiglund to jump. Master Jonkins, of course, merely looked up. Cable strode across the room, not bothering with his cloak.

"Tig," he called, "hie yourself on over to my place and gather up Jube and Bor. We'll be needing them at Mohrdrand's villa—"

"Bor?" the guildmaster raised an eyebrow.

"Big roan gelding with a great white spot on top of his head and a scarred muzzle," Tiglund supplied helpfully, a wide grin on his face.

"You don't say," the guildmaster scrubbed at his beard with a contemplative hand, giving Cable the eye.

"Eh hem," Cable mushed on. "And do you saddle Molly up for yourself," he ordered the boy.

"Where're we going?" Tiglund straightened, brightening.

"*We're* not," Cable told him seriously. "*I'm* going north with the novice mage. *You're* going to drop off the horses and beeline straight to your parents' farm. You gather your family and you bring them..." he turned to Jonkins, who nodded resignedly. "You bring them here. The guild hall should be safe."

Tiglund was looking between the two men, back and forth, his face clouding.

"What we're going to face," Cable spoke before the boy

could ask, "ain't something I'm absolutely certain we can handle. I may not be back. In that case, Tig, Molly's yours. Hell, the whole place, if you want it."

"But Cabe!" Tiglund lurched from his chair. "You're joking, right?" He turned to the guildmaster. "He's joking?"

Jonkins' face was stern when he shook his head. "He's got the right of it, Tig," he confirmed. "And if he falls, it's up to us —you and me— to protect the town."

"Now go!" Cable waved the boy out. "Time's precious. I'll meet you at Mohrdrand's soon's I'm done. You know how to get in?"

He didn't, of course. So Cable explained the way.

Once the boy had gone, the big man sighed and rubbed his forehead. "Bor—?"

"Y'mean me, or the horse?" Jonkins queried dryly, even as he drew the rank thirty an ale.

Cable chuckled despite himself. "I mean, he really does favor you, y'know."

"The gelding."

"Well, not that, I suppose," Cable made his way to the bar, although he didn't take seat. "I'm only guessing, of course."

He took the mug and downed a good swallow while Jonkins stood with his arms crossed. When he'd done, he set the mug on the bar top and wiped his mouth. "Girl hasn't got the bounty token, Bor," he told the older man. "Gave it to the sentinel, she says."

"Well, then, give me—" but Cable was already holding his guild token out.

Jonkins took the token and fed it into the chronicler. This wasn't a usual thing, but it could be done. He brought up the bounty and, consulting a dog-eared book beside the machine, drew a series of glyphs within the field, finally enclosing both the token and the glyphs within a nine pointed star. Then they waited.

It took a moment or two. Jonkins wasn't a mage, he was only following instructions written by one, while the device provided the magical energy. Eventually, though, the token and glyphs began to glow with a faint light. The lights began to pulse, each with its own cadence. The pulses altered, moving into synchronization until they beat as one. The pulse faded until token and glyphs once more shone steadily. The spell faded.

Pulling Cable's token free, Jonkins observed the bounty and nodded. "There you go, Antel," he tossed the guild token to the spearman. "You're officially a member of the party."

Cable nodded, drained his ale, and headed for the door.

"Wait," Jonkins called to his back before he'd gotten three paces. Cable turned and Jonkins tossed him the gold ring. "This belongs to the girl," he said. "Make sure she gets it."
Cable caught the ring and turned back for the street.

"Luck!" Jonkins called after him. He'd need it.

* * *

Within the shadow of a small copse of trees well east and a bit north of Mokkelton, there formed a shimmering pool of darkness. A few seconds only, it shimmered, growing and spreading, until a shambling, hirsute form lunged clear of it. Four more followed, at which point the pool collapsed in upon itself with a soft pop.

The five figures stood for a few moments, acclimatizing themselves to this new place, checking weapons, testing the air with upraised snouts. Two bore ugly short swords, two carried crudely fashioned crossbows, and the fifth, and larger creature, a sword and buckler.

After four or five minutes, at a nod and grunt from the largest beast, they set out towards the west at a ponderous trot.

The Tiniest Wizard

Jack sat cross-legged, draped in his tattered cloak, and cursed softly under his breath. He'd tracked the old mouse in the robes down finally, to ask him about the soul release, and maybe the healing Osmando had mentioned. As much damage as he was taking, that one seemed like it would be pretty useful.

He had, of course, run headfirst into yet another problem. The old guy seemed to speak Tandrian exclusively. Jack couldn't understand a syllable, even in the painfully echoey way he understood Osmando.

Meynardo was still off with his friend sorting their kills, which meant that *he* couldn't help. So there he sat, frustration eating at him along with the cold, the wet, and the ever increasing urge to be moving before his enemies moved.

The mouse mage tried a few more times, speaking more slowly, but to no avail. One or two words got through once he'd slowed to a crawl, but not nearly enough to matter. Finally, the old mouse turned toward where the others were going through the rubble and raised his voice.

A tiny little bit of a mouse broke away from the group and scampered over, bringing up before the old one and looking up. He was about seventy percent house mouse, with a quivering nose and button eyes. But he held himself upright and listened intently to what the old mouse was telling him.

After a few moments, the youngster nodded, turned to Jack, and squeaked. No recognizable words, only the sound of a common mouse. But as he did, Jack heard the words come into his head, something like the way Rosaluna's did, and a bit like Meynardo's, but not quite like either's.

I am Amiandro, Jack heard. *Son of Orimondro, called crook-tail. Grandson of Montenardo, called Longfoot. I speak as the voice of Grandfather Luciandro, called Bright Hand. He of the first generation, son of the master himself. Wisest of the mice of Castle Scarpwatch. The Tiniest Wizard.*

Grandfather Luciandro, he went on, *thanks the human*

person for his aid in our hour of need, and wonders what Grandfather can do for the human person. He turned to look over his shoulder as if to verify his message. The old mouse nodded.

Jack was somewhat taken aback. The obviously high ranking magic user was unable to manage the telepathic spell, but the little kid could do it? And Meynardo as well, obviously. Even Osmando to some extent. Jack had gotten it into his head somehow that telepathy was a high ranking spell and that Rosaluna kind of had a lock on it. Even the rings seemed to be high order items that only she could craft.

But if he'd been wrong and it was more widespread, why could the kid do it but not the elder?

"Tell him he's very welcome," he told Amiandro. "And tell him I was wondering if he could help me learn a few things. Concerning the use of magic."

Amiandro nodded and turned back to the old... wizard, who took it all in, free hand stroking what Jack suddenly realized was a long white beard depending from his muzzle.

After a bit, he addressed the youngster. Amiandro turned to Jack and shook his head sadly. *Grandfather regrets that he is unable, at this time, to do this thing.*

"Might I ask why?" Jack frowned.

Amiandro turned again, again exchanging dialog with the old wizard. Turning back, he addressed Jack. *It is not that he is unwilling,* he explained. *Grandfather begs the human person to understand. It is the words. To properly instruct, the words must be the same. Too slow to go through a youngling. Mistakes make bad things happen too quickly, and there is much danger for all involved.*

That made sense. Another roadblock.

The mouse wizard was speaking again, and the youngster was looking apprehensive, glancing back over his shoulder at Jack once or twice, an uncertain look on his face.

There is a way, the sending sounded hesitant. *If the human person is willing.*

"You don't sound happy about it," Jack pointed out.

I am not, Amiandro answered, nose twitching. *It is not*

something I have ever done before, and it frightens me a little.

"You?"

Amiandro straightened to his full height. *I will be Grand-father's apprentice in a few years,* he announced proudly. *Even now, I sometimes help. But... but not like this.*

"It's dangerous, then?"

Grandfather says not, Amiandro told him. *But possibly painful. Possibly very painful.*

"Then don't—"

There is a debt, the young mouse insisted. *You were in-jured saving us. Should I be afraid of—*

"You don't owe me a thing, kid," Jack frowned. "I didn't do it because of you. I did it because of me."

The youngster clearly didn't understand. He turned to the older mouse and they went back and forth again. For a good while this time. When he turned back to Jack, his face was reso-lute. *I will help Grandfather, then,* he met Jack's eyes squarely, *because of me, and not because of you.*

Jack sighed resignedly. That's what pride did to you. Made you stupid. "Okay, Amiandro," he shrugged. "What is this way you speak of?"

I will share your words with Grandfather Luciandro, he said simply.

"Aren't you already doing that?" Jack was confused.

No, the youngster shook his head. *Show words.*

"You're going to teach me Tandrian, then?"

I cannot do that, the youngster admitted. *I will show your words to Grandfather and he will learn them through me.*

Jack rocked back. That sounded like a horrible idea! "So you're going to look around inside my head and gather up all the words," he wondered incredulously. "And what? Send them to your... to Luciandro? Kid, you do *not* want to go rummaging around in my memories. There's things in there you do NOT want to see, I promise you. I wouldn't put you through that."

Amiandro seemed confused. *No,* he insisted. *Not memo-ries. Words. Words not...* he had his hands up now, framing his head. *Not stored? Kept? Stored. In same place. Only look at words.*

His sendings had been pretty smooth and coherent at the beginning of this conversation, Jack thought. But they were getting more choppy as the conversation went along. The kid must be pretty nervous.

"And Luciandro can't do this himself why, exactly?" he wondered.

Amiandro tilted his head in puzzlement.

"I mean, if you can do this spell, why can't he?"

Spell? The sending bore the wash of confusion. *No spell. I mean, yes, there is a spell to learn, but talking... me talking to you... this is not a spell, it is only the way we are.*

Jack's own confusion was growing. "I don't follow."

The youngster was growing frustrated, it was clear. *Only the young mindspeak,* he said as though everyone should know that. *Mouths not able to make human words, so mindspeak. Once mouth... grows?* He squinted his eyes as though he were trying to see something far away. *Evolves? Once mouth can make words, we make words, and mindspeak goes away.*

Jack had his eyes closed as he took this in. Okay. Part of who —no, what— they were. Monsters, he remembered Osmando saying. Tiny little monsters who wore clothes, worked magic, and raised families. And this master of theirs.... He had a pretty good notion that the master wasn't a mouse. Not even close.

"Are..." he asked hesitantly. "Are you guys constructs?"

The little mouse screwed his face up, struggling. *Maybe? The word doesn't match very well, but I don't know what to look for. Grandfather would know, but he can't see until he learns.*

"Wait a minute," Jack held up a hand. "Until *he* learns? You mean he's going to learn English?"

Yes, Amiandro said, puzzled. *Isn't that what I said?*

Oh. Yeah, it was, wasn't it? Jack put his hand over his face. *Why couldn't I have just bit the bullet and watched the damned subs?* He asked himself for the thousandth time. *Or listened to all the weebs on the boards who insisted the noble path was to invest in lessons and watch in the true anime tongue.* "And how long is this going to take?" he wondered aloud. "I've got things I'm supposed to be doing that I can't just ignore."

The youngster turned. Not long this time. *Two hours, Grandfather says,* the answer came with a distraught squeak. *Maybe more if there are lots of words.*

Too long. "I don't have that much time to waste," Jack told the young mouse. "I suppose we'll have to put it off until there's time."

More palaver with the old mouse, and there was real fear in the mouseling's sending when he once more turned to Jack. *Grandfather says that you will have to make time if you expect to live past the coming day.*

Jack rocked his head back at that. *The hell?*

You are hunting the dark humans from the camp to the south, Grandfather says, the youngster went on. *He says that among them is a dark mage of some rank, and that you will need Grandfather's aid if you hope to defeat him, or even survive his attention.*

Jack lowered his head and closed his eyes, remembering the bandit on the road where they'd found the butchered farmers, and his ragged claims regarding his comrades. Eleven, he'd sobbed. Including a rank fourteen dark mage. Then he remembered what Tiarraluna had done to that selfsame bandit, frying him with lightning until his hair had started smouldering in spite of his wearing of warded armor. Tiarraluna who was only rank ten.

"What can he tell me about this mage?" he asked Amiandro quietly. "Is there no defense against him?"

The mouseling wasn't too happy with that question. He wasn't used to hearing anyone question Luciandro's wisdom. Nonetheless, he turned and conveyed the question. And thus began a torturous back and forth as the human person attempted to worm his way out of doing what he must already know was the right thing.

* * *

Along the road between Rosaluna's cottage and Mokkel-

ton, five shambling figures paused as one, noses raising to the sky. Acute senses led them to the scorched patches of grass where their brethren had fallen. Given the darkness and intermittent rain, that was the extent of their discovery.

The original flit had shown the pair of killers proceeding to the west, and so they followed, keeping well clear of the roadway. None had any idea how they'd find their quarry, insofar as their kind had ideas at all. For the most part, they followed orders, fed, and slept.

The champion, however, possessed a slightly higher level intellect than its troops. It understood its mission. Clear the spawn zone, search, remain undetected by the locals, kill. It also possessed a reader which it had been shown how to use. There would be some sort of mass habitation ahead somewhere. Humans held to them whenever possible. Once within sight of one, they would go to ground and release the twenty flits they'd brought with them. If the quarry remained within, the flits would find them.

Runstable's Enchanted Overland Speeding Wagon

"I really should—" Mohrdrand started again.

You really should not. Rosaluna repeated firmly.

"But I'm the only one who can drive—"

Along with Cable, once you show him the way of it. She interrupted. *You will travel with them long enough to assure that Cable is capable of controlling the wagon and then you will return. But you* must *return here as soon as you are able. You* must not *accompany them the whole of the way.*

"It's not so easy as that, woman," he growled. "Nor remotely simple. Think you controlling so powerful an enchantment is no more than driving a dog cart?"

You will not be teaching him dressage, Mohrdrand, she shot back. *He need know only how to start, steer, and stop.*

"Oh," he put hands to hips. "is that all? And I suppose—"

Mind your tone, old man, Rosaluna cautioned, shifting her eyes to her granddaughter without moving her head. *I do not wish for her to become even more distraught.*

Mohrdrand heaved another in a long line of exasperated sighs, struggling to bring his temper more firmly under control. At times, the old woman seemed to forget that the whole of the world did not share her ability to instantly adjust to impossible tasks.

The speedwagon was an incomprehensibly intricate device that had taken its original creator nearly thirty years to bring to a near complete state, and Mohrdrand another five to get properly working after his acquisition of it. And well should she know, for he'd solicited her aid on more than one occasion in its completion.

"It is to be assumed you wish them to survive the journey?" he asked mock sweetly when he'd gotten himself under control.

Her eyes flared and her lips flattened.

"It's not so simple as rolling a ball down a hill," he leaned in. "Nor so easy as riding a horse down a smooth trail."

Tiarraluna remained as she'd been when Cable had left, and continued to watch the conversation intently, growing ever more apprehensive. She'd never seen Uncle so angry. Not in her whole life. Nor Grandmother, who, while she had no outer voice to gauge anger by, exposed her emotion by way of the grim set of her face and the force with which she gripped Tiarraluna's shoulder.

It was difficult, but not impossible to determine the path of the long argument from Uncle's side only. He apparently wanted to accompany them. Grandmother would seem to disagree. Adamantly and at length. Why, she wondered. What was happening that she wasn't being told?

Mohrdrand had continued his litany of the difficulties in the control of the speedwagon, but Rosaluna remained firm.

I see that a young man is bringing you horses, Old Man, she interrupted at last. *Make your wagon ready. My granddaughter and I have a few more things to discuss in private, and will leave you to it. We will join you in a short while so that we may instruct her in her part of its operation.*

You and I will continue this discussion later.

"Oh?" he frowned, rearing back in his chair. "Am I to be dismissed in my own home, now? No more than a common lackey?" when he was not answered, he harrumphed angrily. "Very well, then, oh great enchantress," he growled. "But mark you, we will *absolutely* continue this discussion. And before there is any leave taking, you may rest assured." he surged to his feet, exasperated near beyond reason, and stomped out.

* * *

Tiglund hesitated just inside the compound gate, bowing to the wizard as the old man stomped out into the yard, slamming the door angrily in his wake. The wizard waved for Tig to follow him toward the collection of strange shapes he was heading for. Confused, Tiglund did not immediately respond. What were they supposed to be hitching the horses *to*?

The wizard was walking in the direction of several things that looked *somewhat* like coaches, but not altogether that

much. For one thing, he saw no sign of traces on any of them, nor anywhere to connect traces. Nor any seats for a driver or guard.

The near cart... carriage... thing... he thought might be the front. It had a sloping glass window stretching across its width. It was otherwise smooth but for a pair of swooping and gold trimmed fenders with large, brass, directional lanterns mounted atop them, one to each side. Those fenders covered obviously steerable wheels, with fat tires like overstuffed leather sausages wrapped around the rims.

It was also the only one with wheels at all four corners, and it had six of them. And had another, with fewer wheels, and they all on one end, mounted on top of it, like a pair of giant, fornicating turtles.

What's more, each of the... wagons, he supposed... were huge. Far too large for a single team of horses to pull, let alone with any speed. The six wheeled coach with the windows and door must have stood nine or ten feet ground to roof, and twenty-five feet front to back. And that not even counting the windowless contraption leaning on its tail like some sort of gargantuan goose dipping its bill to drink. That thing must be twelve feet high all on its own and another twenty or twenty-five feet long.

Tiglund wouldn't bet a bent copper piece the thing would move across the yard with fewer than an eight-up of solid drafts, and he'd brought a pair of glorified farm horses Cable had received as reward for some mundane quest or other.

The wizard had paused and was staring angrily his way, so he ducked his head and followed.

Mohrdrand had the boy tie the horses off to one of the rings flanking the brightwork of the lead motive carriage and showed him how to open the rear doors and lower the ramp. That done, he bade the boy to lead the horses up and inside one at a time.

Cable came to a halt in the gateway in his turn, his mind

struggling to wrap itself around what he was looking at. Tiglund had obviously already arrived, as one the horses was tied off to what Cable hoped wasn't what he thought it was. He knew better of course. What else would it be? He wasn't sure what he'd been expecting a magical wagon to look like, but this was certainly not it.

Skinned in shining black lacquer, with elaborate gold piping, sheets of glass, and an improbable number of odd wheels, it was as gilded as it was long. And it was ridiculously long. How were they expected to maneuver such a thing even through the gate he occupied, let alone through the town's narrow streets and out onto the highway? How had they even gotten it in here?

He'd never seen anything like it. Hadn't even imagined anything close.

Tiglund appeared around the far side of the far end near the horse while Cable was still trying to come to grips with what he was seeing. Tig waved, and he gave a half wave back before finally entering the yard.

Tiglund untied the horse and swung around behind the whatever, so Cable followed. He rounded the corner in time to see Tig leading the horse up into the brightly lit interior. *What? For what possible reason...?*

* * *

The moment the angry wizard had slammed the door behind him, Rosaluna bade her granddaughter to take the chair to her right.

Tiarraluna sat, leaning forward intently in hopes of finding out what was going on beneath the surface of what she'd been told.

Rosaluna regarded the young girl for a long moment, until Tiarraluna had begun to squirm.

Button?

"Grandmother?" the girl responded nervously.

You explained to me earlier that Jack san often spoke to FoeSmite, yes? That at one point, he called and she came to him?

"Yes?" her reluctance to speak of the hero was evident in her tone.

Has she ever spoken back?

"She, Grandmother?" the girl asked, puzzled.

FoeSmite, Button, Rosaluna frowned. *Has she ever spoken to Jack san?*

"As I told you, Grandmother," Tiarraluna responded with a frown of her own. "The first time he called. During the fight with the teufel-things. He told me that FoeSmite called to him. Urged him to summon it. But only that once, and he was sick and dizzy from the poison. Feelings only since that time, he told me. Difficult to sense. He was not entirely sure that any of it was anything more than his imagination."

And you, girl? She asked. *Has she never spoken to you?*

Tiarraluna's confusion was deepening. "No, Grandmother," she shook her head firmly. "FoeSmite does take on something of a glow when Jack is in combat, but nothing I could call communication. And never addressed at me. Why would it?"

Rosaluna nodded to herself, eyes closed in thought. Not ideal. Still, even partially awakened....

She was no less worried about her Button than old Mohrdrand. Well she knew the perils inherent in what was to come. The foes the girl would be racing to face could well end her were she not cautious. Yes, and a bit lucky. And yet the bitterest of pills; there was naught for it.

Dread it though she might, Rosaluna knew with an iron certainty that Button must go to the hero. Her hero. And harsh on her long missing tongue the phrase lay. And furthermore, Mohrdrand must remain behind. More than the hero's fate alone, or even Button's was in the balance if her fears were valid. Still, there were yet things she could do, though she prayed they would not turn out to be necessary.

Here, child, she steadied herself. *Give me your bag for a moment.*

Tiarraluna nervously fetched her new bag and brought it to the old woman.

Rosaluna took the bag and lay it in her lap. Holding the

strap up before her and closing her eyes, she ran a hand along the length of it, seeming to caress the jewels it was studded with. Slowly tapping a cadence against the surface of each one. The process took some time.

Her eyes opened, startling the girl who'd leaned in close in an attempt to see what she was doing. Rosaluna smiled a quiet smile, and passed her old bag to her granddaughter.

"What did you do, Grandmother?" Tiarraluna wondered. "What was that?"

A ward, the old woman's eyes twinkled. *To keep you safe in the direst of circumstances. It is my sincere hope that it never activates, for that would signify that your peril was deadly.*

Now, she began rummaging through her newly made, as yet incomplete traveling bag, *You will need these things if you are to prevail,* and she began to haul things out and explain their nature.

* * *

Cable stood silently at the opening of the strange wagon, leaning against the frame, arms crossed, a frown on his face. He watched silently as the wizard and the boy worked to strap the horses to some sort of strange framework that seemed to be the primary feature of the... what? Wain? Coach? Wagon?

After a few moments, Mohrdrand happened to look his way and straightened, an angry frown warping his beard. "You really should be helping us do this," he spat irritably. "You'll need to know how to both unharness and reharness them once you've finished your journey."

"*How?*" Cable asked with raised brow. "Old man, I'm still trying to work my mind around *why*. Why, for instance, are you lashing the horses *inside*, the damned thing?" he gestured broadly at the animals strapped into near immobility. "How're they expected to pull the damned thing from up in here?"

"Pull?" the wizard measured himself, his eyes going wide. "Whoever said they'd be pulling? Not I, surely.

"Listen to me, Cable," he squared his shoulders and put fists to hips. "Did you think the speedwagon no more than a vegetable cart? A wheeled box to lug manure about? No, my friend, it is far, far more than that, I promise you. The speed-wagon is a ruinously complicated, vastly elaborate wildly magical apparatus, capable of hauling vegetables, manure, *or* adventures, around for distances and at speeds that most cannot begin to imagine.

"The horses do not pull the wagon, Cable," he explained. "They power the engine that pulls it.

"There!" he shot a stiffened arm, pointing between the hooves of the near horse. "The wide belts they stand on. Those belts roll beneath their hooves, pulled along by the movement of their gait, and so the horses themselves must remain stationary. Hence the process of harnessing them in place. The bed beneath the belts has been enchanted with a permanent charm to remove any and all friction, so that the horses need not overcome that impediment as well as the resistance of the sprockets."

"Wait," Cable held up his own hand, halting the wizard mid speech. "Removes all friction? You're talking about Slip, aren't you? Isn't that a high level dungeon trap?"

"That is its most common use, yes." the wizard nodded, frowning, " But it has many others.

"Now, where was I? Ah! There!" he pointed to a place before the horses and hidden by some sort of cabinet. The engine itself. Connected to the belt by sprockets and chains. It converts the rotation of the sprockets into mana... enhances it, multiplies it—"

"Stop!" Cable gave the outstretched hand a shake, a horrified expression on his face. "Just... stop."

"What now?" Mohrdrand looked up from his impromptu lecture, annoyed at the constant interruptions.

"You're talking about Demon Spark, aren't you?" Cable asked, the first hand still out, the other now covering his face.

"Hmm?" Mohrdrand raised an eyebrow. "Greater Demon Spark, actually, but yes. Why?"

"Because it's another dungeon trap," Cable spat, the hand coming away from his eyes. "And a ruinously high ranked one at that.

"Five years, I traveled and fought with the Hero's army," he told the old wizard. "And I never so much as heard of anyone but him or his party delving into a dungeon ranked high enough to encounter demon spark, let alone *greater*. How? How did you find— no, how did you manage to *cast* it? Where did you even find the tome to learn it?"

Mohrdrand straightened and regarded the spearman for a moment. "I didn't," he said matter-of-factly. "The original builder of the speedwagon was responsible. I didn't actually build the speedwagon myself, you see. At least, not its major components. I acquired it in an estate auction some years ago, after the builder's death."

"I see," Cable finally drew in his hand, moving it to his forehead. "Consumed by his creation, then?"

Mohrdrand scowled at the jape. "He died in the service of the sixth hero," he said evenly. "The exact particulars remain uncertain."

"Fine," Cable closed his eyes. "Fine. How many, then?"

"How many?"

"How many traps are built into this infernal rolling grand dungeon?" Cable clarified. "How much of dark magic?"

"Ah," Mohrdrand smiled. "As to that—"

"No!" the hand came up again. "No. On second thought, I do *not* want to know. And please stop explaining how it works. It only makes it worse."

The old wizard stood bemused as Cable worked his way through the situation.

"Just... just show me how to wrangle the thing," Cable sighed at last. "I'll have to make do with trying to pretend it's not a barn-sized clot of dark magic that will no doubt kill me within the day."

They were in the forecarriage going over the vehicle's operation when Rosaluna and her granddaughter, having finished their talk, made their way out into the yard. Cable was growing a bit surly as the sheer magnitude of the energy wreathing the wagon ate at his nerves. For, while Mohrdrand had honored his request and stopped explaining the minutia, the very nature of the controls spoke loud their own warnings. The air within the forecarriage's interior was charged with tension.

And then Rosaluna passed a hand over a pedestal between the front and rear benches, causing a latch to click and a cover to rise, exposing what could only be the life stone of a high-ranked monster nestled within. One look was all it took. Nothing smaller than rank eighty had dropped that, Cable thought to himself, his face closing down harder than ever.

Tom Black

Jack and Luciandro Have a Talk

They'd been at it for awhile, and all three were growing frustrated. What's more, as his agitation grew, the youngster's translations became more hesitant, less reliable. Jack was forced to admit that, if he were to gain anything positive from the wizard, he'd have to do so directly. And what *had* been getting through had convinced him that he'd be better off learning what he could than going in alone against what was looking like a far more dangerous group than he'd been anticipating.

Grandfather says that this would go more smoothly if you used a focus, Amiandro suggested, his sending tinged with equal parts relief and trepidation.

"I don't have one," he shrugged.

The little one turned to consult his elder before turning back. *You have amber, Grandfather says,* he sent. *He can sense it, Grandfather says.*

Jack rocked his head back a bit. He hadn't known that was possible. "It's not exactly mine to use,"

Another consultation. *Grandfather asks if he may see it,* Amiandro relayed. *It feels strange, Grandfather says.*

Jack gave it some thought. Then he shrugged. What harm could it do? The mouse wizard was almost certainly better equipped to figure the thing out than he was anyway. He dug through his pouch and retrieved the shard, passing it to the youngster, who passed it to the older mouse.

Luciandro's eyes widened as he examined the gem. He rattled off something to the youngling without looking up.

Grandfather asks where you acquired this thing? Amiandro queried.

"It's a life stone."

Now Amiandro's eyes widened. *What sort of creature dropped such a stone?* He asked without consulting his elder.

Jack took a deep breath before answering. He wasn't sure they'd believe him, given what Tiarraluna had told him. "An ungifted farmer who'd been killed by these bandits I'm hunting," he said, voice level.

Amiandro took a moment to digest that before relaying the information. It was clear he wasn't sure was he being lied to or told the truth.

After a further moment, Luciandro's eyes rose to meet Jack's, a hard glint to them. He nodded. He, at least, believed. He went on at some length to his apprentice before the youngster turned back to Jack.

Grandfather wonders, did you avenge this man? He queried, obviously leaving some things out.

Jack gave it some thought. Had he? Or had he simply...? "I killed the man who killed him," he admitted at last. "Whether it was avengement or something else, I can't really say. It might just have been.... No, let's just leave it at that."

Amiandro stared up at him for a few heartbeats, his little face screwed up in a peculiar expression. Then he turned and conveyed what Jack hoped was his message to the wizard. The way the kid seemed able to look into his head, it might have been something completely removed.

Grandfather says that he will wait until he may speak to you directly before requesting the rest of the story, Amiandro broke into his introspection, holding out the amber shard. *But for now, you should be able to use this life stone without harm to either of you. He will show you how.*

Jack shook himself and looked to the wizard.

Luciandro was casting about in the mud, looking for something. Eventually, he picked up what was either a small pebble or a large grain of sand. Looking up to be sure Jack was watching, he made a show of holding the fingers of his right hand rigidly straight, forefinger and ring finger slightly beneath the middle finger. Sort of a triangle. He waited for Jack to mimic the action. Which he belatedly did.

Now Luciandro took the pebble and placed it between the three fingers, at the first knuckle. It took some squinting before Jack could see what had been done and copy this action.

More consulting before Amiandro came in close to examine Jack's grip. He nodded, turning back and assuring his elder that the gem was being held correctly.

You are supposed to place the tips of your fingers against the top of my head, Grandfather says, the little guy was shaking. *And to try and empty your mind, if you can. Or to concentrate on something that you know, that will free your mind from wandering... Grandfather says.*

Jack had to squint to understand what was being sent now. He thought he understood. He hoped he did. He reached down to gently place the tips of the fingers holding the amber shard against the tiny grey head.

As for emptying his mind, he'd never been able to wrap his brain around meditation, but he thought he understood what Amiandro had meant about concentrating on something he knew. His initial thought was to go through staff forms, but he quickly discarded that notion. He didn't trust FoeSmite to stay out of things, and he *sure* didn't want *it* involved.

Sword forms, then. He closed his eyes and wondered which set, growing more accustomed to how easily he could bring forth each and every one he'd ever studied. Sabers first, he decided. He started picturing himself going through the nine guards. Then the nine cuts, and then the thrusts. And on and on. Once he'd gone through the lot, he moved to rapier. Then rapier and dagger. Small sword, Long sword, sword and shield, Then....

It is done, Amiandro broke his concentration, his sending feeling exhausted.

"Huh?" he shook his head and drew back. "Already? I thought—"

A new voice caught at his ears. "It's been nearly three hours, Jackson Grenell," the old wizard said aloud in American English, complete with Midwestern accent. "You've got quite a vocabulary."

The voice sounded like him if he'd inhaled some helium. "Uhm...."

"Side effect of the spell," the wizard shrugged. "It'll go away before long, as the words and syntax sort themselves out in my head."

"Right." Jack closed his eyes for a moment and rubbed at

the lids. He had a colossal headache. Opening them, he looked to the sky. The rain had stopped, but it was still pretty overcast, and he didn't see much of the moon beyond a bit of a glow above the clouds. "We're looking at, what, around midnight, d'you think?" he asked.

"Roughly," Luciandro replied. "Now, you wanted to learn the soul release?"

"No time," Jack told him. "I'm up against some pretty substantial opposition, and I've already given them way too much time to get set."

"Not sure you really understand your position, then," the mouse said.

"Right," Jack acknowledged. "The mage. How big a problem is he gonna be, and what do I do about him without any useable magic of my own?"

The old mouse gave him the eye and shrugged again. "Alone? Get killed. Even if you had magic, given what Meynardo has told me, at your rank you wouldn't stand a chance against him."

Jack's shoulders slumped and he lowered his head. There it was. *Some hero*.

"With my help, on the other hand," Luciandro continued, bringing Jack's head up. "If we get a little bit lucky and our timing works out, I suggest putting an arrow into his forehead." He poked a stiffened finger just above the bridge of his own muzzle. "Right here." He lowered the hand the finger was attached to and smiled. "I've found that that generally sorts just about anyone out, wizard, mage, dire hare, or ogre."

"Just that easy?" Jack asked, not really believing it would be anything of the sort.

The mouse chuckled without humor. "If we can get close enough without being spotted. If he's somewhere where we can get a line of sight on him. And if you can make the shot quickly and on the first try," he paused just an instant for effect. "Then yes."

"I'm smelling a whole lotta if coming off this process," Jack grumbled.

Another shrug. "You have to understand, Jackson Grenell," the wizard said. "I've been fighting nonstop for three days, using mana at an unsustainable rate. Now, after pulling your language from your head, I've even less remaining.

"What's more, in order to get your large carcass close enough to make the shot, I'll be burning through what remains to me much more quickly than I'll be recovering it. Unless you've got some spare potions you aren't using."

At Jack's negative, he went on. "I'm afraid I won't be able to deal with even a rank fourteen on my own unless you're willing to wait a few days for me to regain my full measure. Which I know you aren't.

"So," and he spread his arms wide. "I will attempt to get us close enough to the camp without your being seen by the scrying spells he's no doubt pouring over at this very moment, if they're as worried about you as you say. Beyond that, I'm afraid, I'll be of little more use.

"I won't be able to fully stop him from casting any sorts of attack magic, for instance," he went on. "And it goes without saying that you won't be invisible to the naked eye. Only to the scrying spell."

"So where does that leave me?" Jack wondered half to himself. "Fried, froze, or blasted?"

Another shrug. "One thing I *should* be able to do even then is to weaken his wards. For a moment only."

"Which means?" Jack perked up.

"You will have one chance. If, once I drop the spell concealing you from his magic, you can loose an arrow quicker than he can complete an attack spell or warn his compatriots, he'll be trying to cast or call with an arrow buried," and the finger went back to his forehead, "right here. I should think that would make casting quite a bit more difficult. I know *I* wouldn't want to try it."

So, a snap shot, then. How far could he manage that sort of thing with that sort of precision? "I'm gonna need to be pretty close," he murmured.

Luciandro frowned. "How close?"

"Unfamiliar bow," Jack ticked off on his fingers. "Dark. Tired." he quirked a lip. "Twenty-five, thirty yards, maybe."

"So," the old mouse mused. "Inside the camp."

"Well inside," Jack affirmed. "Given what I saw of the layout this afternoon. And I'm not sure how well I'm going to be able to pull that off with the bunch of them already on the alert.

"And we don't even know where the guy is, so we won't know where I'll need to be, or even if I'll be able to see him from anywhere I'm liable to be able to reach."

He sighed heavily, almost a cough. "No matter, I guess," he grumbled. "Not like I have a choice, is it?"

Luciandro ran the fingers of one hand through his wispy beard. *It's actually just like that,* he thought to himself. There was no true reason the camp must be taken tonight. Only the drive within the breast of the sentinel. He foreswore to mention this, however. The man was already strung taught as a bow-string. *Wait a moment!*

"Meynardo!" he called with some volume. To Jack, he held up a forestalling finger, smiling.

Meynardo arrived a few moments later, panting, to bring up before the wizard. "You wished to see me?"

"I know you must be weary to the bone," Luciandro addressed him. "But have you any energy left at all?"

Meynardo narrowed his eyes, cocking his head. He looked up at Jack, then back at the wizard. "What will you of me, Luciandro?" he asked evenly.

"We were wondering where their mage might be hiding himself," Luciandro told him. "And I was thinking, wouldn't it be fine if I had, say, a ranger somewhere about who could sneak into the bandit camp and locate him for us."

Meynardo sighed, allowing his shoulders to slump. "And I suppose you'll be waiting right here for news?"

Luciandro smiled benignly.

Meynardo spared Jack another look and a nod before bowing to the older mouse and turning away, shouting, "Osmando! How many arrows do you have left!"

In a matter of moments, quiver partially refilled, he was

off into the taller grass to the south.

Luciandro nodded and regarded his new friend. "There," he smiled. "Now we have some time. Young Meynardo is quite swift, but even he will be some time running all that way and back, not mentioning the time involved in searching the camp and avoiding their cats."

Jack unclenched his teeth. *Fine.* "Alright," he sighed. "Teach me to free souls."

The mouse wizard shook his head. "I think, before we begin teaching you magic, I'd like to see your stats and skills, if you don't mind."

"Fine with me," Jack shrugged. "Don't see how, though. I understand you don't have a window here, nor do I see one of those readers anywhere."

Luciandro frowned and had another go at his beard. "I beg your pardon?" he said in wonderment. "Do you mean to say you're out here with no token or idea of your abilities?"

"Token?" Jack repeated. "Oh," and he fished his guild token from his pouch. "You mean this?"

"Ah," the mouse nodded. "Then you are an adventurer after all. Wait. Are you trying to tell me that you can't *use* the token? And you don't know how to free souls. Minor healing?"

At Jack's negative, he snorted. "What sort of guild do you belong to where they don't teach the most basic of tasks?" he wondered. "What sort of dunderhead would sent a new adventurer out into the wilds without the least notion of how to survive?"

Jack had to think about that. What sort of dunderhead, indeed? "The guildmaster was kind of upset at my class assignment, I guess," he offered.

"Assignment?" the mouse wizard's voice rose. "Jackson Grenell," he assured the man. "Classes are not 'assigned'. Classes are recognized. They are as intrinsic to who you are as your very blood. If Jehsha's Window recognized you as a sentinel, it was because you were already a sentinel. Your guildmaster should have known this."

"He might have," Jack admitted. "But it doesn't seem to

have mattered. He might also have expected my companion to explain things to me. She was a rank ten advanced novice mage."

Another snort. "So he allowed a student to take on an apprentice, eh? What could have *possibly* gone wrong with such endeavor?"

Jack had to chuckle at that himself.

Rosaluna's Confession

The back door opened, and a weary Mohrdrand let himself in. Rosaluna looked up from the fire. *So Cable has learned control of the Runstable's, then?* She sent.

Mohrdrand couldn't completely hide his glare. "I give them an eighty percent chance of arriving at their destination without overturning the wagon and being killed, yes."

Her eyes narrowed, but she held comment. *There is food on the table beneath the heating bowl,* she sent. *Eat something, you must be famished.*

He spared her a look, but turned for the dining room. The old woman stood and made her way slowly into the kitchen to fetch some tea.

She sat with him as he ate, face inscrutable, neither drinking nor eating herself. Finally, Mohrdrand could stand it no longer.

"Rosaluna," he said around a mouthful of soft bread. "What is *wrong* with you?"

She raised her eyes to him, one eyebrow going up.

"Look here, old woman," he said in a tone that clearly indicated his anger remained but lightly tamped. "I've known you for sixty years. I know how you are. I know your foibles and your eccentricities. And I've been trying to ignore it, but something is clearly wrong with you. Has been since you sent the wandering bird to warn me of my approaching guests, and probably before.

"You've been acting off. Hiding things. *And* being even more bossy than is your wont, which is saying something."

He glared for awhile longer. Long enough to take another mouthful of food, chew and swallow. When she didn't answer, he pushed the plate away and lay his forearms on the table. "Is it just the boy?" he wondered. "Does having him about cause you *that* much pain it's addled you?"

Her face drew into a fierce frown, but she remained silent.

"The boy thinks he was at your cottage for three months while you healed him," he accused.

"*I* was expecting you to arrive with your cartload of product more than eight months gone at the latest," he followed. "So you had him at least *that* long." Another pause. "Just how close to death *was* he when you found him?"

Her shoulders sagged and she let a long breath out. *As near as does not matter,* she finally responded without energy. *Had I found him a quarter hour later than I did, there would have been nothing even I could have done.*

She went on after a long pause. *I did what I could to keep him from knowing because he* would *not be* still! She looked up and directly into his eyes. *Had he realized how long....*

Truthfully, Mohrdrand, she sighed. *He should still be at the cottage, not wandering about slaying monsters. He should be another two or three months recovering before venturing forth to so much as walk to town.*

But I could not... tears began to form. *I did not have the strength, Mohrdrand,* she admitted. *Do you understand? Not to have him there. Not to remember... Not enough to hold him against his will.* She wiped the damp from her eyes with a handkerchief. *I could feel him chafing, wanting to be gone. Into Jehsha knew what, for no particular reason. Just like all the rest. Just like....*

"So you lied to him." it wasn't a question.

I... did not tell him the truth, she admitted. *And allowed him to draw his own conclusions I kept him from realizing how badly he'd been injured so that he wouldn't lose hope. And in the end, I foisted him off on my Button when I could no longer bear the pain.*

"So why take him in to begin with?" he wondered. "By your own admission, people die, Rosaluna. You sent him off to me, you said, knowing that he probably would. Why go to so much trouble and heartache for someone you clearly... dislike? Someone you already think is as good as dead?"

She had no answer for that. *It...* she struggled. *It never occurred to me to do otherwise, old friend,* she told him. *That is*

who I am, you see. I could no more leave him there to die than he can avoid charging into a suicidal battle the moment one presents itself.

"That isn't all, though, is it?" he accused. "You forget, old woman, that my memory is still very good. When I visited you the other day, you were filled with sly musings, and secret knowings."

Rosaluna rose and returned to her seat beside the fire, where she sat quietly, gazing into the flames. Wiping the occasional tear.

Mohrdrand retrieved his plate with a grimace, shoveling down the remainder of his meal without so much as tasting it. Finished, he brought plate and cup to the kitchen and returned to join her by the hearth. He sat and glared.

"You insisted that I be here," he accused. "In Mokkelton. When I'm clearly needed elsewhere. Why? Button is not here to frighten now, Old Woman. It's just us two old dabblers, and we've faced down more than low level bandits on our own more times than either of us can count. What are you afraid of?"

She turned to him, and her expression caused him a start.

I am not afraid, Old Man, she assured him. *I am terrified.*

He blinked a couple of times at that pronouncement. Of all the words that might have escaped her lips, those, he would never have expected.

"What—?"

I... have... friends, Mohrdrand, she told him slowly. *Quiet friends. Secret friends. They tell me things. They have been telling me things over the past months. Darkness is rising once more. In the absence of protectors, darkness is rising.*

Abruptly, she sat up straight, squaring her shoulders, and her face went stony. *Know this, Old Man,* she admonished. *I do not cling to this life for my own sake. Nor for yours. Nor for the people of Mund. Do you understand?*

Left to my own devices, she sent, *I would allow myself to fade. What, after all does this world hold for me? Most all that I have ever loved is gone. I am one old woman, surely the world would continue to spin without me.*

Gladly would I venture forth to the next plane, or even oblivion were it only me. Hear this, then, she pressed, stabbing a stiffened finger his way. *I live on for one reason, and one reason alone....*

"Button," he finished for her.

Button. She nodded. *All that I do, I do for her. I have attuned myself to her for her protection. I have made myself strong for her survival. I have developed spells that allow me to project my energy into her very core in times of dire need, such as when she faced the otherworld monsters on my road.*

And yet, she deflated, her hand dropping to her lap, *in the end, I gave her over to a madman. And sent them both forth into the teeth of the darkness.*

"What *darkness*, Rosaluna?" Mohrdrand pressed. "You've now alluded to that twice. Surely mere mid tier bandits—"

Far more, Mohrdrand, she warned. *Far more.*

"But Mohrtgauth is dead."

Yes, she sent. *The current idiot killed it, finally. But think, you, Mohrdrand. How did he kill it?*

"Yes, yes," he nodded, "we've been over this. He swept the world clean of every fighter, mage, and healer he could lay hands on and brute forced his way up the Dark Road and into the Obsidian Fortress, where he slew the Demon Lord using a composite spell cast by five hundred mages simultaneously and channeled through him and his special power."

And what did he leave in his wake?

Mohrdrand's eyes went wide.

And now they're gathering, she clasped her hands together in her lap. *With or without their lord, the old lieutenants are gathering. Mohrtgauth may be gone, Mohrdrand. Their generals. But how many of the lesser blights upon Mund remained unaddressed? Bypassed? They are gathering under new leaders. With, now, none to stand in their way.*

"Except for," he stroked his beard.

Children, Mohrdrand, she finished for him. *A few scattered children barely into their power. And One misplaced hero whom Jehsha has snatched from oblivion. Who cannot be everywhere, and who has the caution of a housefly,* she scowled. *And who has my Button.*

"Why have you kept this a secret?" Mohrdrand demanded. "Surely—"

And who would I tell, Mohrdrand? She wondered. Should I alert the guild? What would Jonkins do? Warn the new king? Who no doubt knows already, given it was his plan to leave the dark lord's forces run loose so as to preserve his army's strength for the final battles.

No, old friend, she shook her head slowly. *Bor Jonkins would ask me what I intended. And he would worry.*

"You can't know that."

Oh, she tilted her head. *Can't I? What are his other options? Fortify the town? With what? Higher walls, thicker gates? Nothing an ungifted can construct will stop them.*

Reinforce the guard? With whom? There is no one, else they would already be reinforced.

Evacuate the citizenry? To where? Mokkelton is the sanctuary, old friend, she cautioned him. *Were there any possible steps he could take to mitigate the forthcoming crisis, I most certainly would have informed him. But there are not.*

"He could...." But, thinking hard, he couldn't come up with any either.

I will also tell you another secret I've been keeping, old man... she sighed. *I sent a wandering bird to the capitol before even our new hero arrived.*

"And?"

The bird returned within a month, for it was one of my strongest. No message accompanied it.

Mohrdrand fell back in his chair with a gasp. "So we're abandoned, then?"

It would appear so. Along with the entire eastern region.

I have been twisting my head around the problem, Mohrdrand, she sent. *In whatever moments I might spare from* the tasks of keeping wandering heroes alive or preparing Button for her journey.

"And?"

I... there might have been a way, she confessed. *Once. Once, when I was young. When I was far less frail. Now? Now, there is forlorn hope and ruin.*

I cannot find a solution, Mohrdrand, she sighed and settled back into the chair. *Not one with an acceptable outcome. And so I pretend it will all turn out alright somehow. And I fear. And I lash out from time to time, because fear is a thing I've grown unaccustomed to over the decades since I... over the decades.*

Still, she sent, *should the town be attacked, the two of us might at the least slow the horde where I alone would not.*

Mohrdrand's hand was at his beard again, his mind racing. "What gives you reason to believe that Mokkelton, specifically, is in danger?" he asked. "And how large is this horde of which you speak?"

The presence of the bandits, of course, she replied. *Ask yourself,* she went on. *Why are mid rank bandits wandering about our countryside, hmm?*

There can be but little of interest to them here. There is little of experience to gain for such as them from the slaughter of ungifted. And certainly no great treasures to be garnered from looting traveling peasants or farmers in the hinterlands.

It's likely, therefore, that they're some sort of advanced guard for the larger force. Mokkelton, as the town nearest the Heroes' Glade is an obvious target for destruction given its relative lack of defenders.

As to the size of the horde? I cannot say for certain. Only that one of Mohrtgauth's greater lieutenants, a Drugand named Grishnuk Oggza, was seen some months ago in the vicinity of Oria, accompanied by at least fifty lesser drugands and a score of other dark creatures, along with a scattering of human soldiers.

That number is likely to have grown in the intervening months. Possibly significantly.

Mohrdrand stood abruptly and began to pace, hand still at his beard. Every once in awhile, he'd pause and turn to her, as if to say something, but then hold and continue pacing. The force she'd described, even had it not grown, would easily be sufficient to sack the town, given its current state and defenses.

"You should have told me sooner," he growled at the last, not turning his head. "*Me*, at the least, if no other."

She did not immediately answer, staring instead down at her clasped hands. *I will concede,* she sent at last, her tone as near contrite as he'd ever heard it. *Up until the moment you demand to know my sources.*

He did turn at that, spinning in place to glare down at the top of her lowered head. That had been an interesting caveat.

* * *

At that moment, some sixty lenn west of Mokkelton, and nearing the crossroads that would have them heading north towards the ferry station, the Runstable's speeding wagon sat quietly in the middle of the road while the horses rested.

The journey through the town had been... a trial in the bizarre coach do to its length and height, taking far longer than it should have. And that with the wizard driving. He who owned the insane contraption, and, it was to be presumed, knew its operation.

The real trial, however, had begun once they'd cleared the north gate. That had been when Mohrdrand had pulled the thing to a halt and vacated what he'd called the driving seat, motioning for Cable to take his place — a thing which he'd been loathe to do. In the end, of course, there'd been naught for it. They'd had a place to be and the wizard had insisted that he would not be able to accompany them the whole of the way.

True to his word, an hour into the journey, and already an improbable distance from the town, he'd ordered Cable to pull up.

The spearman had watched the empty patch of air through which the old wizard had vanished for some long time after he'd gone before coaxing the horrid contraption into motion.

Now, here they were, near two hours farther along and already two days journey from the town by regular means.

In the horse wagon, Cable was stowing the fold away water trough with shaking hands. Twenty minutes, the wizard had insisted. At least twenty minutes of rest after the first two hours. Well, that time was up, and while the horses seemed ready enough, Cable, himself, felt in no way prepared to move on.

He'd fought against veritable hordes of monsters while following the hero, and never had his nerves been tested like this. Even the wounds that had nearly spelled his doom hadn't affected him in such manner.

Back in the cabin, he settled himself into the driving seat. He twisted towards the rear section to regard Tiarraluna, a thing that was possible because, against all convention, they were both within the coach. "Are you ready, lass?" he asked nervously and with a heavy sigh.

He was still not entirely confident in his ability to pilot the contraption alone. Particularly given they were soon to arrive at the end of straight and level road.

The girl nodded, not looking up from the tome she was studying, and so he turned to face through the wide glass that spanned the front of the carriage. With some trepidation, he mashed down on the leftmost pedal sticking up out of the floorboard, stirring the long stick to his right until its base lay firmly within the slot marked 1 on the diagram plate screwed into the dash panel beneath the glass.

With another, deep, almost gasping breath, he eased his foot down on the longer, rightmost pedal of the three before him. Presumably, this action would, in some way, coax the horses into motion, though he felt no trace of it, nor could he see a trace of it.

The only indication he had that the pressure was working was a large brass needle moving slowly within a jeweled dial inset into a brass cabinet below the forward window. The same

cabinet the 'shifting' diagram was screwed into.

Once the dial had circled to the proper number, as per the wizard's instructions, he eased the left pedal slowly up, and the whole of the long coach lumbered into motion. The whole process flew in the face of everything he'd ever known about wagons or carriages, and this being the seventh or eighth time he'd seen it happen wasn't helping.

Easing further down on the right pedal, he watched the road racing toward him, bathed in the glow of the twin directional lamps affixed to great, sweeping fenders arcing over the fat wheels. The wagon was difficult to control as there were no reins, but only a large, tri-spoked wheel as big around as a wash tub stuck onto the end of a thick shaft that disappeared into the floor just forward of the three pedals.

The needle of the dial reached the shifting point, and he let his right foot up and mashed down on the left pedal again, sliding the stick into the slot marked 2, before easing up with his left and easing down with his right. He repeated the ordeal with the slot marked 3.

There were nine such slots in the floor, connected by a central slot. Mohrdrand had cautioned him, though, against going past the third of them with only a single pair of horses, and only at the low side of the dial, lest they exhaust the beasts and founder them. That was fine with Cable. That range was already vastly faster than he'd any desire to travel.

Before long, they were once again hurtling through the darkness at a pace no living horse could match. Cable held on for dear life, jaw clenched, white at the lips, eyes wide, nerves taut as the string of an overdrawn bow. Constantly running through his mind was the solemn vow that he would walk back to Mokkelton barefoot before ever he came near this infernal rolling dungeon again.

At this rate, even staying to established and paved roads and going the long way 'round, they'd reach the ferry station in a little over four hours more, and that with another stop to rest the horses midway along. Less than eight hours total for what should be more than a three day journey. Four more terrifying hours, granted.

He wondered, with that small part of his brain not repeating his vow, why he'd never heard of anything like this before tonight.

The Wizard's Apprentice

"Now," Luciandro squared his shoulders and grounded his staff. "What say *I* take you on? Temporarily, at least."

"You mean as your apprentice?" Jack's eyes went round. "Won't Amiandro have something to say about that?"

"I'm not suggesting you spend the next decade at my knee," Luciandro said. "I'm suggesting that I teach you the basics, insofar as I may. I remind you that I —we all here— are considered monsters. Not beastkin, not demihumans, monsters. As such... let us just say that our manipulation of magic, and the types of magic we may manipulate, are not altogether the same as those who are considered otherwise. The basics, however, are mostly from the essentia school of the neutral college, and so all may cast them without opposition."

"*Considered* monsters?" Jack asked. "Osmando said the same thing. Considered as monsters by whom?"

"Why, Mund, of course," the wizard seemed surprised at the question. "The world has rules, Jackson Grenell," he gestured with his staff. "And we must follow them, whether we like them or not. That is your first lesson.

"Now," he nodded towards the token in Jack's hand. "I will show you how to read your guild token, and show you some of the tasks you may use it for."

"That might be easier said than done," Jack confessed. "Given that I neither speak nor read the language, I doubt I'll be able to do much with it."

"Yes," the old mouse stroked his beard. "That will be a problem.

"Tell me this, Jackson Grenell," he asked. "Forgive me if this sounds rude, but how do you come to *be* in this place without knowing anything? Did you simply wake up one morning and decide, 'today I shall travel to a far off land I know nothing about and go bandit hunting?'

"Don't get me wrong," he hurried. "I mean no disrespect, and I'm obviously more than glad you're here. I'm simply very confused, and the condition vexes me."

So Jack took a deep breath and gave him the story, or the bare bones of it, as quickly and concisely as he could. He was still working on the assumption that time was precious.

"That..." the old wizard clasped his grounded staff with both hands, "is quite the....

"And you really have no idea how you got here or why? I mean, *here*, as opposed to somewhere else?"

Jack shrugged. "As I said, my working theory is that I got shoved here so I could be taken care of if the bus missed."

"Doesn't make sense," Luciandro frowned. "Why go to so much trouble? I know from my master that passage between the universes is difficult and costly to manage. Far easier to simply punt you into the void between and be done with you. No air in the void. Very little light. Nothing solid. You'd be irretrievably dead in thirty or forty minutes."

Jack had no answer to that. "Maybe because my attacker was a demon lord?" he posited. "And they can't resist going for the Rube Goldberg attack? Even when a simple projectile between the eyes will get the job done quicker and easier?"

"Actually, that might be it," Luciandro nodded.

"In any case, we need you versed in at least the basics of self preservation and adventuring before we can proceed with any hope of success, so we may as well get going. I'll read your information to you. Later, perhaps, should we all still be together and alive, I'll have our youngling teacher help you with learning to read."

It was a testament to how normalized Jack was becoming to the bizarre nature of this world that he didn't find the notion peculiar.

"Now, firstly," Luciandro's hand disappeared within his robes for a moment and reappeared holding a smooth stone about the size of a grain of Japanese rice. "Hold your token thusly," and he demonstrated, holding his own between his fingers, much as Jack had been shown to hold the shard of amber, although this time, palm up.

"Now," he went on once Jack had mimicked him, "while

holding it flat, pour a bit of mana into it through your fingers, as you did with the language spell. But this time, keep your mind on the task at hand. You'll want to be thinking about yourself, and your powers and their measure. The stone will recognize your flavor and produce a depiction of your abilities and classes, along with your basic information and current experience."

Jack nodded and held the stone level before him, sending out the mana trickle. Wavering at first, but solidifying quickly, a smaller scale duplicate of the field he'd seen in the guild hall was projected into the air above the stone. It was still gibberish except for the rifleman class and rank, and, oddly, a list of the weapons he'd qualified in when he was on active duty. All the English text remained translucent and difficult to read.

Luciandro's eyes went round, and he let out a whistle.

"Those are some impressive... not to say unbelievable figures," he said in a breathy voice. Then he gave Jack a look and turned back to the guild token and its display field. "But, then again, I've never seen a hero's status field before."

"I dunno," Jack said. "Guildmaster Jonkins seemed to think it was pretty unbelievable himself. Presumably he'd met at least the last hero at some point, given we're all supposed to have appeared in the same place, and Mokkelton's the first town. Of course, he didn't seem to view it as a good thing."

Luciandro was peering up at the field, face stern. "Be that as it may..." he answered. "I'll read this off to you, and give you, so far as I can remember, some sort of reference so you might see where you fit in the grand scheme of things.

"To begin," he nodded, "I don't suppose I need tell you your name, age, or eye color, yes?

"Your health, it rates as three hundred-fifteen points. That's quite good for a human of your rank. I'd expect the norm to be somewhere in the neighborhood of two hundred to, say, two-fifty for a run of the mill human adventurer at rank nine. Your mana is even better at four hundred fifty-one. Mage territory, that.

"Let's see, now. Strength is fifteen, owing to a plus two bonus from your sentinel rank. Normal range for an adult male human, if I'm remembering correctly, is between seven and eleven. So you started out strong, and your class gave you a further boost.

"Your agility is up at the same level. Fifteen, with two of that coming from your class. Agility is a measure of your flexibility, fluidity of motion, and speed. Again, a normal adult human male will average between four for the epically clumsy and eleven or twelve for the acrobatically inclined. You started at thirteen.

"Of course, before you twist something patting yourself on the back, your average housecat has an agility rating of around forty.

"Perception is nine," he gave his beard a stroke. "You notice things, and recognize what you're seeing, I'll wager. I'm thinking not much gets by you. Humans tend to wander from dullards at two or three, to an alert six or seven.

"Jehsha says your intelligence is twenty-five, hmm? That's at the upper end of humanity as a whole, but not outside of normal parameters. Let's say, idiots begin at around five, the average run of peasant wanders the world at ten or fifteen, and the seekers and movers up around twenty to thirty, although those thirties are rare birds indeed.

"Your wis— er... wisdom. Yes. Well, I mean... five isn't *so* bad. It's at least average. And I'm sure it'll come with time, yes?" he ran a finger inside his collar and gave it a tug.

"Endurance, now. Basically a combination of stamina and perseverance. Yours is... well, it's not bad. Six. At least it's better than an ungifted, although not by all that much. It's possible that you're not yet completely healed from the ordeal you told me about, and the stat will improve over time.

"Your toughness is fourteen, though. And an unmodified fourteen at that. You must have been through some sore trials, Jackson Grenell.

"Toughness is a facet of strength, but not tied to it. Meynardo, for instance, has a toughness of twelve. At its core, it's a measure of your ability to withstand physical or mental force and push through.

"Given a fourteen toughness, I don't imagine your low endurance will hinder you overmuch when times are hard, although I'm sure you'll enjoy it less. A base human will normally have a toughness of between four and ten, depending on how much hardship they've endured over their lives.

"Your charisma is thirty-two. Low for the gifted, but in the upper end of the ungifted. I won't go into all the variables that go into the rating, but I can tell you that the ungifted rarely rate past forty. The gifted, on the other hand, range from around thirty to up in the neighborhood of fifty, in part because of the power and mana they exude." He paused to give Jack a good, long look. "Maybe if you smiled more?

"Chance. Luck, if you will. Serendipity. The degree to which fortune favors you. Yours is thirty-two percent. While the number may seem low, it's actually quite high. You must have survived some very calamitous events, Mister Grenell. Even beyond your transportation to Mund, to have raised it this high.

"And finally," he looked up, "your magical affinity. That is to say, the strength of your affinity. Your ability to wield magic at all. Twenty-eight. Now," and he paused to order his words. "Magical affinity isn't so simple as a base stat. No, it's a balance. You've to weigh your ability to wield, that's the twenty-eight in your case, with the affinity you have for a given school, as well as the opposition of its polar school.

"For instance, if you were attempting a spell of the conjuration school for which you have an affinity of, say five, your castings will be more powerful than one without the affinity, but with the same power, and you'll probably cast it at a lower rank.

"On the other hand, were you to attempt a spell from the curse school, which is in opposition to your affinity, you'd need more mana for a lesser effect, and would likely need to gain more ranks to cast it at all than one with an affinity for curses. And you'd end up with a less powerful curse at the end."

While Jack was absorbing the mountain of data the old wizard had just laid in his lap, said wizard was examining the field of Jack's guild token, stroking his chin, one hand still on his grounded staff.

"You want me to give you the particulars on the colleges and schools of magic you've affinities or oppositions in, or your elemental affinities and oppositions? Given you seem to know a single, minor spell of the abjuration school, which you don't seem ever to have cast, I'm thinking it might be a waste of our time at the moment."

Jack didn't hesitate. "Probably not necessary. I doubt I'd understand much of it anyway. Can I at least learn free souls and minor healing with any of them?"

Luciandro waved a hand. "Both are from the school of essentia, so, yes."

"Then, no," Jack shook his head. "Let's move on to whatever's next."

"That would be weapon skills and ranks,' Luciandro said, "although some of them appear to be inactive and in some script I cannot read, which is a bit disconcerting."

"Okay, skip those," Jack told him. I already know about those."

"If you say so," Luciandro sighed. He'd have liked to understand what that strange script said, but he supposed he could wait.

"This next section details your classes and their special traits. Sentinel is your primary, as you said. Its description is quite... extensive," he raised an eyebrow, but Jack nodded for him to continue.

"Alright," the tiny wizard sighed.

"Primary Class: Sentinel. Special traits: Plus two to strength. Plus two to agility. Plus two to endurance. Which, as expected, is where the bonuses came from.

"Adaptable: You may apparently use any out of class weapon or armor you find at a rank penalty of minus two below your lowest ranked certified skill, and gain experience and skill with them.

"Courageous stand: Your weapon and defensive skills increase by three percent for every enemy that you and your party are outnumbered by. For example, if you're alone, and fighting three enemies your skill will increase by six percent. You'll also be getting five percent more experience for every five enemies in battle range, whether you're fighting them all or not.

"Self Reliant: Whenever you're questing alone, even if you're still nominally a member of a party, you'll accrue experience ten percent faster than normal. Any other party members you have will continue to accrue experience at normal encounter rates.

"Insane courage: You'll never fail a morale or fear check." he looked up again from his reading. "Not sure that one even needed to be noted.

"Grim Resolve...." The mouse went silent as he read, casting glances up at the human as he did so. It took him a moment or two before he could bring himself to continue. "We'll... skip that one for now, hmm?" he smiled uncomfortably. "Get back to it later, yes?

"Now, uhm... Tracking, plus ten percent. So, you can track, and do so ten percent better than you might otherwise, I suppose. Wilderness craft, plus five percent. Self evident, yes?

"Detect Life. Ah," he nodded. That would explain how you can tell there are no enemies about, yes? I'm going to assume you already know what it is and how to use it.

"Mentor," he nodded again, contemplatively. "That's an interesting one, but somewhat in depth, and your rank isn't yet high enough to make use of it. Still want to hear it?"

"Not right now," Jack told him. "I'll wait until I *can* use it. Which will be...?"

"Ah," Luciandro checked. "Rank ten."

"How close am I?" Jack wondered.

"Depending on how things go in the next twelve hours," Luciandro mused. "Do we all live, and none of them get away, I'd say along about the time you turn in your bounty token and collect your quest reward."

"I'll wait, then," Jack decided.

"Good choice," the mouse nodded. "That's it for sentinel, then. There's a description here for your artificer secondary class, but I don't see you building any magical engines before morning, so we can probably wait until we're done at the camp. The third? I can't read it, it shows that it's inactive, and aside from some gibberish up in the weapon qualification section, it's not displaying any specifics."

"That's it, then?"

"As far as what the token tells me," the mouse nodded. "Yes. There are a few other things that it can be used for, though. As I understand it, given that I've never actually *been* to a human town, the token will allow you tax free entry into any village, town, or city in the realm. It can be used for a single free meal per day at any guild hall. In company with a bounty token, it can allow you to requisition supplies from some of the royal quartermasters at a discounted rate, or even free, depending on what sorts of nuisances your bounty has you chasing.

"Finally, it allows you to accept spot quests in the field. If you will hold your token out to me, Jackson Grenell?"

Frowning, Jack lowered the token to where the old wizard could reach it. Luciandro reached up with his own token and solemnly intoned, "Jackson Thomas Grenell, I request that you become my apprentice. As well I ask that you protect and guide myself and such of my people as survive to some new home where we may be safe."

He paused for a moment, waiting. Then he chucked his chin to where the two tokens pressed against one another. "You're supposed to say, 'I accept' now."

"Oh," Jack stiffened. "I accept."

The tokens took on a momentary glow before going quiescent.

"And now," the mouse heaved a great sigh, "I shall teach you how to release souls, and possibly minor healing should there be time before Meynardo returns."

Focus

Jack was sweating, his whole arm aching, but the aura was finally beginning to sheath the dead hare. Luciandro looked on closely, silent for the first time since Jack's efforts had begun.

The aura dissipated, and Jack let his breath out in a whoosh. It had seemed so easy when Osmando had done it. Or Tiarraluna, come to that, once she'd come to the realization that she couldn't brute force the jaegers over the rainbow.

He asked the tiny wizard about it.

"Well," the mouse told him seriously. "It was your first time doing magic of any sort, was it not?"

"I suppose," Jack nodded. "I mean, I tried a couple of times, but without a focus—"

"And there's the second reason," Luciandro nodded, a smile splitting his face.

"But, I have this, right?" Jack was confused.

Luciandro nodded again. "For what it's worth," he acknowledged. "But that isn't exactly a focus yet, Jackson. It's the beginnings of one at best.

"See, there are reasons mages don't wander the countryside with pocketsful of unmounted jewels," he explained. "There's method to the creation of a focus, and reason behind it. We can go further into that at some point when we're not so pressed for time as you seem to be at the moment.

"Suffice to say, even a poorly crafted focus would more than halve the mana requirement for that spell you just cast. And the amount of will required would also be lessened considerably."

Jack looked down at the shard of amber. There seemed to be an inner glow to it, still fading. He looked to the mouse.

"Try again," Luciandro ordered. "Repetition will make it easier, even without a proper focus. And if you're going to be struggling, a lesser tier, rank one spell is the thing to struggle with."

Ten dire hares in, with another ten at least to go, and Jack was gasping for breath, sweat pouring down his face.

"That's enough for now," the tiny wizard commanded. "The rest will abide for the time being. Meynardo will be returning soon, and there are a few things left to do."

"Are your people about ready to move yet?" Jack asked as they neared the shattered village, Luciandro perched on his shoulder. There was a lot of activity, but he wasn't making much sense of it.

Luciandro cast about the ruins of the village as they approached. "Nearly," he said.

"There is another task we must complete before we leave, however, if you would grant us the time."

Jack gave him a suspicious side eye, but shrugged. Meynardo wasn't back yet, so there wasn't much he was going to do anyway.

"We cannot hope to keep up with your horses on foot," the old mouse said. "And the wards on the saddles make it very uncomfortable for any of us to be near them, so at the moment, we cannot ride."

"You ride horses?" Jack was amazed. "Wait. The *saddles* are warded?"

"They are, but you miss my point, I think," Luciandro said dryly. "You must weaken the wards on at least one saddle. Once that is done, anything slower than a trot will be manageable with some small adjustments. The third rank of **Manipulate wards (Lesser),** however, is a level that is beyond you at the moment."

"Why me?" Jack wondered. "Aren't you a rank thirty wizard? Should be child's play, right?"

"Human wards," Luciandro explained. "Human magic. Only a human may remove them. I could explain, but it would take some time, which again...."

"We don't have," Jack scowled. Mission creep, oh, how he hated it. "Fine," he grumped. How do I do that?"

"A small bit of preparation first, and then I will show you," the old mouse nodded, smiling.

They had reached the remains of the village where they'd done the language spell. Jack lowered the old wizard to the ground. Luciandro clapped his hands and Amiandro was there, swaying slightly, but fully erect on his hind feet. A quick patter of instructions in Tandrian, and the youngster was off, shouting to his brethren.

Luciandro trudged over to a wide patch of flattened grass, clearly exhausted. Jack could almost feel his own bones creak as he watched. "Your focus, if you please? Luciandro beckoned.

Jack crouched and laid the stone in the old mouse's cupped hands.

"Fascinating," The old wizard mumbled as he examined it. Looking up, he was smiling. "No signs of damage, you'll be happy to know. Even after all of that. Apparently he's accepted you. This stone should work just fine."

"He?"

"Life stone, didn't you say?"

"Ah."

"Were there contention, there would be clouding in the stone at the least, after all the mana you've poured through it. Cracks, perhaps. But it remains clear and smooth. It will do just fine until you find something stronger."

By this time, the area around them was filling up with mice. Each of them was carrying something. Some scrap of clothing, some strand of grass, some plant stem. Some of the females had clipped off strands of their own hair. While he was wondering at this, Jack felt something race up his arm. Before he could react, he felt a tug, and caught a glimpse of Amiandro racing back down his cloak with a hank of his hair.

The potbellied mouse he remembered from the initial rescue shouldered his way through the crowd, a large, for him, hammer in one hand. Behind him followed a younger mouse, nearly as burly, carrying a smooth strip of some silvery metal about an inch-and-a-half long and half an inch wide, with a wrapped handle on one end.

"Hold out your hands, please?" Luciandro requested.

Jack gave him the eye, but the tiny wizard nodded towards the ground.

"What's going on?" Jack asked as he eased forward to lay his hands uncertainly, palms down in the sodden grass.

"A gift," Luciandro smiled. "A small token from a village to its savior."

"I wasn't expecting—"

"And yet," Luciandro interrupted.

Fine, Jack's shoulders slumped and he watched the two burly mice approach his grounded hands.

"Try to project some mana," Luciandro prompted. "You needn't try anything complicated. Just will some flow. This time through the entirety of both hands and out through all of your fingertips."

"Haven't we been over this?" Jack asked.

"Not this," Luciandro corrected him. "The first was you acting as a source. Any touch would have done the job. The second was you learning a basic spell with an untuned stone. That was *meant* to be difficult. This is something else."

Jack gave him the hairy eyeball. What was it with these Mundians that they all felt compelled to make everything harder than it needed to be?

Still, he closed his eyes and imagined electricity flowing down his arms and out his fingers. Power, right? Maybe? Without the amber, he wasn't sure it was possible. Straining, with the twenty iterations of casting soul release behind him, though, it seemed as if he felt a slight tingle.

Luciandro moved forward and placed a hand on each of Jack's fingers in turn. "Ah, this one," he instructed the burly mice, indicating the middle finger of his left hand.

Jack opened his eyes and tried to figure out what they were up to.

The older mouse with the hammer gestured and said something up to him.

"Lift this finger, please?" Luciandro requested. "Just a bit? And you needn't hold out the other hand anymore."

Jack settled himself more squarely, and raised the finger

half an inch or so. The old mouse laid his hammer aside and took the hank of Jack's hair from Amiandro. He straightened it out, feeding one end under Jack's finger and around, knotting the ends and leaving the tails hanging.

A female mouse with a babe in arms stepped forward from the crowd, tilting her head and sliding her hand through her long hair, speaking quietly to the old mouse. He nodded and snipped off a small, full length bundle. Another female stepped forward as the first stepped back. She'd already cut some of her own hair and she passed it to the old mouse, who affixed it to one end of the hank he already had in some way Jack couldn't discern. Another, younger female came forward with her own contribution. And so it went.

Once he had a bundle long enough, the old mouse turned back to Jack and began braiding this new bundle with Jack's own hair, sliding the original loop around as he twisted the new material around it. This knot was smaller, and laid hard against the first.

The next group to come forward was mixed. Some of it was more hair, some of it was cloth. Some of it even plant stems of some sort. Regardless, the old mouse made a cord and wove it around Jack's finger, braiding it into the two already there.

Every surviving member of the clan donated something, be it a belt, hair, a portion of clothing, or in one case, a collection of flower petals. Somewhere during the process, Meynardo showed up out of the darkness and held forth a long strip of his green coat and the feather from his bycocket hat. Then Osmando proffered the sleeve they'd torn from his shirt when they'd set his arm. At the end, Luciandro stepped forward and pulled the sash from his robe, passing it forward.

The old mouse, whose name Jack had yet to learn, twisted the band a few more times to get it laying the way he wanted and stepped back to give it a final appraisal. He nodded, whether to himself or his assistant, Jack couldn't say. But he picked up his hammer and stepped forward again.

This time the assistant came with him. He slid the silver bar between Jack's skin and the band of donated material as though he knew what he was doing. The old mouse paused, his off hand laying against the edge of the bar and swung his hammer.

It was all Jack could do not to cry out. The tiny hammer hit like he'd slammed his hand in a car door! A cascade of blue-white sparks burst forth from the contact point, lighting the nearby area and the attentive audience. The second blow wasn't quite the shock, but it hurt just as much.

The process took awhile. The form was apparently five or six blows for a given width, with the assistant raising or lowering his end of the bar. After which the older, what, smith? Slid the band half an inch along and went at it again, each blow deliberate and precise.

What had begun as a ragged band of junk slowly took on a glass smooth, multihued laminate finish. Once the ring had been forged the whole way around, it looked smooth as glass and shone with a faint, inner glow.

The bundle of knots were gathered at the top, and even as Jack was wondering what they were planning with it, the old smith called to the crowd. Osmando plodded forward, an angry scowl on his face. With an unhappy look up at Jack, he doffed his bedraggled hat and removed the silver band, passing it to the smith.

The silver band was hammered down around the circumference of the bundle of knots, and the assistant with the silver bar moved forward again. It only took Jack a few moments to realize what they were doing with the tail ends of the knots. They were fashioning a setting for the amber shard.

Luciandro carefully set the shard within the nest of stiffened fibers, examining and adjusting it a number of times before he was satisfied. He nodded, then, and the smith moved in, different tools in his hands. Some sort of tongs, Jack thought, and a smaller hammer.

Moving with utmost delicacy, the smith gripped each strand in turn, gripping and twisting, tapping against the tongs with the hammer. Jack lost himself in the process. Mouse, the little guy might be. Construct he might be. But the smith was a craftsman, and Jack could appreciate a craftsman in whatever form.

Once the amber shard was solidly affixed, Luciandro moved back into place, sprinkling some sort of powder across the surface of the setting, and passing his hands slowly through the air above the now shining bars. Jack felt power flowing in through his skin, and stifled a grimace. A lot of power.

The whole ring took on a golden glow, and Jack felt heat radiate out from it. And then Luciandro spat out a harsh sounding string of what seemed like gibberish, and the ring darkened, expanded, and then contracted. Three or four times, it did this, before settling into a size that felt snug, but not tight.

Luciandro dropped to the ground, his rear hitting the grass with a thump. "It is done," he groaned. Looking up, he ordered, "try to remove it, Jackson. Think, 'come off' while you're doing so."

Jack followed his instructions and the ring slid off like it was three sizes too large. Sliding it back over his finger, he felt it snug down. He gave it a tug, but without the accompanying thought, it wasn't moving. He pulled it off again and admired it.

It was beautiful. What was the term they used back home? Micarta? He slid it back over his finger and smiled like a twelve year old kid who'd been handed his brand new hunting rifle just in time for opening day.

"Now," Luciandro wheezed, "pick me up and we'll see about those other carcasses before I teach you **Manipulate Wards**."

Tom Black

Home Stretch

Learning to use the ring, certainly compared to merely holding the shard, was simplicity itself. Jack found that he could simply point and recite the spell without much force or mana flow at all. Within seconds, the aura would form and the dire hare fade.

They weren't dropping much in the way of gifts, though. Not like the haul he'd seen Osmando raking in.

"Take into consideration the size disparity between Osmando and the hare, Jackson Grenell," Luciandro pointed out when Jack asked about it. "One on one, *you* could probably throttle a dire hare with your bare hands, could you not?

"Just one?" Jack allowed. "Sure, probably."

"Now imagine Osmando trying it."

"So...." Jack paused while he sent the next hare on its way. "...The quantity of the gift is a reflection of the disparity of power between winner and loser?"

"Quantity, quality, and the experience earned for freeing the soul," Luciandro explained. "Although, in the case of the experience differential, the variation is dwarfed by the earned experience variance of the battle itself. You earn far more experience defeating a foe larger or of a higher rank than yourself than for an equal contest or battling a lesser foe.

"For Osmando, for instance, defeating a creature many orders of magnitude larger than himself gained him far more experience than you gained from defeating one a fraction of your own. And a concurrent increase in gifts"

Which explained the jaeger drop sword, although he'd pretty much figured that out already.

The ward spell proved a different matter. It wasn't so much that the spell was particularly difficult, as it was that it was a third rank spell; the highest rank of **Manipulate Wards (Lesser)**, while Jack's mana manipulation skill remained solidly at rank one. It didn't help that ward manipulation was somewhat finicky.

It took him a couple of tries, and taught him the valuable lesson of what a failed casting's backlash felt like while it was still low ranked enough not to kill him or melt his hand off the end of his wrist. Or, indeed, any of the myriad of other lurid fates Luciandro regaled him with as he danced around in pain, blowing on his scorched fingers.

"Worry not, young Jackson," the tiny wizard called as Jack cursed his way through the aftermath of another screwup. "**Self healing** is up next, and now you'll have a target that will easily show you how well you've learned it."

Jack gave him the evilest of evil eyes he could muster. "I already have plenty of holes in me we can use as test subjects," he rasped. "Anyway," he lamented. "Wouldn't it be easier for me to just flat out *remove* the ward and for you to put a *fresh* one in its place? I mean, you're the one who put up the wards that kept this place safe, right?"

"I'm husbanding my mana," the mouse told him. "So that I'll be able to help you with the bandit mage. As it is, it will be a tricky thing with what little I have remaining, and what little will naturally refresh on our way there.

"Now," the mouse ordered, "if you're quite finished flailing about...? Again."

By comparison, **Self Healing (Lesser),** the spell most adventurers commonly shortened to **Lesser Healing** —although it was technically its own spell, and completely different— was a breeze. There wasn't even a spoken component. Concentrate on the injury, aim the mana, and hum a short, easy to remember tune. Even the focus wasn't particularly necessary, as none of what it focused was leaving his body. He was essentially swapping MP for HP, at the rate of three to one.

Higher ranks would grant more favorable exchange rates as well as allow him to heal more serious injuries. Eventually, should his abilities not peak beforehand, he'd be able to cast a version that would initiate autoheal and leave it running in the background while he fought.

Luciandro couldn't tell him whether he'd ever reach that level of power, though. "Every creature," he explained, "has a peak, beyond which it cannot climb. For the vast majority, human, beastkin, and beast alike, that peak is rank zero.”

“Not much of a peak,” Jack grunted.

“But a peak, nonetheless,” the mouse assured.

“I will tell you a secret now, Jackson Grenell,” the old wizard confided conspiratorially. “That I know because of who and what I am, and who my master was.”

Jack tilted his head to better hear the soft whisper, since the mouse was once more riding on his shoulder.

“There is no such thing as an ungifted,” Luciandro told him.

Jack straightened his head abruptly and turned to look the tiny wizard in the eye.

“No,” Luciandro assured him. “It is true.

“In the vast majority of Jehsha’s creatures,” he clarified. “The gift is vanishingly small. But it is there. Life, itself is the gift, and the gift is life. If you wish, we may discuss this further, and at length, for I feel it something you will eventually need to know, given who you’ve found yourself to be involved with. But not now, for it is a long tale, and we’ve not the time.

“For now, it is enough to know that, for most, the gift is so vanishingly faint that they may do nothing with it, useful or otherwise. So faint, that their crystals are, essentially, invisible to all but the most potent of appraisal skills. Their talents likewise so small that they cannot even see the crystals of others.

“For those we call ‘gifted’,” he raised a finger for emphasis. “The gift burns brighter, its effects are more pronounced. But even for these, there is a peak. No one knows where this peak lies for any of them... for any of us. We only realize when we notice that we are no longer advancing, regardless of how hard we strive.”

“So a baked in, hard limit,” Jack decided as he examined his freshly healed hand.

“Weelllll,” the mouse shrugged. “Hard*ish*. There *are* ways to enhance the gift. If one knows the secret. My master knew this, *and* the secret. It was instrumental in the creation of my people. You see, Jackson,” he held a hand to the side of his mouth as though imparting a deep secret. "I, *myself*, was once an ordinary mouse."

Jack narrowed his eyes. "Ordinary? Sorry, I'm having trouble picturing that."

Luciandro smiled, just a bit. "Would you believe an extraordinary, but common mouse?"

Jack shrugged, nearly dislodging the tiny wizard. "We'll go with that," he grinned.

The horse didn't seem to know quite what to make of the situation. It kept turning its head to examine the gaggle of mice clinging to its back. Jack was forced to smack its nose a few times as it reached around to bite before it got the idea that it probably shouldn't do that anymore. Once underway, there'd be no problem, as the beast's head would be held forward by the lead rope tied off to Jack's chestnut.

He'd pulled his own blanket roll from the back of the chestnut's saddle and draped and folded it over the saddle of the bay the bandit with the massless mace had ridden. He'd folded and tied the ends to make a couple of troughs in the cloth for the mice to nestle into.

There hadn't been any sort of camping gear on any of the saddles he'd found thus far, which was why the fifty-odd of mice were nestled in *his* bedroll. He wasn't all that happy about it. They *were* still mice. But he wasn't about to say anything, and he sure wasn't going to begrudge them the aid after all that had passed.

Around half of them had to satisfy themselves with just hanging on to the rough weave out in the open. Jack noticed that, even after his having modified the ward, they were still staying well clear of the rough gemstone at the leading edge of the saddle.

"So," Jack heaved a great breath, sitting his saddle at last. "We done here yet?"

Luciandro, perched on his left shoulder, nodded. "There is nothing left for us here. Such of our dead as we could find have been laid to rest in the old sanctuary, and such belongings as could be salvaged are on the last horse."

"And we aren't leaving anybody behind?" although he already knew. His detect life skill was showing no signs of life within more than a mile.

"No one alive," Meynardo sighed from his right shoulder. "We searched far out into the grass for more bodies, but found none."

"So we're off then," Jack nodded and clucked the chestnut forward.

"More towards the east," Luciandro warned. "I cannot hide you *and* the horses, so we dare not close within around, say, two miles of the camp before we hide them somewhere."

Jack gave him a glance, but swung the reins, bringing the chestnut's head a bit farther to the east.

* * *

Tiarraluna winced as she hobbled back and forth beside the Runstable's, trying to relieve some of the pain from her legs without being forced into the use of magic. She was loathe to use the least drop of mana, not knowing what she might expect to encounter at their destination.

The northern road was far rougher than the eastern, and the speedwagon had thrown them about a bit, although Cable hadn't allowed their pace to slow overmuch. He was currently out in the bushes on the far side of the road throwing up.

Three quarters of an hour, Uncle had told them. The minimum length of the second rest period for the horses. After this next run, they'd have to lead them out of their carriage and allow them a couple of hours to rest without the bindings before they'd be of use again. By then, of course, they would have reached their destination.

While she wasn't exactly certain where they were just now, they couldn't be much more than an hour from the old ferry station at the speed they'd been traveling. She wondered whether Cable would race right into the place, or stop short to come upon them ready for a fight.

Given that she could clearly hear his tortured retching, she decided it would probably be the latter. He would, no doubt, wish to take some time to compose himself before entering battle.

Within five or six minutes, Cable was done feeding the bugs and back inside the rear carriage, caring for the horses. This time, as they drank, he examined each leg in turn, running his hands along them, checking for injuries.

This whole being lashed into place and running on a moving platform was madness, and he had no notion of what sorts of injuries the animals risked engaging in it. So he made extra sure.

He figured they were about thirty lenn from the ferry station. Fifteen from their turn back to the east. Looking to the slowly clearing sky, he decided they'd probably strike it just before dawn. He yawned reflexively.

Shaking his head, he fished a bar of what looked like compressed grain from his jerkin pocket, gnawing off a large chunk. Even as the flavor washed through his mouth, an electric tingle spread along his jaw and down his neck. Alchemical restoratives weren't a replacement for rest or sleep, but they were certainly an extra boost if neither of those other two were available.

Swallowing, he shook his head again and rolled his shoulders, feeling his strength returning, bit by bit, second by second. He took another bite and chewed while he watched the horses drink. Just this one bar wouldn't bring him back to his full capacity, but it would bring him well along the way.

Glancing up and over, as though he could see through the solid wall of the carriage, he wondered when the last time the girl had slept might have been. He had a couple more of the bars in his gear aboard the dungeo —he winced, hunching his shoulders— wagon's cabin. He'd give her one as soon as he'd finished seeing to the horses.

While Tiarraluna seemed quite unaffected, Cable's stomach started to turn the moment he set foot upon the wagon's step. *Crawl*, he decided. He'd *crawl* back before he drove this monstrosity an *inch* further than was absolutely necessary.

In a few more minutes, they were once again roaring up the road, bouncing like a babe on her mother's knee over the rough cobbles. Or possibly like a barrel rolling down a rocky slope.

Hang on, kid, Cable thought as he clung for dear life to the aiming wheel. *We're comin'!*

In the back, without the need to pilot the wagon, Tiarraluna continued pouring over the tome, fretting silently. **Greater Heal** was the spell she was studying at the moment. Completely different from **Healing (Greater),** or, indeed, anything she'd ever heard of. It would seem to stand alone, with neither tiers nor ranks to divide it. It was beyond anything she'd thought herself capable of. Yet Grandmother had assured her she would be able to learn it. That was good, since she feared that, when finally they'd come to the ending of this wild ride, she would need it.

* * *

In the old ferry station, Bear the Mauler gazed angrily up into the cloud bedecked sky, a vitality brew in his hand — his third of the night. It'd be coming on dawn in a couple of hours, he decided. Glancing over his shoulder, he grunted.

"Nothing yet, Boss," Hurgus yawned.

Where the hells are *they?* Bear wondered. *Do I need to send up a damned signal flare to draw them in?* Growling, he stepped once more into the drizzle to make sure his men were still awake. And alive, in case their mysterious adversary had somehow snuck in despite Hurgus' scrying.

* * *

From just within the treeline half a mile or so east of Mokkelton, the five invaders stared towards the city walls. There was where the trail led. The leader grunted a command and it and its subordinates each spread their arms wide. Another command, and, four from each of them, twenty nearly invisible shapes leapt from their backs and arms, taking to the sky.

The flits resembled stingrays in a broad sense, uniformly about half a meter across, and perhaps seven centimeters thick at their centerlines. Transluscent, nearly transparent, they swam up through the air with an undulating grace.

They'd already been programmed at a basic level. They'd section off the city into twenty grid squares, and each would circle over one such square until they either picked up one of the targets, or needed to be refreshed. At either point, they'd return here, and the champion would scan each with the reader.

Now, About Those Bandits...

Following Meynardo's directions, Jack made his way south, dozing in the saddle. It had been a long day atop another long day, with little of sleep between. And that not particularly restful.

Freed from the pressure of learning the new magic he'd been taught. Freed from the necessity to sit still when he needed to be moving, his mind was wandering. As it often did, it found the nightmares, ever-present in the corners and recesses of his mind. The things he hadn't wanted young Amiandro to see.

Luciandro, riding his shoulders clung tightly as he groaned and twitched and lurched, but didn't move to wake him. Rest he needed, even poor rest. Meynardo was perched atop the chestnut's head, between its ears, steering the horse by way of tugging with all his might on the headstall and whispering to the beast. He, at least seemed possessed of boundless energy. Or, possibly, that was his rank twelve toughness coming to the fore.

Luciandro wakened Jack with a small spark to the ear, and he jerked upright, scowling down at the robed mouse.

"I *did* try calling," the mouse insisted. "But you were too far into your slumber to hear."

Jack kept scowling as he looked up at a familiar tree. They were back where Meynardo had first found him. "How long was I out?"

"Not long. Less than half an hour. With you asleep, the horse found its own pace."

First things first. He climbed down from the saddle and moved back to help the villagers down from their horse, giving his neck and shoulders a good shake on the way to clear his muzzy head.

He lifted the majority of them up into the lower branches of the tree, save only for the few warriors who remained whole. Those four who, along with Meynardo and Osmando had survived their decoy missions during the siege, and who would be assisting in the attack. Osmando, given his arm, would remain here.

Then he draped the blanket roll over the branches above as a sort of tent. "You're sure about this?" he asked Luciandro as he bound the edges to various suckers protruding from the branches.

"They'll be safe up there," Luciandro assured him. At least for the time being. Safer than we'll be, certainly. The wards on the saddles will keep any itinerant predators away."

"What happens if I get killed?" Jack asked, not for the first time. "What happens if *you* get killed? What do they do then?"

"I would suggest you don't get killed, then, Jackson Grenell," Luciandro told him without humor. "That is lesson.... where are we now...? Twelve? Yes, that is lesson twelve. Don't get killed. I will endeavor to do the same."

"Not funny."

"Nor was it meant to be," the mouse frowned. "We are in your hands, Jackson," he reminded. "Make no mistake. If you die, in all likelihood, we all die. Keep that in mind going forward, please, and don't spend your life foolishly.

"Now, I've been meaning to ask you," he addressed the man once his fellows were safely stowed. "What are your plans once we've dealt with the mage?"

Jack plopped down to his former seat at the base of the tree. It was still wet, but the rain had lightened to no more than a heavy drizzle. "My original plan," he said offhandedly, "was to draw them out one at a time until they wouldn't come out anymore, and then go in after the rest."

Both Meynardo and Luciandro stared openmouthed at him.

"That's a *terrible* plan!" Meynardo accused. "What sort of sentinel *are* you to be so foolish?"

Jack shrugged. "It's what I had," he admitted. "All I knew of the place this— yesterday afternoon, I guess, now, was what I could see from outside the station. I didn't know how many were in there, how they were armed, or what sorts of skills they might have.

"All I knew for sure was that any of them, picked at random, could probably kick my butt in a stand up fight. So I wasn't planning on giving any of them one of *those* until it was absolutely necessary."

Luciandro had his hand over his eyes, shaking his head. "Perhaps I put too much faith in you," he mumbled.

Jack shot him a look. "Maybe you did," he said with a trace of fire. "I was doing okay until I got called awa—" Even as the words came out, he regretted them, his heart lurching in his chest.

"Disregard that," he sighed. "I don't regret an instant of what I did, and even if you hadn't helped me as much as you have already, I'd do the whole thing over again. Every time."

"Still," the mouse's face was stern. "You cannot simply *hope* your way to victory."

Jack looked to Meynardo. "I no longer have to," he chucked his chin at the younger mouse. "I now have access to a scouting report from a renowned and stealthy rank eight ranger."

Meynardo twitched and measured himself. "A renowned, stealthy, and hard-*assed* rank eight ranger," he corrected. At which point, he waved in the direction of the others and crouched down to begin drawing a map of the ferry station in the mud at the base of the tree, where it wasn't quite so wet, and thus still somewhat firm.

"Corral is here," he said. "Stable here. Behind are a number of wagons and carts in no particular order. There *is* room enough between them, however, to get through if you're careful."

The other four fighters arrived, then, and Meynardo paused, straightening to address Jack. "Oh, of course. Jackson," he waved in the direction of the newcomers. "You haven't officially met my friends, have you?

"Allow me to introduce, Sharamandro," and he indicated the mouse in question with an outstretched hand. This one was garbed similarly to Osmando, and bowed with a flourish of his wide hat.

"Elonardo," a slightly younger mouse in a jacket similar to Meynardo's and likewise without pants. Elonardo bowed and doffed his soft cap.

"Jupitorano," a more gangly specimen garbed some-where in between.

"And Fitupitro," a stouter mouse with tall boots, dark pants, and a tabbard, who bowed and swept his slouch hat in a theatrical manner.

"Along with Osmando and myself," Meynardo explained, "they're what remain of our fighting force.

Jack nodded to each of them in turn. It was telling that Meynardo hadn't included the whole lineage spiel he normally went through. He must be nervous, indeed. None of them were wearing armor. All had small knives, or maybe swords, and all carried bows.

"You should know, Jackson," Meynardo cautioned, his head bowed. "We will aid you so far as we can, but...." he looked up and his face was guilty. "We have twenty-three ar-rows remaining between us, and only Jupitorano's arms and bow are long enough to use the six he has left."

"Hey," Jack reached out to nudge the mouse's head with a gentle fingertip. "I *was* going to go in there alone. I'll be thank-ful for any help I can get."

Meynardo smiled forlornly and fist bumped Jack's finger before turning back to the map.

"Here," he drew a square on the far side of the general oblong he'd used to encompass the station. "is the old station-master's house." he looked up at that. "Cabin, really. Little more than a shack itself. Two rooms, oiled leather over the windows, here and here. One door, here. And it's an actual door, no just a hole in the wall with a blanket hung over it.

"Cats here, here, here, and here," he stabbed the stick into the ground at various points to indicate the locations of the hated enemies of the mice. "Although they may have moved since then. You know cats."

While the other mice nodded solemnly, Jack tried to hide his smirk. Nor did he care about cats. And he already knew there were no dogs.

"Two shacks," Meynardo was still sketching. "Here, and here. Open fronts.

"When I was there earlier, the bandits were scattered out at the edges of the camp, hidden to various degrees," he indicated positions along the outskirts of the camp. "Presumably waiting for us to show ourselves. All had bows and a goodly number of arrows. all wore enchanted armor, none of it below rank ten.

"Their leader was ranging about the station, going from one to another of them in no particular order. No bow. He wore high ranked steel armor and carried an enchanted sword and shield.

"You others," he nodded to his compatriots, "you know your parts, yes?"

The other mice nodded.

"Off you go, then. And be careful."

And off they went. Jack took a moment to wonder how Meynardo had ended up in command given the obviously higher ranks a couple of the others bore. But it didn't really matter, did it?

"They'll infiltrate the camp ahead of us and attempt to set themselves up in hiding within bowshot of at least some of the bandits," Meynardo told him. "Give them a ten minute or so head start," he warned. "We want their hands steady when they draw their bows.

"When the fight starts, they'll attempt to distract the enemy for so long as their arrows hold out. As will I once we arrive."

Jack nodded. "Leaving me free to engage the mage and, presumably, the leader before I have to worry about the rest.

"And, speaking of which," he added, where *is* the mage? Did you find him?"

"Yes," Meynardo said. "He's in the stationmaster's cabin," he stabbed the stick down. "Square in the middle of the main room, hunkered down over his scrying circle." He looked up, then. "Unless we can figure out how to get him out of there, I don't think you're going to get a good line of sight for a bow shot. Not unless you're standing right outside the door on the porch."

That was unwelcome news. "How close can I get to the building while staying in cover, at least?" he asked.

"Through these trees here," Meynardo drew a line. "And up between the carts to the corral," he said. "Across the corral to here. You'll be within about thirty yards of the cabin from there. I can lead you." he looked up again. "How good are you on the trail?" he wondered. "We dare not make too much noise."

"What kind of ground—? Never mind," Jack answered. "I'm pretty sure I'll be fine over wet leaves."

"How long will it take to lead him there?" that was Luciandro. "I remind you that I have to shield him from the scrying spell until the mage is dealt with, and my mana reserves are still quite low."

Meynardo gave the man another look before turning to the wizard. "We're still around a lenn and a quarter out," he said. "So, thirty minutes to the outer ring of the camp?" he ventured. "Being careful to avoid notice by the watchers. Another ten or fifteen minutes around through the trees to within bow range? Maybe a bit more, depending on what happens on the way."

"Don't worry about the more," Jack told him. "Anything happens, I'm gonna want you guys to make yourselves scarce while I deal with it. At that point, the jig will be well and truly up already, and stealth won't be an issue anymore."

"I'll try to see that such things don't happen," Meynardo assured him.

Luciandro nodded without speaking, and hobbled away towards the base of the tree.

As the minutes ticked by, Jack had a thought. "Any way I might be able to get a shot in through the window?" he wondered of Meynardo.

"Through the oiled leather? Meynardo asked dubiously. "It's not exactly transparent. I doubt you'd be able to see more than vague shapes through it."

"How thick is it, though?" Jack asked. "Thick enough to foul the arrow?"

Meynardo had to think about that. It hadn't been something he'd specifically examined. "I... don't *think* so?" he didn't sound too sure. "And you'd have to be careful of your line. You wouldn't want to accidentally hit any of the captives."

"The *what*?" Jack's voice went flat, and his face drew into hard lines.

Luciandro had been huddled against the tree, while they waited to move, meditating. Gathering his strength. He was an old mouse, and still not recovered from the exhaustion of the past days. Even moreso than Jack, he was weary, and the coming contest would tax him to his limits. The tone of Jack's voice brought him to full consciousness in an instant.

"The... the captives," Meynardo rocked back. "The stolen girls. The ones you're here to rescue, yes? Isn't that why you're here? To rescue them? They're in the back room of the stationmaster's cabin."

"You ready to go, Luciandro?" Jack asked without turning his head.

"Jackson...."

"It's too soon," Meynardo insisted. "The others won't be in place in time."

"We'll work it out," Jack hissed through his clenched jaw.

Meynardo looked to Luciandro, but the old wizard shook his head silently.

Grim Resolve, Luciandro thought. He'd hoped to avoid its overt presence, but it looked as though that was not to be. Meynardo's innocent slip had triggered it. He could feel the pall of it radiating out from the man, and he fought for calm.

Ready or not, shielded or not, the man was about to make his move, and they would be carried along with him or left behind.

"Ready, Jackson," he sighed. "pick me up, if you please.

I'm far too weary to walk, and I'm far too old to run."

Jack scooped him up and placed him on his shoulder, where the wizard took hold of his collar and began the spell that would shield them from the enemy mage, struggling to concentrate against the pall of the sentinel's curse.

Showdown

"**A**nything?"

Hurgus raised bleary eyes to his boss. "Any interest in mice?" he wondered. "Looks like a few of 'em heading this way. Other than that, just what I've already told you about."

Bear lifted his hand to give Hurgus a thump, but didn't bother. *Mice.* He snorted. *Let the cats worry about 'em.*

Out in the darkness, Jack crouched behind the rails of the corral, hugging the deeper shadows. He'd just seen a hulking brute in three quarter plate with a shield hanging from one shoulder wander into the stationmaster's cabin, and wondered if that was the bandit leader.

"You see his rank?" he whispered to Luciandro.

"Eighteen," Luciandro's voice was thin and brittle. "Place me on the ground, Jackson," he wheezed. "We haven't much time left, so you must hurry if you expect my aid with the mage.

"Once you take your shot, run. Meynardo will help me to get clear. I'm afraid I won't be of much help beyond that."

It had taken them longer than it should have. The bandits were more alert than they'd expected, given the hour. Their leader must have been up their asses the whole night to get this kind of dedication out of them. But he was here now.

Meynardo had been right about the window. He couldn't see much through it. Light and vague shapes, no more. But his detect life skill may as well have been a ten thousand dollar thermal vision scope for the clarity he was getting this close in.

The lines of the figures were sharp and clear. He could easily tell the big rank eighteen from the hunched over mage, from the huddled forms in the back room. If only he could get a little closer.

"Boss?" Hurgus looked over to Bear, a quaver in his voice and a pleading look in his eyes.

"Oh, alright," Bear groaned. "I don't conjure nobody's

gonna cover a whole lenn while yer in th' privy. But be quick about it."

Hurgus lurched to his feet, and turned for the door.

The hell? Jack saw the mage's silhouette shift, its head rising up to clear the window, and without conscious thought, he straightened, drew, and let fly, all in a single motion. He was still riding the follow through when he heard a yell to his left and something sliced through the web of his left thumb. He hit the ground scrabbling for the back of the corral, ducking beneath the legs of the nearest horse and clawing his way across the mud for the back rail.

He heard more yelling in his wake. Words he couldn't understand, but whose intent rang loud and clear. And the voice was coming closer.

Farther off, another, deeper voice, started yelling something, voice bleeding anger.

He cleared the back of the corral, and hit the ground rolling. Staggering to his feet, he turned and nocked an arrow, pain lancing up his arm as the blood-slicked bow pressed against the slice in his hand.

Looking up, he sucked in a breath. One of the bandits was perched on the far rail of the corral, straddling it, his bow already aimed, an arrow already at full draw. He was still yelling, but his voice cut off with an abrupt, "*OW!*"

The shot went well wide and high, sailing out into the trees. Jack's return shot didn't, and the bandit rolled over backwards into the mud of the yard.

Jack spun and legged it into the trees, ducked over and smiling grimly. *Some*body had put an itty bitty poisoned arrow into that clown's neck just as he'd been about to put his much larger one into Jack's middle. *Thanks, Meynardo,* he thought. *I owe you one.*

* * *

Hurgus hadn't taken a full step before an arrow sliced through the window covering and buried itself in through his ear. He crumpled bonelessly to the floor without so much as a whimper.

Bear couldn't immediately come to grips with the sight, and stood frozen for half a second.

Then Timony started yelling and running across the yard, "I got'im, I got 'im!"

"NO, you fool!" Bear launched himself for the door. "Don't you *follow* 'im!"

He bounced off the doorframe and out onto the porch just in time to see Timony let fly wildly into the trees with another arrow, his right hand going to his neck as he spun his head to his right. An instant later, he was rolling backward off the corral and into the mud, an arrow sticking up out of his chest.

"Alright," he hauled up on the porch, raging. "I've had enough of this! I'm done playing with this ghost in the rain and the dark."

Raising his voice, he called out to his remaining minions. "HIE! Back here, all of ya! Now!"

"You! Flost!" he ordered the first of them to appear from the rain drenched trees. "You and Membry bring them wenches out. All of 'em. Strip 'em down and string 'em up yonder by the corral. See can we get 'em screamin'. He's close in now, at least. That'll bring him the rest of the way, I'll wager. You others, hunker down and find cover so's he don't just pot us from th' trees."

"Even the little 'un, Boss?" Flost wondered.

"You punch drunk?" Bear snarled. "She ain't no wench, now, is she? *Product* is what *she* is. The *wenches*, blast you! Now go!

"Likes to pick us off one by one, eh?" he muttered while his two subordinates hustled into the cabin. "Let's see how good he is with all of us to oncet."

* * *

Jack was back in the trees a hundred yards or so, where he'd left FoeSmite before going in. He was cinching a bandage

around his left hand, one end of the cloth rag in his teeth, when he heard the commotion start.

He'd heard the leader calling them in a few minutes earlier, though he'd not understood the words. What else *could* he have been doing? So much for their brilliant plan, huh? There wouldn't be any tiny little archers distracting the bad guys from hiding now that the bad guys were all displacing. But the chance for that shot had been too perfect for him to pass up.

Then the first scream split the night, and his blood went chill.

Snatching up FoeSmite, he shimmied 'round the tree he'd been hunkered beneath and arced in towards the camp for a better look, crawling low on his belly through the slick grass, FoeSmite gripped at the end in one hand and trailing behind.

They'd thrown ropes over a hanging limb near the corral and had already hoisted one of several naked girls up by her wrists until her toes left the ground. She hung limp.

The screaming was coming from the second, who they were still about hoisting aloft, none too gently. Even as he watched, one of the bandits snapped at her with a length of rope, the crack of its impact ringing clear even through the rain. Her screaming intensified as fresh blood ran down her rain-slicked flesh.

Two more girls were being held ready, the last of them still being stripped of what crude garments they'd allowed her up until now while she wept bitterly.

Something changed inside him in that moment. Something that had been building for most of his adult life. Building from his time in the desert, watching the horrors inflicted on the sex slaves the jihadis had captured and held. Building from the tales of the grooming gangs running rampant throughout Europe, preying on young girls, and protected by the so-called law. Building from the legions of sex traffickers who ran the southern border of his own country like a route, all the way to the halls of government in the east and the dens of the glitterati in the west. Tens of thousands of innocents tortured and abused every year for the amusement of the sick and twisted.

Faintly, a chime sounded in the back of his head, followed by a clear voice. Calm, feminine, like the helpful guide in a GPS navigating app. He should have been paying attention, but his whole consciousness was focused on the hulking rank eighteen with the sword and shield, laughing and waving as the terrified girls were strung up one after another.

New skill acquired, the voice informed. *Status affect.* **Cold Rage.** *Speed, plus ten percent.*
Strength, plus ten percent.
Agility, plus ten percent.
Perception, plus ten percent.
Auto-cast **Ignore Wounds (Minor), rank one.**
Duration: *one hundred-eighty seconds.*
Cooldown: *four hundred-twenty seconds.*
Skill cost: *two mana points per second.*
Skill cost: *one health point per second.*
Cold Rage, *Once initiated, cannot be cancelled while MP or HP remain.*

The chime sounded again.

New skill acquired. Secondary affect. **Ignore Wounds (Minor), rank one: Ignore Minor Wounds.**
Duration at rank one: *two hundred-forty seconds.*
Skill cost: *zero-point-five mana points per second.*
Effect: *Minor wounds suffered will have no effect on user while status is active. Intermediate wounds will be reduced by half their normal effect*
Caution: *Ignore Wounds does not prevent wounds, nor heal them. All wound effects will manifest upon status expiration.*

A third chime.

Bonus: Equipped item: Ring: *Blessing of the Children of Scarpwatch.*
While equipped, Blessing of the Children of Scarpwatch decreases the cost of all casting by ten percent. May be combined with other bonuses.

* * *

"Oh," the Mauler laughed menacingly as he stalked to

the hanging girls. "This won't do at all, *will* it? We needs 'em *all* screaming, *don't* we?"

He slung his shield and moved to the nearest of the wenches. The farm girl they'd only taken earlier in the week. The strongest of them, she was. Not yet completely drained. He knew she had some yell left in her, but she refused to more than sob. Closing on her, he hauled his free left arm back to see could he clout her loud.

"Boss!" Membry called to him in a nervous voice. But he'd already seen the movement from the corner of an eye.

Turning, he watched the dark figure rise from the grass. All hooded, cloaked, and scarifying, he was. Except he wasn't, was he? Confusing was what he was. A hand came up, swept the hood clear, and undid the brooch holding the sodden green cloak at the neck, allowing the garment to slide from armored shoulders, giving Bear his first good look.

Tattered, stained armor, helm, sword, dagger. All of them obviously well higher than rank zero to his well-trained eye, beat up though they were. And yet, no life crystal. Not even a shimmer.

And that stick. Held crossways at the figure's hips, seven long feet of it and glowing dark carnelian red, crimson veins so bright as flowing lava coursing its length. Obviously enchanted to a stupid high degree, that stick.

But no crystal. Was the figure a construct of some sort? Couldn't be a grubber, could it? Not with them weapons. Then the figure looked up, and The Mauler stifled a gasp. Its eyes! The whites of its eyes were glowing like pale fire.

* * *

On the far side of the station, Ephram saw the glow of the eyes, and turned quickly away. "Yep!" he nodded to himself as he spun. "Higher Golem. Madwoman's back, alright! Good luck, boys!"

He was shedding his already loosened armor as he ran the ten steps to the end of the pier, and was into the river and swimming hard for the other side by the time any of the others had time to move.

* * *

Jack took his first step and the four lesser bandits arrayed around the yard stepped out of cover and let fly, all at once. He ducked and weaved, FoeSmite spinning baton-like too fast to see, intercepting every one. One deflected arrow, bounced from a pauldron, one dug into the ground between his feet, the remaining two sailed clear.

He twisted his upper body, drew back his arm and released, slinging FoeSmite spearlike straight at the rightmost of the bowmen, going nearly to a knee with the force of the throw. He struck his target in the helm, the blow knocking the helm clear and rocking his head back, toppling him into the dirt.

The instant FoeSmite struck and rebounded, Jack called it back, catching it as he regained his feet, spinning with the catch and releasing at a fresh target as he came full circle.

FoeSmite twirled away like a flying buzzsaw blade, whistling through the air and striking a second bandit hard at the juncture of neck and shoulder as he was nocking an arrow for a followup shot, snapping his neck and near tearing his head from his shoulders before caroming away. Jack recalled the staff an instant later, smiling grimly as it changed course in mid-air and returned to him.

The Mauler had unslung his shield by this time and charged. FoeSmite slammed into Jack's hands barely in time to block the first powerful blow of the heavy sword. A second came down almost too swiftly to counter, but Jack was moving nearly as quickly now, his reflexes supercharged by the layered bonuses. This blow he parried to the side, following through with a whirl and a strike.

The Mauler got his shield down in time to save his legs, but the glowing staff struck with such force the rank sixteen shield buckled and was dashed against them in any case, knocking him back a couple of paces.

Another, lesser volley of arrows was coming in, and Jack wasn't able to completely block them. The first, he managed to divert so that it scraped along his brigandine, but the second was biting into his thigh even as FoeSmite shattered the shaft

midway between head and fletching. He didn't even look down to the wound. He looked up instead. Into the eyes of the frightened bowmen.

But the Mauler was coming in again, dashing his ruined shield into Jack's face as he charged. From there, they each forgot about the others.

Even with his current buffs, Jack was in nearly all ways clearly outmatched by the rank eighteen. All but one. FoeSmite.

Bear the Mauler wielded a magical weapon of his own. Unnamed, it was, but powerful in its own right. A rank fifteen bastard sword of uncommonly rare quality and possessing two upgrade slots, both of which the Mauler had filled.

Durability took up the primary, and sharpness the secondary. The Mauler was an old hand and understood that the sharpest of blades would do no good if it broke. With the shield gone, he bore it now in both hands, and its speed was the greater for that.

The sword, with it's high rank and upgrades, ignored Jack's much lower ranked brigandine, and the mail beneath it as though they were common cloth. Its every bite drew blood, its every touch clawed at his life, already wicking away under the grip of his status effect.

For all the damage he was doing, though, the Mauler was in little better position. FoeSmite had been caught up in the status effect. *Its* rage, however, was in no way cold. Under the impetus of Jack's enhanced abilities and deadly concentration, every strike against the bandit chief's armor sundered steel. Every kiss pulped flesh and crushed bone.

More, with each exchange, each block, each bind, wherever wood touched steel, it was the steel that gave way.

The two remaining archers, Membry and Flost, they were, were visibly shaken as they watched the duel, drawing together unconsciously. Each had an arrow nocked, bow half drawn, but neither could do much more. The combatants were too close together. They moved too quickly. Almost too quickly to follow, let alone target.

And then the agony came. Some invisible foe began

peppering them with tiny slivers, each of them delivering the pain of a cave wasp's sting. Turn as they might, neither could find the least trace of what might be attacking them. And the attacks kept coming.

A minute and a bit into the fight, the bandit leader cried out for the first time. A few seconds later, he went down to a knee, desperately beating back the stranger's attack,

Membry and Flost found their breaking point. Between their leader going down, and the rain of agonizing pain, they looked to one another, nodded and spun on their heels to leg it into the trees, not even bothering to catch up horses.

Had the two held but a few more minutes, they'd have seen their chance. For if Bear the Mauler was done, Jackson Grenell was little better. His final strike, the one that ended the duel, had come at the cost of three inches of steel in his belly, right through the steel plates and rings. Cold Rage had expired, and the last few seconds of Ignore Wounds were ticking off. He had nothing left.

He sank to his knees, and back onto his heels, FoeSmite held upright before him as the bandit leader flopped over and lay crumpled in the dirt a few feet away.

The Mauler lay where he'd fallen for a moment or two, pain taking up his entire world. his legs were broken, each of them in multiple places. And his arms. Ribs, too, more than a few. His left shoulder joint felt like jagged glass sawing through his flesh. He was frothing blood at the mouth, so he knew he'd one dead lung. But at least only one. Everything between his chest and knees was pure, acid dipped agony.

The crystalless monstrosity had gone still, finally, its eyes losing their unholy glow. Maybe he'd done for it at the end. Maybe he wouldn't be dying here in the slowly falling rain after all. He had potions in the cabin. Some of them very powerful. And magical charms that would speed healing, or even mend bones.

He didn't even bother trying to get up, though. Shrugging himself over onto his belly, he scrabbled slowly towards the cabin with the half arm he had left, hoping against hope that the false grubber didn't simply wake up, come over and crush his skull with that damned cursed staff as he crawled.

He was nearly to the cabin when the thing toppled to its side in a spreading pool of crimson, but he didn't stop crawling. He didn't get to those potions quick, he wouldn't get to them at all.

Of the two who'd run, only Membry made it out of the camp.

As Flost was pelting through the tangle of wagons, a small form leapt onto his shoulder from one of them. Before the man could realize his peril, Meynardo drew and let go his last arrow into the man's carotid artery from less than an inch away. He leapt clear as the man stumbled, rolling and springing to his feet as the human crumpled, twitching.

While it was true that the poison wasn't normally strong enough to kill a human, there were some exceptions. Delivering it directly to the brain was one of them.

Staggering back to the twitching human, Meynardo drew his knife. Small, it was, but razor sharp. He'd eventually make it through to the jugular if he worked at it. After that, it was only a matter of whether the poison or blood loss killed him first.

The Mauler finally reached the cabin and disappeared inside. The camp fell into silence, broken only by the sounds of the falling rain and the soft moaning of the hanging captives.

Help Arrives

The silence didn't last long. It was broken within minutes by the squalling of the station cats as they were hunted down and sent packing. The arrows wouldn't kill them — he mice had too few remaining— but they'd be painful enough to keep the cats away for a good long while.

Once the cats were seen off, the tiny warriors raced to the side of their fallen champion.

Fitupitro was the first to reach him. He immediately laid hands on him and began casting intermediate healing, greater. At his rank of twenty, it was the strongest healing spell he knew.

Sharamandro reached him next, and began his own casting of the same spell.

Even with the both of them together, they knew that it was a losing battle. They hadn't the mana to heal something as large as he was of as many wounds as he had. The best they could hope was to stave off his death for a few moments longer. But that didn't mean they wouldn't try.

Jupitorano and Elonardo arrived together and made as if to cast, but Fitupitro ordered them off. "Find some thread or something, and a needle. We need to begin closing these wounds quickly! Check the stationmaster's cabin."

The two of them dashed off.

Luciandro hobbled up, leaning heavily on Meynardo. "Have a care you don't touch that stick," he warned them unnecessarily. They'd seen what it could do and weren't about to get anywhere near it.

"Meynardo," Luciandro ordered. "Go to the cabin and see if you can find any potions or elixirs. Have a care to stay clear of that rank eighteen. I'm not sure he's dead."

Meynardo nodded and ducked under the old wizards arm, pelting off across the station yard.

Meynardo found Jupitorano and Elonardo crouched beside the cabin's door.

"The big one is still alive," Jupitorano whispered.

Meynardo barely slowed. "into the back room," he called over his shoulder at the other two as he veered around the dead mage and his magic circle. "Find bandages and medical supplies if they have any."

He swung wide around the other bloody lump against the far wall beside a cabinet and an overturned chest. It rolled its head and stared owl-eyed at him as though it couldn't quite decide whether to believe what it was seeing or not.

He ignored it as he went up the far side of the rough hewn cabinet beside which the body lay. He wasn't sure what he was looking for. The humans apparently stored their potions differently than his people, and none of them bore labels he could decipher. The lot of them had very colorful names, but none was particularly informative.

Then he saw them. Scattered and broken, a number of empty bottles surrounded the groaning figure of the bandit leader, whose eyes were still fixed on him. Meynardo made a rude gesture, which caused the eyes to widen.

There were still a number of similar bottles atop the cabinet. He chose the largest one there that contained red liquid, the typical color of healing potions. This one was of a deep, almost burgundy hue. Hopefully, that meant a higher order potion. He took it up. It was heavy!

Now, how was he to get it down without breaking it? A quick search revealed nothing on the cabinet's surface with which he might fashion a sling. Glancing over the side, the only thing that looked like it might cushion the fall was the bandit leader, and he was mostly covered in steel plate armor. "Hey!" he called down. "Reach up here and I'll hand you down a potion!"

The bandit looked to be thinking about whether he believed what was happening for a few seconds, and Meynardo saw his arm twitch, then quiver. Then fall back to the floor.

"Good!" Meynardo grinned. Then he grabbed the bottle, spun 'round a couple of turns, and hurled it with both hands onto the dirty mop of the bandits hair, where it bounced free with a hollow 'tonk', and clattered to the floor. He followed, leaping clear of the bandit, who was now struggling to move his other arm to catch at the spinning potion bottle. *Hah! As if!* Meynardo caught up the bottle and was off across the floor, heading for the door.

He met Jupitorano coming out of the back room, a human-sized spool of rough thread held in both arms. Elonardo was hot on his heels with a long needle that looked none too clean. The three of them nodded to one another and scampered out into the mud with their prizes.

Bear the Mauler stared out the empty doorway for awhile after they'd disappeared. *Did that... was that real?* He wondered. He allowed his head to flop around on his neck, taking in the array of vials, bottles, and charms scattered about and atop of him. He'd never taken so much of so many different things all at once before, and was feeling quite strange.

His eyes went back to the doorway. *That must be it*, he thought. *Side effects. Heh. Talking mice of all things.* He wondered which of the poorly understood concoctions was doing it, or if it was a combination. Later on, if he lived, he'd have to ask— No, he'd not be able to ask Hurgus, he supposed. Maybe he'd find another, better mage. Hurgus hadn't been worth much in the end.

It took three of them to get the potion into Jack's mouth. Even then, laying on his side as he was, Luciandro had to throw a spark at his Adam's apple to trigger a swallowing reflex and get it to where it would do some good.

"Meynardo!" Luciandro gasped. "Elonardo! Find his fingers! The middle, ring, and small fingers of his right hand." He waved vaguely about the yard. "They're out there someplace. If we're quick enough, we should be able to reattach them."

This was the tableau that Cable and Tiarraluna beheld as they emerged from the trees beside the road, having left the speedwagon well clear of the camp and come in on foot.

Tiarraluna cried out at the sight of the bloody blue lump

in the center of the yard, hiking her robes and racing heedlessly across the mud, splashing it liberally across the white and magenta cloth. His health bar looked completely empty! The only reason she could be sure he yet lived was that it remained visible at all. And there were vermin crawling over him!

She brought up to an ungainly halt when she spied the small, maroon robed figure in the tall wizard's hat blocking her way. It was holding a staff aloft, the jeweled end glowing brightly.

"Make your intentions known!" the high-pitched, but no less ominous voice demanded. "You will not approach our hero—"

"He is *my* hero," she shot back, bringing her own staff to full light and holding it before her. "And you *will not* keep me from him!"

The tiny figure took a step back with a gasp, and then leaned forward, eyes going wide. "Lady Luna?" it demanded. "How are you still—?"

"I am Tiarraluna Galbradia," she told it, chin going up. "And I am Jackson Grenell's party leader."

The glow from the creature's staff dimmed. "Then go to him," it said, stepping aside. "But do not touch the staff. Nor my people who are helping him."

"I know full well about the staff," she growled as she passed, breaking into a run. "I helped to create it!"

"Do not touch it!" he called to her retreating back. "It is the only thing keeping him alive!"

She was at Jack's side in an instant, barely pausing as the mice made way. "You had better not die, you fool," she wept with quiet intensity as she laid a hand upon his chest and the glow of Lesser Greater Healing began to enfold him. "Do not *dare* to die! I forbid it!"

Another pair of mice came out of the darkness, bearing his missing fingers. Without addressing her, and careful to avoid the still-glowing staff, they gently laid them against the bloody stubs from which they'd been sundered.

Cable, meanwhile, raced immediately for the tree from which the naked girls were hanging, drawing his belt knife.

The nearest of the girls also looked to be the strongest, so he saw to her first, and had her feet on the ground swiftly, ignoring her nakedness for the moment. She seemed largely intact and was still able move on her own.

She helped him with the others, who were farther gone. They worked together to cut them down and lay them as gently as they might in the mud of the yard and the rain.

His healing spells weren't anything like as powerful as Tiarraluna's, but they would suffice for such wounds as the girls had suffered, at least for the moment. His helper shrugged into the rags the bandits had so recently torn from her while he attended the others.

That done, and again with her help, he got them, one by one, into the cover of one of the open shacks and out of the weather.

He was searching for dry clothing when he found Bear the Mauler in the cabin, slumped in a corner near a rough cabinet and an overturned chest, surrounded by a scattering of potion bottles and healing talismans. Several of the potion bottles nearest him were dashed open and empty. A number of the talismans lay against his bruise mottled skin, glowing softly. Some of them were two deep.

The Mauler wasn't in much better condition than when he'd managed to overturn the chest. Worse, come to that. Even powerful potions took awhile with injuries as severe as his were. Even left alone, it would yet be some time before he could move well enough to reach the remaining potions or healing aids. Longer still before he'd be able to move or fight. All time which he was now not going to get.

"Well, then," he coughed, frothy blood dribbling from his chin as he looked up at the rank thirty standing in the doorway. "This'll be it then, I suppose."

"Suppose so," Cable nodded. "Well past due, *I'd* say."

"You catch those bloody cowards lit out and deserted

me?" the Mauler wondered, his head lolling against the wall.

"One of 'em," Cable nodded again. "Not much fight left in 'im, though.

"You the lot sacked Weilei's Crossing?"

"We are," the Mauler tried semi-successfully to nod. "An' Tullbury. An' Ch-Cheslisston. Piney Grove. Few others."

"I figured," Cable's voice came flat.

"...the chaos *was* that thing?" the Mauler asked after a tortured breath or two.

Cable chuckled, though there was little humor in it. "One of them other world heroes," he informed the bandit leader. "Sentinel, this one is."

The Mauler's eyes widened. "*Sentinel*, is it? Well, now, ain't *that* just my luck. Did I kill him at least?"

"Not that I noticed," Cable shook his head. "Healer's working on him now."

"Damn," the Mauler let his head flop back against the wall. "Well, get it over with, then," he told the tall man. "Too late t'do it painless or quick, so just get on with it."

Cable didn't answer. He simply stepped forward, raising his spear.

"One last thing," The Mauler asked, staring up at the poised spearhead, his voice calm. "You seen any talking mice about? Wearin' coats, 'n' hats 'n' little bitty swords?"

Outside, Tiarraluna was crouched over the still form of Jackson Grenell, struggling to assay the extent of his injuries without relaxing her concentration on the spell. There were so many, though. *Too* many. How had he kept moving long enough to *acquire* such an array of wounds?

His armor was shredded, his helm split. The shaft of an arrow protruded from a gaping hole in his thigh, as though he'd stirred it around after it had buried itself in his flesh.

"Uncle was right," she sniffed around her tears. "You *are* an idiot."

A faint shadow fell over her and she looked up. It was a bedraggled girl of about her own age, rain-slicked black hair stuck to her head, dirty rags hanging from her shivering body. One of the captives, obviously.

"What are you doing out here?" she demanded, her voice ragged. "You should be out of the rain, at least, lest you catch your death."

"Not until the hero is safe," the girl's voice was no less ragged.

The girl dropped to her knees opposite Tiarraluna, reaching down to begin undoing the buckles and straps of the armor with shaking hands. She managed to get the brigandine opened and moved aside, but the mail was problematic. There was no way to get it clear without moving him, which was obviously not a good idea. Then one of the strange mice she'd been seeing crawled within the torn mail and stood, holding it clear of his skin. Another moved to the other side, and did the same, giving her room to work.

She settled back and hunched over to shield the needle and thread she'd brought with her from the drizzle. "T-Those animals," she sniffed as she fed a length of thread through the needle's eye under the bright glow of the jewel in Tiarraluna's staff. "They didn't even bother to search our wagon. Aft-after they'd murdered my parents for it. Just parked it t'other side of the corral. S-so I fetched papa's doctoring kit.

"That... that awful man, he cut this one up something fierce while they was fighting. He'll need t'be sewed up, I think, even with your magic, won't he?"

Tiarraluna was struggling already with her task and the unfamiliar spell, and neither the girl's talking nor the presence of the strange mice was particularly helpful. But nor was she wrong.

"It will help," she said through clenched teeth. "The less blood he is losing, the sooner I may begin to heal him."

Before long, the former captive was tying off the thread she'd used to stitch the first wound. The deep one in his middle. She'd had to sew it together in two layers, like her father had taught her to do with particularly deep wounds, and leave the stitches loose to allow weeping. She'd done it often enough over the past year, although only on cattle before this.

Cable showed up as she began on the second of the deeper slashes, crouching and laying a number of talismans and potion bottles beside the still form they were working on. "Found these in the cabin," he informed them. "Along with a little girl, tied up in a corner. Put her in the shack with the others."

"That'll be my sister, Juniper," the girl with the needle said without looking up. "Is she alright?"

Cable took a second to answer, observing as she leant close over Jackson Grenell's body, struggling to stitch him up through the rents in his mail. Raising an eyebrow at her assistants.

"She's about as fine as can be expected, I suppose," he allowed. "She says they never messed with her or anything. Just kept her tied up and let her know she was to be sold."

"Could you find something to cover him, please, Cable?" Tiarraluna asked then. "We dare not move him just yet, and the rain is not helpful."

"Right," he nodded and moved off to try and find a tarp or something.

Recovery

Jack opened his eyes. He lay in a grassy glade, beneath the shade of a spreading ash tree under a bright summer sun. He smelled water and fresh grass, and heard the chuckling of a stream somewhere nearby.

He didn't feel any pain at all. That didn't make any *kind* of sense. He turned his head slowly to take in his surroundings without moving anything else. There, to his left, was the stream. Just seeing it made him thirsty. To his right....

There was a naked girl relaxing against the side of the ash tree's trunk, long, dark green, curly hair tumbling down her back. Which, he noticed now that he was paying attention, was also green. And ever so slightly translucent.

The whole of her, in fact, from the myrtle green of her hair to the tea green of her skin, to the sea green of her finger-nails, were all shades of that same color. Including her emerald eyes, which were currently glaring at him from her scowling elf-in face.

"Uhm...." he ventured cautiously. "Hi?"

She crossed her arms and turned her head away with a toss of her hair. "Hmmph!" she grunted.

Okay, he decided. *That's the way it is, eh?* He started to roll onto his side so he could get to his feet.

"Don't move, you idiot!" she snapped, once more glaring at him, her skin tone darkening, her eyes glowing. "You'll die if you move. Just stay still until help comes and I can see you gone from here!"

"What...?"

"Don't talk to me!" she hissed. "Murderer! Monster! *Treekiller!*"

What the hell was she talking about?

* * *

Jack opened his eyes. Darkness and pain. How many times was this now? But he didn't recognize the roof, and the place smelled of stale booze, rotting food, and rancid sweat.

And death. He wrinkled his nose and stifled a sneeze.

Taking stock and considering the great heaping piles of pain, he decided he was probably still alive, although he didn't see how. He was pretty sure he'd been dead. That sunny glade.... Not heaven as he'd have expected it, but nice enough, and definitely not of *this* world.

He became aware of a weight against his thigh and looked down. Spreading silver hair bisected by a band of orchid. Where the hell had *she* come from? And why was she sleeping on him?

"Finally awake, are we?" the whisper came from directly beside his right ear.

"What's going on?" he whispered back. "Where am I, and how long was I out?" he flexed the fingers of his left hand. "And why am I still holding FoeSmite?"

"In order," the mage answered. "The stationmaster's cabin, four days, and because it was all that was keeping you alive for the first three."

Now he did turn his head, looking into the glowing, button eyes of the little mage. "How's that again?"

"You were drawing mana from the staff," Luciandro informed him. "Don't ask me how. Not enough to heal you, it nonetheless kept you from passing completely through death's door until your friends arrived."

He looked back to Tiarraluna, sleeping, her head turned slightly in his direction. Her face looked hollow and drawn.

"Friends?" he whispered, eyes drooping. "Plural?"

"Another adven—" but Luciandro didn't finish. Jackson was already asleep.

The next time Jack's eyes opened, both Luciandro and Tiarraluna were gone. What's more, FoeSmite was leaning against the far wall propped up in the corner behind the doorway. There was light coming through the oiled leather window covering, and the door stood open, allowing bright sunlight to shine through.

For the second time since arriving on Mund, or was it the

third, he was unsure of how much time had passed.

As he lay there quietly, a strange girl with black hair, and wearing a clean, homespun dress entered from the porch, carrying a shallow clay pot. She must not have noticed that he was awake, probably because she never so much as glanced towards the bed. She had eyes only for the staff in the corner.

"Oh," she whispered, "*there* you are, *aren't* you. So lovely, so powerful. I saw how you thrashed those bad men, yes I *did*. With your beautiful glow. Like an avenging *angel*. I brought you something to show you how much I appreciate you."

Jack was still trying to work out what the hell she was going on about when she reached for the staff. He lurched upright, his arm lancing out to summon the deadly weapon before she could touch it. "No!" he yelled.

The girl whirled to face him, holding FoeSmite in one hand, the clay pot in the other. "Oh!" she exclaimed. "You're awake. *Jehsha*, you gave me a fright. I'll fetch the mages straight away." She set the clay pot on the floor and placed FoeSmite's butt inside before hurrying out into the yard.

Jack stared dumbfounded for a good minute and a half, before shaking his head and flopping back down onto the mattress. He hadn't been able to understand much of what she'd been saying, but he could read body language and facial expressions as well as the next guy.

Able to crush tempered steel and shatter bone, he thought, chagrined. *weak to flattery. Good to know.*

He was lying on his back, staring at the ceiling by the time Tiarraluna came charging in, Luciandro on her shoulder. The lurch had cost him. Apparently, however long he'd been out, it hadn't been long enough, and his stomach felt as though there was a sword blade still in it.

"Jack san," Tiarraluna's voice caught. "How do you feel?"

He looked up into her worried face and smiled in spite of himself, as his heart started thumping. "Alive?" he ventured hoarsely. "Not sure how, though. And it still feels like I should be dead."

"You very nearly were," she admonished. "Such that neither good Luciandro nor myself can understand how you are not."

That caused him to raise an eyebrow. He remembered the ash tree and the naked green girl. "How many gods does Mund have?" he asked.

"Only Jehsha," she answered, puzzled. "and Torhahm, the dark god of the demons, I suppose. Why? Does your world have more than that?"

He almost shrugged, but stopped himself. His memory of the fight was hazy, and he still wasn't sure how torn up he might be. The pain washing through him suggested a lot. "Depends on who you ask," he wheezed. "Even those who'll say only one won't always agree on who it might be. So, no naked green girls?"

Her eyes narrowed. "No, Jack san," she whispered, voice even. "No naked girls of any sort. Why do you ask?"

He didn't much like that look. Lot of information in that look that he wasn't ready to acknowledge. "A dream, I suppose," he said. "How bad is it?"

"Dreaming of naked green girls?" she asked archly. "Very bad, Jack san. Naked girls of any color are generally considered to be troublesome for such as you."

It was at this point that it occurred to Jack that he was understanding every word she was saying, in spite of his having sent the translating ring back with her. Belatedly, he checked his right hand so see if she'd slipped it back on while he'd been out.

That stopped him for awhile, as he examined the metal brace and the bandages that covered his forearm, wrist, most of his hand and all of his fingers save the thumb.

He looked up without saying anything.

"That Mauler fellow cut three of your fingers off at some point during your fight," Luciandro informed him casually. "But we found them and put them back on." Then, after a moment, "it will take some time, of course, before they're fully healed, even with magical aid."

He remembered Tiarraluna's warning back during his guild testing. *Accelerates natural healing.* "How is it I don't—?

Never mind," he allowed his hand to flop down on the bed, wincing as it struck the rough cloth.

He checked his left hand, and there it was, beside the focus the mice had made.

Tiarraluna gasped and leaned forward quickly, raising his tunic clear of what Jack realized was a spreading stain of crimson. *Oh,* the thought struck. *That don't look good!*

"You must refrain from sudden movement," Luciandro warned, as he leapt to the bed and moved to aid Tiarraluna.

They were at it for awhile as Jack lay back and let them work. At some point during this, he faded out again.

Darkness. No, not quite. There was a lamp on the far table, turned down until it gave off barely a glow. This time he made sure not to make any sudden moves. He turned his head slowly in that direction. Was that a huddled form laying atop the table beneath the lamp? "Hey," he whispered, feeling his stomach pull uncomfortably.

"Shhh!" the figure returned with an oddly discordant tone. "The mages are asleep. You don't want to wake them."

"Meynardo?" he whispered back. "What's wrong with your voice?"

The mouse leapt from tabletop to a chair and then to the floor. A moment later, he was climbing the blanket to the surface of the bed, bringing up beside Jack. He was different than Jack remembered. Taller. Less... mouse-like. And he was wearing pants and a shirt.

"What d'you think?"Meynardo asked when he saw Jack looking. "Millie made them for me."

Jack nodded approvingly. "Now all you need is somebody too make you a pair of boots."

There was another change. The difference between what Jack was hearing inside his head and what was coming out of Meynardo's mouth were further apart. Not as bad as Osmando's, but it still made Jack's ears itch.

"I ranked up," Meynardo's excited whisper caused Jack to grin. "Several times, actually. I'm rank twelve now! Nearly to thirteen!"

"Good for you," Jack congratulated him. "And thanks for saving my life out there."

"Hey," Meynardo waved him off. "What are friends for?"

"We get them all?" Jack wondered.

The smile was gone. "You killed all but four, and you came *very* close to killing their leader. Nice shot with the mage, by the way," he added. "You caught him so off guard, I believe your arrow entered his mind before the thought he might need to raise a ward could.

"Three of them fled," he continued. "I killed one of those. The spearman killed another. The third, I'm afraid, had the good sense to bolt so soon as he saw you, and was well gone before any of us had a chance to pursue. Oh, and the spearman finished off the leader."

"Finished off—?" Jack frowned. "Damn! I thought I'd killed him."

"He had a good number of healing items secreted here in the cabin," Meynardo told him. "Otherwise you would have. You broke nearly every bone in his body." Then his smile returned. "On the other hand, once he... ah... no longer needed those healing items, we were able to use them to keep *you* alive until your friends came for you."

"Yeah," Jack frowned. "Friends again. I know Tiarraluna, but you said something about a spearman? I don't know any spearmen."

"No?" Meynardo straightened. "But he is from your guild, and is apparently a member of your party."

"*My* part— Wait... did you get his name?"

"Cable," the mouse told him. "Antel Cable."

"Okay," Jack nodded carefully. "I know who he is, I think. He was supposed to be gone on a quest. I suppose she found him in Mokkelton and corralled him into helping."

"How are you feeling?" Meynardo asked.

"Like I got tossed off a tall cliff inside a bag of sharp knives," Jack frowned. "And like I haven't eaten since the *last* sentinel walked the land. I'm hungry enough to eat a raw buffalo with the skin on. Hooves and all."

"The first, alas," the mouse told him, "I can do nothing about. "The second, however," he nodded. "I'll see what I can do."

With that, he turned and scampered down the blanket to race out into the night.

That same black haired girl showed up some short time later, bearing a tray, this time, rather than her clay pot. She brought it quietly to the bed and, with a quick curtsy, laid it on the blanket beside him.

Some sort of roasted meat cut into heavy slabs, thick slices of rough, dark bread and hunks of some off white, pungent cheese. And a mug that smelled almost like beer, if the term were sufficiently tortured and the beer sufficiently raw.

She brought a chair from the table and set it beside the bed, careful not to make too much noise.

"No," he started to say. He wasn't about to be fed like a baby by some strange girl. But when he moved his right hand, he remembered. Yeah, okay, he wasn't cutting any meat or cheese with that hand. So he settled back with a defeated sigh, and let her feed him.

Meynardo settled himself on the far side of the tray, grinning like an idiot at the spectacle, while occasionally cutting free a piece of meat or cheese with his small knife.

"Six days," the mouse told him around a mouthful of cheese. "You were going to ask how long, right?"

Jack narrowed his eyes. "Yeah," he said. "Six days? Total, or since I last passed out?"

"Total," Meynardo laughed. "You actually *are* getting better, I'm told."

"You were dead," the mouse told him seriously. "Make no mistake. I heard Luciandro tell you that you were at death's door? Jackson, you were inside death's *house,* with your staff braced crossways against death's front doorframe while death strove with all its might to drag you in by your ankles. According to Luciandro, the grip you had on that staff was all that kept your soul in this world."

Cable introduced himself the next morning. He was so cheerful, Jack wanted to hate him just on general principles, but he couldn't do it. He wondered idly what the man's charisma stat was as the guy went on and on in his friendly, booming voice.

"Don't worry, young sentinel," Cable assured him within moments of meeting him. "The lion's share of the experience for killing the Mauler is yours."

"I didn't...."

"I can't believe you took out so many of those midranks by yourself. And Bear the Mauler? On your own? You have any idea what the bounty on that evil bastard's head was?"

"Who....?"

"And those friends of yours," Cable went on. "Where did you find *them*? I've never *seen* such high order constructs, and I traveled with the Hero's army for five years."

"About them...."

"Oh, but won't old Bor Jonkins be tickled when you bring *them* to the guild hall!" Cable was still going, leaning back and slapping his knee. "I can just *see* his face when they completely ignore his famous demon trap and hie themselves right on between the bars to set up house in his back rooms!"

"I was going to...."

"Anyway," Cable slapped him on his knee and stood, sweeping up the chair and sliding it towards the table on his way out. "I've been out here too long with the town largely unprotected. Got to ride back to Mokkelton and fetch that hairbrained wizard out here to pick up his infernal rolling dungeon, so I can get back to work. Jehsha knows *I'm* not driving the cursed trap collection back!"

"Yeah," Jack sighed at the empty doorway out which the big rank thirty had vanished. "Nice talking to you." He turned to his tiny translator and shook his head. Meynardo just shrugged.

By his ninth day in the noisome cabin, Jack was missing Rosaluna's cottage. He was sick to death of the stench, the uncomfortable tick mattress, and most of all, the chamber pot. He made every effort to not think about how that particular enterprise had been handled during the six days before he'd awakened.

His tenth day was more eventful, and he had less time to bemoan the conditions of his medical imprisonment. Tiarraluna spent most of it fussing over him, tsking in a very familiar manner, before finally addressing him.

"The majority of your more minor wounds are well along towards being healed naturally," she ordained. "And your four most dangerous wounds are sufficiently healed that it is probably safe for you to begin moving about, so long as you are careful. Your fingers will take longer.

"It is likely that we will be able to move you back to Mokkelton in another few days.

"You did extensive damage to your thigh by fighting on with a war arrow buried in it near to the bone, so do not put much weight on it, nor attempt to move quickly.

"Cable made you a crutch before he left. I suggest that... no, I *insist* that you use it. And please limit your movements to the absolutely vital."

"Yes, mother," Jack sighed, not bothering to look over for the scowl he was sure would be his reward. "How about fresh air, then?" he wondered. "Is crawling out of this stench a thing I might be allowed to consider vital?"

Her voice, when it came, was stern. Measured. "Your imagination rivals your battle prowess, Jack san," she gritted. "Good Millicent has scoured this entire cabin to the bare wood in the time you have been here. That stench, I would hazard, is you."

He squinted his eyes and ducked his shoulders before raising an arm and taking a sniff. Okay, no. Rank as he was, it wasn't him. But, looking around, he had to admit, it might not be the cabin either. It might even be a memory, associated with another time and place, and brought forth by the familiar pain of his wounds.

"Can I go outside anyway?" he asked in a pleading voice that was nearly genuine.

She settled back in her chair with a great, put upon sigh. "I am sorry this has taken so long," she apologized stiffly. "But I am not primarily a healer. Normally, it would have been beyond me entirely, and I would not have been able to save you at all. But grandmother gave me a tome—"

"So I have the old woman to thank again?" he moaned.

Her eyes narrowed further. "That is a problem?"

"More debt piled on top of what I already owe," he observed solemnly. "A debt I'll already be a long lifetime repaying, and probably still come up short."

She tilted her head, frowning. "What, exactly do you expect you owe her, Jack san?" she asked.

He looked at her like he was waiting for the punchline. "All she's done for me—" he began.

"—She has done because she is incapable of doing otherwise," Tiarraluna finished for him. "To act in any other way would be to ignore who she is. You owe her nothing. She expects nothing."

He sighed quietly. He did owe her. He couldn't let that go. But he wouldn't push it. Not now, at least.

"Now," she leaned in and regarded him sternly. "We must speak of your shiny new ring."

Millie and Juniper

"There are two girls here," Tiarraluna told him. "Who were taken when their parents were killed on the road a day's ride east of here a few days before you stormed this camp."

His eyes went wide.

"And you wear on your finger the life stone that their father left behind when I released his soul."

He hadn't an answer for that. Not one he trusted his voice to convey.

"His name was Johannes," she informed him. "And they would like to meet you. Formally, I suppose, as the eldest has already met you more than once."

"Do they know?" his voice was tight.

"It was not for *me* to tell them," she answered.

He drew in a deep breath. "Go get them, then, I suppose."

She nodded and left, leaving him to stare down at the ring, wondering how much to tell them.

Tiarraluna was back after only a short time, with two girls in tow. The first of them was the familiar black haired girl who'd fed him, and seemed so enamored of FoeSmite. The other might have been nine or ten, with the same black hair, although hers was done up in pigtails.

Meynardo was there as well, as he had become Jack's defacto translator.

The older girl stopped well clear and curtsied. Then she fed a gentle elbow to her little sister, who jumped, looked up at her, and then copied the motion.

"I'm Millie," the older girl pronounced. "And this here's my little sister, Juniper. We calls her Berry sometimes."

The little girl scrunched up her nose at her sister and turned to Jack. "Juniper," she stated positively. "I don't like Berry, much."

Jack nodded to each of them in turn. "Jackson Grenell," he provided, although he figured they already knew, given the length of time they'd all been here.

They all stood there staring at one another uncomfortably for awhile, before Millie curtsied again and said, "we wanted to thank you, Mister Grenell," she said awkwardly. "Fer saving us and all, y'know?" she looked to her sister and nudged her again.

"Thank you, sir," Juniper curtsied in her turn. "We thought sure we was goners 'til you showed up."

"Yes," Jack stumbled. "Well... you're welcome. I'm happy I made it in time."

He looked beseechingly at Tiarraluna, but she held silent. "We... uh... found your parents," he said at last, drawing gasps from both girls.

"We consigned them to Jehsha," Tiarraluna finally came to his aid. "And saved such of their belongings as we could," and now she nodded to Jack.

"He fought them," Jack told the girls.

Millie snorted, tears seeping from the corners of her eyes. "I saw," she said softly. "To protect Mama. Fat lot o' good it did him."

"He saved us all," Jack told her seriously.

Both girls gasped. "How can you say that?" Millie demanded. "I watched that horrible man chop him up out there on the road!"

Jack held up his left hand, turning it so that they could see the amber stone. Millie reached out a hand, palm open, as though she could feel it radiating something.

"He fought them," Jack repeated. "And he drew blood. And probably because of that, he dropped this life stone when Tiarraluna released his soul."

Now Juniper was reaching for the ring, tears flowing. "Papa?" she sniffled. "That's papa?"

"His life stone," Jack confirmed. "And because he dropped it, my friends were able to create this ring for me. To focus my magic. And because of this ring, I was not only able to kill your captors, but survive the process. *Only* because of this ring."

The girls came forward and laid hands on the ring. "She..." Millie struggled to speak. "She told me... I didn't really believe... it *is* Papa," she smiled. "I can feel him in there."

Jack turned to Tiarraluna, raising an eyebrow as the girls held his hand and let out their sorrow. She shrugged. *She* hadn't told them anything like that.

"This stone is rightly yours," Jack told them gently after they'd cried themselves out.

"No," Millie sniffled, looking into his eyes. "You keep it. Papa would want you to. H-He was a good man. He was always helping people. Let him help you help folks."

"Was that true?" Tiarraluna asked some time later, after the girls had left. "Or were you only telling a story to make them feel better."

He took the ring off and handed it to her. "You tell me," he told her. "See what your appraisal skill says."

She drew in a breath when she examined the ring and saw its properties. "This is..." she faltered. "Ten percent is a substantial bonus, Jack san. And my appraisal calls it a unique item. How can that be? "

He placed the ring back on his finger, and pointed to his pouch on the cabinet beside the bed. "Could you hand me my belt pouch please?" he asked.

He withdrew his guild token and brought forth his stat field, somewhat to her surprise. "I still can't read it," he admitted. "But tell me what you see."

"Your..." she straightened in her seat. "You have ranked up! How did you—?"

"Now look at my health and mana," he prompted. "And then go down through my skills and find something called Cold Rage."

She did so, with some prompting for him to move between screens, her eyes growing wide. "It is a unique skill, Jack san," she breathed. "How have you managed two uniques in the span of two days?"

"Now," he nudged, still not answering her questions.

"Tell me what would have happened if I'd fallen under the effects of Cold Rage without that ring on my finger." He'd already been through all this with Luciandro and knew what she'd find.

Her breath caught.

"No," he answered her, then. "I wasn't lying. I told that girl the truth. Without that shard of amber, I'd have dropped dead in the middle of my fight with the bandit leader, and nothing you or your grandmother or anybody else could have done would have saved me. As it was, I nearly did anyway, or so I'm told."

The fact that, for all intents and purposes, he *had* died, she kept to herself. Certainly nothing she or the mice had done had kept him from crossing over in those first hours after her arrival.

* * *

"You saw her *that* time, didn't you, Berry?" Millie demanded of her little sister outside in the yard.

Juniper gave her a look and squared on her, putting her hands on her hips, eyes still wet and red. "Saw *who,* Millie?" She demanded. "There wasn't nobody in there but the mage lady and the hero. You're seein' things again."

"Am not!" Millie insisted. "And anyway, remember when I told you what she said about Papa? And now we know it fer true, don't we? Straight from the hero's mouth! Where'd I hear it then, if not from the green lady?"

"I dunno," Juniper was unrelenting. "All *I* know is that there ain't no green lady livin' in that crazy stick. *Listen* to yourself, Millie. Cain't nobody *else* see no green lady. Just you. Don't you think if she was real, some one o' those powerful gifted folks *mighta* seen her at least once?

"Just you don't touch it again, er you'll get in all *kinds* o' trouble! I heard the mouse folk say that it's all kinds o' dangerous, and that it breaks anything it touches."

Millie seemed to not even be paying attention anymore, gazing instead in the direction of the stationkeeper's cabin. "She won't hurt me," she whispered after a bit. "She likes me. 'Sides, she's lonely. She misses her friends. She's happy to have somebody to talk to.”

“Ain’t no *she*!” Juniper throttled a yell. “It’s a *stick*! Didn’t Papa and Mama always warn you about alla this talk o’ spirits and haunts? Too much imagination, Papa said, didn’t he? What if these folk find out you see things ain’t there, Millie? What’ll happen to you *then*, huh? What’ll happen to *me?*”

Millie turned back to her and clucked her tongue before heading for the shack where the other three girls were staying until somebody from town could fetch them all back. Illie, the girl who’d been here longest, wasn’t doing so well, and needed constant looking after.

The little mouse wizard was doing his best, but he didn’t hold out much hope. He’d about fixed her body, but her mind was broke, and might not ever mend.

Juniper belatedly followed, still frustrated and sad, and wanting to take it out on someone. “If you’re so sure there’s a green lady,” she demanded, “why not tell the hero? It’s *his* stick.”

Millie didn’t even turn. “She’s powerful mad at him fer some reason,” she said without hesitation, like she didn’t even need to think up a reply. “Says she hates him, but I don’t think she really does. Why save him if she hates him so?

“Says he killed her, but then says he saved her, and that he’s tied her to him somehow, some way she don’t really understand. And she can’t even talk to him because of how weak she still is, ‘cept when he’s all riled up, and *then* he don’t listen.”

“What about the mage lady, then?”

Now Millie did turn, but just her head. “She don’t like *her* even more’n she’s mad at *him*,” she giggled. “Calls her ‘Little Miss Fancy Frock’, almost like she’s jealous.”

Juniper followed quietly for a few paces, and then popped up with, “So how’s about Mister Luciandro?” she demanded. “She mad at *him*, is she? Er jealous? Hmm?”

Millie sighed as they reached the shack and she lifted the curtain. Truth was, she was more than tired, in body and mind. Juniper wasn’t but half wrong, she thought. And she knew that the little mouse wizard wouldn’t, probably, be able to see the green lady any more than any of the rest of them. Truth was, she was afraid.

They didn't none of them understand. The green lady wasn't the only spirit she'd ever seen. Not by a long ways. Nor was she the only one she'd talked to. Or who'd talked back. Or who she'd had fun with.

Ever since she was a little girl, she'd been able to see things nobody else could. Fairies and forest spirits and the like. And nobody'd ever believed her. Not once. Papa had even taken her to the city once, to have a mage look to her. To see was she maybe gifted after all. The mage had laughed, and shook his head, and Papa had taken her home.

She'd about convinced herself, eventually, that they were, the all of them, right, and that she was just crazy. So she'd started in pretending to not see them, like Mama had always wanted. Neither she nor Papa had wanted word to get out that maybe Johannes and Sellia's little girl was touched in the head.

And then she'd seen the hero fight the bandits who'd murdered both Papa and Mama, and she'd seen the green lady helping him do it, flashing from place to place, changing the course of what was left to her of her tree, returning it to him when he called. She, Millie knew, was real. She had to be. She was moving things about. And so she'd started to believe again.

Then, at the end, she'd lain beside him in the mud, the green lady had, holding onto his hand, to keep him from passing over while the others worked on him. When Millie herself had worked on him. And she'd thanked her, in her ethereal voice that sounded of a breeze wafting through the leaves of the forest.

Didn't matter what any of them thought anymore. Didn't matter if they thought she was touched. Not even the hero would keep her from her new friend.

* * *

Jack and Tiarraluna, meanwhile, were still pouring over his guild stone's field. The revelation of his having somehow ranked up already had surprised her, along with some of the skills and attributes he possessed.

This was the first time she'd had an opportunity to really examine the totality of what Jehsha's window had seen in him, and she was having some difficulty crediting it.

"Sure," he complained after they'd gone through the lot, including what Luciandro had skipped over back at the shattered village. "Big Jack Grenell, the scary sentinel. The great, all powerful *HEE*ro." he let out a half-raspberry. "So how come I keep getting my ever loving ass kicked every time I fight? I thought heroes were supposed to be, like, super strong and able to defeat armies and sh— stuff."

She tilted her head and looked at him strangely, quite taken aback. "You keep getting your... how did you put it? Ever loving... behind kicked, Jack san ," she told him with a lilt in her voice. "Because you are an idiot."

"Beg pardon?" his eyes narrowed and his face drew in.

"Jack san," she ventured. "What is it, exactly, that you believe the ranking system is used for? How is it you imagine it is applied?"

He narrowed his eyes further. Condescending tone, fake question, precise enunciation. All the earmarks of a trap. Still, "Keeps track of your progress as you learn things and gain experience, right?" he ventured.

Her expression didn't change. "In part," she allowed. "But why would such a thing be needed?"

He wasn't up to playing this game. He was tired and in pain, and whatever she'd done to him earlier to take the edge off had long since worn off. "You tell me," short and flat.

"Say," she ventured in that same lilting voice, "as an example, you have two fighters who want to fight. One of them, in white, is rank ten, and the other, in black, is rank three. Who would win?"

Ah. He saw where this was going. "Probably the ten," he said.

She nodded. "In all likelihood. Suppose, then, they were both rank tens? One in black, the other in white. Who would win?"

"Alright, alright," he relented.

But she wasn't through with him yet. "And now," her voice grew sharp. "Let us suppose that a magnificent idiot of rank nine, wearing mismatched and lower rank armor picked a fight with *NINETY-SEVEN RANKS* of hardened villains," her volume rose. "Each and every *one* of them equipped with high ranking gear and weapons, and all of them *waiting* for him?" she leaned in, face angry. "Which side of this battle do you imagine would emerge victorious, my magnificent idiot? Hmm?

"*This* is why the boards at the guild hall are arranged as they are," she pressed. "*This* is why we are encouraged not to engage foes many times our own ranks unless we have no other option.

He wanted to defend himself. He'd been doing okay, all things considered. Up to when he'd faced that rank eighteen, anyway. But Tiarraluna was on a roll, and she wasn't ready to stop.

"Which is why I say you are an idiot." she accused. "Jack san, do you not *understand*? Each and every one of those you have fought since we started out from the town, given the rank disparities, *should* have killed you with little problem, even did you face them one at a time.

"Those teufel-things on our way to town *did* kill you," she waggled a finger. "Make no mistake. Were I not there with you, even did you somehow have FoeSmite already, you would certainly have died from the poison.

"Where we found the girls' parents, any one of the bandits outranked you by significant margin, and all possessed better equipment, save only for FoeSmite. One on one, any of them *should* have bested you with relative ease. And yet you felt completely comfortable fighting them *all at once*!

"Charging into this camp?" her voice continued to rise. "They should have squashed you like a *bug*! Even with your amazing band of mice," her voice gained stridence. "A *bug*, Jack san! That Mauler person was *double* your rank! *Double!* And, according to your friends, you simply walked up to him and allowed him the first strike! With his minions all around you! Idiot? Idiot is *much* too feeble a word—!"

"Okay!" he raised his good arm between them as if to fend her off. "Okay! I surrender. I'm an idiot."

She struggled to calm herself, but her eyes were still blazing when she spoke again. "Were you an ordinary man," she whispered hoarsely, "you would be dead two dozen times over. Do not attempt to feel sorry for yourself because you are not heroic *enough.*"

Three days later, Jack was awakened by a commotion in the yard outside. He rolled painfully out of bed and grabbed the makeshift crutch.

The yard was filled with activity and horses. One of the riders, a boy of fourteen or fifteen, wearing brown brigandine and a conical helm with a gold filigreed nasal, brought his horse to the porch. "You'd be the sentinel, then?" he asked. Jack just about understood him and nodded.

"Name's Tiglund," the boy announced. "Master Jonkins set me to fetch the lot of you back to Mokkelton. These others are here to help pack up your booty and fetch it back, along with the rescued captives. We've even brought a sprung carriage, for Cable has let us know you were sore injured in the fight.

Jack nodded again. The majority of that had gone right by him. "Tiarraluna," he said slowly. "Party leader. Tell her."

Tiglund laughed and turned away to search for the young advanced novice mage.

There was some consternation when the mice appeared, but Tiarraluna put a stop to it before any accidents happened.

The stripping of the ferry station took the rest of the day. The townsmen stayed in one of the open shacks that night. The one the girls weren't using. The following morning, the lot of them harnessed the wagons, gathered up the livestock, and set out on the west road for town.

It would be a trek of several days, as they were in normal wagons or riding normal horses, rather than a swift magical engine, but at least they'd seen the last of the ex bandit camp.

* * *

And they're well gone? Rosaluna inquired from her position atop the city's east wall.

Well gone, Lady Luna, the gray, humanoid figure with the pale, glowing eyes confirmed from the treeline outside of Mokkelton. *Five of us will remain near, following. They have left the province and are continuing westward for the empty lands.*

Whatever the newly arrived human told them seems to have convinced them, somehow, to flee, even to abandoning many of their belongings in their former encampment. Some of us have gathered it up and are conveying it to the old storehouse.

Good, she nodded to herself. *And those other things?*

The figure turned to survey the carnage behind it. The five crystalless corpses lay broken and still in the stained grass. The figure's companions ranged around them, silent. Some of the companions had been damaged, but none had fallen.

They have been eliminated, Lady Luna, it sent.

Excellent, she allowed her smile to widen. *Convey the bodies to my cottage and await me there. Preserve them. I shall return within the week.*

The gray figure nodded and bowed towards the town, although it knew not whether its mistress could see it.

Turning, it relayed her orders to its companions. The corpses were loaded onto the backs of some of the multi-legged variants and the lot of them turned away from the town. They would travel straight through, for such as they needed no rest.

Atop the wall, Rosaluna Galbradia heaved a great sigh and turned away, her mood lighter than it had been in months. There was *that* problem solved. At least for the time being.

She would now have additional time to fashion more of her servants. Enough, in all likelihood. The next time the creatures of the fallen demon lord decided it might be a good idea to invade, she would be ready for them, and there would be no need to trouble Mohrdrand, Jonkins, or that weasel of a hero king squatting off to the west in his glorious, hollow capitol.

He wanted to abandon the east? Fine. *She* would protect it. And he'd better steer clear in the future.

And *best* of all, her secret yet remained hers alone.

Hail the Victorious Hero

The assistant driver leaned over and gave the side wall of the carriage a good, strong rap. Jack jerked awake and glared owl-eyed around the cabin. Three of the former captives, whose names he now knew were Illie, Nenum, and Josimie, were seated in the rear seat, across from where he lay crosswise in the front.

He yawned and struggled not to stretch. The trip had been rough, despite the so-called springs of the carriage, and he was feeling some beat up. Hard to believe it had been less than two weeks since he'd walked into the bandit camp in some sort of battle haze.

He carefully levered himself upright, and leaned out the window, knocking on the side wall in his turn.

The assistant driver leaned over again and let him know they were nearing Mokkelton, pointing over his shoulder. Jack recognized the words Mokkelton and soon. The rest, not so much. He was flying solo for this run, as Meynardo was riding in a separate wagon with the rest of his people, and Tiarraluna was riding with Millie and Juniper in their parents' wagon.

Millie was supposedly teaching her to drive, but who knew what they were really up to?

Jack nodded and slid his head back inside, where an uncomfortable silence awaited him. Two of the girls were not unfriendly. They recognized him as their savior, and had thanked him before the whole cavalcade had left the ferry station.

The third, however. Illie. She broke his heart, and he couldn't help but wish the two farm girls had taken her in their wagon. She sat quietly, staring vacantly ahead, with a thousand yard stare. She didn't speak, she didn't move. Whatever they'd done to her.... He'd seen that look before, back in the desert. He stifled the curse before it could well to the surface. He wouldn't show any anger where she might see.

Deep down in the pit of his stomach, he heard a soft whisper. *Ah* it hissed. *Late again.*

He'd killed them way too quick, the thought ran through his mind again. And way too clean.

The caravan caused quite the commotion when they brought up at the city gate. It took some time as the townsman on duty worked his way along the wagons, horses, and livestock, counting and tallying the fee.

It initially came to quite a bundle. Then Tiglund flashed his guild token and Tiarraluna flashed hers, and they explained where it had all come from. The gatekeeper shaved a considerable sum from it. He was under orders from the mayor as well, it seemed.

Jonkins was out front of the guild hall to meet them, having been alerted by a runner sent from the gate upon their arrival. He put both hands to his head when he saw the size of the train, then waved the drivers around behind the hall. By the time they'd gotten them all sorted out, the stable was full, the yard was full, and there were animals tied the length of the rail out in the street.

Jack remained in place as a couple of town women appeared at the carriage's door and helped the girls down. He gave them time to get clear and for Meynardo to show up before dragging himself and his crutch down and into the enclosed yard of the guild hall.

"Survived, huh?" Jonkins voice assailed him from the rear. Joke was on *him*. Jack's detect life skill had already placed him, so poor Jonkins didn't get the jump he was after. Instead, Jack turned and gave him his old infantryman's deadpan. "Nope. Killed me dead." The *real* joke was that he wasn't lying.

Jonkins let out a huge guffaw, and nearly slapped Jack on the back before he could stop himself. Even now, the sentinel looked like the low rent side of the underworld. "C'mon in, lad, let the others get things sorted out here. Gauging by the volume, I'm pretty sure you won't miss whatever they charge for the service."

"Is there beer?" Jack asked quietly.

"Ale," Jonkins raised an eyebrow.

"Good ale?" Jack came right back. "That doesn't taste like it was brewed this morning by an unwashed gremlin using his loincloth to filter the hops?"

Jonkins snorted, a hand going to his mouth. But he nodded. "*Very* good ale," he chuckled.

Jack nodded and shuffled into motion, "then I believe I'll accompany you, guildmaster," he said. "We have some things to discuss."

Jonkins paused at that, standing stock still while the sentinel gained a couple of paces on him. When he followed at last, his face was less jolly.

"I apologize," Jonkins tried to gain a march as he drew a mug for Jackson Grenell. "I should have allowed you to get a better look at your token before shooing you out. Uhm, he drinking, too?" he pointed to Meynardo, who'd resumed his place on Jack's shoulder.

"I am," the mouse announced, scampering down Jack's good arm and setting a tiny wooden mug on the bar.

Jack stood quietly, not touching his ale while Jonkins clumsily filled the mug and placed it on the bar. Nor while Jonkins drew one for himself.

With the guildmaster once more before him, then, he finally took up his mug, staring directly into the old battler's eyes while he lifted it to his lips. He took a deep swallow and set the mug down on the bar before speaking.

"That's *one* of the things you should have done," he said. "Along with making sure I knew how to *read* the damned thing. Or how to release souls. Or, maybe, cast **Self Healing**. Just in case I might run into the odd... oh, I dunno... *bandit?*"

Jonkins winced at the first accusation, the wince deepening with each subsequent point.

"This the drink you owed me for cracking the quarter-staff?" Jack inquired levelly after another swallow.

Jonkins squared his shoulders and lowered his head. He didn't at this point, say anything. What was there to say? That he'd fouled up his most basic of duties. Almost, he thought to point out that he'd sent the boy out with an experienced mage, who should have been capable of teaching him all of those things, but then he remembered the state she'd been in when he'd found her in this very room a couple of days later.

"You sent out a student, expecting her to teach a student," Jack pointed out as though he could hear his thoughts. "That's a bad plan. This something I need to worry about going forward?" he asked, voice flat. "Because, if it is, I think we might be gonna have some trouble."

He finished his ale and pushed the mug across the bar.

Jonkins refilled it and looked up at him, face equally hard. "I'll take that from you *this* time," he said. "Because I was wrong, and I can see you're in a lot of pain." He paused while Jack took a few more pulls on his drink. "But in future," he glared, "you need to respect your elders a bit more."

They watched each other, neither budging, while the commotion outside echoed at the edges of their awareness. "And I'll do my best not to send you off unprepared again," Jonkins finally grudged. He held out his hand, then switched to his left when he realized Jack's right was unavailable.

"Now, lemme see your guild and bounty tokens," he ordered when they'd released their grips. "And the life stones."

Tiarraluna found them there some time later, frowning at the loose way Jack was holding himself against the bar, and the droop-lidded expression on his face. "Why are you standing up, you lunkhead?" she demanded. "There are forty chairs in this room."

Jack looked blearily about and nodded, taking half a step before nearly going down, holding himself up by clutching at the bar with his good left hand.

With a scowl that could almost be heard, she stomped over and got herself up under his arm to half drag him to a chair, bringing another for him to put his leg up onto.

"And *you,*" she glared at the guildmaster. "Drunken? At *this* time of day?"

Jonkins started a denial, but it turned into a belch, so he

just shrugged.

It took less time to sort the plunder at this end due to the sorting it had gone through at the front end. All that remained by late evening was the disposition of the mice and the two farm girls, the other three having been taken in by townfolk.

Millie and Juniper were relatively easy. They would stay here and help Jonkins keep the place clean against the return of the missing adventurers. Perhaps later, when things were quieter, they'd settle somewhere nearby on some abandoned farmstead outside the town.

Jonkins was thinking about it when Tiglund stuck his oar in the water, vouching for them in no uncertain terms, while casting sideways glances at the older girl, who blushed at the attention. Juniper, of course, started in teasing with blazing speed, nearly getting a swat from her sister for her trouble.

The mice were another matter. True to Cable's predictions, they sprung the rear demon trap coming in, but ignored it, simply walking between the upthrust bars. Its designer hadn't expected such *small* demons.

Jonkins goggled at the lot of them. Even moreso when Luciandro stepped from the crowd, presented his token, and asked for admittance to the Mokkelton guild for himself and his people in unaccented Tandrian.

Much to the surprise of all concerned, the reader not only accepted the token, but updated it. Without a mirror attuned to them, unfortunately, there would be no way to apply any of the benefits of the new ranks. Silently, both Jonkins and Luciandro turned to regard Jack, who suddenly felt a chill run up his back.

For the time being, the mice would take up residence in one of the lower rooms, which could be warded against the particular dangers they'd to contend with beyond those normally faced by larger residents.

They held the auction five days later, out in the street

before the guild hall. By day's end, everything they were likely to sell was sold. As predicted, the salvaged arms and armor remained. No one could use them, so no one bid on them. Not even the merchants bothered, since who would *they* sell them to? Which led to Jack's and Jonkins' current discussion. There was ale on the table, though neither was drinking to excess this time, and the remains of a meal. Off to one side of the tabletop, Meynardo, Jack's perennial companion these days, and the reason this discussion could take place at all, was seated at his own setting, his tiny wooden mug before him.

"How many gifted you figure are here in Mokkelton, or in the surrounding area?" Jack wondered of the guildmaster. "If I have my math right, there should be three or four gifted kids between twelve and fifteen wandering around at *least*, in addition to the city guards and Tiglund."

Jonkins thought about it for a bit and nodded. "Sounds about right," he allowed. "What of it? We've already been through this."

"What's keeping them from presenting themselves, do you suppose?" Jack asked him seriously.

The guildmaster shrugged. "Could be none of 'em knows they're gifted. Could be they suspect, but can't afford the fee for the test. Could be any of a number of things."

"How much have I got banked in your vault?" Jack asked, although he already knew.

Jonkins narrowed his eyes. "You suggesting what I think you are?" he asked.

"Put out notices, flyers, broadsides, whatever you guys call them here. Call anybody in who even *thinks* they might have a gift. You see the *least* sign of a crystal, put 'em in front of the mirror. I'll set aside a chunk of my account and you take the fee out of that. And keep going 'til the money runs out, however long that takes."

Jonkins let out a loud guffaw. He couldn't help himself. "Who're you, now, the bloody *king?*" he laughed. "It ain't your job, nor your obligation to feed adventurers to the guild."

Jack shrugged. "Sentinel," he reminded. "My job is

whatever the hell I decide it is. And if I decide that what protects the most people is having more protectors, who're *you* to stop me?

"Anyway," he snorted. *"What* king? I haven't seen a trace of this king or anybody who works for him since I *got* here. Seems to *me*, we're on our own out here. Am I wrong?"

The laughter cut off short, and Jonkins' face went serious. "I have to send half of the fee to the capitol," he told Jack. " That's the extent of his royal Heinie's assistance. I need some of the rest of it to help run this place and keep things repaired. But I'll eat a quarter of any fees you pay. You may be the sentinel, but I *live* here."

"Great," Jack stuck his good left hand out for the shake. "Now, where might I find a good armorsmith?"

Another chuckle, and Jonkins stuck his thumb over his shoulder. "Nearest one I know is a month's hard ride west."

Jack's shoulders slumped. "I need to repair that armor I brought back," he said. "What are my alternatives?"

Jonkins rocked his head back. "Why? What good is it to *you*? Most of it won't fit, and you can only wear so much armor."

Jack smiled. "Well," he said. "Since I can't sell it, I thought I'd give it all away."

"So, you're not only going to pay their fees, but you're going to equip them? It'll be *years* before the *best* of them can use any of it, even *if* you could figure out how to fix it.

"Good point," Jack stroked his chin, thinking. "How about you hang on to it until we can find somebody who can fix it, and hand it out as needed to any I sponsor?"

"I c'n do that, I suppose," Jonkins allowed. "Same with the weapons, I suppose?"

"Give first pick to Tig and Cable," Jack told him, "but otherwise yes."

"And how do we go about training these youngsters?"

"That's a hard one," Jack admitted. "If only we had a couple of gifted types who knew their way around the basics of weaponry and combat. Guys who might take a few hours a week to help the newcomers along...."

"You're suggesting a school?" Jonkins had a go at his beard. "I mean, I can help any who have the knack with sword or spear, I suppose. I might even be able to use the dolls to show the proper forms of other weapons, since they're already programmed to test for them.

"Antel can train them in spear and shield," he added. "A bit of basic magic, and fieldcraft.

"Tiglund, young as he is, is some punkins with a bow, and near as good on the trail as Antel. His father was a hunter, y'see. Oh, he's not up to *your* standards, sure, but for a rank four, he ain't bad. And compared to anybody just walked in off the street, he may as well be a master."

"Great," Jack smiled. "Let's call that a plan, then. What d'you think about two hundred gold rondels to start?"

Jonkins jaw dropped. "That's... that's the whole of the special bounty you earned from taking down that Mauler Gang," he said, shocked. "I thought you needed all the money you could lay hands on to get you to the capitol?"

"I've got plenty more," Jack waved a hand. "Besides," his voice lowered," I can't leave yet. There's things going on here that look to need some attention. I can't just dip out and leave them undone. Even knowing what's waiting for me on Tarr and how important it is that I get there soonest." he stared down at his mug for a long minute before taking a hefty swallow. "You understand casualty math, don't you Bor?" he asked in a somber tone.

* * *

Jack leaned back against the wall, one arm out to either side along the back of the ornate bench, careful of his right hand, still swathed in bandages. He was mixing it up between staring out across the busy square and up into the bright summer sky.

Now that he was in town and surrounded by people, he was picking up Tandrian pretty quick, and so he was listening to the general hubbub around him with a detached air.

He still hadn't decided what to do about his rank up. He

didn't want to rush through the choices without knowing more about how things worked here. Bad enough he'd gone into this last mission woefully unprepared. That wasn't happening again. Or so he told himself.

Tiarraluna hadn't returned from her grandmother's yet, although he wasn't sure why that should matter. Or, in any case, he wasn't ready to address why it might, quite yet.

They'd disbanded the party better than a week back, after splitting the treasure and experience, but the girl had somehow wrangled a promise out of him not to go anywhere until they'd spoken again.

He'd decided to himself that, now he was getting along better with the language, he could go on alone. He had decent gear now. A couple of reasonably good horses and tack. Even money enough to last awhile, despite his current expenses.

It wasn't like she wanted anything to do with him, after all, was it? Far as *she* was concerned, he was either a monster, a murderer, or an idiot, depending on her mood, or what he'd done most recently.

Even Meynardo had gone back to his own people now that Jack's constant need for a shoulder mounted interpreter had passed. He still wasn't getting everything, but he was getting enough, and more was coming through all the time.

Of course, it wasn't like he *could* move on yet, was it? He was still receiving medical care, although now it came from Mohrdrand, and the old geezer was charging him for it. At least the old man was allowing him to live there for free while he did it.

Superficially, all but his fingers were fully healed. Magic had traditional surgical medicine beat by a substantial margin. But superficial wasn't whole, as he'd recently learned.

So, given there were no quests on the board that obviously threatened death to the citizenry, in whole or in part, he was trying to take it easy and allow his body to finish mending before he took it out for another endurance rally.

He was, of course, currently moping around town trying to throttle his urge to be on the road regardless of all this high thinking. He glared at the crutch propped up against the bench beside him as though this whole mess were *its* fault, and tore another chunk out of the meat bun he'd picked up from a stall on his way to wherever the hell he thought he'd been going. Right. Take it easy. Nothing to it.

He was still chewing, head back, eyes aimed skyward, when he heard the whine. Looking down, he had to wonder whether he was *seeing* things now. It was a corgi. A genuine, honest to god, no foolin' orange and white Welsh corgi. It was filthy and looked half starved. It was staring longingly at the last of the meat bun in his hand.

What the hell? He tossed the food with a short flip of his wrist, and the dog snatched it out of the air with an audible snap of its jaws. It then proceeded to jump up onto the bench beside him and sit, staring out into the street, tongue lolling.

Jack looked over frowning. "If this were a normal isekai," he muttered, "you'd be my comedy relief spirit guide."

The dog looked up and tilted its head. "Name's Bob," it said in a casual voice. "And let me tell you, Jackson Thomas Grenell, you are one hard man to locate."

Epilogue

nine months ago

Iktchi-Chi came to herself slowly. She was tumbling through a space neither light nor dark. Featureless to the naked eye. Dotted around in all directions, however, clearly perceived with her faerie sight, star-like bodies of rippling color swirled in a grand cavalcade, each at their own pace, each along their own path, yet all combining in the same grand dance.

Her heart fluttered with dread. She'd been caught up in the spell! The cursed human had dragged her along, intentionally or not, into the void between worlds. The flickering lights weren't stars, they were portals. Portals, each of them, through which travelers between realities entered or left the worlds beyond.

Except you were supposed to be *guided*, she knew. *Aimed* at the *very* least. The void wasn't meant to be occupied. It was meant to be traversed, and that as quickly as possible. It would not long sustain life. Even the life of a lost devil girl. Harsh, the demon realm was, but it was nothing to the void, which was, itself, nothing, and she didn't belong here.

She caught intermittent glances of the human as her tumble brought him into her line of sight. He was tumbling as well, but in more of a ragdoll fashion, trailing a spiral cloud of blood. She couldn't tell if he was dead yet, but he was certainly dying.

She cursed him without feeling. To have been freed after so many long centuries, only to end up here.... She withdrew the curse, then. Doomed she might be, she thought. But she was *free*. At last, she was *free*.

The void wasn't completely empty. Nothing really is. There wasn't much, true, but perhaps, if she stretched her wings and snapped them hard enough...

Suiting action to words, she straightened her body and unfurled one batlike wing. The left for no particular reason. At the moment, she was tumbling backwards, and she didn't much care for that. Stretching the wing as far as she could, straining hard, she beat down with enough force to make her wince. Well.... Now she was tumbling side over. Another, then.

Gradually, after several iterations, she managed to both correct her direction and stop her tumble. She was facing forward, at least. She knew this because the human was some short distance ahead and to one side, and the blood cloud was trailing past her.

It was a shame he was dead, the thought passed through her mind. He was kind of cute. In a pale, mortal sort of way. Yes, she thought as his face came periodically into view, he was... had been now, she supposed, definitely a cute one. And he'd been nice, she remembered. More than nice. He'd been... special.

As she was contemplating the waste of having had to kill such a yummy human, a great hand shot forth from one of the flickering lights. She had barely enough time to allow her eyes to go wide before the immense hand snatched up the tumbling human and withdrew, unaccountably drawing Iktchi-Chi along with him. The spell! They were still connected by the spell!

Iktchi-Chi opened her eyes slowly, groaning softly in the back of her throat. She hurt all over, and her right wing felt broken. Everything was green. No, not everything. Just most everything. She'd somehow landed in a tree of some sort, it seemed. Looking down over her shoulder, she frowned. Very high in a tree. Ordinarily, that wouldn't be a problem. Not with both wings working. Just now, on the other hand....

She floundered along to the farthest reach of the canopy that would hold her weight, looking down. She frowned. There was a great whopping dire wolf with golden eyes down there, staring back up at her, and it didn't look happy to see her.

"I don't suppose you'd be willing to allow me free passage out of here?" she called down in high lupine.

To be continued

in Book Two:

What Do You Mean the Demon's Not

the Antagonist?

Tom Black

Magic Wheel

LIGHT
LIFE
INVOCATION
ABJURATION
CONJURATION LIGHT
CHARM
ELEMENT OF AIR
ELEMENT OF WATER
NEUTRAL
ELEMENT OF FIRE
ELEMENT OF EARTH
CURSE
CONJURATION DARK
DEATH
NECROMANCY
DARK

EVOCATION
ENCHANTMENT
DIVINATION
TRANS MUTATION
NEUTRAL
ALCHEMY
ESSENTIA
ILLUSION
ALTERATION

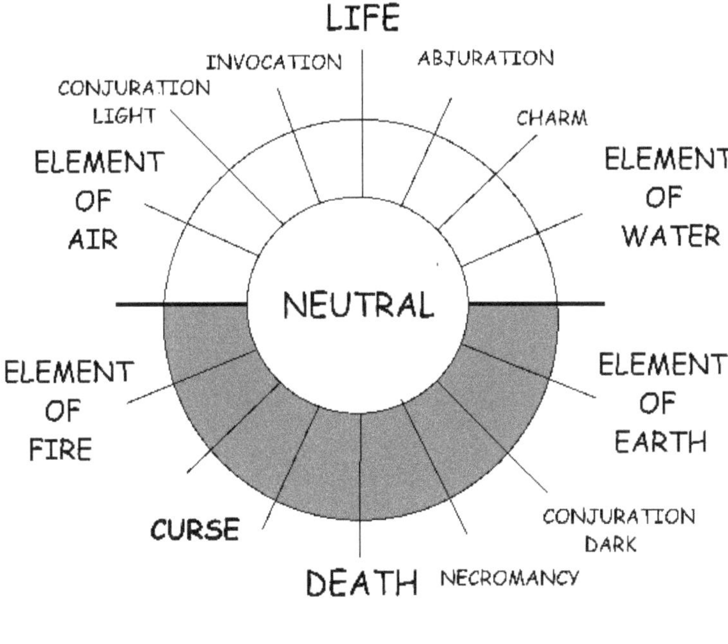

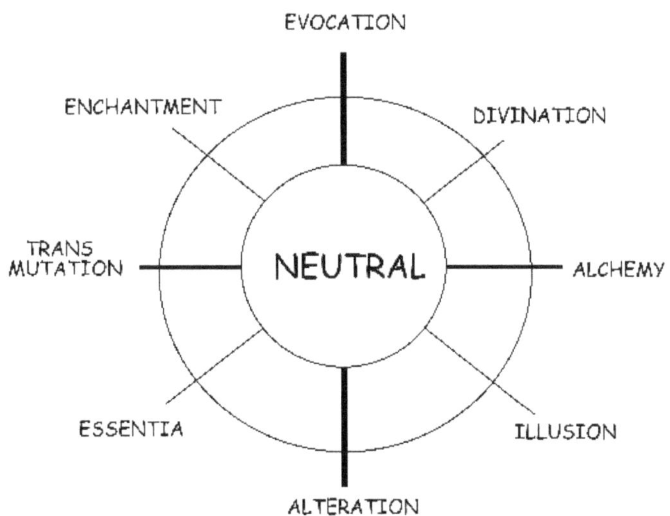

Glossary

Days of the Week(Mundian week has eight days):

Sofsday.
Hornsday.
Soolsday.
Grippensday.
Hoffsday.
Erochsday.
Lamsday.
Jesha's Rest.

Months of the Year:

Months on Mund are a bit peculiar, at least in Tandera. They basically have eleven months of four weeks each, and a special, twelfth, festival month in the fall after harvest that's only two weeks long.

Beginning at the winter solstice, they are:

Sae's Awakening. Frequently shortened to Awakening.

Deep Frost. Or just Frost.

Jehsha's Warming. Generally shortened to Warming.

Rain's Freshening. Generally shortened to Freshening.

Farmer's toil. Frequently shortened to Toil, or Planting. Planting season.

Summer's Dawn. Sometimes shortened to Sundawn.

Torhahm's Fire. Named for the dark god of Mund. Midsummer is pretty hot in Tandera.

Dragon's Fury. Sometimes called Dragon's. Yep, just Dragon's.

Festival. Once a grand harvest festival, these days, it's just another month.

Autumn's Waning. Frequently shortened to Waning.

Snowfall.

Jehsha's Glory. Frequently shortened to Glory.

Money:

Tandrian cash is pretty much universally accepted, at least so far in our story. The odd foreign coin shows up here and there, but not often enough for me to create multiple systems of currency.

The form here is, Name, followed by abbreviation, followed by colloquial name, followed by approximate value compared to the US Dollar (given I'm an American, and its value is familiar)

Copper Common (CC): Copper washed zinc. Normally shortened to 'copper'. About the size of a

US nickel. ($0.01)

Copper Real (CR): Larger coin, higher copper content. About the size of a US quarter. ($0.10)

Copper Rondel (CRD): Still larger coin, higher copper content. About the size of a newer US

half dollar. ($0.50)

Silver Common (SC): Small silver coin. Normally shortened to 'silver'. about the size of a US

dime. ($1.00)

Silver Real (SR): Larger silver coin, about the size of a newer US half dollar. ($2.00)

Silver Rondel (SRD): Still larger silver coin, about the size of an old form US silver dollar.

($5.00)

Gold Common (GC): Small gold coin. Normally shortened to 'gold'. About the size of a US

Dime. ($10.00)

Gold Real (GR): Smallish gold coin about the size of a quarter. ($20.00)

Gold Rondel (GRD): Large gold coin about the size of an old form US silver dollar. ($100.00)

1 CC. Smallest unit.

1 CR = 10 CC.

1 CRD = 5 CR = 50 CC.

1 SC = 2 CRD = 10 CR = 100 CC.

1 SR = 2 SC = 4 CRD = 20 CR = 200 CC.

1 SRD = 2.5 SR = 5 SC = 10 CRD =50 CR = 500 CC.

1 GC = 2 SRD = 5 SR =10 SC = 20 CRD = 100 CR = 1000 CC.

1 GR = 2 GC = 4 SRD = 10 SR = 20 SC = 40 CRD = 200 CR = 2000 CC.

1 GRD = 10 GC = 20 SRD = 50 SR = 100 SC = 200 CRD = 1000 CR = 10000 CC.

Tom Black

About the Author

The author has been, in no particular order; a farmer, a machine operator, a car mechanic, a truck driver, a cook, a waiter, a soldier, a salesman, a computer tech, a network engineer, a teacher, and a shopkeeper. He's traveled in six countries and forty-seven of the fifty states. Now, he's delivering food... go figure!

Tom Black

Preview of Raiders of the Black Sun

FARM BOY

"**D**AAARRRnaaan!" the voice rang clear and bright as a peeling church bell on Sunday morning. There was no immediate response.

"DARNAN!" and the chime struck harder, more strident.

Darnan Palanna sighed wearily but made no real effort to move. She'd found him pretty quick this time, he thought. Maybe he was getting too predictable.

He was a well set up young man of some five feet and ten to the top of his head —tall for the times— and dressed for hard work, though he was currently doing no such thing.

His rough, white, collarless shirt was wrinkled and sweat-stained and his brown canvas dungarees muddied halfway to the knees and frayed at the ankles. The heavy brogans on his feet showed more mud than leather, for the sky had been spitting rain off and on all day long. Only the bright red suspenders holding up his pants gave him any real color, although they too showed the occasional darker stain. A faded tan newsboy cap perched atop his head, its bill giving shade to his half-lidded eyes.

"Over here, Mailyn!" he called over his shoulder without moving more than his head.

Mailyn Entigh flounced over the rise behind him, following his voice — all five and three of her, swaddled in heavy, grease-stained blue coveralls three sizes too large, a clanking tool belt slung from her hips, and hobnailed boots that seemed over-large on her small feet.

One of the long barreled Norbertson flechette rifles that no colonist dared leave the built up areas without was balanced casually over her shoulders, one hand draped loosely over it on either side, in the manner of a shoulder yoke, minus the hanging buckets.

She was nearly seventeen —not that you could tell it beneath the baggy clothes— and she was either Dar's best friend, his accomplice, or his sidekick, depending on who you asked, what the pair had been up to most recently, and how much evidence had been left behind in their wake.

"They're late again, aren't they?" she asked, plopping to the grass beside him with a soft bounce and jiggle that he really should have noticed.

"Very," Dar rose up on an elbow and pointed down and to the northeast, well out beyond the jagged green edge of the island and much lower in the sky. "They're just now coming up to leeward."

A silvery shape cut the air only twelve or fifteen hundred feet above the roiling fog of the mist sea. One of the Westerling heavy packets, slender and long, and running a good eight hundred feet lower than the minimum altitude her rating called for. The eight engines flanking her shining hull vibrated at their maximum RPMs, pushing hard against their cruise and lift ratings. Their huge, multi-bladed metal propellers whirled the scattered streamers she was cutting through into long corkscrews behind her as they struggled to push her up and into the prevailing westerly winds.

"Hmph!" Mailyn snorted merrily. "Late, low, and slow."

"I'll say," Dar answered. "And look up there."

He pointed up higher and closer in, at a darker, squarer, deeper ship tracking along the same heading, but up at the twenty-two hundred foot mark that the Westerling should be maintaining and nearly five miles to the fore. "They're going to lose their escort if they aren't careful."

Mailyn watched the destroyer's shape cut the scattered streamers of low cloud — watched the smoke trailing from multiple exhausts as her powerful diesel engines hurled her along through the air at a good forty knots.

"You mean the escort's going to run away from their charge if they don't start paying attention," she said dismissively." Who is that anyway?" although she already knew.

"Looks like Kestrel," he said. "See," he leaned in close so she could follow along his pointing arm. "She's only got six banks of fifty millimeter automatic cannon along her quarters, instead of Peregrine's eight, to make room for the extra main battery mounts. And three extra four inchers on her upper decks to chase the high flyers.

"She mounts three ventral turrets along her centerline instead of two, see? And twin mounts to boot. Add those to the three dorsal turrets, and she carries twice Peregrine's main battery guns. five inch by fifty-four calibers, too, not those antique four-point-sevens. Those five by fifty-fours can reach right out!

"And Kestrel has room for two extra Lampreys in her launch bays. And the new MK IV's at that." He was almost giggling. "She's almost more a pocket cruiser than any old backwinds destroyer!"

Mailyn curled around to rest a hip on the grass and prop herself up on a stiffened arm. Leaning her head against his upper arm, she made a big show of sighting along it, assimilating the information while oohing and aahing appropriately. Dar could pick out every ship in the Imperial Ninth Western Fleet at range, just by the way it shouldered the wind. He never tired of waxing prolific about them and she never tired of listening to him do it. This despite being well able to match the feat ship for ship, gun for gun.

"What do you suppose they're carrying?" she asked casually without moving her head.

Dar shrugged. "Hard to say," he said. "Take a lot of weight to drop a ship that big twelve hundred feet. If I had to hazard a guess, I'd say ore of some sort. Not iron, I don't think — not with Kestrel for an escort. Silver maybe. Maybe even a mixed cargo with some gold from the Federly mines. We're close enough to Eastmarch now for that. Although... I'd think they'd have a couple of Lampreys flying CAP if they were hauling gold, wouldn't you? In case they got jumped?"

she snorted. "What pirate is going to jump a falcon class RN destroyer, Dar?" she laughed. "Do they even *make* that much liquor?"

They sat that way for awhile, quietly watching the packet struggle along under her unusually heavy burden, before Dar thought to remember why it was that Mailyn might be here when she was supposed to be working for her father back at the garage. Turning to her, he noticed her head still resting on his shoulder and stiffened, his nose nearly touching hers.

Feeling his reaction, she jerked her head clear and sat up straight, making a production of straightening and retying the mop of her unruly black hair away from her blushing face — pretending great concentration to cover her embarrassment.

"Your father sent you?" Dar's voice didn't quite crack.

"Well," she said in a subdued voice, "he did sort of wonder where you and his shipment of sweet grain had gotten off to."

He sighed again, looking at his wristwatch and drawing in a sharp breath. Tarnation! Maybe she hadn't found him so quick at that. Had he really been out here for more than three hours already? Damn! He'd have to hurry if he was going to make the scheduled delivery time.

He stood slowly, brushing dirt and grass from his dungarees. He reached down and helped Mailyn to her feet, somewhat distractedly, still half watching the destroyer and her charge sailing the sky against a backdrop of cloud banks and far-off islands, their shadows undulating along the variegated and roiling surface of the mist sea far below.

"Tell your father that I'll have his grain in the silo by dusk, as promised," he told her seriously, still holding her hand.

She nodded, leaning in very close, looking up at him. Close enough that he could smell her breath. She'd been chewing mint or something, he thought.

Her sloe eyes were close enough that he could pick out the details of their irises — almost feel the phantom tickle of her long lashes against his chin. When had her eyes gotten so deep and so green? And this close, pressed up against him the way she was, the baggy coveralls no longer hid the fact that she was growing up. And when had *that* happened?

He shook himself clear of the improper introspection and backed a pace, face flushing.

"Dusk," he repeated hoarsely.

"Dusk," she whispered somewhat breathlessly. "Did you want to—?"

"No!" he said quickly. "No, I won't have time. I have... lessons tonight."

Her eyes got very bright. "Ooh, can I come?"

"What?" he leaned back. "No! Lessons, I said."

"Well I know what 'lessons' means when you say it like that, Darnan Palanna!" she shot back happily. "You're going to visit the old pirate to learn more piratey things!"

"He's not a—!" he got control of himself quickly, taking a deep breath and another backward step.

"Nobody knows exactly *what* he is!" Mailyn retorted gaily. "He *could* be a pirate for all that you know!"

"No!" he shot back.

"Can I come?" she pressed closer.

"We've been over this, Mai," he insisted. "He isn't somebody who just takes to anybody who happens along. You don't even know him."

"I've seen him around," she sniffed. "I've even spoken to him. Once. In any case, I know what *you're* learning from him. I can see it in the way you carry yourself — the way you look at things differently than the rest of us. Like it's all some sort of challenging game and you're a master gamesman sorting through the possibilities. And I want to learn too!"

He was growing angry. She'd been pestering him about this forever, it seemed. "Then why not ask him yourself?" he demanded for perhaps the thousandth time.

She flipped her hair mischievously. "Because he's scary," she giggled. "Besides," she added airily, "*I'm* not his student."

He squinted at the non-logic of that. "It is precisely *because* I'm his student that I *cannot* ask him." he insisted, "and precisely because you're *not* that you *should*."

She leaned in very close again and smiled, eyes sparkling. "But I'm not *his* best friend, Darnan," she said sweetly.

He sighed again. "No," he insisted, trying with little success to ignore her suddenly all too grownup body pressing against him.

Taking in a breath that was all but a gasp, he took her by the upper arms and pushed her away, trying to clear his suddenly swimming head.

"You can't come. It would be rude of me to invite you, and *Kisêyiniw isn't someone you want to be rude to. Not if you value your hide."

"But...?" she clasped her hands together and locked her elbows, pressing her hands down between her legs and leaning in still closer.

Had she been wearing coveralls that fit, the tactic might well have been more successful. Given her close proximity, however, and built upon her previous efforts, it was successful enough. He leaned back, giving her space. She'd been watching her older sisters at work again, it seemed. She was trying to manipulate him like a regular girl would. That it was working made him even angrier.

"I'll ask," he told her quietly, measuredly, finally. "If he says it's alright, you can come with me next time. Is that good enough?"

She smiled broadly and skipped forward to plant a peck on his cheek before he could react. "Perfect!" she laughed.

And then she was off over the hill to reassure her father that his cargo would be in the proper place at the proper time after all, pausing only long enough to scoop up her Norbertson gun on the fly.

Dar turned his flushing face to cast one last look over his shoulder at the airships and froze, realizing abruptly that he'd backed nearly to the edge of the island. Holding his breath, he

---

* with the ê pronounced like the "e" in "berry"

took a long, deliberate step inland before turning back to face the mist sea some thirty-two hundred feet below. He felt a small shudder run through his body.

The edge was fairly stable here, it was true. But it wasn't like Plubenda was a ship, was it, forged from high steel or crafted of mistwood? It was mostly New Victorian highrock, like every other island in the sky, its very bones laced with the ore that kept everything drifting above New Victoria afloat.

Pieces could and occasionally did break free and float off. Chunks were known to come loose and shoot upward like bullets for several or a hundred feet before achieving neutral buoyancy, cold-cocking anybody in the way with some considerable force.

People, however, didn't float so well. It would be a long, cold fall down to whatever mystery lay beneath the mist, did something down in it not eat him on the way.

Gathering himself, Mai's sudden and befuddling burst of femininity completely forgotten, he bent down for his own Norbertson and plodded determinedly over the rise, pushing the heavy packet, the destroyer, the mist sea, and his dreams of adventures above it from his mind.

He was a teamster again, with all of the breathtaking excitement which that entailed. And that would have to do him. For now, at least.

He did not look back again, and so he missed the swarm of small red specks dropping down from the high strata like hurled stones, reflecting metallic glints in the late afternoon sun. At this distance, and with the shoulder of the island between them, he couldn't even hear the explosions as their dive bombs took Kestrel from the fore port quarter, shattering her armored high-steel decking and starting fires in the forward magazines before her crew had the time to react to general quarters.

He was almost back to his balloon wagon and its cud-chewing draft beasts when Kestrel swelled with internal explosions and broke apart, sending her crew and anything made of mundane materials plummeting downward as the shards of her ruined highware scattered upward and outward, trailing smoke and flame.

Almost quicker than the eye could follow, all that remained of Kestrel was a slowly spreading black smudge of oil smoke blowing eastward on the wind.